Mistress of Manningtor

Also by Connie Monk

Season Of Change
Fortune's Daughter
Jessica
Hannah's Wharf
Rachel's Way
Reach For The Dream
Tomorrow's Memories
A Field Of Bright Laughter
Flame Of Courage
The Apple Orchards
Beyond Downing Wood
The Running Tide
Family Reunions
On The Wings Of The Storm
Water's Edge
Different Lives
The Sands Of Time
Something Old, Something New
From This Day Forward
Echo of Truth

Mistress of Manningtor

Connie Monk

PIATKUS

Copyright © 2002 by Connie Monk

First published in Great Britain in 2002 by
Judy Piatkus (Publishers) Ltd of
5 Windmill Street, London W1T 2JA
email: info@piatkus.co.uk

This edition published 2002

A catalogue record for this book is available from the British Library

ISBN 0 7499 0615 4

Typeset in Times by Palimpsest Book Production Limited,
Polmont, Stirlingshire
Printed and bound in Great Britain by
Biddles Ltd, Guildford & King's Lynn

Chapter One
1938

Theo Sullivan was enjoying himself. Not that there was anything unusual in that, for he accepted any opportunity life presented and, with natural good humour, made something pleasurable out of it.

On that morning in early June he had left home as dawn sent the first deep mauve streaks to colour the eastern sky. From South Devon to the Berkshire Downs was a long drive and he was determined that they should arrive ahead of the furniture which had been loaded onto the lorry the previous day. Part of Theo's pleasure came from the opportunity to put his foot hard on the accelerator of his Riley, part from the break with routine, but perhaps most of all – although he wasn't aware of it – from the warmth of Albert and Tessa Humphries' gratitude that he was putting himself to trouble on their behalf. All in all, the day couldn't fail. A roadside breakfast of boiled bacon sandwiches and Thermos tea might not have been what he would have chosen, but the side of his nature which enjoyed seeing the pleasure he gave to his companions overcame thoughts of the laden sideboard at home.

Tessa watched admiringly as he bit into her bacon and mustard offering, glad that she'd cut off the crusts. How many people in his position would have put themselves out as he had? Albert had worked for Sidney Sullivan since he'd set up his coach business in 1919, and right from the beginning she remembered what a dear, pretty child Theo had been – Sidney's nephew, poor little fellow with no mother and a father who, from the way local gossip went, he might have been just as well off without. In those days the name Sullivan's Coaches had owed much to hope and confidence, for there had been but the one bus and Albert to drive and maintain it. Soon a second had been added, the route extended, a second driver engaged. But Albert had been the first and, as time went on and the company grew and prospered it was he who had been put in charge of the depot. If Theo had endeared himself to her, so he certainly had to his uncle, who often proudly brought him to the workshops where even as a child he'd been welcomed by any of the staff on hand, delighting in his outgoing friendliness. Tessa had seen him there often enough for, like him, she liked the cheery atmosphere of the workshops.

Remembering how things had been, then looking to the shapeless future, she was scared. It was one thing to be brave and cheerful while Theo was still with them, but in another day or two he'd be gone, and they would be by themselves miles from all they'd ever known. But as she packed the remnants of the picnic breakfast into her basket there was nothing in her expression to hint at her fears. Nearer the truth, Tessa's thin face was never a mirror to her thoughts; pale, thin, round-shouldered, she gave the impression of frailty which was far from the truth.

'On we go,' Theo beamed, standing up ready to offer assistance to Albert, who had been seated on the step of a stile.

'You help the missus and her packages; I'll manage.' And so he would. It would take more than an empty, pinned-up trouser leg to beat Albert Humphries. A giant of a man, ruddy complexioned and with a ready smile that hid images of the future every bit as terrifying as Tessa's. 'And now we've done eating, Samson better be given a couple of minutes to stretch his legs.'

'I'll get him. No traffic about, he'll be all right off the lead.' Theo said it with more hope than confidence, for the Humphries' large, well-meaning retriever cum sheepdog was, in Theo's opinion, utterly crazy. As if to prove him right, once out of the car Samson mounted the step vacated by Albert, leapt the stile and was away across the field. Despite all the calling and whistling, it was ten minutes before he came back, tail swinging, a large stick in his mouth and a look of hope in his eyes.

'Don't take it away from him,' Tessa said, 'he's found it, so let him bring it in the car with him. I'll see to it that he doesn't chew it up and make a mess.' Today she was all too aware of what it was like to drive away and leave the things you'd loved behind you.

2

So they were settled in the Riley, Albert in the front with Theo, Tessa, the basket, Samson and a two-foot long stick in the back. The next time the car stopped they would have arrived and they would see for themselves what sort of a place Heathfield Cottage was. Would the neighbours be hanging over their gates to watch the van being unloaded? Well, they'd not see much to interest them there, for Heathfield Cottage had come to her as it stood. Apart from clothes, linen and bedding, all they'd had carried out to the van yesterday had been treasures she couldn't bring herself to part with: the pretty little table Albert had made when they were first married, the standard lamp, the fire screen she'd embroidered, pictures, the canterbury that had come to her from her aunt, china, ornaments and her few bits of silver – for inheriting the cottage from a bachelor she didn't like to imagine its contents. Anyway she could no more live without her treasures than she could live without the clothes that comprised her wardrobe. Maybe they weren't up-to-date fashions like those glamour pussies who grinned from the pages of all those movie magazines, but they were *hers*, part of her life. She had to accept the changes, she had to get used to a new way of living. Firmly, Tessa believed that Fate mapped out your pattern and you had to accept it, like it or no. And a kind Fate it must have been that had ended her cousin Augustus life only weeks after Albert's accident. 'You can always put his cottage up for sale,' was what Albert had said. But Tessa knew better. If Fate took a hand like that, then it wasn't for them to twist things around to suit themselves. A cottage of their own instead of renting as they always had in Moorleigh, a few pounds behind them to eke out the pension Mr Sidney had insisted on paying Albert . . . and here she was, feeling sorry for herself; she ought to be ashamed. As if he read her thoughts, Samson gave his tail an extra fierce wave and put his front paws on her lap so that he could reach to lick her face.

Less than an hour later they reached Heathfield Cottage. There were no neighbours watching; there were no neighbours. It must have been more than half a mile since they'd turned onto the bumpy lane in Wickley Cross and there had been no sign of a house until they reached Heathfield Cottage. Then, looking ahead of them, the lane seemed to narrow into a track that appeared to be going nowhere.

'Work to be done here, that's for sure,' Tessa put a note of vim and vigour into her voice as she took stock of the overgrown garden and sadly neglected cottage.

'All the time in the world to do it, my dear,' Albert was just as determined not to be beaten. All this had come about on *his* account, that was something he couldn't forget.

'I'll stay a few days if you'll put up with me,' the ever-cheerful Theo told them. 'We'll soon lick it into some sort of shape.'

The early summer day was glorious, the haze hanging over the downs on either side of the road hinting at a wonderful world beyond. Another half mile and Anna would be at Wickley Cross where she would turn left into the rutted lane that led her home. She could always leave her bicycle in the back yard of Alfred Harmann's shop and travel to town on the special market-day bus, but except for when the roads were icy, no matter what the elements threw at her, she preferred her independence. Wednesdays gave her a freedom quite different from any other day. Not that her movements were restricted; they never had been. With six days of every seven spent mostly alone deep in the silent solitude of the country (for in such surroundings she didn't consider the distant lowing of cattle or the occasional bark of a dog as breaking the silence), even as a child she had thought of Wednesday as 'special', a day that brought hope of some added adventure. There had been almost no traffic on the narrow road from Wickley Cross to Brindley, so on a suitably small bicycle she had been allowed to make the trip on her own. With more than enough money to cover her needs and a shopping list written by Mrs Short carried securely in the purse attached to a strap that hung around her neck, she would set off on her mission with a feeling of importance; and no one at home had considered it might be seen as strange for a child on her own to order her own lunch in the Olde Copper Kettle café. She had loved the bustle of people and the cries of the stallholders. Childhood behind her, she no longer anticipated adventure, yet subconsciously that bubble of excitement still lurked. Somewhere out there 'life' was waiting for her – perhaps this would be the day Fate led her to its path.

Having bought the first strawberries of the season and some clotted cream to go with them, a bag of potatoes no bigger than alley marbles and with skins that came off at a touch, on that particular Wednesday she'd still had enough left to eat roast beef in the Olde Copper Kettle and put sixpence in the barrel-organist's collecting box. With economy playing no part in her outings, she always made sure that any luxury she brought home would be sufficient not just for herself and her grandfather but for all of them: themselves, Mrs Short, Lily and Potts too.

After pretty well an hour's hard pedalling, with less than a mile to go, she turned off the road onto the last stage of her ride. The lane was rutted and the basket strapped to her handlebars felt heavy, so no wonder she wasn't able to save herself when a large, shaggy dog rushed barking towards her, his tail flailing in excitement. She wobbled, and instinctively put out a hand to save her shopping, but it was too late.

'Samson! Sam, come here! Oh dear, I *am* so sorry. He's excited, you see, we're only just moving in.' As agitated as her dog was excited, Tessa Humphries hurried from the front garden of Heathfield Cottage. Anna was sprawled inelegantly on the stony lane, showing a pair of beanpole thin legs and with her shopping scattered around her. Her assailant was apparently delighted to have her at ground level and proceeded to lick her face in greeting. 'Wretched animal! I always stand up for him, but I think Albert's right: sometimes you'd think he hadn't a ha'porth of sense.'

'He's already apologised.' Anna laughed, her initial anger at the onslaught melting, probably overtaken by the sharp pain in her ankle and the sting of a grazed knee. Once on her feet she'd feel better, she told herself, mustering up her dignity. 'The only damage is that my handlebars need straightening but I'll soon do that.' She spoke brightly, determined to stay on top of the situation in front of the stranger. Heathfield Cottage had been empty for ages, but she remembered how as a child she used to hate passing in case the owner was about. Could this pasty looking woman be something to do with him? Seldom did she see anyone at all on the long, uneven lane; to meet a stranger was a rarity indeed. Then, her bicycle retrieved, as she held the front wheel between her legs, preparing to straighten the handlebars, a voice called from the jungle that used to be a front garden.

'Wait, I'll do it.' If it was a rarity to meet a stranger, to meet one like this was surely the heaven-sent moment she'd imagined. Her first impression was that he was handsome, but within seconds that first impression had been overtaken by a second. Aesthetic, that was the word that sprang to her mind; he had the face of a poet, with fine features, the long upper lip of a sensitive mouth, eyes as dark as coals. There was something in his appearance that suggested he came from far away, that his roots were in the Latin races. Perfectly capable of straightening her own handlebars, she surprised herself just how willingly she let him take her place while she brushed the dirt from her gingham dress and ran her fingers through her short wavy hair in an effort to present a better picture. He was well dressed with an eye to modern fashion, his blazer pocket bearing a gilt crest that looked more than anything like crossed propellers (perhaps they were supposed to be oars?), his pale-fawn trousers immaculately pressed, his shirt a gleaming white and open at the neck to allow for his cravat. He may have had the face of a poet, but not the attire. His two-tone shoes shone as though they had never made the acquaintance of mud, while his voice was in keeping with his well-turned-out appearance. Those were the thoughts that chased through her mind in the seconds it took him to cross the lane.

'I'll take my silly dog back in the garden,' Tessa said, smiling affectionately at Theo. Always the same, bless him, she wouldn't wonder this young lass would be the same as all the others. Like flies round a honeypot they were, and no wonder.

With the handlebars straight Theo turned his attention to Anna.

'You've grazed your knee. You must come back to the house with me,' he said, in a voice that told her he wasn't used to argument.

'I'm not hurt, not really hurt. I just fell awkwardly. Anyway, I'm nearly home. I live just along the lane.'

'Even so, I shall drive you home.' To him his voice sounded masterful; Theo was enjoying himself.

Dunsford House, where Anna lived with her grandfather, was the nearest house so there was no logic in his suggestion. That and Heathfield Cottage were the only two dwellings in the long lane.

'There's no need. I'm perfectly all right, honestly. And I'll be home in no time.'

She might as well not have spoken. With the bicycle propped against the hedge that divided the lane from Farmer Gingell's top field, he had started to gather up her scattered shopping.

Fortunately the strawberries had come to no worse harm than spilling from their punnet into the brown paper bag; the potatoes had spread further and he was busy collecting them while Samson, who had again escaped, this time by wriggling through a gap in the hedge, barked with excitement as he nosed the tin of clotted cream, his hind quarters wagging out of control at the discovery of his game.

'I'm not letting you ride. Sit down again and wait while I collect the car. It's only across there in that jungle of a garden. I've been seeing the new owners settled at Heathfield Cottage.'

Curiosity getting the better of her, she sat on the grassy verge and watched him wheel her bicycle away. What made her fall in with his instructions so easily? She didn't try to find the answer – it was enough that today had broken the usual Wednesday routine. In no time she heard the low throbbing of the engine and an open-topped Riley, with her bicycle lifted onto the back seat, reversed through the opened gates in the overgrown hedge that divided the wilderness of a garden from the lane.

'There's no need,' she muttered, 'honestly, I'm fine.'

'If we only did anything out of necessity, what a dull time we'd have. Humour me. And Sam, it seems he wants to come too. He'll have to share the back seat with the bicycle. He means no harm, you know, his trouble is that he has the brain of a sparrow.' He shifted the position of her bicycle to make room for Sam, but he needn't have bothered, for the dog stood on his hind legs, his head forced between theirs, the nearest thing to a canine grin on his face.

She wished the drive home were longer. Cycling it would have taken perhaps five minutes, allowing for the fact that she had to walk the last uphill part. In a car the journey was nothing.

'I've come for a few days to see Mr and Mrs Humphries settled in to Heathfield Cottage. I understand it's been empty a long time and he's not able to be much of a help.' Theo Sullivan managed to combine driving with taking stock of his passenger. Slightly built, arms and legs thin as matchsticks, yet by anyone's standards she was a delight to look at with her high cheekbones, her tawny brown wavy hair cut into a fringe that emphasised eyes which were surely of the exact same colour, thick lashes and straight clear-cut brows. An artist might have imagined painting her, a poet might have waxed lyrical about her elfin-like appearance –

7

and yet neither would have captured a quality in her character quite at odds with her waif-like build. Theo was enjoying himself. 'Perhaps we ought to introduce ourselves. I'm Theo Sullivan and, as I said, I'm here to see the Humphries settled. And you?'

'My name's Anna Bartlett. I live with my grandfather at Dunsford House. That's its chimney you can see above those trees.'

'Just you and your grandfather?'

'Oh no. There's Mrs Short and Lily, then there's Potts who helps Grandpa and does things in the garden when he has time.'

'And where do you fit in?'

'Pretty uselessly, if I'm truthful.' She took a peek at him. Willingly, or more truthfully, eagerly, she acknowledged that she liked what she saw; she only wished he meant to make his home at Heathfield with the couple he seemed so concerned about.

'How long have you lived here? There doesn't seem much at Wickley Cross. Don't you find it lonely?'

'I can barely remember when I didn't live here. My parents left me with Grandpa while they went on holiday to Italy. I was only three, so it's pretty well all I remember.'

'Some holiday!' Idle conversation, for it could hardly be of interest to him when he was only here for a day or two.

'They only went for a month or so. But there was an accident. They were out at sea on a friend's sailing boat with a party – they loved parties – and there was a fire on board. My grandfather told me how it had happened long afterwards. He showed me the letter he'd kept that their friend had written to him. They'd been quite near the shore, but not near enough for anyone to row out to them in time. When they couldn't put out the fire, they'd all dived into the water and made for the beach. And that was the last anyone saw of them. Mother couldn't swim; my father must have tried to save her but both of them were lost.'

'That was dreadful for you.'

'I wish I'd been older so that I could remember them more. I just have a hazy recollection: parties, people, rushing about, that's what they liked. I expect I should have hated that sort of life.'

'And here? Have you friends living close? It seems completely isolated.'

'I've always been used to just myself for company, being on my own was no problem.' She brushed his concern aside. Talking to strangers was a rare thing for Anna; the experience was exciting for even though she'd not been used to mixing with people she knew nothing about shyness. 'We're almost there, the gate is just round the bend.' Any second it would be over, he would unload her bicycle and drive away.

Instead, he braked and brought them to a standstill before they reached the bend in the lane.

'You said you're staying a day or two,' she said almost without thinking. Anything to make the moments last. 'Where do you really live? Have you taken some time off from your work?'

'I live in Devon, just outside a place called Moorleigh. Moorleigh is hardly more than a hamlet, so you won't have heard of it. It's only a few miles from Deremouth, the coastal town.'

'What do you do?' Curiosity got the better of manners. Anyway, what did manners matter? In a few minutes he'd be gone, but she wanted to keep him talking, to give herself things to remember. 'I mean, how do you earn your living? You have to go to Deremouth – or Exeter?' She felt pleased with herself that she remembered enough about where Deremouth was to know that if the place he called Moorleigh was near there, then it couldn't be terribly far from the city.

'I don't *have* to go anywhere. My work – if you call it that – is at home. My uncle runs the business; I naturally spend time there. I suppose I grew up with it.'

'A farm, you mean? So you know all about living in the country.'

'Indeed I know about the country. Yes, we have a farm.'

'You don't look like a farmer.' She smiled at him when she said it, as if to take the sting out of her words. 'I mean, you don't look like any of the farmers around here. I expect that's because you've got scrubbed up and dressed to bring Mr and Mrs Humphries. I only ever see any of the local farmers in their working things.' By this time she had forgotten that half an hour ago she'd not even met him! She supposed either Mr or Mrs Humphries must be a relative, which must be why he could free himself so easily from the family business.

'Mr Humphries was forced to give up work recently. They know no one in this district, but they were insistent that they should move here.'

Why had they chosen to come to neglected Heathfield Cottage?

'They will be our neighbours so I shall call to welcome them. That must have been Mrs Humphries I saw.'

'I shall be grateful if you'll do that, Miss . . . ? I say, do I have to call you Miss? I'm sorry, I forget what you said your name was.'

'Anna Bartlett. Just Anna will do.'

'Anna,' he repeated, 'It suits you. But the Humphries – they've never actually lived in a town, although this is worse than quiet: it's isolated. Surely you must have found it lonely?'

'Have I? I've never known anything else.' She considered his words. 'As long as I always closed the gates and never walked on any crops, I've been allowed to go wherever I like on my own, but I've never thought of that as being lonely. I suppose I made up the friends I wanted. That's not loneliness, it's almost magic. It brings to life all sorts of wonderful things. I've always read a lot, so there was no limit to the people I made my friends.'

'What about school?' He looked round at the empty fields, imagining the downs beyond. 'Living here, you must have gone away to school – surely you weren't taken all the way to Brindley each day?'

She supposed courtesy made him attempt to show an interest. But she talked willingly: anything to put off the moment when the car would drive away and she would be left with – with what? It was true that as a child she'd never consciously been lonely; it was also true that even as an adult she'd never lost her faith that somewhere, some day, 'life' waited just around the corner. Now, on this day that had brought such a break with the routine of her Wednesday trip, she was horribly aware of that isolation he talked about. But she needn't let herself think of that – not yet.

'School?' She laughed at the question. 'I've never been inside a school. When my parents left me with Grandpa, Miss Sherwin was already looking after me. I told you, they were very social people, a child must have been a dreadful inconvenience. Miss Sherwin was a sort nursemaid cum governess. She'd been a schoolteacher, but I think she liked the idea of just one child to look after. We had lessons every day, just baby ones at first. I expect it was quite different from proper school but I bet there's lots I know that I wouldn't have been taught in a classroom. Of course there was plenty we didn't bother with. She taught me to use a sewing machine and make my own blouses and skirts;

10

she used to say that would be much more useful than stitching nothing but embroidery. I learnt some French – not like I would have learnt it at school, or so she said. She taught me sentences, first just a few, then gradually I learnt more so that we had a rule that on Tuesdays of each week that was the only language we were allowed to speak. Even Grandpa joined in sometimes. Poor Mrs Short,' she added, laughing as she spoke, 'she "couldn't abide Tuesdays", that's what she used to say. You'd think she would have tried to learn so that she could talk too, wouldn't you? But she used to stay tight lipped and disapproving.' Then, another chuckle. 'I expect a Frenchman would have thought we sounded funny, although I believe I know enough to manage if ever I cross the Channel. But mostly it was literature. With Miss Sherwin I found out about loving books. Stories are alive if you let them open the door into their world. So, you see, that's how I've never been short of friends.'

'Tell me about your grandfather. Tell me about what you do with your days. Not just what's gone. But now.' He was surprised to hear himself asking.

'There's nothing to tell you about my grandfather. Really my parents had an awful cheek dumping me on him even for a month or so when he'd come to live here for peace and quiet. That's really all he's ever asked. He never needs people, books have always been his world. He used to be a classics master. Long before I came to live with him ill health had forced him to give up – that, and I suppose age too. That's when he bought Dunsford House, looking for peace in his old age. But I don't think he could ever refuse my mother anything, so he had a three-year-old thrust on him. And after that, there was nowhere to send me.'

'Children always think their grandparents are ancient.'

'Yes, but he really was. He was, oh I don't know, forty something, when he married. So was my grandmother, but she died when Mother was tiny. As Mrs Short says, Grandpa's longevity is quite remarkable.'

He smiled. What a quaint combination she was: one moment as prim as no doubt this elderly grandparent expected and the next as excited as a child.

'And this Miss Sherwin, is she still with you?'

'Giving me lessons?' Anna laughed. 'Silly. She's been gone for ages. She found a job in a girls' school in Reading. I've

11

seen her since she left, of course, but she belongs to *them* now, not to me.'

'So you look after your grandfather?' What an unnaturally tedious life for a pretty young girl. His stay with the Humphries was getting more promising by the minute.

'Sometimes I think I'm not very useful at all. Mrs Short takes care of everything; she's been with him since she was just a girl herself. Even before my mother was born Mrs Short was there. Of course, she has help in the house but she's in charge. Then there's Potts, who helps my grandfather with things he can't manage.'

'And you say you aren't lonely?' he prompted, certain a lot remained unsaid.

In that, he was right. Never had she been so near confiding in anyone as she was at that moment. But she overcame the temptation. He might patronise her, laugh at her!

'I may not run the house for Grandpa,' came the prim reply, 'but I'm not empty headed enough to find my life boring. Only boring people get bored – that's something else Mrs Short says. My days are very well occupied.'

'Don't you ever want to spread your wings and fly?'

If she did, she wasn't prepared to tell him so.

'Growing up in the country doesn't mean you have to become a cabbage. I read the newspaper and discuss with my grandfather what's happening in the world. We like to know what goes on, not just what we are going to have for dinner.'

He laughed, surprised to find himself enjoying a companion so naïve.

'Here comes Mrs Short, looking for me.' There was nothing in Anna's manner to tell him of the sudden nosedive in her spirits as she groped for the door handle. Theo was ahead of her and by the time she climbed out he was holding the door open. Always the junior member of the household, she was unused to such treatment; it added to the magic of an afternoon that in another minute would be no more than a memory.

Amelia Short advanced on them, criticism in her every movement. A tall woman with youth put firmly behind her. Her dark hair had silver wings at the temples and was pulled tightly to be pinned in a bun on the crown of her head. Straight, tall, slim, confident; but what right had a housekeeper to speak to Anna as she did?

'And about time too!' Amelia said, pointedly ignoring Theo and his car.

'I've enjoyed talking to you.' Equally pointedly he spoke just to Anna as he lifted her bicycle to the ground and stacked her shopping in the basket.

'Did you get my cotton?' Again he might have been invisible.

'Yes, of course I did,' Anna answered, unperturbed and clearly used to the housekeeper's manner. 'It's in my purse. Goodbye Theo, and thank you for the ride. Tell Mr and Mrs Humphries I am looking forward to calling on them. I'll give them a few days to get settled first.' Then, taking her bicycle from him, she followed Mrs Short and he heard the gate click shut behind them.

Back in the car Theo found Sam sitting bolt upright in the front passenger seat, his face carrying a message of hope. Now it's just us, any chance of a walk? he managed to convey.

'All right, old fellow. We'll find somewhere to turn, then you can have a run. How's that?'

Apparently it was the answer Sam had wanted, for his mouth opened wide enough for his long tongue to loll out as he panted in anticipation of things to come. Further along the lane Theo found a field gateway wide enough for him to turn the car then, remembering his promise, he stopped the engine and got out, followed closely by his excited friend. He really ought to get back to the cottage – he'd come to help. But it was pleasant enough out here, throwing sticks for Sam, letting his mind wander back to the elfin-like creature who'd been dropped into his path just when he'd considered the next few days promised nothing but dull jobs that Albert Humphries could no longer do himself. Ten minutes of freedom, then his conscience prodded harder. So Samson, complete with yet another stick, was persuaded into the car and they returned to Heathfield Cottage where Theo changed into a pair of corduroy trousers, rolled up his shirtsleeves and attacked the undergrowth with a scythe. He worked with energy, but his mind wasn't on what he was doing. Two or three days could easily stretch into a week if he decided that was what he wanted. Female company was always his for the asking, so what was so special about the elf? Tomorrow he'd 'test the water'; he might well find her no fun at all. His decision made, he concentrated on the overgrown nettles.

13

Anna meanwhile couldn't so easily put the afternoon out of mind, indeed she didn't even try.

Dunsford House had seen a great change since a time more than 300 years earlier when the solid, stone edifice had been built as a row of three, or perhaps even of four, labourers' cottages. So it had continued until the mid-nineteenth century when accommodation had been built adjoining the farmyard for the workers. Desolate and unloved, the old cottages had stood empty. And that's how they had been when, some sixty years later Cuthbert Hamilton's life had been knocked off course. Just as his daughter had married and he'd been left on his own – with the exception of the faithful Amelia Short – ill health had finally brought about his retirement from the public school where he had taught. Amelia had kept house for him since she'd been in her twenties, so he had taken it for granted that she should accompany him as he viewed properties in a quest to find one to become their new home; and it had been she who had had the vision and had persuaded him that the centuries-old building, isolated from neighbours, could be converted to suit his needs. With little interest in looking towards the future, he hadn't asked himself why she wanted them to bury themselves so far from any trace of human life. He'd simply been relieved that someone else was making the decisions. While they shared a rented villa in Brindley, builders had set to work converting the erstwhile labourers' dwellings. The row of cottages had been transformed into a gentleman's residence, one that gave no hint that it wasn't just as it had been built at the time of Elizabeth I. The house had needed a name – something else Cuthbert had left in Amelia's hands. Her maiden name had been Dunsford, so that had been her choice.

'Who is this young fellow I understand brought you home?' Cuthbert asked Anna as they sat together at the dining table eating their strawberries and cream. There was more criticism than interest in the question. Mrs Short had reported that she had been brought back from market in some strange man's car. Not at all the way to behave! At his time of life he ought not to have worries thrust on him. And look at her now, sitting there so straight, trying to look as though butter wouldn't melt in her mouth. He may be old but he was neither blind nor stupid. The

14

girl was bursting with excitement. Who the devil was the fellow and what was he doing taking up with a girl out on her own?

'He is staying at Heathfield Cottage for a few days, seeing some elderly friends are comfortably settled. I suppose it must have been sold at last; I wonder what happened to old Mr Cummings. Theo – that's who I met this afternoon – is very concerned about his friends; he says they've not been used to living anywhere so quiet. He was glad when I said I would call on them.'

'An elderly couple, you say,' he mused, feeling a tug of affection as he looked at Anna. What sort of a life was it for the child here? He'd done his best. Of course he had, she was his darling Elizabeth's girl. And she tried not to make a nuisance of herself. But it was no use pretending. He was nearly four score years and ten; getting through each day hampered with the infernal pain of joints that didn't want to move was burden enough without having a girl at her end of the scale looking to him for companionship. It wasn't right, it wasn't fair – not to her and not to him either. If Elizabeth could have seen into a crystal ball and known what the outcome of that Italian holiday would be, would she have left him to care for the child? But if she could have seen what the trip would bring, then she wouldn't have gone at all. Just think of it – if Elizabeth were still here, here in the flesh just as she was always here in his heart. She'd be forty-three, his darling little girl forty-three. Instead there was just Anna, something about her appearance so like her mother it tore at his heart to look at her. Yet there the similarity ended. Remember how Elizabeth had loved parties and company. This child knew no one, was unprepared for life. Had he failed her? How could she tell good from bad when she'd had no experience? Just look at her, prim as a Sunday school teacher yet with eyes like stars, stars put there no doubt by some bounder who'd spotted her in town and made her acquaintance. She needed friends of her own age. Nothing more dangerous to a girl than a head full of dreams.

'Elderly friends, you say. Pity they're not younger people with a family. Everyone needs company of their own age.' And from the way he said it Anna took his words to be a reminder that her company fell short of his needs. 'It's not right, a girl of your age hanging around here, doing nothing with your days.' She knew from his tone just how disgruntled he was.

15

'It's not that I'm lonely for company, Grandpa, but you're right. You know how often I've suggested looking for work. There must be *something*. I may not be trained for anything special, but I'm not stupid. I could soon learn a job.'

'We won't go into that again if you please, Anna. There's no need for you to earn a living. I'm not so impecunious that I can't afford to keep you and give you pocket money. Young women today seem to have no sense of their place in society. I know, I know,' raising his hand to silence her before she had a chance to interrupt, 'women make fine nurses, yes and teachers too; certainly there are fields that are acceptable. But for any of those you require the sort of academic education you lack. What sort of nonsense do you suggest? A shop girl? A waitress? Do you imagine I'd allow you to cycle seven miles each morning to sit in some miserable office doing the bidding of an employer who would treat you as an inferior? We'll hear no more of it, if you please. I promised your dear mother that I'd look after you while she was away. Then the Lord took her life. All these years I've kept my word to her. I lost her mother, then I lost her, and in their place I have responsibility for you. Are you seriously expecting me to break faith? Just eat your strawberries and we'll say no more about it.' Then as a parting shot, 'I'm surprised that you haven't a better mind than to let yourself become bored.'

'I'm *never* bored.' She heard herself saying it for the second time in a few hours. Could she be running away from the truth?

Cuthbert settled back into his habitual silence. Urging him into some topical discussion was important to Anna; somehow she saw that as her contribution to his care. As she'd told Theo, she read the newspaper avidly and she encouraged her grandfather to interest himself in what was going on in the world. Internationally, they had gone down the road of the Hitler Youth Movement, the creation of the Luftwaffe, the new German 'people's car' made by Volkswagen. She scoured the newspapers, drawing his attention to a changing scene abroad and at home: the new innovation of frozen food – not yet on sale in Brindley or Wickley Cross; the talking television that had been on display at the Radio Exhibition – something that was hard to imagine as neither of them had ever seen television pictures; the fire that, a few months earlier had destroyed Crystal Palace and had led him to recall memories of his youth; they'd aired their views on the latest sculpture

16

by Henry Moore, they'd both read Evelyn Waugh's *A Handful of Dust* which she had given him for his birthday (an event he refused to be seen as a cause for celebration) and discussed it earnestly. Then there had been the abdication of King Edward, who gave up the throne for love of an American divorcee, Mrs Simpson: differing views, perhaps, but he had brought her up to listen and respect other people's opinions. A few months after that all the household had gathered around the wireless to listen to the coronation of George VI and Queen Elizabeth, their Union Jack nailed to a tall pole she and Potts had erected in the rosebed and seen by no one but themselves. Often in these discussions, her views and her grandfather's were complete opposites, but that never mattered. Between them was respect and, perhaps more than either of them realised, an undemonstrative affection. On impersonal subjects she could often lead him to talk; but anything personal and his interest immediately evaporated. His day-to-day living was no more than something to be endured – and she accepted that she fell into the category of day-to-day living.

This evening she was glad of the silence that settled at the end of her fruitless suggestion of looking for work, for it enabled her to let her mind wander where it would, taking her thoughts to her new acquaintance, reliving every moment. She liked the way his dark eyes seemed to ready to smile, and the way when the message reached his mouth it turned up at the corners. His voice was on 'laughter alert' too, even though it was deep and authoritative; his near-black hair was neither straight nor curly. He was no more than average height, yet he seemed taller because his back was so straight and his air so confident. And his hands, remember his hands, slender, beautifully kept and yet not effeminate. She smiled to herself as these thoughts drifted across her mind. Everything about him was right, everything fitted his personality just as it should. She had met no one like him – the heroes of her acquaintance lived simply in her imagination. As a child she had conjured up images of the figures of legend; only as she'd grown up had the subtle change come, developing with the literature she consumed and coming alive in the fantasies she created as her pen flew over the pages of her exercise books. And as she dreamed, as in her mind she conjured up such heroes, heroines, situations of tragedy and joy, never for a moment did she doubt that Fate would guide her to such a man. With all the naïve trust of her inexperienced youth she believed that today she had reached the milestone she had known waited along her path.

Amelia Short heard a car draw up in the lane, then the slam of its door. From the window of her sitting room she watched as Anna looked up from where she was weeding the border, let her hoe fall to the ground and went out to greet the young man who'd brought her home the previous day. The housekeeper's mouth was set in its habitual firm line as she weighed up the situation. Nothing to complain about in his looks, all the signs pointed to his being well heeled, but how much could you judge from appearance? In any case, a smart dresser like that would surely have had a girl or two in his sights before this. What interest could a young man of that ilk have in Anna? She didn't come out of the same mould as the sort of modern misses he would very likely be used to. Wonder what he's saying to her to put that look on her face? Too trusting, that was the child's trouble. Well, of course she was. What did she know about the way a man can treat you? Amelia pulled herself even straighter, if that were possible, as if she meant to take her thoughts in hand. You mustn't judge everyone by the way you were used, she told herself. This fellow, Theo Sullivan, hadn't the old gentleman said Anna had called him, he's fine enough to look at – too fine by half! But looks! Hah! Looks were the trouble. Give a man a pair of boss eyes or a nose like a strawberry and no girl would see him as God's gift. And as for Anna, the good Lord knows what nonsense all that reading has stuffed into her head. The old gentleman and me, we're about all she's ever known; just us and Alice Sherwin to fill her head with a lot of books and daydreaming. Well, I tell you what, Amelia voiced a silent opinion, good enough child as she might have tried to be, this house would settle down comfortably if she could find herself a husband and move on. A good husband, mind you. And that's more than can be said for most of them!

Moving slightly out of view she watched as Anna and the visitor stood talking, seemingly taking stock of the garden and the work done there. Now why would that be? Ah, now they were sitting on the bench under the sycamore tree – talking, still talking. Amelia would like to have changed places with that blackbird who was busy making his tea on a worm only a foot or two away from them. Young Anna, she seemed to be having a lot to say for herself – now what was he writing down in that notebook of his?

Had she been able to hear, she would have been reassured.

'I can't be away too long, but before I go back to Moorleigh I want to be sure they are going to manage. Albert Humphries has been with the business since the start. It was while he was working for us that he was hurt. You can't put a thing like that out of your mind. We have a responsibility for their future.'

'Hurt? Badly hurt? Was it with some sort of farm machine?'

'Farm? No. He was at the coach company –'

'But you said yesterday that you had a farm.'

'I expect you misunderstood. There is a farm, but my uncle owns Sullivan's Coaches; that's where Humphries worked. I've known him since I was small, nothing I liked better than to go to the depot. The world of transport is exciting, Anna. Think of the changes, the advances, in travel. But I was telling you about Humphries and why I can't go back until I know he can manage. You see the accident happened in the depot, when an inexperienced driver put a coach into reverse instead of forward gear. Humphries was trapped behind it, his leg crushed – and ultimately amputated. So you understand why it is I feel concerned for him.'

She nodded. Her hero was proving not to have feet of clay.

'What made them move so far from Moorleigh?'

'Fate, that's what Mrs Humphries says. She inherited Heathfield Cottage from some distant relative just when their lives were at a turning point. I wish it were nearer, or I wish they'd sold it and stayed where they were. But she is a great believer in life working to a set pattern and she saw the timing as fortuitous.' He laughed as he went on, 'Tessa Humphries is the sort who bows to a new moon, never walks under a ladder and who goes into a panic if she sees one magpie and no sign of its partner. In her mind I believe superstition and religion are one.' Then, the smile gone as quickly as it had come, 'You won't forget to speak to your gardener when he comes tomorrow. If he can manage two days a week for a while, the garden at the cottage can certainly use him; but even one day would be a blessing. I've hacked away some of the overgrowth, but I know it will depress Humphries to see the place needing attention and not be able to do anything about it.'

19

'When I call to see them, if we get on well enough, I might be able to persuade them to let me help too.'

'I can't ask you to do that.'

'No, of course you can't. But you can't stop me offering.'

He not so much looked *at* her as *into* her, his scrutiny making her uncomfortably aware that she had no idea of his thoughts.

'You say you're never lonely, but I can't believe it. These days plenty of women find work – wouldn't you rather do that than potter about here on your own?'

'It's not like you think.'

He shrugged, looking at her enquiringly, expecting her to elaborate on such a sweeping remark. Not for the first time she was tempted but, just as she had before, she resisted. If only she had the confidence to talk about the way she spent her solitary hours; but she hadn't. When she was ready she would send her work to be read; criticism and rejection from an unknown professional she could accept, accept and build on; but the thought of mockery from her grandfather and, she realised, even more importantly, from Theo, who had come into her life just as she'd always known he would, would be unbearable.

'Do you think I might meet your grandfather?' Theo changed the subject.

She took him indoors and introduced him to Cuthbert, sure that he would make a good impression and looking forward to seeing her grandfather charmed as he couldn't fail to be.

'No need for you to stay, Anna my dear. Off you go back to your weeds or whatever it is you are doing out there in the garden. We can manage very well on our own. Isn't that so, Mr Sullivan?'

'Indeed, sir, I've already made Anna waste half an hour's hoeing time. And please, not Mr Sullivan. My name is Theo.'

She left them, dismissed just as she might have expected when she'd been a child. Angry and disappointed she took up her hoe, but this time she brought it to work on the flower bed beneath the open window of the sitting room. She wanted to be part of what was being said yet she had no intention of letting them know she was nearby, so she had to stay out of their vision, which meant that although she could hear their voices she couldn't tell what they were talking about. One thing was certain: her grandfather's voice wasn't agitated, nor yet filled with self-pity; once she actually heard him laugh!

20

Already near perfect, in her estimation Theo was raised even higher.

The next day he took her to Heathfield Cottage, and after that most days they worked together there in the garden. He was surprised just how much fun he was having. He took her driving and called casually to collect her to come dog walking with him. Altogether he stayed ten days, leaving with no mention of coming again. Tomorrow he would be swallowed up in his busy life, the hours they'd spent together would mean nothing to him. For Anna, to remember her stupid faith that Fate had sent Samson bounding at her bicycle was humiliating.

Always alone, yet never lonely; that's what she'd told him, believing it to be the truth. Her company had come from the characters who peopled her imagination. She knew them so well, not just how they looked or what part they played in the plot of the stories she wrote, but how they thought, their likes and dislikes. None of that had changed, and yet now for the first time there was mockery in the solace she'd always found alone with her exercise books. This was how her years would pass, not with reality, not with real love. Fantasies, make-believe, that's what her life was built on and, for the first time, it failed her and she knew cold loneliness. All this because of a few wonderful hours with Theo Sullivan when she'd let herself rush headlong into the romantic adventure she longed for. He'd probably known and secretly laughed at her! Now she had nothing, she had less than nothing.

Chapter Two

From her first week at Dunsford House, Anna had been taught
the lesson of self-control. In a home where noise was frowned
on, even a three-year-old had had it drilled into her that tears
were something to be ashamed of, so she had learnt to bite her
lip and hide her feelings, at both joys and disappointments alike.
With childhood behind her it was second nature to her to live on
dreams that she shared with no one.

As the days of June went by and there was no word from
Theo, no one knew what his silence meant to her. She spent
her time just as she always had except that whereas before that
magic week she had been able to lose herself in the characters
she brought to life as she walked the lanes or scribbled in her
notebook, now they were an empty mockery. But no one guessed
her misery, there was nothing different in the determined way
she pedalled off to Brindley, worked the treadle of her sewing
machine as she turned the gingham she brought back into a dress,
clipped the hedge, cut off the first deadheads of the early roses,
or led her grandfather to discuss the news they listened to on the
wireless. On the surface everything was just as if Theo had never
come into her life (And more's the pity, Amelia Short thought,
a well-set-up young man like that could do very well for her –
and without the hustle and bustle of a young one in the house,
we could settle down comfortably enough, more than comfortably
enough. Quite time the old gentleman had a bit of peace, him and
me too.). The only addition to Anna's old routine was that she
sometimes called at Heathfield Cottage on the pretext of asking
if Tessa Humphries wanted eggs as she was on her way to Mr
Gingell's farm, or to Wickley Cross, so was there anything they

needed from the butcher? There was nothing in her manner to hint at her real reason for calling, her hope that she might be told there had been a letter from Theo and some hope that he was coming again. Any mention of him always came from one of the Humphries, who enjoyed reminiscing about their good years when Albert had been in charge of the coach depot, years when Theo had endeared himself to them so firmly. But as to mention of a letter from him, there was none. June turned to July bringing no word.

Then, two days into the new month, as suddenly as he had departed, so he returned. What was so different about this visit and his first? It was hard to pinpoint, for they had spent hours together each day when he'd been at Heathfield Cottage before. Yet there was a difference and when, this time after only two days, he returned to Moorleigh, Anna knew that before long he would be back.

For the average motorist the distance from Moorleigh to Wickley Cross would have made the journey an event. There were some from the Home Counties, the Midlands or even beyond who might make the journey to the West Country for their annual holiday, but Theo proved himself different from the average. A sports car to drive, the open road before him, and no distance was too long. As the weeks of summer progressed, without warning he would arrive at Heathfield Cottage, sure of his welcome and more than sure of Anna's delight when, unannounced, he walked through the garden gate of Dunsford House. Sometimes he'd stay over the weekend, but one visit in August lasted more than a week. Anna supposed that being part of a family business gave him freedom, just as it gave him a feeling of responsibility towards the faithful Albert Humphries. Stanley Mount, who worked at Dunsford House on Fridays, spent his Mondays bringing the cottage garden back into shape and, after that first visit, when Theo came to Heathfield, he did little more than sleep there. There was no doubt why he came so often: he came to be with *her*. She soon realised that he never committed himself to time and place, and always drove away with no mention of coming again; but by that time she was sure he would return.

Through the early weeks of September the countryside was damp and dreary under a heavy laden sky. It didn't surprise Anna that there was no sign of him, for somehow the magic of their time together had belonged to the golden days of summer. Then two things happened, coinciding and, in her mind, dependent upon each other: daylight brought misty sunshine; the ground was damp, not with rain but with morning dew and by midday the temperature soared, the garden once more filled with birdsong and the scent of summer; that was the day Theo returned. No mention of how long he meant to stay, but she'd come to know that he never looked ahead and planned. They took each day as it came. Sometimes they met soon after first light by the stile to Farmer Gingell's top field where she'd always been allowed to hunt for mushrooms; sometimes they walked the downs with crazy Samson leaping and bounding after rabbits, both real and imagined; sometimes they picked blackberries; it was always her job to find enough for bramble jelly at Dunsford House, but now there was also Heathfield Cottage with its apple crop waiting for blackberries to be added for Albert's favourite jam. Anna wouldn't let herself look beyond each perfect day.

It was an unseasonally hot morning when Theo had been there almost a week. The damp start to the month was forgotten, the muddy ruts in the lane had become rock hard and the sun beat down on the parched earth as if it were still high summer. By noon they were climbing into a punt at Goring, the Riley parked in a shady spot near the pathway to the river, a picnic hamper stowed aboard and not a cloud on their horizon. His prowess with the punting pole was just one more thing to add to his list of perfections. How handsome he was, his olive skin tanned, bareheaded, the sleeves of his white shirt rolled above his elbows, his cravat taken off, leaving his shirt open at the neck. He was all she had dreamed of as she had grown up on a diet of the great lovers of fiction, so perfect in every way that she was frightened to look ahead. To imagine a future with Theo was like tempting cruel Fate; to imagine a future without him was like losing faith. She touched his neatly folded blazer that lay at her side. When they walked together, sometimes they would loosely link hands; when they came to a stile he would climb it first, then as she stepped over he would lift her down. Did he guess how she willed him to hold her? He showed no sign of it. They might have been brother and sister, childhood friends. But even to have that much of him gave her this feeling of joy and fear, fear that when the wonderful summer was finally gone so too would Theo be.

'See that willow tree?' He cut into her daydreams. 'Let's tie up under that and eat our lunch.'

'I'll hold the branches out of the way while you steer us in.' She turned her back on him as they came near the overhanging tree, poised to make an archway for them to reach their secluded spot. Not that there was any sign of activity on the river – except for the weekends the punting season was over and the only occupants of the water meadows were bovine.

The magic lasted. They ate the food Tessa Humphries had prepared after Theo's early morning drive to Alfred Harmann's village shop at Wickley Cross. He produced a bottle of Burgundy which he'd bought and transferred to the picnic hamper when they'd parked the car.

'No glasses I'm afraid. Have you any objection to drinking wine from a picnic cup? Mrs Humphries insisted no picnic is complete without a flask of tea and I didn't like to offend her and tell her I'd got something better. Anyway, the cups will be useful.' Then, about to pour the tea away, 'You don't want this stuff do you? You'd prefer wine.' It wasn't a question.

'Today demands wine,' she said, laughing. Then, seriously, 'If we could hold time still, this is the day I would want to last for ever.' If only he would say he wanted it too. But he said nothing, only looked at her silently in a way that made her clench her teeth tight together in an effort to hide from him what was happening to her.

Somewhere upstream a moorhen called but apart from that there was no sound except the lapping of the water against the gently rocking punt. When he suggested they walked on the bank she agreed, not because she wanted to leave the isolation of their hiding place so much as dreading his teasing if he knew what it meant to her to be here, alone with him.

It seemed though that walking wasn't what he had in mind; only yards from the willow he sat down, still holding her hand and pulling her to the ground next to him. They shared the field with a herd of Jersey cows that came to drink nearby, one or two of them glancing in a disinterested way as they passed.

'You're what Nanny Harknell would call a funny ossity,' he said, looking at her with affectionate curiosity. 'Penny for your thoughts?'

'Nanny Harknell?'

'Never mind Nanny. Tell me what you're thinking, sitting there so quietly.'

Something in the way he said it put everything else out of her mind. Her throat felt tight, her arms ached, she wanted to touch him, she wanted –. '*My* thoughts? First tell me yours,' she whispered, for she seemed capable of nothing louder. His face was so close to hers, he was looking at her mouth, at her slightly parted lips. She moved nearer, now she could feel the warmth of his breath. His mouth covered hers – or did hers cover his? It wasn't the first time she'd felt this strange aching yearning. But today, here in the solitude of the meadow, she was conscious of their having come closer – any moment he would say the words she longed to hear. He loved her, he must love her or he wouldn't kiss her like that; she could tell it even in the way he breathed, in the way he caressed her. Her fingers moved on the back of his neck, his warm hand cupped her tiny firm breast first through her blouse and then beneath it, his fingers fondling her hardened nipple and waking desires that tingled in every nerve, that took away her power to think and filled her with emotions she didn't question. Reared in the country, she understood and accepted the ways of nature. But nothing prepared her for the wild, hungry need that flooded through her – and through him too, she knew it did. If she'd grown up with companions of her own age she would have been more aware of the lines drawn by convention. Had she not been in love with Theo then the situation would have been different; she wouldn't have been lying on the sun-baked ground, listening only to the voice of instinct, consumed by emotions outside her knowledge, beyond anything she had ever experienced, even alone with her dreams or the loves of the characters she created.

'Theo,' she whispered, to say his name somehow making him part of the half-understood longing that blinded her to all else.

'Darling, darling Anna,' he mumbled, his mouth almost on hers, 'I want you, dear God but I want you. Now . . . I want you now . . . now this very moment.' It was as if he talked more to himself than to her.

When he fumbled with the buttons of her blouse she undid them rejoicing as he looked at her nakedness, glad that in this heatwave she'd worn neither brassiere nor slip. His mouth tugged at her nipple and when she felt his hand on her leg she guided it.

26

Surely all those heroes and heroines of the great romances must have known this consuming need just as she and Theo did.

The sun beat down on them; the cattle wandered back into the shade on the far side of the field. When Theo moved onto her, she pulled him close, closer, his flesh in her flesh. One body – one spirit – she felt exalted. Never had she known such exquisite agony, there was nothing in her world but this, this, *this*. 'Dear God, but I want you,' his words echoed and re-echoed. He loved her. The rest of her life would be just as wonderful as this, belonging always to each other.

Afterwards they paddled in the river, he with his trousers rolled up above his knees and she holding her skirt high. They splashed water over each other laughing like excited children, full of sudden vitality. Then they returned the punt to the boatyard and, almost silently, drove home. What was there to say? Words had no place after the wonder of what they had shared.

'You'll come in and talk to Grandpa,' she said when finally he drove her home. It wasn't a question. Of course he'd want to speak to her grandfather: he'd ask for her hand in marriage, partly out of courtesy and partly because she was still four months off twenty-one and his consent was necessary. After today nothing would ever be the same again. There would be a wedding to arrange, a future to plan.

'Not this time,' he answered. 'I've been away too long – this evening I must face the road and drive home. If I don't hang about I can be on my way in under an hour.'

'But does Mrs Humphries know you're leaving today?'

'She will,' he laughed, 'when I tell her. Don't look so puzzled, little elf.'

'I just think it's a bit inconsiderate.' Pride made her hide her own hurt. 'She will have cooked a meal for you –'

'Something I shall have to sacrifice if I'm not to be on the road half the night. So out you hop, my pretty one.'

The wonder of the afternoon might never have happened.

'When are you coming back?' Even pride couldn't stop her asking.

'Soon, I dare say. Don't pin me down, Anna. It's easy enough for folk like you, no responsibilities, time always your own.'

The way he leant across her to open the car door seemed only one stage removed from ejecting her. So, head high she climbed out and slammed the door closed.

'Good girl,' he grinned, half closing one eye in something resembling a wink. Just for that second the intimacy of their hour by the river was back with them.

'Come back soon.'

'It's a long way,' he teased, 'promise to make it worth my while.'

She wished he hadn't said it. His words made a joke of what was precious. Or hadn't it been like that for him? Was what they'd done a normal way for a couple to behave? I know so little, she told herself angrily, that's the trouble. How can I expect to write great, worthwhile books when I don't even know if what we did was what men would expect if they were alone with the girl they loved? With all my might I willed him to say he loved me; but he didn't. No, but then I didn't actually say it to him either. He must know that I do, or I wouldn't have wanted us to love each other like that.

The sound of his car had faded by the time she clicked the gate closed and started up the path to the house.

That night the hot weather broke with a thunderstorm, one that put a final end to summer. The changing colour of the leaves painted the country with a hint of gold and, just as it had after his first visit, a month went by with no word from Theo, by which time another fear was casting a shadow, one that grew darker with each passing day. Was it so easy to get pregnant that it could happen the very first time? Or had her regular cycle been upset because she'd made love and was no longer a virgin? There was no one she could talk to – all she could do was hope with each new day that the worry would be lifted. Please, she begged silently, make Theo come back so that I can talk to him. I may be worrying for nothing. Am I worrying for nothing?

The countryside seemed to be permanently shrouded in mist. How could she expect him to drive all that way in the fog? If he doesn't come by next week I'll write and tell him – I'll have to, it will be the end of October. But it's not the way I wanted it to be. All right, she argued with herself, I know he does love me, remember how wonderful it was – but knowing it isn't the same as hearing it said. I want him to ask me to marry him, and me to say yes because it's what I long for more than anything in the world; but asking me because he has to and me saying yes because of a baby, would make it not the same no matter how much we might love each other. But perhaps when you make love for the first time it makes you miss a whole month. If only I knew someone young and married, someone I could ask questions like that. Instead she cycled to Brindley and sat in the Public Reference Library reading medical books that were beyond her understanding in the vain hope of finding an explanation – other than the one that became increasingly certain. Theo was her only hope. Perhaps he'll come today, was her first thought each morning, or tomorrow, as the hours of each day went by.

As October drew to a close there was nowhere for her to hide from the truth. Ought she to write to him? How long would it be before he could be spared from the coach company? Was she being fair to him not to tell him?

Then came the morning when she got out of bed, the room seemed to reel and she was assailed by nausea.

'You look a bit humperty this morning,' Mrs Short greeted her as she came downstairs half an hour or so later feeling limp from a bout of sickness. 'Not going down with anything, I hope.'

Anna felt all the world must suspect what she was trying to hide. Of course, she told herself, they have no idea. It's only because I feel guilty that Mrs Short seems to be looking at me in such a knowing way. She'll expect me to eat breakfast.

'The old gentleman's having his in his room. I'll tell Lilly to bring your kippers.'

The smell of the fish wafted into the hall. Anna clenched her teeth, frightened to speak, wanting Mrs Short just to be gone so that she could retreat back to the lavatory before she lost the battle. Yet five minutes later, finally alone at the table, she realised how hungry she was. Kippers, crusty bread spread thickly with butter and a cup of strong black coffee restored her.

But Mrs Short had watched her starry-eyed adoration of Theo through the weeks of summer. With the exception of the 'old gentleman, bless his heart', she mistrusted all men. Had her brief marriage to Jimmy Short left her widowed and with happy memories, then Anna's early fears might have gone unnoticed; but Amelia had fled when she could no longer stand being used as an unpaid housekeeper and a licensed receptacle for his perverted

29

lust. Cuthbert Hamilton's gentle respect had done much to dim her memories, but worrying about Anna brought them alive. Hadn't she known from when she'd first clapped eyes on Theo Sullivan that he spelt trouble? Trouble. Was that the truth? Was the girl in trouble? It became Mrs Short's duty to watch and listen. With no mother to take an interest in the girl, someone had to do it. She'd had no first-hand experience of pregnancy, but she'd read plenty of letters in her weekly magazine: she knew the signs.

'A word with you, Anna. Just come inside my sitting room and close the door.' Such a request was unheard of and immediately Anna was on her guard.

'Is something wrong? Something wrong with Grandpa?'

'Only thing wrong with him, bless his heart, is that he's lived too many years to deserve worries. It's you I'm concerned with. Now, answer me truthfully. No fobbing me off with it not being my business. If I don't try and look after you then the Lord alone knows who can. You and that Theo Sullivan, have you been doing things you shouldn't?'

'No. It's narrow minded and beastly to call it that.'

'Ah, so I was right. And now the young bounder has gone off and left you in the cart. Is that about the size of it?'

'Mrs Short, you aren't being fair to him. When he comes back I'll tell him. We shall be married – not because of the baby, but because we love one another.'

'Oh my dear Lord, what can we do? You're just an ignorant child, knocking twenty-one or not. And as for me, what do I know about how to rid you of something like this? Nothing. Nothing and no one who can help us.'

A minute earlier Anna's reaction had been anger, anger partly based on fear. But those last words – 'who can help *us*' – touched a vulnerable spot.

'It'll be all right, Mrs Short.' It took all her effort to hold her mouth rigid, somehow the effect making her voice expressionless. 'Any day Theo will be back. Then I'll tell him. It's going to be all right.'

'No use dilly-dallying. You get a letter off to him.'

'I don't want to do it that way. It would be like greeting him with it the moment I see him. I want us to talk about being married first.'

Mrs Short's sniff spoke volumes. 'What we want and what

we get aren't always the same thing. Oh dear, oh Lord. I had my doubts about him right from when I clapped eyes on him. Too smart by half. Can't trust a body who sets such store in his own appearance, that's what I thought. But the old gentleman, he seemed to take to him.'

'Of course he did. Theo is – is –'

'Enough of that. I don't want to hear all your lovey-dovey thoughts, child. What we've got to do is see if we can't shift this bit of trouble. But how? The good Lord only knows! How late are you? Jump about, make yourself ride up hills, put a bit of strain on yourself.' She untied her pinafore, then retied it more tightly as if that somehow gave her new strength to face what had to be done. 'Damned men, all they have to do is pull up their trousers and walk away leaving their troubles behind them,' her uncharacteristic choice of words bringing home to Anna what the situation would do to the household. 'And trouble, that's what it is, make no mistake! Not just for you but for your poor dear grandfather, yes and for me too. What an upset for the house! You ought to be ashamed – self, self, self, that's all young people ever consider. All very well for you, come what may you'll get over it. But the poor old gentleman at his time of life. It's not fair. He's not deserved an extra worry like this. Well, off you go, I've said my say. I blame myself – me and your Miss Sherwin, between the two of us we don't seem to have taught you the difference between right and wrong. Well, off you go, I said. I've more to do than stand here wasting my time.'

Seeing that Anna had no intention of telling her grandfather until she and Theo were married, she didn't consider there was any need now to worry him.

'It'll be all right Mrs Short,' she said, making sure her voice exuded the confidence she clung to. 'When Theo comes we shall be married; until then there's no need to say anything to Grandpa. Honestly, it's not *trouble*.'

'I've said my say. Now I have work to see too. This house doesn't run itself.'

Each time Anna came face to face with Amelia she held herself ready for interrogations which didn't come. No reference was made to the situation as another week passed with no sign of Theo. Her daydreams were overshadowed with a fear she tried not to acknowledge. What if he didn't come? Suppose something had happened to him, some dreadful accident in his car? She'd have to go away on her own, her baby would be cold-shouldered because it was illegitimate – her baby, *their* baby, born because they loved each other. It must be because he had work to do that he didn't come – he wasn't free like she was. As soon as he could get away he'd come back to her – she mustn't doubt.

Then came the day when returning home she saw the Riley outside Dunsford House. He must be indoors with Grandpa; she imagined them together as she ran the final hundred yards of the lane and up the path that led to the side door. Once inside, it wasn't her grandfather's voice she heard but Mrs Short's coming from behind the closed door of her sitting room.

'You've harmed the child enough. If you have any consideration except for yourself, then you'll shoulder your responsibilities. But if you need pushing, then my fine sir, you'll be pushed and make no mistake.'

'You wrote to me. How did you know where to find me?'

'I called on your friends at Heathfield Cottage. Oh, not to tell them. You don't think I want local gossip about Anna, stupid girl though she is. So I wheedled your address out of them and sent for you. And don't think I shall hesitate to write to your family, to that uncle the Humphries seem to think so much of. Take your choice: either marry her quietly or have an extra push from him. The end result will be the same. You've made your bed and I'll see to it that you lie on it.'

Into Anna's mind flashed Theo's first encounter with Mrs Short when he'd brought her home after falling off her bicycle. He'd made no secret of his opinion of the housekeeper's greeting. Now, with no thought for anything but protecting her 'poor dear gentleman', she was speaking her mind in the way that came naturally to her. Anna burst into the room.

'Don't, Mrs Short. Theo's come, I knew he would. I told you he would.' So why was it so hard to look at him? She moved to his side, her hand almost touching his. Please make him take my hand, make me know that it's all right, that he doesn't mind things being like they are. Please.

But he didn't. Instead, he spoke just to Amelia. 'You've said what you wanted to say. Now, leave us.' He was used to his word being obeyed immediately; Mrs Short looked as though she had no intention of being turned out of her own room. '*Now*, if you please,' he added with no smile in his voice. This time she turned and left them.

'Is what she says true?' There was no way Anna could avoid looking at him. His dark eyes were always so ready to smile, yet now what she saw was more like anger.

'I don't know what she said,' she mumbled.

'Of course you do. You've clearly discussed it with her. Why else would she have written to me?'

'Theo, she asked me, she asked me point blank – and I couldn't lie could I? I mean, soon they'll all know.'

'Christ! What a bloody mess!'

She turned away from him. Was he saying he didn't love her? Hadn't what they'd done been important to him like it had to her? Had he seen it as just a way to spend a hot afternoon, like mushrooming had been the way to spend the early morning of the day when the cowfield had been wet with dew, or scrambling in the hedgerows for the first blackberries to ripen for Mrs Humphries to add to her apples?

'You don't have to marry me,' her words fell into the silence, quiet and firm.

'Of course we shall have to marry.' His hands were warm on her shoulders, she wanted to cry, she wanted the earth to swallow her. If only she could clear from her mind the proposal she'd imagined. 'We haven't any choice, Anna, either of us. If you're sure you're going to have a child, then we both have an obligation.'

'Don't have to –' What a fool she was, Anna who never cried felt the hot tears on her cheeks.

'Darling Anna, please don't cry. It's my fault. I knew what I was doing, you were just an innocent.'

'No Theo, I wasn't. I knew. I wanted it more than I've ever wanted anything. Thought it mattered to you too.'

'Come on, Anna, dry your tears. This is no way to start a marriage, eh?' Something of his old cheerfulness was back. 'Tell you what we'll do: I'll stay with the Humphries until after we're married then I'll take you home with me.'

'But I thought you had a family, people who'd want to be at your wedding. Being married isn't like – like going on a day's outing. It means that they have to see me as family. You can't just take me home – as if you've been out to do the shopping.'

33

He laughed, yet she felt there was no humour in the sound.

'You can say that again.'

'Then oughtn't you to see that they're here? Or would it be better if we married in Moorleigh? I don't expect Grandpa would feel up to coming to the ceremony wherever it is. We have to be sensible.' But there was nothing sensible in the way her mind was racing: it was really going to happen, she would be with Theo for the rest of their lives, Mrs Theo Sullivan. Fighting down that heady thought was the echo of his words 'We have an obligation'. That's all she was to him, an obligation. 'Getting married isn't like buying a dog licence, it takes weeks. Having the banns called, making a bridal gown –'

'What a lot of bosh! I'll see about a special licence and fix up at the registry office. It can all be over in days.'

She knew she was being emotional and childish, but the sound of the bells, herself dressed in white and being showered with rose petals, had been the unchanging finale to her dreams.

'You'll need your grandfather's written consent but that should be easy enough. There must be a registry office in Brindley. Come on, Anna. Nothing's a bigger waste of time than kicking against the pricks. Will being married to me be so terrible?'

'It's what I want more than all the world.' She lost the last vestige of control as turning towards him she clung to him. 'It's what I've wanted for ages. I've been imagining it – like other people, I mean, you asking me, me having a ring to wear and making plans. That's what people do, isn't it.' Then, wiping her eyes with the palms of her hands, she forced her voice back in control. 'There's room at Dunsford House for your uncle – and is there an aunt too? Will they be able to come at such short notice?'

'They'd say the same as you did: it takes time to plan a marriage. Anyway it's not up to them to tell me what I can or can't do. It'll be a lark, seeing their faces when I drop you on them.' And from the way he was smiling it was clear that he managed to derive fun even from his present situation. There was no logic in her reaction, but somehow his looking on it as 'a lark to drop her on them' isolated her from his world. 'Dry your face and we'll go and put a pen and paper in your grandfather's hand, make him write his consent.' Then, with that boyish and ever-ready smile that seemed to draw a line under all trace of

34

emotion, he added, 'Then you'll be my property. Do you see me as a lord and master?'

'And me as your willing slave?' She made an effort to match his mood as she rubbed her face hard with the bottom edge of her cardigan.

'I say, perhaps things aren't so bleak after all!' But wasn't his tone that bit too bright? Then, his manner changing with the subject, 'Have you tried anything? Taken anything, or whatever women do? If we'd been at home Sylvia might have been able to put you on to something that would get us out of it.' Sylvia? Who was Sylvia? A cousin? A girlfriend? 'Who'd have thought, Anna, that ten minutes of sunshine on that scratchy cowfield could have landed us in a mess like this?' He didn't seem to expect an answer, which was as well. 'Let's go and speak to your grandfather. No, better still, you wait outside. I'll do the right thing and ask for your hand in marriage – he'll like that, he's probably been waiting for it. Then, when we've got his permission, we'll put a pen in his hand. With winter coming he can't expect me to keep driving all this way just to walk the muddy lanes with you. He'll think that's why we want to get married right away.'

But Cuthbert was less anxious to hand Anna over than Theo had expected.

'I've nothing against you, my dear chap; I don't want you to misunderstand me. But I must insist you give yourselves time. The child has met no one, her conception of life probably comes from the Brontë sisters. Many a young woman is experienced at twenty, but – I'm putting this badly – she's had no mother, no one to guide her, talk to her about what marriage entails.' Clearly he was embarrassed.

'Anna is ready for marriage. Keeping her shut up here for a long and boring winter would serve no useful purpose.'

'I must ask you to let me be the judge of that. Willingly, gladly, I will give my consent to your betrothal. During the winter months you will find the journey arduous, I realise that. If by spring you are both wanting to rush into wedlock, then I shall be satisfied. A relationship that can't remain strong through a few months apart is not worth the name.'

In the hall Anna stood with her ear to the door. Often enough her impatient anger had flared at her grandfather's dogged refusal to fall in with her plans, whether it had been her longing for a pony, Farmer Gingell's offer to give her a kitten of her own, her ambition for the independence of earning her own living – nothing had moved him.

'You needn't worry about her, sir.' Even without seeing him she knew just the way Theo's eyes would be smiling. 'My family will love her and I will take great care of her. She'll often come back to see you.' His family? She knew so little about his home, only that he lived with the uncle who owned the coach company. But, of course, once they were married they would look for a place of their own. Could Theo afford to think of buying a house? Next spring when she was twenty-one she would inherit everything her parents had left her, money which for more than seventeen years had been held in trust. The thought gave her spirit a boost, reminding her that she would be an asset to their future. Those things Theo had said – had she tried to get rid of the baby? And worse, far worse, his spontaneous 'Christ! What a bloody mess!' Surely they came from shock at what he'd just heard. She'd had weeks to get used to the idea, but remember how she'd felt in the beginning, how frightened she'd been as she faced the truth. Once they were properly together, loving each other like they had on that glorious afternoon ('ten minutes of sunshine on that scratchy cowfield' echoed again, which she tried not to hear), they would hold nothing back from each other; she'd *make* him feel the same as she did; she'd *make* him thankful even for the way they were having to start. But what was her grandfather saying?

'I've said my last word. Take her out and buy her an engagement ring and I'll give that my blessing. Now, that's enough. Let that be the last word.' Always his way of drawing a line under any question of his authority.

'I'm afraid that's impossible, sir. Anna is pregnant.'

Silence, silence when surely Anna could *hear* the beating of her heart.

'Dear God!' Never had she heard her grandfather speak like that, his voice unnaturally strong. 'If I were a young man I'd take a whip to you. Fornicator – rapist – disgusting lust –'

'No, Grandpa,' Anna burst into the room. 'It's true, but it wasn't like you make it sound. I want to marry Theo, I want to be with him always. I want his baby.'

'You stay out of this. You disgust me, the pair of you. Go along.

Outside when I say.' With a struggle and using both his walking sticks, he pulled himself to his feet. 'You should be *ashamed*. Elizabeth's child, my Elizabeth's own daughter bringing shame on her name like this.' As suddenly as he'd found his strength, so he lost it. 'What's the use? Nothing I can do.' He seemed to wilt, collapsing back into his chair, his energy drained. 'Helpless . . . old . . . lived too long . . . failed her . . . Elizabeth.'

'No Grandpa, you've never failed her.' Anna was on her knees in front of him. 'She'd want me to find happiness. Forget about the baby, that's not why I want to marry Theo.'

'I've no choice,' Cuthbert muttered brokenly. How pathetically thin his hands were, the knuckles standing out as he gripped his two sticks in an attempt to disguise how he trembled. A million memories crowded into Anna's mind: always he'd been strict, but never unjust. She'd told Theo that as long as she could remember her grandfather had been old, but today it hurt to see his frailty. She wanted to reach out to him, to lay her warm hands over his as if that way she could transfer some of her own healthy energy. But she realised now what she had always accepted without question: he avoided physical contact. As a child when she had been sent to say goodnight to him his words had never varied: 'Have a good night's sleep. Off you go.' No kiss. Only her faithful Miss Sherwin had ever kissed her goodnight or taught her to say her prayers. So many thoughts and memories crowded her mind. Of course he'd cared about her, she was her mother's daughter. And because she was her mother's daughter the hurt she was doing to him now was all the greater.

'When it's all behind us, Grandpa, you'll see how glad you are – not just for me but for my mother too. She'd want me to be happy, you know she would.'

'Lived too long,' he mumbled, 'should never have seen this day.' Then, making a supreme effort and looking coldly at Theo, 'You give me no choice, I'll do as you say. Somewhere I failed. No moral guidance. The girl needed her mother . . . my little Lizzie trusted me to take her place. It ends in *this* –' His face crumpled, silently he wept. Forgetting his constant aversion to physical contact Anna laid her head on his knee, her arms around his thin waist.

Theo had come back just as she'd prayed and dreamed,

but she'd never imagined this was the way their life together would start.

No time was wasted. Theo spent the next day making urgent appointments, making arrangements – and giving himself no time to consider the enormity of his commitment nor yet what the alternative might have been. At Dunsford House Anna was aware of disapproving silence. She told Mrs Short that, just as she'd believed, she and Theo were to be married within days; but she made sure she told her out of her grandfather's hearing, for his silence on the subject, indeed on any subject as he sat gazing into space, made it impossible for her to broach the subject in front of him.

With the licence in his pocket and the appointment made with the registrar for the following Thursday at half past eleven in the morning, Theo brought the news of the arrangements.

'You'll come with me won't you, Grandpa? Theo will drive us in his car. It's no distance to –'

'No, no. I shall stay here. You might have forced my consent out of me, but that's an end to it. You know my feelings, you know my shame for you and for myself too that I could have failed to guide your morals. No, no,' he raised his hands as she opened her mouth to argue. 'Let it go. I can't take any more. All I ask is peace. And you bring me trouble like this. Why didn't the dear Lord take me before you did this to me?'

'Grandpa –'

'Don't argue with him,' Theo cut in. 'If he doesn't want to see you married, then we can manage without him. What about his man, Potts, do you call him? He'll do as a witness.'

'No.' Anna wasn't prepared to have her decisions made for her. 'If Grandpa doesn't feel up to it –' purposely she worded it like that, giving him time to restore his almost lost control or even to change his mind '– then I'll ask Mrs Short. She's my friend.'

Theo raised his eyebrows, his eyes bright with laughter. Friend? He could have given her a more accurate description.

So it was that on Thursday morning at two minutes to half past eleven Anna, Theo and Mrs Short arrived at the dingy office of the Brindley registrar. Together the three of them walked up the stone-flagged corridor to the room to which they were directed, the silence accentuated by the sound of the steel tips on the heels of Mrs Short's best shoes. To be honest she'd be glad to get home and take them off. Never does to buy in the sales, she thought as she tried not to let it show how they pinched her corn. Nearly two years she'd had them and worn then not half a dozen times. Had to do her best for little Anna. Silly child getting herself into such a mess, and there was the poor old gent at home – having a quiet cry she wouldn't mind betting. Not a bit what the child should have had for a wedding: no bells, not a bit of cheer, just this registrar man looking at them over the top of his half-moon spectacles – and sizing up the situation, no doubt about that. Thank goodness the dear old gent wasn't here to see it. In no time it was done, the promises made (for what they were worth!). The registrar opened the communicating door to a room where throughout the short ceremony someone had been typing.

'We're ready now, Miss Roberts, if you will spare a moment from your work.' Then, as they waited for the typist to appear, 'I believe we might get a glimpse of the sun later. Indeed we don't want to plunge too early into winter, do we?' He addressed his remarks to Amelia, but he needn't think she knew no better than to join in a lot of silly chatter in the middle of Anna's wedding!

Then came the signing of the register, the only sound the scratching of the nib on the paper as the bride and groom signed, followed by Amelia and the unknown typist brought in to be a witness. Then it was over; there was nothing left but for him to shake hands with the 'happy couple' and wish them many happy years. Small hope of that, in Amelia's view. It was a wedding so unlike her own; she wasn't prepared for its disturbing effect nor for the way her mind carried her back through the years between.

Just remember how sure of yourself you were when you made your vows – vows made before God – not like this with some official looking more like a draper making his silly chit-chat. Made your vows, then broke them. With my body I thee worship, that's what Jimmy had declared, his voice strong and sure; and had she had stars in her eyes like Anna had today? Little Anna, stars in her eyes – and trouble in her belly, poor little mite. Men! All the same, the lot of them. Or were they? Was it that I picked the rotten apple from the barrel? No worship about the way he used me, that's for sure. Yet for all my promises, it was me who cleared off. Love, honour and obey, that's what I vowed. There must have been a time when I believed I loved him, just like Anna thinks she loves this too-handsome-by-half young fop. Honour? If ever I honoured him, it hadn't been for long and as for obeying, well surely no decent woman would have obeyed the things the dirty bugger had wanted. What if, like Anna, I'd got myself in the family way, would I have gritted my teeth and made the best of things? Is that what Anna is doing, for all her wild talk about love? Please God don't let it go sour on her, don't let her get used like I was. And, please God, I know I broke my solemn word – love, honour, obey, I broke the lot – forgive me. Oh, not for leaving him – You must have been as disgusted as I was with the things he tried to get up to; but forgive me for not loving him. Perhaps that's the crux of it. If you love a man – oh no, love or not, there's right and there's wrong. Please look after young Anna; she's had a rum sort of life and it seems to me there's something not natural about this young spark not inviting any of his family. Ashamed of them perhaps? What sort of a home is he taking her to? Yet the Humphries spoke highly of that uncle of his. Oh dear, oh dear, why couldn't she have met some nice farmer's son, someone from round these parts? And the dear old gentleman, pretends he only wants peace and quiet, but I know just like You know, he loves that girl like as if she was the shadow of his beloved Elizabeth – beloved and spoilt too, that's always been my opinion, just between me and You.

The typist was thanked and returned to her room with the folded pound note Theo had slipped into her hand. All that remained was to return Mrs Short to Dunsford House.

'The master's taking a rest,' Potts greeted them as the car drew up. 'Off to sleep by now, I expect. He left a note for you, Anna, and said don't hang around; he'd rather you got straight on your way with such a long journey. An excuse, if you ask me. I think he didn't want a farewell.'

'I'll just creep into his room and see him. If he's asleep I'll not wake him.'

His eyes were closed. Gently she bent over him and laid her lips on his forehead, thinking as she did so how strange it was to be kissing him.

'I'm going, Grandpa,' she whispered. 'Please don't be sad. It's

40

going to be all right.' Then, when there was no sign that he had heard her, she added, 'God bless you.'

She left the room as soundlessly as she'd entered it. Before she reached the bottom of the stairs he was struggling to his feet, all pretence of sleep gone. What a stupid coward he'd been. All the years he'd held her at arm's length. Now it was too late, she'd gone. He'd call her back, he'd tell her – tell her – what could he tell her? How much she meant to him? That she looked just like her darling mother? That he really loved her? But you don't tell a grandchild you love her, she ought to have been able to take that for granted all her life. Ought to – but had she?

'Anna,' he called as he stumbled out of his bedroom bearing heavily on his sticks, 'Anna, wait.' There was no reply. The front door was open, everyone was outside. He'd surprise her, he'd get there before that lusting devil carried her away. 'Anna, wait. I'm coming down.'

In the lane the engine started. Letting his sticks fall, he grasped the rail for support in his rush to get downstairs. He didn't hear the Riley draw away.

'It's not grand, but it will do us,' Theo said as he dropped their suitcases on the bed. The Boar's Head was a country inn with only three letting rooms, but to Anna it held all the sophistication of a grand hotel. Grand or humble, to her hotels were an unknown. Perhaps in her early childhood she might have slept away from home – in fact, even with her vague recollections of her parents, she was sure she must have – but since she'd been 'dumped' on her grandfather every night of her life had been spent in her own bedroom.

'I think it's lovely.' Any momentary sadness she'd felt as she'd driven away from her past had been forgotten in the hours they'd motored.

'We've only another hour or so to drive.'

'It's not even four o'clock. I'm glad we're staying here, but why didn't you want to finish the journey? Had you told your uncle to expect us tomorrow?'

'No.' He pulled her to sit by his side on the bed. 'We'll arrive when we're ready. I want us to have tonight first.' Oh, that was better! That was the sort of answer to fit into the picture she'd created, akin to a moonlight proposal and his words of undying love. 'You say, had I told my uncle. No, I've not told any of them.'

'Them?'

'We're quite a tribe,' he answered. Imagining the 'tribe' at home she detected a smile in his voice, but rather than being reassured by it she was instinctively put on her guard.

'Theo, I don't know anything about your family. You said there was a farm – yet you work for your uncle in the bus company. Did you go to live with him when you started to work there?'

'What a tangled mess of nonsense you've managed to weave,' Theo laughed. 'My uncle was younger brother to my father. We Sullivans have deep roots in the area, deep roots and many branches. Manningtor has been home to all and sundry of the family since the beginning of time.'

All and sundry? So how many of them were there?

'I just wish you'd told them about *me*. Perhaps they won't want me inflicted on them.' Was she still to be no more than someone to be suffered? 'Just till we can get our own home, I mean. It seems awfully rude to drop me on them and take it for granted –' One look at his changed expression and her sentence faded into silence. 'Theo?'

'I told you: my father was the elder son. So it was he who inherited the Park. For generations it has been the nest the Sullivans have looked on as their natural roost. My father died when I was twelve, I'm his only son. Naturally I was his heir – and it continued to be home to those who were already there, just as it continued to be looked on as a haven for those who've broken away, a place for them to come home to. When my father died my uncle became my official guardian. And now – well, you'll understand when you come to know it.' If she'd had dreams of a home of her own, they came crashing to the ground. 'Like it or not, you are mistress of Manningtor – that comes in the same package as having to marry *me*.'

It must have been his choice of words that made her so sure his smile was forced.

Under a leaden sky they drove the last few miles. By morning she felt ready to face his family, indeed she felt ready to face any hurdle Fate had in store for her. With the previous night behind her, the devils of doubt had no power. On that September

42

afternoon by the Thames she had believed his nearness, the sense of belonging, had been the ultimate joy. What had happened to her the previous night had been – silently she tried to find a word to encompass the wonderful and unexpected thing that had happened to her.

Neither of them spoke as he drove, every minute bringing them closer to a future that to her was impossible to envisage. Not that she wanted to waste her thoughts on imagining the unknown; instead she let them go where they would. With the bedroom door locked there had been nothing in her world but the two of them. In her dreams she had only half understood. Only days earlier she had felt bruised by his referring to their 'ten minutes in a scratchy cowfield', but then she'd had no idea of the wonder of really knowing each other, nothing held back. All that she was had been in those moments, every inch of her body, every thought in her mind, every beat of her heart. Even then she hadn't been prepared for the miracle that had happened to her. And in the morning, as she'd woken to the sound of the dawn chorus, woken just as he did, so it had happened again. It hadn't needed that glorious journey of discovery they had made the night before; that morning without a word he had moved onto her, as if the day had started where yesterday finished. So it had, so it always would. As the memories crowded in, so her determination grew. Perhaps without a push from Fate, they may have taken longer to get to where they were now; but she would make him glad of what had happened, just as glad as she was.

'Down that hill to the left is Deremouth,' Theo told her. 'The next turning on the right takes us to Moorleigh.'

She mustn't fail him. His family must become her friends.

On both sides of the lane was heathland, then they came to the village of Moorleigh, a cluster of houses and cottages nestled around the green, with a village shop and bakery at one end, alongside a stone building she recognised to be the school. Another right turn, a small and ancient church, then up a long hill past buildings bearing a painted sign announcing they belonged to Sullivan's Coach Company; then they came to a long stone boundary wall.

'Almost there, the gate is just around the bend.'

And so it was. Only it wasn't 'the gate'; he should have said 'the gates'. Wide wrought-iron gates standing open at the end of a long straight drive. Her horizons had been so narrow, the limits of her experience no further than an infrequent visit to Reading and once or twice in her childhood with Miss Sherwin to Oxford. Nothing prepared her for this.

'You mean – you mean you *own that*?' Mistress of Manningtor, he'd said!

A few yards along the drive he stopped the car and turned to her. It wasn't often he sounded as serious as he did as he told her, 'Own it, you say? There's a difference. On paper I own it, but in truth I have a duty and one day it will go to my eldest son. Suppose we'd not married, suppose this child is a boy – my son, but not my legal heir. You can see now, Anna, why it was I said we have no choice but to make the best of things.' Then, his expression changing and his smile back in place, 'And we will, we *must*.'

Only pride made her sit an inch taller and look him squarely in the eye.

'Indeed we have no choice.' She spoke with quiet dignity, seeming to hear Mrs Short's so often repeated 'What can't be cured must be endured'. Mrs Short, her grandfather and his so frequent 'And let that be an end to it, if you please', the familiar rutted lane, the seldom-broken quiet of Dunsford House, the silence of the familiar fields and woods, the imaginary and unfailing friends who lived within the pages of books she'd grown up with – all of it gone beyond recall, as lost to her as last night's miracle that had been destroyed by his words.

Chapter Three

Theo called it the place they all came home to. There were only five people in the morning room when he ushered Anna in, three women and two men, but she felt herself overwhelmed. The large, lofty room with its long windows and carved stone fireplace was no more than background. The conversation stopped dead as they entered but there was no doubt of their pleasure at Theo's return.

'Theo, my dear!' Anna's impression was of an austere-looking lady who was seated near the blazing logs and who greeted him in a strong contralto voice, holding a ringed hand in his direction. 'We thought you'd deserted us. And not a word from you in all these days. You said you'd be away just one night. Was something wrong with those people – Hunter? Humphrey? I forget the name. And you've brought us a visitor?'

'More than a visitor, Aunt Kath.' He might have considered marriage an unavoidable obligation, but there was no doubting the fun he was having dropping his bombshell on the family. 'This is Anna, my reason for staying away so many days. I want you –'

'What a tease he is,' the youngest of the three women, a tall brunette, came towards Anna with her hand extended. 'Don't believe half he says. I'm Sylvia, his sister.'

'Half-sister,' the contralto put the handsome brunette in her place, by which time Anna was thoroughly confused.

Sylvia went on as if there had been no interruption, 'Is this brother of mine on his way to give you a lift somewhere? Has he brought you for lunch?' Then without waiting for a reply – for which Anna was glad – she turned back to Theo. 'You've timed your return perfectly. Nadine is expected at the farm this

45

afternoon, in time for tomorrow's hunt meeting. Was it telepathy that brought you home or have you been in touch with her?'

If Anna was confused, Theo at least was enjoying himself.

'Didn't I tell you we were quite a brood?' he laughed, speaking to Anna. 'Before you lot interrupted me I was introducing Anna – Anna Sullivan.'

Immediately the matriarch from the fireside was on her feet, both hands outstretched.

'Sullivan? Which branch of the family, my dear? Where did Theo find you?'

'He found me at Wickley Cross.' Some inner strength came to Anna's aid as she spoke to the room at large and no one in particular. 'We've known each other for months, we met the day Mr and Mrs Humphries moved into their cottage.' Then, the light of battle in her eye as anyone who knew her would have recognised, 'Why do you imagine he's been visiting so often?'

Pint-sized, skinny as a waif, having the audacity to take that tone! Kath Sullivan stood to her full height as if the inches between them made her authority unquestionable. Young minx! Who did she think she was? Some twig on a lesser branch of the family tree, no doubt.

'Indeed,' she boomed. 'What dear Theo does with his time is his own affair and,' with a lovingly tolerant look in her nephew's direction, 'I'm sure he's been managing to find himself some amusement. Girls go down like ninepins before him, they always have; life is a game to him. Isn't that so, Theo, you rascal? I believe Sylvia enquired whether you'd be staying to lunch. Is that the plan, Theo?'

'It certainly is. Lunch, tea, dinner, breakfast –'

'Really, you are too bad, Theo!' His sister (half-sister? Anna wished she'd found out more before they arrived) said. 'So inconsiderate bringing an overnight guest with no warning. You really don't show a scrap of consideration for the running of this house.' Then, to Anna, 'Do forgive me, I don't mean to sound inhospitable, but really he ought to *think*.' From her manner it appeared the responsibility rested on her shoulders.

In the way Anna had noticed occasionally before, Theo's expression changed. The smile vanished and his dark eyes looked coldly at Sylvia.

'Perhaps, Anna, I ought to have carried you over the threshold or whatever tradition demands, then they wouldn't have been so slow-witted.'

'Carried her –?' The third woman in the room spoke for the first time, 'Anna Sullivan? You mean you and Theo are married?' Another one with two hands outstretched in welcome, but this time Anna turned to her in relief.

'We were married yesterday. He wanted me to be a surprise.' She felt small and insignificant before these three robust women: Sylvia, tall, broad, brunette and handsome; the matriarch, angular and autocratic; then this one, plump, comfortable, her mousy fair hair more frizzy than curly, her front teeth set far apart, perhaps in fact no older than Sylvia but matronly before her time. The one thing they all had in common was confidence. Hiding behind an unfamiliar shield of dignity she was far from feeling, Anna held herself as tall as her five foot one inch allowed and surveyed the assembly. 'I'm sure I'm a shock to you all – indeed, so are you to me, for Theo told me almost nothing about his home – but I'm sure when we know each other better we shall learn to be friends.'

Sylvia's eyes – eyes as dark as Theo's even if they were only half-brother and-sister – were bright with anger that seemed to Anna completely unreasonable; the elderly lady Theo called Aunt Kath pursed her lips, keeping her opinions to herself; the plump and motherly one beamed her approval.

'I'm sure we shall all be friends.' This time it was one of the two men who came forward, a man whose hair was thinning while his waistline was thickening, his hand outstretched to take hers. 'If you hadn't been warned, then we're a bit much for you to take in in one fell swoop, I dare say. But, get to know us and we're pretty harmless. I'm Matthew, Theo's cousin, just call me Matt the same as everyone else does. This is my wife, Thelma,' he put his arm around the friendly woman's shoulder. 'My mother – she'll be Aunt Kath. Sylvia has introduced herself and this chap is Francis, her husband. They live at Home Farm but take no notice of that; they're here as often as not. There are more but, lucky for you, none of them are home for the present. Enough to be going on with, eh?' Then to Theo, 'You're a dark horse. All these months and never a word. Still, you're to be congratulated. Quite time you got yourself a wife, isn't that so, Sylvia?' His light-blue eyes were bright with laughter as he looked at his cousin, whose only

47

reply was to set her mouth in a tight line that made Anna forget she'd thought her beautiful. 'We wish you well, both of you. Isn't that so?'

'Welcome among us.' Aunt Kath's words said welcome, but her tone couldn't quite get in step. 'And you, young man, you know Sidney and I wish for you everything your heart desires. If this is your choice, then we shall make her welcome in the family.' To Anna it seemed more than apparent that 'his choice' was a disappointment.

'You're nearest the bell, Francis. This demands a glass of bubbly,' Matthew's jovial voice ordered. 'Pity Father's not at home too.'

'Champagne can wait,' Theo countermanded, 'but ring for it anyway. First I want the staff in the hall. Ready for it, Anna?'

'For what?' Staff, he said. A house like this – mistress of Manningtor he'd called her. He'd meant what he'd said. If he was the owner, then that must make his wife mistress. But look at these women – even the plump, jolly one who was called Thelma – all of them so sure of themselves. Which one of them decided on the menus, controlled the running of the household? The matriarch was Aunt Kath, the bossy one was Sylvia, the natural homemaker was Thelma. So where would *she* fit in? Was she frightened? No, she told herself, not giving herself time to look the question in the face. Surprised, overwhelmed by the size and grandeur of the place, but not frightened. She had one meaningful objective: to make Theo truly love her and be proud of her. Nothing and no one was going to come between *her* and her goal.

Her courage held as the staff were summoned and lined up in the marble-floored hall to meet her. The elderly butler showed no expression, and she suspected that his opinion was in line with the family's. As for the others, rightly or wrongly she'd shaken each of them by the hand and repeated their names, mentally writing each one in an attempt to sear it into her memory. And all of them from the housekeeper down to Grant, the inside/outside and none-too-bright bottom of the pile who picked up all the jobs no one else wanted, seemed pleased to see her. Her spirits rose.

'Fetch the mistress's luggage in, Grant,' Mrs Gibbons, the housekeeper instructed, 'and look lively now. Where do you want them taken, Mr Theo sir?'

'Leave them upstairs in the gallery. No! Open up what used

48

to be my parents' room. I'm sure my sister will say the bed needs airing, but I'm sure you can produce enough bottles and warming pans to sort that out, Mrs Gibbons. Do you want to see the room now, Anna, or shall I introduce you to the gardens?'

'The garden, please.' Then, before she followed him to where he was already opening the front door, she turned back to the staff. 'I'm sure we shall all get along well.'

'Indeed ma'am, we're here to help you in any way we can,' Mrs Gibbons told her, imagining the reception one or two of those 'high and mighties' had probably treated the poor child to. If the girl was the one Mr Theo wanted, then those below stairs would make sure she had an easy ride while she was getting used to things. Smart enough little dresser, yet there was something about her that made the housekeeper sure Manningtor overwhelmed her. Well, back below stairs she'd have her say to the rest of them, make it plain that the mistress they served was Mr Theo's new wife. 'It'll be a real pleasure to put that lovely room back into use again, Mrs Theo, ma'am.'

'Thank you, all of you,' Mrs Theo ma'am answered, with an incline of her head that carried a message of dismissal and disguised such a silly fluttering of excitement.

'Come on outside, Anna, come and get acquainted with your new surroundings.'

For a man who had been pushed into an unwanted marriage, he was keeping remarkably good humoured. Willingly Anna let him usher her out through the heavy front door to the terrace, then down the wide steps.

'Why didn't you warn me?' Even out of earshot she spoke quietly, more unnerved by the last half hour than she let herself admit.

'Warn you of what?

'All this. Theo, it's not just a house – it's – it's an estate.'

'Did I ever say it wasn't? Manningtor was built more than two hundred years ago. A distant ancestor earned a vast fortune out of wool and wanted the world to see his success. I told you, it's been home to the Sullivans for generations. I inherited it, but none of us will ever own it. We are custodians, one generation for the next. Look, Anna, I don't want to keep repeating myself. I suppose you imagined getting married and having a neat little home, a husband who went off to work in the morning and came home in the evening, probably two children –'

'You don't know what I imagined. You don't know anything about me.'

'Probably not – nor you about me.' Standing on the vast expanse of grass, some twenty yards from the house, they faced each other.

'We shouldn't have got married. I could have looked after my baby on my own. I'm not beholden to you, you know. Before it's even born I shall have inherited everything my parents left. I could have bought a house. Anyway, there are other things I want to do with my life. Being Mrs Theo Sullivan isn't the be all and end all.' She could feel the threat of tears. It was so hard to sound calm and confident when in her mind anger battled with hurt, uncertainty battled with the need to make him see her as something other than a young and naïve child and, above all else, she longed to see his eyes smile at her. But they didn't.

'You may have all the gold of Midas,' he said, brushing her remarks aside, 'that doesn't concern me. What you mean to do with your life doesn't concern me – at least, it wouldn't have concerned me except for this turn of events. The fact is, the child isn't *yours* any more than it's *mine*. But more important than that is –' he made a sweeping movement with his hand '– all this.'

'They don't want me here. Oh, Mrs Gibbons and the staff, they were fine. I know they'll help me get used to things. But the others, they looked down their long noses as if you'd picked up some . . . some . . . some stray mongrel and taken it home to their pedigree kennel. Well, I don't care. I'll show them!'

In vain she'd been looking for the smile to come back into his eyes, but now while she was intent on venting her anger on the Sullivan household, she was unprepared for his sudden laugh.

'Anna, you'll make circles around them. Now then, take one long look at the house, and tell me in all honesty what you think. Like it or not, you are its mistress.'

'Why, it's beautiful. All this, the surroundings, the building, you don't have to ask. You know how beautiful it is. But what do I think? I think if we had been married for the usual reasons I would have been confident of the future, I would have been keen to take on the responsibilities that went with being your wife. Yet there's no sense in that. Your family manage much better than I would.'

50

'Anna, the staff will look to you as mistress. You won't find it easy, but it shouldn't be beyond your intelligence. This is important. It's *your* side of the bargain.'

'A bargain you didn't give me any choice but to accept!'

'Don't let's go over that again. This is where we're at – and from here on it's up to us to make life worth living. I want you to be happy – heaven preserve me from a moaning woman!' He sounded impatient. Theo Sullivan was used to getting his own way: a few minutes with his family had made that very clear to her.

'I've never had any responsibility in running my grandfather's house, so it's no use imagining I can suddenly rule the roost here – even if any of them wanted me to interfere.'

'It makes no difference what any of them want – or us either – you have to rule the roost, as you call it, like it or not. Are you frightened, is that it? You obviously made a good impression on the staff; at least that's a beginning.' Then his scowl vanished as he looked at the great house, majestic in the autumn sunshine. 'It's built of local granite, solid and unchanging. To me it's perfect – but not everyone thinks so. Red brick and they'd think it beautiful, but granite isn't friendly; that's what my young sister Alex says.'

'It looks impregnable. It's more than beautiful, it's awesome. And I do understand what you say about duty and responsibility, all that sort of thing. I truly will do my best, Theo. I'm sorry I sounded beastly.'

'No more than I did.' Then, with an unaffectedly boyish grin, he added, 'Perhaps we're both unnerved.'

'Do you suppose they're watching us? Mrs Short always used to peep round her curtain if she thought anything was going on in the garden.'

'Why should they do that?' he laughed.

'I suppose because I'm not what they wanted. Do you know what I wish?'

'Don't keep me in suspense,' and this time his eyes were smiling just as she'd wanted.

'I wish I was four inches taller and beautiful – a proper shape, not scrawny like I am. I wish I were a *success*, so that when you'd mentioned my name they'd immediately known who I was and been in awe of me. A great writer or a famous actress or head of a big company.'

51

'In such heady circumstances our present situation is hardly likely to have arisen. Can you imagine such a creature having time or inclination to romp in the sunshine by the Thames? After lunch I'll take you to meet Nanny. She's living in an estate cottage now that Matt and Thelma's two are away at school. I want you to like her, Anna. She'll come back into her old rooms, of course, once the child is born.'

'I may not want a nurse for the baby. That's what mothers are for.'

'Now you're being silly. By the way, do you ride? If you don't, living here you'll want to.'

'All I've ever ridden is my bicycle.'

'Sylvia will teach you. She's a wonderful horsewoman.'

Remembering Sylvia, Anna was quick to retort, 'I don't know that I have any interest in learning. I've never had the slightest inclination.'

'You know your trouble?' he laughed, 'You're hungry. That's what Nanny used to say if any of us were grouchy. Come on, let's go in. We'll continue our tour of inspection when I take you to see her this afternoon. Once you've had lunch you'll find the world looks a brighter place.'

Imagining lunch with the Sullivans en masse, Anna's appetite deserted her.

'His trouble is, he's always had his own way,' Sylvia grumbled as she and Francis walked back to Home Farm.

'If there's one thing a man ought to have his own way over, then surely it's his choice of a wife,' he answered, his good humour undented by the fact that his sister Nadine's willingness to fill the role had been overlooked. 'In general terms I expect you're right, though I imagine from Aunt Kath down everyone has always bent over backwards to do his bidding.'

'I know he had a rotten time after Mother died; so did Lance and I. But always it was *Theo*, anything to keep him from fretting. And their reward was in seeing his pleasure. Well, now they can sit back and enjoy his pleasure in this girl he's got entangled with. Honestly, Francis, can you see her ever shaping up to run a home like Manningtor? Whereas Nadine –'

'Darling Sylvie, Nadine had battles enough with our parents persuading them to let her train. Now she's qualified and doing well, even if she fancies herself queening it at Manningtor, believe me she'll soon recover. That's Nadine for you: she'll battle if there's a chance of winning but if she knows the chips are down and she has no hope then she'll decide it wasn't what she wanted.'

'What a convenient nature!' This time Sylvia laughed, taking hold of his hand and, for no apparent reason, feeling better about the situation. 'I expect it was partly that I would have liked her to be living here, someone belonging to *you*. But this Anna creature, who is she? Was she something to do with those people he used to pretend to be helping? We know nothing.'

'Theo is nobody's fool, Sylvie. And perhaps it's the family's fault that he didn't tell them until afterwards. They've always expected to do his thinking for him. You know what I think? You know what I intend to do? We ought to try and relax the poor kid instead of all looking at her as if she's standing before the Spanish Inquisition. She may turn out much better than first appearances suggest. At least we ought to give her the benefit of the doubt.'

'You're a nice man, Francis Chadwick. I'll try, honestly. But first we have Nadine coming this afternoon. If anyone understands her it ought to be you, so let's hope you're right and she'll accept being cast aside with good grace.'

'Cast aside be damned. She's an attractive young woman, and like all attractive young women who've come into Theo's path, he has enjoyed playing up to her. If he'd intended anything more permanent he would have made a move in that direction ages ago. So, you'll be a good girl and try and smooth that poor child's path. Aunt Kath takes a lot of notice of what you say.' Then, at Sylvia's reluctant silence, 'Please darling. This is Theo's home, it's Theo's choice. You're in a no-win situation.'

'Run away and amuse yourself,' Nanny Harknell gave Theo a gentle but not-to-be-argued-with push in the direction of the door. 'Take the log basket and set about seeing to some fuel for me; show this new wife of yours that you aren't too good for a hand's turn of man's work.' Her adoring expression took any sting from her words but, with a view not of her face but of the back of her head with its tightly anchored hair pulled into a bun reminiscent of Queen Victoria's, Anna knew nothing of that.

53

'He has no need to prove himself to me, Miss Harknell. I saw the way he worked to help Albert Humphries.' But she might as well not have spoken. Then she saw Theo give his old nurse a cheery wink, a sign that the point scored had been his.

'Off you go, now.' And off he went. Even if he'd returned to Manningtor a bachelor he would have called at Brook Cottage to see Millie Harknell, just as he would have split logs for her fire. Theo was fond of his family, even Sylvia with her patently obvious matchmaking designs for him with her young sister-in-law Nadine. But Nanny was different. She had always been there for him, the one to bind his cuts, dry his tears and hear his troubles. It had never occurred to him that she had any interest beyond *his* world; even now, a grown man, he took for granted his importance in her life. To him she was just Nanny, the rock that formed the foundation on which he'd built his cheerful trust in life.

'Now we've got rid of the boy, let me take a good hard look at you. Not a choice I expected – not what I feared, might be nearer the mark. Sit down, child. If you're to be mistress of his home, then you and I would be best to get acquainted.'

If Nanny Harknell was surprised at Theo's choice of a bride, Anna most certainly was at the sort of woman who had been given control of his upbringing. Her mind jumped back to Miss Sherwin: gentle, reserved, kindly; and from there another leap and it was with Mrs Short: austere, avoiding anything hinting at emotion, dignity in her voice and in her bearing. Nanny Harknell's appearance might have been more in keeping with the wife of a farmer than the one responsible for the welfare of the heir of Manningtor. Her dazzlingly white afternoon pinafore was tied round her comfortably plump waist to protect a plain black dress, the only relief a gold locket hanging from a chain around her neck. If she'd been introduced as Manningtor's head cook, it would have been more believable.

'What did you make of each other, you and the family? Young rascal he is, always has been, bless his heart. Fancy dropping you on them like that. I'd stake my last ha'penny he'd never so much as mentioned you to them. To me, yes, he'd told me about meeting you. Not that I took much notice, wherever Theo goes there's always a pretty girl all too willing to make sure he enjoys himself. Good and bad, the boy has always come to me with his troubles.'

54

'Troubles?'

'What child gets let off without them? And him, poor mite, losing his mother when little Alex was born. Too old, that was the trouble with the poor soul; not natural for a woman of her age to be brought to bed in labour. That was the start of all the sadness. Up till then there couldn't have been a happier house in all the land than Manningtor. Has the boy told you about his father? Or is that why he's handed you over to me?'

'I don't know anything about any of them.'

'Young scamp. Never gives a thought to other people.' But it was said with tolerant affection as if inconsideration were one of his endearing charms. 'No, that's not fair, he wouldn't wittingly hurt a soul. Put a bit of trouble in front of his face so there's no missing it, and there's no one kinder. But never sees beyond the end of his nose. You know the creed he lives by? Well, of course you do, you wouldn't have tied your life up to his if you needed me to explain him to you.'

'I know he puts Manningtor above everything else, Miss Harknell. I know he loves to have fun and looks on life as a gift to be enjoyed.'

'Nanny, not Miss Harknell, if you're to be one of the family. I said just now he told me about you – well, I take it to be you he talked about, a girl he'd met and gone about with while he was helping poor Albert Humphries. I took very little notice, that I admit. Always there has been a girl of some sort ready to add sunshine to his days. That's what concerns me and I don't mind admitting it. A bit of fun, harmless fun, that's one thing; marriage . . . if you'd asked me, I'd never have thought he was ready for marriage.'

'Perhaps you don't know him as well as you thought!' Anna retorted, touched on a tender spot.

'I reckon I know him as well as anyone ever will. But I admit to being knocked off balance by today's news. He's shown more sense than I'd feared he would, I'll give you that. Between ourselves, I was afraid he'd fall into Nadine Chadwick's net: she's been trawling for him plain as the nose on her face. That's Sylvia's sister-in-law, Francis's sister. Before long you'll meet them all. I wouldn't bother giving that one the time of day – Nadine I mean, not Francis, nothing wrong with him. As for the rest of the family, you'd never find better. Young Theo,

55

bless him, he's always been able to make circles round them – round me too, although I'd not let him hear me say it. So, young Mrs Theo my dear, you've got a lot to live up to if you're to be accepted as good enough for the young rascal.'

'Families never know the whole of a person,' Anna made herself answer in the voice of quiet confidence she'd so often resorted to in the topical discussions she'd had with her grandfather, especially when she'd been less than certain of herself.

'I seem to think the boy told me you were something of a loner, hadn't much in the way of family?'

'I have a grandfather.'

'And kept yourself in wraps, no doubt, so that the old gentleman only knew what you wanted him to know. Yes, you're right about families, my dear, it's not till we get away and stand on our own two feet that we become whole. I dare say that's why I'm uneasy about Theo marrying suddenly like this when he's known nothing but home and family. Only has to snap his fingers and he's had girls like bees around a honeypot. But marriage no more entered his pleasure-loving head than it did his father's before him – that was, not until he'd lived double the time Theo has.'

'I didn't *make* him marry me, you know.' Was it anger, hurt or fear that made Anna speak like it? 'I told him I could very well manage on my own. To hear the way you talk, you'd think he was no more than an empty-headed playboy. Obligation, duty, those matter to Theo.' Fiercely on the defensive, increasingly aware of how it was she'd come to Manningtor, she chose her words carelessly. Was she being fanciful in taking the older woman's penetrating scrutiny as evidence that she had guessed the situation? 'I'm not dependent on him, I told him so. It was Theo who insisted –'

'That's enough!' As if she were talking to a badly behaved child, Nanny raised her hand to emphasise her command. 'Those are things that are between no one but you and him. But I'll ask you one question, just one and I want a truthful, swear before your God, truthful answer. Do you love Theo?'

Anna knew the question was asked simply because Millie Harknell cared. An honest question deserved an honest answer and somehow stripped her of her fight. 'Yes, Nanny, I do love him. And one day he's going to love me too.' What was she saying? It was as if she had no power to stop herself. 'I'm having

56

his child, you guessed that, didn't you? I could see it by the way you were looking at me. That's why he married me. Not for me, not because he's in love with me. An obligation, that's what he said. Not to me but to this child. Now you're thinking, where's my pride?'

'No, child, I was thinking no such thing. I was thinking that for all his flighty ways, he's shown a bit of sound sense at last. One tip I'll give you: stand up for yourself. You say he talks of obligations, well you have one to yourself as well as to the child he's given you. This son – or a daughter come to that – needs to look up to both its parents. If Theo *insisted* on marriage as you say, then it's up to you to take your rightful place as his wife. Not just one of the family, but Mrs Theo Sullivan. You have your own position in the house to uphold.' Then, with a smile aimed at turning them into conspirators, 'And when I'm back in my old rooms there at the big house, I'll see to it that no one forgets. Till then, it's up to you, child.'

If her words were aimed at boosting Anna, they fell short of their mark. For a second she was about to make the spontaneous retort that she didn't expect to have need of a nurse for her child, but there was something about Nanny Harknell's faithful affection for Theo and the family that stopped her.

'Now it's my turn to tell you something about Manningtor,' Millie Harknell moved the conversation on, closing the door on what had led up to the unexpected wedding. 'Like I think I said earlier, there was a time when there couldn't have been a happier establishment in the land than Manningtor. Theo's father owned the estate, a bachelor some years older than Mr Sidney, the one who's always given all his thoughts to that coach company as if he hadn't two ha'pennies to rub together. Perhaps he hadn't, for all I know: younger sons don't come off too well sometimes. But he and the master always got on well. Anyway, I was telling you how things used to be. Before I came down to Devon I looked after Sylvia and her older brother Lance. He's been out in America for years, found himself an American wife and is raising a family. Never talks of visiting, so I doubt if you'll meet Lance. Well, as I was saying, I looked after the pair of them. Their mother was widowed when Sylvia was barely old enough for school. Never strong, but with the nature of an angel. Her roots were somewhere in the sunshine of the Mediterranean, a real Latin

57

beauty she was. When Terence Sullivan met her all his bachelor ways flew straight out of the window. Fell in love with her like only a man old enough to know better could. She was just turned forty and he was I'd guess some ten years more. Ten months into their marriage she was brought to bed with Theo. I remember how it worried me. She was fragile as a butterfly. I'd been with her when Sylvia was born, I knew what a fight she'd had then, and this time she was pretty well ten years older. But Theo, he came into the world good as gold. A son for Manningtor, now wouldn't you have expected them to be content? Content? Oh, but they seemed more than that. Like I told you, you could feel the happiness in that old house. Then she fell pregnant again. Theo was coming up to five. Another baby at her age would put a strain on any woman and, I told you, she was fragile. A build not so unlike your own, not some strapping, broad-hipped sort who drop their young easy as the cattle in the fields of Home Farm. Forty hours she was in labour, every minute of it the sort of hell none of us will ever forget. I doubt if she even lived long enough to hear Alex's first cries. And for Manningtor, that was the end of happiness. I doubt if Theo has talked much to you about his childhood, has he? Once his mother was taken, it was as if the master's spirit, his soul you might say, had gone with her. If Theo knew what was good for him he kept out of the way and, as for Alex, he never forgave her for being the cause of his misery. Took to the bottle, poor man. Drink, gambling, anything rather than be here at home. And for the peace of Manningtor, it was better the poor broken creature stayed away. Mrs Sidney, Theo's Aunt Kath, you know, she took over the running of the household and Sylvia grew up able to take responsibility. Thank God they did, or who knows the sort of rundown state things would have become. These days, of course, Sylvia is along at the farm, but she and her husband seem to see it as all one place. Now there's Mr Matthew's wife too. And as far as the estate goes, Theo grew into the job easy enough.'

'What happened to his father? I'd rather ask you than Theo. He hasn't told me anything.'

'Naughty boy. He had no business not preparing you. He was no more than a child when the poor master met his end. In his cups as they say, he staggered out of some drinking hole he used to frequent in London, never a thought for the traffic. Out of the door and straight into the road. It was a taxi that hit him. And I dare say it was the greatest the mercy, for there was nothing in his life. Of course there could have been: happy memories, two beautiful children from his marriage, the care of Lance and Sylvia if he'd needed to feel he was doing something for his beloved Emily. But no. He hadn't the gumption, the staying power. The greater the happiness, the greater the fall from the heights to the depths, I dare say. Theo is his father all over again. If he hit trouble – and please God he won't – I don't know whether there's enough inner strength in him.'

'Theo won't hit trouble. Nanny, you mustn't worry about him. Anyway, of course he's strong.'

''Tis to be hoped you're right. Now, I hear the kettle singing; I'm making a pot of tea. Go and tell him we've done talking about him, he can come back in now.'

It didn't enter Theo's head that being so recently married this 'honeymoon period' might be different from any other. The day after their arrival he went out hunting with Sylvia, Francis and his sister Nadine.

'What are your plans?' Thelma asked Anna, her manner relaxed and friendly. 'I wondered whether you might like to drive into Deremouth with me – there are one or two things I want. Then perhaps you might be interested to call in at the coach station. The sooner you get acquainted with everything, the better. Are you coming, Mother?'

'No, my dear,' Aunt Kath – or Mother as she was to Matthew and his wife – declined. 'Take this child and show her the sights.'

Anna wished they wouldn't refer to her as the child – first Nanny and now Aunt Kath did it. Right on cue came a tap on the morning-room door.

'Come along in,' Aunt Kath called. 'Ah, Mrs Gibbons, come in. You've come with the –'

But before she could finish her sentence, and probably in an attempt to save any unpleasant awkwardness, the housekeeper held a handwritten sheet of paper towards Anna. 'Today's menus, Mrs Theo, madam. I'd like you to glance over them and tell me if you'd prefer anything altered.' Of course there was embarrassment, there was no way of avoiding it.

59

Kath put on her spectacles and opened the morning paper as if she'd been waiting for just that moment. Thelma looked on, her sympathy divided between the matriarch who'd been ousted and the inexperienced girl who found herself thrown in at the deep end – and a non-swimmer too, judging from her expression! Anna's first reaction was to turn to the others, but almost before the idea had time to form itself she remembered what was expected of her. Mistress of Manningtor, and this was her first test. Help me sound as if I know what I'm talking about, she thought, help me to strike just the right note, help me to do it so that Theo's people won't see me as some pushy upstart.

'I think it all sounds very nice, Mrs Gibbons. I know it's all wrong and silly of me, and I expect I'll be the only one who likes it, but if you have any apricots – I think dried ones will do but I don't know much about cooking – with the lamb, could you also ask them to make an apricot sauce?'

'I'll tell cook, madam. Apricot you say? Instead of the usual mint sauce?'

'Oh no, as well as. The others might not think it's such a good idea. But at home one day when they realised they couldn't find enough mint in the garden, that's what they did. And I loved it. So after that we always had apricot with lamb; it really goes very well. If you haven't any apricots in the kitchen, never mind this time.'

'I'm sure we have, madam. And if not, Grant will ride down to the village and get some. You shall have your apricot sauce.'

'Lovely. Thank you, Mrs Gibbons.'

Anna was pleased with herself; she'd got over her first hurdle. More than got over it, she was sure she'd taken a stride into finding a place for herself here at Manningtor. Hurdle number two was the one she dreaded: facing the reactions of Aunt Kath and Thelma, who must see her as a usurper.

'Did I manage all right?' It was useless to pretend they didn't know how new she was to authority. Only when she'd asked the question did she force herself to look at them.

'Splendidly,' Aunt Kath folded the newspaper and gave up all pretence that it had held her interest. 'I admit, yesterday when Theo dropped you on us, I foresaw difficulties. You're young and I'm sure inexperienced. But, my dear, you need have no fears – and neither need we. The house will be in capable hands.'

'Mrs Gibbons could have made it difficult for me. But I felt she was friendly.'

Thelma relaxed with relief. She too had feared trouble. 'If Mrs Gibbons is behind you, all the rest will take their lead. About Deremouth, do you like the idea of a morning out?'

'I'd love it. I have a letter I want to post to my grandfather. And – both of you – thank you. I must be a horrible shock for you, but I truly mean to make a success of what's expected of me.'

'And so you will. Yes, you were a shock; not just you as a person, but to arrive home and drop a bombshell like that, well of course it was a shock. Why the young rascal couldn't have introduced you to us before, to us and the people on the estate too, then had a proper wedding, I can't think. There should have been an announcement in *The Times*. The local paper will soon be on your heels, but that will only give the gossips something to wonder about. People are so quick to think the worst; I don't mean *us*, I mean people who only know what they read in the newspapers. It's not fair on you to put you in that position. But Theo has always been a law unto himself – and truth to tell, we wouldn't change him. When I think of some of the flighty pieces he's involved himself with, then I say thank God he came to his senses.'

'The others were no more than playthings to him, Mother.' Thelma saw no sense in raking up his past indiscretions. 'I'm sure he'd never been in love until he found Anna. And as for marriage, I doubt if the thought ever entered his head.' Then, with a laughing shrug, she added, 'All those worries we've wasted and all the time he had more sense than we gave him credit for.'

Never in love until he found Anna – for one moment she wanted to tell them the truth. But she mustn't. In seven months' time, when her baby was born, would they believe it was premature? Believe it or not, that would be the story they'd make sure was put around.

'I understand Sylvia is taking Nadine into Exeter for the fast evening train back to London. She says she only came down to go hunting and is anxious to be back in the clinic.' A statement, but it gave no hint of Aunt Kath's views on Sylvia's sister, a tall handsome young woman, a professional physiotherapist.

'Hunting will lose its appeal, I wouldn't wonder.' Thelma chuckled, collecting books she wanted to take back to the lending library at Boots. 'Now then, coats on and I'll introduce you to Deremouth and the coach station, Anna.'

As they drove down the long lane to Moorleigh they heard the distant call of the huntsman's horn and caught sight of the riders. Thelma braked by a field gate so that they could watch.

'Living in the country, I wonder you never rode,' she said. 'Do you paint, or sew, or – or what?'

'I hate being asked, because really I don't do anything. Oh, I make my own clothes, but that's always been because it's easy to buy material in Brindley market but the only dress shop there is terribly dowdy. Apart from that there's nothing to show for what I do with my days. That sounds so negative.' A quick glance at Thelma and before she could stop herself she rushed on, 'And there is something else, something I've never told anyone before, not Grandpa, not Theo.' What was she saying when twenty-four hours ago she hadn't even met Thelma Sullivan? 'I write. Perhaps nothing I've done is any good, I've never sent it to a publisher to find out. But sometimes I've thought that what I write has been all the more from my heart – does that sound stupid? – because I didn't know anyone to make friends with; no one else, I mean, just the people in my books.'

'And you've not even told Theo?' Thelma put the car into gear ready to drive on. 'Why?'

'I suppose because I'm scared he'd laugh. What I do may be bad. The people I write about and the things that happen to them are *real* to me. He might not believe in them. I mean, no one but me might believe in them. I don't know why I told you. Promise not to say anything, not even to Matt.'

Thelma promised and Anna was sure she wouldn't break her word. Somehow it was comforting to know she had shared her secret and it put Thelma into a category of her own, a confidante, a *friend*.

'Does Theo spend much time at the coach station? Mrs Humphries used to talk to me about his being there.'

'When he was young I think he used to tag along with Matt. Father took his responsibilities very seriously and poor Theo had precious little male company. But it's up to him to tell you about his childhood; his mother had been dead some years by the time Matt and I were married. But, yes, he used to enjoy going down to the coach station, the men all knew him, everyone made a fuss of him.' There was no doubting her affection as she said it. 'It would be hard not to be fond of Theo. These days he doesn't go there, and in any case there's usually something to take his time on the estate. Until he was grown up, of course, Father looked after it, or sometimes Matt, being that much older than Theo. One thing is certain, as a child or now, you never find Theo sitting around doing nothing. He likes to cram all he can into each day.' As if its entry were stage managed, an aeroplane few overhead. 'He's told you about the flying club, of course.'

'You tell me.'

'Just how keen he is? He has his private pilot's licence. Fast cars, aeroplanes, horses more frisky than most people could master, he really is a mad cap, bless him.' Thelma was his cousin's wife, probably no more than a dozen years older than Theo, yet such was her motherly nature that she spoke of him with the loving tolerance usually kept for the hare-brained exploits of the very young. 'I'm not going to ask if you drive a car, I know you won't have had the opportunity. But living so far out of Deremouth it's really a *must*. Would you like me to teach you? Or does Theo want to be the one to do it?'

With her hands gripped tightly between her knees as if to hold back a sudden rush of excitement, Anna beamed her thanks in the direction of her new friend.

'If you would, it would be wonderful. From what you say there will be lots of time when Theo will be occupied, so let's not tell him. Let's keep it a surprise from all of them. Can we?'

Matronly Thelma may have been but she was as excited as Anna at the prospect of what they intended to do. Perhaps her excitement held a special quality because driving lessons were to be a secret from the family – and that had to include Matt. And not just driving lessons: they were only half the secrets, there was Anna's trust in confiding about her writing too.

It was unheard of for her not to share all the events of her day with Matt, but loyal to her promise she kept Anna's secrets. As they got ready for dinner that evening she would have loved to have told him, knowing that he'd never break a confidence. But she'd given her word. So as she dabbed the powder puff across her healthily rosy face she turned the conversation to Alex.

'Did Mother show you Alex's letter?'

'Humph. Off to Austria for Christmas with some woman she works with. What do you make of it? Wouldn't you think she'd want to come home this year of all times? Personally, I see it as a slight on Anna. If she'd visited for a weekend during term it wouldn't be so bad. And how will Theo feel? She's always doted on him, now she can't even be bothered to come and meet his wife.'

Thelma looked at him affectionately, loving his male lack of intuition.

'Poor Alex. Jealousy is such an unhappy thing. And that's the trouble you may be sure. Fasten the buttons at the back of my neck, there's a dear. As you say, she idolises Theo – well, of course she does, we all do.'

'Humph, so she may. If it's jealousy she's suffering, she ought to be ashamed of herself. Can you imagine Dee taking that attitude when Sam finds a sweetheart?'

'Of course not. But ours have the security of loving parents. Poor little soul, Alex must have felt so – so bruised by the way her father treated her.'

There was no unkindness in Matt's laugh. 'If one of them was bruised, I'd say it was Theo, the times he came in for his father's temper.'

'Just talking about it brings it all back. Aren't you grateful for our own family? I was frightened of him myself when I first came here. I know he was sick with misery, but you wouldn't think one person could so poison a household.'

Grateful for their own family, she'd said. Oh, but she was. She must never allow herself to get so contented that she forgot to appreciate. And from the way her eyes smiled when they met Matt's there was no fear of that.

When next morning at breakfast Theo announced that he was going to the flying club the family knew from experience they'd see no more of him until evening. It presented a golden opportunity for Anna's first driving lesson. With the learner's plates she and Thelma had bought in Deremouth hidden in the boot, they went towards the moor where the roads would be empty at that time of year. And so began a new chapter in Anna's progress towards the independence she'd always longed for, and when Sylvia kept her promise of offering friendship and suggested teaching her to ride, she was ready to take that in her stride too. Add to that the time she spent in the estate office with Theo, familiarising herself with the filing system, sometimes with two fingers hammering out any letters he wanted on the typewriter, and the only thing almost pushed out of her mind was her escape to the characters of her own creation. They were there in the background, but for the moment she was learning to *live*.

Her dreams of life with Theo were very different from the reality, yet with each day her confidence grew and even though he never spoke those words she longed to hear, yet she was happy. Her days were full, each one ending with the satisfaction that she had learnt something, bettered some skill, become more at home with the ways of Mannington. More than that, each one ended with lovemaking that fulfilled her to the very depths of her being. She would drift into sleep believing that it must be the same for Theo even if he weren't aware of it. Otherwise surely he wouldn't be as eager as she was for their nightly lovemaking, and how could it be like it was for him, carrying him to a climax as glorious for him as it was for her? So Anna was happy, refusing to let herself dwell on words like duty or obligation. Each day she rode; almost each day she and Thelma went out in the Morris.

She didn't rush to tell the family about the baby. Always thin and scraggy, as Mrs Short had said, only she herself could notice the first slight changes in her body. Would Theo lose respect if estate tenants thought he had been forced into an unwanted marriage? And the baby, perhaps a boy and heir to what Theo held so dear, how would he feel if he were ever to know he'd been the reason for their marriage, he'd been their 'obligation'? She tried not to dwell on the thought.

Clad in her brand-new jodhpurs and hacking jacket, she strode purposefully towards the stables where Sylvia was already waiting, both mounts treading the ground in a sign of their eagerness to be off.

'I was out here early so Dilly is ready for you. I've put the jumps out – I think it's time for you to get the feel of them.'

Anna felt her tummy turn over. So far she'd learnt to control Dilly, the mare, in the paddock; on instruction and with Sylvia watching closely, she had managed to convey to kindly Dilly the order to walk, to canter or to trot, even occasionally to gallop; she had turned her to the right, then to the left. But all that had been on flat ground. Her mind flew to the few times she'd seen the hunt and watched the horses flying over the hedges. Her hands felt clammy with terror.

'Sylvia, I'm not ready. Supposing I get thrown!'

'What rubbish. The jump is hardly off the ground. And if ever there was a docile horse it's Dilly – *anyone* could get astride her and she'd take care of them. Now, once round the paddock then take her into the jump.'

Relief at seeing the bar was in truth hardly off the ground gave Anna confidence; Sylvia's inference that her progress was due less to her than to Dilly gave her determination. As she cleared the lowest jump she felt she was soaring to the heights she had admired when she'd watched the hunt.

'Was that all right?' she shouted, sure that it had been.

'Yes, you sat well. Round again and jump it just once more then we'll have a proper ride. I promised Uncle Sidney I'd drop a package in to the repair shop in Moorleigh.'

Five minutes later, another successful 'jump' accomplished, Anna was ready for anything. If only someone were here with a camera, imagine how proud they'd be at Dunsford House if they could see her. Not that Grandpa would let it show that he was impressed, but Anna felt she had come a long way and grown into a new understanding since she'd left home. Dear Grandpa, was he missing her? 'Missing all your silly chatter,' he'd say. Out through the wide wrought-iron gates they went and down the long lane towards the village. From this height she saw the world quite differently, she felt invincible. Above them an aeroplane flew low on its way to make its customary circle round Manningtor. Theo! In that moment, sitting so proudly astride Dilly, she understood his need to show off. No wonder she smiled as she rode. From this height she had a clear view across the hedges on either side of the lane, on the right to the distant fields that were part of Home Farm and to the left Deans Farm, part of the estate but cultivated by a tenant farmer.

'I wonder why Uncle Sidney first started the coach company,' she mused. Surrounded by all this, who would want noisy, smelly, petrol engines?

'The younger son. You know how they used to say the first son inherited, the next one went into the Church and the third into the Army. He has an independent streak, and would never have let himself be planted in some profession not to his liking. Just after the war, when he started with only one coach, it must have been quite an exciting thing to do. Where any normal man gets excited by the smell of perfume, I bet the only thing that made his pulses race would be fumes from those buses. When the eldest inherits it's hard on the rest of the family. Look at us lot – can't pull ourselves away from Manningtor. All except Alex, who's too ambitious not to want to earn her own way. Here's the workshop, I'll just slip in with this package.'

I'm not nervous on Dilly, Anna told herself as she was left alone, and at that moment she believed it to be true. Certainly from Day One, fear hadn't been part of the exercise. But this was the first time she'd found herself in an empty lane, no one here except herself and Dilly, no one within earshot. Just beyond the entry to Sullivan's depot a gate into a recently ploughed field was open and, in a leisurely way, she walked Dilly across so that they were on the grass verge leading to it.

It was then that she heard what turned out to be a coach coming up the hill from Moorleigh village, making hard work of the climb as it approached the repair depot and every now and again backfiring as if the strain were too much for it. Dilly's ears went back, her tail swished as she tossed her head.

'All right, Dilly,' Anna leant forward, stroking her neck in an effort to calm her – to calm herself too, if she were honest enough to admit it.

The coach was almost at journey's end, the driver changed into first gear to turn into the gate and then came a bang like cannon fire. With a loud neigh Dilly was on her hind legs, then, with no warning, she galloped through the open gate and, as if all the devils in hell were after her, started across the furrowed field where each ridge was piled higher than the jump which had made Anna feel so cock-a-hoop less than an hour before. Jolted out of the saddle, she was almost lying on the mare's neck, all semblance of control gone, fighting just to hold on.

'Stop her, please stop her. Help me.' She heard her voice, heard it break in a whimper. At the far end of the field was a hedge.

'Make her stop, please don't let her jump. Help me to hold on. Please help me.'

Behind her was the sound of pounding hooves, but she couldn't look round. Instead she closed her eyes. For all her frantic pleas, hope and reason both deserted her.

Chapter Four

'She did well.' Back at the Home Farm Sylvia reported the tale to Francis.

'A blessing she was thrown clear. We've all had a few falls in the early days, and although you give her a lesson most days it only adds up to a few hours. To be thrown from a bolting horse is enough to put her right off.'

'Oh, but it didn't,' Sylvia laughed, holding her face towards him so that he could light her cigarette, then relaxing onto a narrow wooden bench against the wall of the implement barn – or as near relaxing as it allowed – as she watched him bolt a replacement plough share into position. 'I don't know who was shaking most, her or Dilly. But she's got guts, I'll give her that. When I told her that the only thing to do was to get straight back on I could almost feel her girding up her loins ready to do battle. I made sure our ride home was a very quiet plod. I wasn't going to let her see how sorry I was for her, but honestly I took my hat off to her – or I would have if I'd been wearing one. I could almost feel the way she was gritting her teeth at every jolt but she kept a sort of set smile on her face.'

'There's more to that girl than meets the eye,' Francis muttered, his interest more on the job of tightening the nut on the plough share. Then, satisfied the job was done, he added, 'But what attracted young Theo to her in the first place, I can't imagine. Plucky she made be, but she's not what you'd think of as a sex symbol. Up to now his taste has always been more, shall be say, blatant.'

'That's not how I'd describe Nadine.'

'Any interest in Nadine was in your mind, my love.'

Sylvia shrugged, a sign of acceptance. 'Thinking of one or two he's played around with, I dare say we should be counting our blessings for the one we got landed with. They're a strange pair, though, he still goes his own way just like he always has. She insisted on seeing to Dilly herself when we got home, you know.'

'Where is she now?'

'I told her to go and have a hot soak. But she'll be bruised – and stiff as blazes.'

'She must thank her lucky stars it was a newly ploughed field and the ground still soft. I'm glad you got back in time. I'm just off to get a few bits from Gowers,' he said, naming the agricultural engineering firm on the road to Totnes. 'How do you fancy a drive?'

'I fancy it very well, if you wait while I fix my face.'

'Your face is fine.'

'Beauty is in the eye of the beholder. And something tells me they don't see me quite that way at Gowers.' Which was undoubtedly true, for Gowers, like most local traders looked on Sylvia as 'Mrs Too-Big-For-Her-Boots' or something along similar lines; indeed, those working at Manningtor, and sometimes even the family, took much the same view. Francis knew her better.

'Buck up then and tart yourself up. Five minutes, no more.'

'Yes, sir,' she pursed her lips in a departing kiss and went into the cloakroom leading from the farm office to repair her always immaculate make-up.

If she and Francis considered Theo and Anna an ill-assorted pair, that wasn't so far different from the family's view of their own partnership. A good-looking and intelligent child, Sylvia had developed into a handsome and confident adult, a first-rate horsewoman, one who had many an admirer and showed no interest in any. All that had changed when Francis Chadwick had become manager of Home Farm. More than ten years her senior, he was a true son of the soil, only emphasised by his training at agricultural college, his pleasant appearance owing more to good health and good temperament than to symmetry of features. Within weeks of knowing him, her mind was made up. And when Sylvia's mind was made up, nothing could change it.

Married for ten years, they had no children. Whether that was by design no one knew and, always holding herself slightly aloof, Sylvia wasn't the sort of woman to confide, even to warm and friendly Thelma.

Lying back in the bath, Anna closed her eyes and gave herself up to the caress of the hot water. It had probably been less than a minute between Dilly's terrified bolt and the second when she'd given up the battle to hold on and had found herself flying through the air to fall onto the deeply furrowed earth, but it was a minute that couldn't be erased with the comfort of warm water. In truth, neither could the ache in her muscles, the deep pain in her shoulder and back. By the time she had hit the ground Dilly was already over the gate into the next field where, fortunately, the change in the surface must have broken the mare's demented rush; yet Anna felt as if her back had been crushed by pounding hooves.

Under the water she pressed her hands against her still-flat stomach. Somewhere in there her baby was safe. So grateful, she thought to herself, then, certain that all was well and her thanks said, she let her mind wander where it would. Think how everything has changed in just a few weeks. Before Theo knew about the baby – and when she heard the echo of his words 'obligation', 'we have no choice' she pushed them away – even *I* didn't understand, didn't know I'd feel like I do now. My baby: a living person, mine to love. When I used to pray so hard for Theo to come back, a baby was just a reason for making us marry and be together. Forgive me for not understanding – and thank You for keeping it safe. If only Theo loved me, really loved me, not as a sort of easy daytime companion or else someone to make love to at night, but loved me as part of himself. You've helped me with everything else, I beg, yes really beg You (beseech, isn't that the way they say it in prayers?), please help in this too. I'll do my part, I'll try hard, well, I do already, but I'll make an even bigger effort to be all he wants and feel like he does about Manningtor.

Eyes still closed she sank into the comfort of the water, feeling it wash over her stiff shoulders, giving herself up to the pain of her aching limbs.

'Anna, Anna, are you all right?' Who was calling her? She was walking on the sloping lawn with Theo's arm warm around her, a pram standing in the shade of the sycamore tree. 'Anna? Can you hear me?' Her eyes shot open, bringing her back to an awareness of pain and cooling water.

'Yes, Thelma, I'm fine. I think I went to sleep.'

'You mustn't get cold or you really will stiffen up. It's nearly lunchtime; Theo is due back.'

'I'll get dressed. Thanks for waking me.' Such a bright voice, nothing to suggest that she felt as though a carthorse had kicked her in the base of her spine. 'I'll be down in five minutes.'

'You really are all right, dear? Perhaps you ought to have a quiet afternoon in the warm instead of us going out?'

'No, let's stick to our plans, Thelma. Concentrating on my lesson will help me forget my bruises.'

So, lunch over, Thelma drove her off in the Morris, then a mile or so away from the house, like a pair of conspirators, they changed places. This was her tenth lesson, one of great importance, for Thelma had decided the time had come for her to take them the whole way to Exeter. A red letter day. Had it been yesterday, Anna would have been wild with excitement, but today it was all she could do to concentrate, to change gear at the right time, to circle her hand out of the window to indicate a left turn or to hold it out straight to indicate a right. She could sense that Thelma was watching her with concern but somehow that helped to strengthen her resolve.

'I want to go into Boots,' Thelma told her as they neared the centre of the city, 'pull up over there, can you.' Then, when the car came to rest by the kerbside, 'Well done, I felt utterly safe. You did everything right, I'm proud of my pupil. Go on like this and we'll soon arrange for you to have your test. I want to show you off – I'm looking forward to impressing them when they find what we've been doing with our afternoons.' Anna forced a smile. 'I say, you look really rotten. In Boots I have to change a library book for Mother, then I'm going to get aspirin. We'll go and have tea somewhere and you can dose yourself.'

Aspirin and a cup of tea swallowed, Anna tried to believe the pain was dulled. And so the day dragged on.

Theo was anxious. He'd fallen from his pony sometimes when he'd been learning, and had probably yelled if he'd hurt himself, but he'd pretty soon got back on and tried again. And so had

72

Anna, according to Sylvia – except that with her there had been no yelling. But he didn't remember ever looking like she did. Her thin face was ashen, there were dark smudges under her large eyes, eyes normally mirrors to her mind yet now dull and expressionless. There was nothing elfin-like about her tonight; she looked haggard, plain.

Always at night she longed for the moment when he turned towards her. Often they kept the light on, every sense alive to the thrill and adventure as with no inhibitions they followed instinct. To Anna the thought that they were 'knowing each other' in the biblical sense added an unspoken sanctity to the act of lovemaking.

'I won't touch you,' he tried to sound reassuring, 'try and get to sleep.'

She bit her trembling lip, thankful that he'd turned his back and was reaching to put out the bedside light. Won't touch me, that means he won't make love to me. But for him it's got nothing to do with *love*. I want him to touch me, I want him to hold me, I want the comfort of his sharing how frightened I am. But all I am to him is a *thing*, someone always there for his sensual pleasure – his carnal pleasure. If he can't have that, he doesn't want me at all. I suppose it's my own fault. What would have happened if I'd not been as desperately keen as he was that afternoon – a few minutes in a scratchy cowfield, that's all it was to him. And even now, after weeks of being together, night after night – she couldn't bear even to remember the joy she'd thought had been the same for them both. 'I won't touch you,' the words echoed. Already, with his back towards her, he was settled for the night. A hot tear escaped, she held her mouth stiff and clenched her teeth. Soon his even breathing told her he was asleep.

She must have drifted into sleep too, for when she was jolted into consciousness the waning moon had risen and was lying on its back, high in the sky. Ever since her fall she'd been wracked with pain, but nothing had compared with this! Her first instinct was to wake Theo, but reason came hard on the heels of instinct. She must get up, she must get away from him, somewhere by herself where she wouldn't have to fight for control to be silent. Each breath tried to turn itself into a whimper. Perhaps if she knelt down, bent double, it would feel easier, perhaps, perhaps. Barefoot and with eyes closed, as if by shutting out the near darkness she could cut herself off from this new agony, she crept from the room and across the corridor to the bathroom. She had tried to hold on to the belief that she'd bruised her back when she'd hit the ground just as she could already see she'd bruised her shoulder. But now the pain that gripped her groin in a stranglehold put all thought of her fall out of her mind. She might escape Theo and lock herself in the bathroom, but there was no escaping what she was frightened even to contemplate. If she'd imagined there could be pain like this, it was when she'd let her mind jump forward to mid-summer and the birth of her baby. Sitting on the edge of the bath she leant forward, elbows on her knees, her face buried in her hands. Can't stop crying, can't stand up, she heard herself whimpering like a whipped dog. Looking down she saw a stain of blood on her nightdress.

That was the beginning. Time ceased to exist for her.

Am I going to bleed to death? That would be a let-out for Theo – he doesn't want me, not *me*, I'm an obligation. My baby – I wanted my baby. Why did You let it happen? So much blood – not just blood, it's my baby – why did You let it happen? You could have stopped it, You could even stop it now and make all this be a dream. But You don't care, You let it happen. How much blood can I lose before I die? No baby – nothing – no one.

Nature is very resilient. How long Anna wept, how much blood she really lost, she would never know. At last cold broke through her misery and with it came a glimmer of resolve. She wasn't going to bleed to death, things were as they were and if that was the hand that had been dealt her, then it had to be the one she played.

Back in the bedroom the only sign of the passage of time was again the moon's journey across the winter sky. Groping in her drawer she found what she was looking for and in another minute or so she was getting back into bed, feeling the chill of the sheets. She felt drained, empty of emotion.

'You're like ice,' Theo's sleepy tone told her she'd disturbed him.

'Yes.' Oh, but she was. Body and spirit, she was like ice.

'Poor old you,' he was more awake now, his normal good-natured and casually well-intentioned self. 'You'll be stiff as blazes in the morning. Don't ride for a day or two. If you like I'll take you with me to the flying club – I don't mean I'd take you up, but you might like to watch. Better than moping around the house feeling sorry for yourself.'

'Sorry for myself,' her rasping voice came as a shock to both of them, 'yes, I am sorry for myself!' She felt the threat of tears and had no power to hold them back. She didn't even try. 'My baby's gone. Not going to have my baby.'

Like a jack-in-the-box he was sitting up.

'But why? You got up from the fall none the worse except for a few bruises.' What she had said seemed to be filtering slowly into his half-awake mind. Then, lying down again he drew her into his arms. 'Don't cry like that. It's rotten luck, but we'll get over it. Don't cry, Anna.'

'So I've let you down. That's what you think.' In her misery she needed to hurt herself. The confidence she'd been building during the last weeks left her, she was the girl he'd married out of duty – duty not to her, but to the child. Now it was gone.

Only a few hours before, she'd longed for the comfort of his arms and of his understanding. Now held close against him she was aware of his sympathy but not his love, and she was too numb with misery to care.

'Now you've got no need to keep me – only married me because of –'

'Shut up.'

'Won't shut up,' she wept, knowing she was behaving badly, needing to behave badly, having no power to act any other way. 'It's all right for you, having an heir was all the baby meant to you. It was *me* it belonged to, it was *mine*. Nothing to do with you until after it was born. All it was to you was a mistake, an obligation, the outcome of ten minutes in a scratchy cowfield, that's what you called it. It was *mine*, part of *me*. Now I haven't got it. I prayed and prayed – shan't any more – never any more. If there's a God, he could have stopped it happening. But he didn't. Gone, before it even had a life.'

'Don't cry like that, Anna,' he said again, he who always wanted happiness for those around him. 'Of course it matters to me. We have to say "This is where we're at," and we have to make a go of things. We know how to do that, don't we.' She heard the smile in his voice, as if he was placating a

75

hysterical child. 'We've done it once and we'll do it again. We get on well, I thought you were beginning really to care about the place here.'

'You're trying to be kind.' In the depth of her misery she managed to hide her heart behind the shield of that prim tone that had always been her defence. 'We both had a reason, a duty; that duty is gone.' But her control was short-lived, her evenly spoken words were lost in a snort she couldn't hold back. 'And I'm not going to be one, a duty, an obligation, I'm *not*, I'm *not*. I've got to be *me*, I've got to find a life.'

'Find a life? I thought that's what you were doing here; I thought you were getting to care about Manningtor; I thought you were interested in what you did; I thought you fitted in and were happy.'

''Course I was. Knowing Thelma and the others, learning about Manningtor.'

'And me?' She didn't answer, perhaps he didn't expect her to. When he turned onto his back, she did the same. Side by side they lay there, bringing to her mind the stone effigies of a long-dead local squire and his wife in Brindley church. 'We have to build a future.' There was no angry resignation in his tone, no emotion of any kind. It seemed the incident was closed.

But then, she told herself, what she'd said was true: losing the baby wasn't tearing him to pieces like it was her; he hadn't known those moments of wonder she'd felt as she'd inspected the first hint of change in her small, thin body and known she shared it with another being.

'Perhaps Mrs Humphries is right, perhaps Fate is what builds our future and there's nothing we can do about it.'

'Rubbish,' he laughed drawing her closer and speaking in that good-natured tone designed to give cheer, 'we'll soon be back where we were. And next time you'd better steer clear of Dilly.'

He meant to be kind, she knew he did, but the misery of her body was at one with the misery of her restless mind.

That had been the second week in December, and already the house was gearing itself up ready for preparations for Christmas which always started as soon as Sam and Delia came home from school. Sam was the first to arrive, a fair-haired, jolly-faced lad just as Anna expected a son of Thelma's would be. The only thing he appeared to have inherited from Matthew was his build – tall, broad-shouldered and, if his genes were to have any influence, the promise that one day his youthful strength would develop into the heaviness of middle age.

'Mum's pleased as Punch, having you here,' without preamble he said to Anna, the first time they found themselves alone together. 'She never moans,' then with a chuckle, 'I don't think she ever learnt how. But I'm pretty sure she misses having Dee and me about the place. She'll be able to mother you to her heart's content. Is that what she does?'

'I don't know about mothering, I can well do without that. But she and I get along really well, I know she's my friend.'

'And you're hers – I know that's how she feels from the way she writes about you,' he said, beaming. 'That's good. I know it's daft, but I always feel mean leaving poor old Mum when I go back to school. I suppose it's because I always look forward to the start of term, getting back to my mates, you know, and, even though she never says, I know how much she hates it when Dee and I go. Dad's always busy, he and Grandpa are so wrapped up with the business. Mum seems out on a limb. The others are fine, don't get me wrong. Aunt Sylvia's in and out all the time but really hasn't time for anything outside her own affairs,' adding with a laugh, 'battling for Hollywood-type glamour on a farm must be a full-time job. Gran – oh, she's great, she and Mum get on really well and I'm not criticising any of them. It's just that I've always felt sorry for Mum, the one who's married into the family. Gran was managing everything before my father brought her here, so there was no responsibility waiting for her. But now she's got *you*. You're birds of a feather.'

Despite herself, Anna laughed. So much for being Mistress of Manningtor!

The next day Matt waited on the station platform at Exeter St David's for Delia. At twelve she was nearly three years younger than Sam, and holding a very special place in her father's heart. When the train slowed almost to a halt and the doors were thrown open, she was out before it even came to a standstill, waving to her father, then lifting her suitcase from where it was blocking the exit and dumping it on a seat so that, unhampered, she could run the length of the platform and fling herself into his arms.

'Got here!' she exclaimed unnecessarily. 'Saw you before the train stopped. Case is over there.'

'I'll get it,' he told her. 'Early. Wanted to be sure.'

Their first moments were always like that: short sentences, half formed but wholly understood. He retrieved her abandoned suitcase, then holding tight to each other with linked arms, they made for the queue at the exit. Her return ticket was punched, his platform ticket collected, and they were out in the square where his car was waiting by the kerb.

'Home again, Dad,' another unnecessary statement as she wriggled comfortably into the seat by his side. 'Tell me everything. What's she like, this wife of Theo's? Is she a dreadful bossy boots ready to keep us all in our places?'

'Anna?' He sounded genuinely surprised. 'Of course not. But what's she like? you say. I've not given it a lot of thought. She's young, but then of course she is. A bossy boots, you say. She doesn't give me that impression. Your mother says she's getting a good grip on what's expected of her.'

'Oh, Mum wouldn't recognise a bossy boots if it jumped on her toes,' Dee scoffed. 'Anyway, isn't it stupid, just because she's married to Theo we are all expected to look on what she says as being important?'

'Now, Dee darling, don't set out to make an enemy of her just because of the way he dropped her on us.'

'I expect she's in the club.' She turned just far enough to see her father's expression as she said it, knowing she was playing with fire and enjoying the experience.

'I don't like to hear you talk like that. It's not attractive.' The tone of his rebuke was mild, but she knew from his frown that her 'worldliness' had impressed him.

'That's what it's called. I know because Molly Dawson's parents had to sack their maid during the summer holidays. Molly said that's what they called it – in the club.'

'I dare say they did. But I don't like to hear you repeat it. And in Anna's case I shouldn't think for a second it's true.' Not that he hadn't wondered the same thing himself when such an unlikely specimen had been dropped on them. Granted she had a certain charm, touchingly young and patently doting on Theo.

And as for Theo himself, who could tell how he felt? Certainly marriage had done nothing to alter the way he spent his days.

'Humph,' Dee was disappointed. A shotgun marriage had promised to be a meaty piece of gossip to take back to school. She wasn't prepared to relinquish the idea too easily. 'Well,' she pressed her point, 'why else would he pick up with some friend of the Humphries and not even bring her to meet the family.'

Matt laughed affectionately, his left hand stretching out to Dee with no effort on his part. His little girl was growing up, but what a joy it was to have her here with him again. 'You know Theo,' he said without criticism, 'he makes his own rules.'

'Anyway, what's she like? Is she ravishingly beautiful? And don't tell me you haven't even noticed *that much*.'

'I would have, if she were. In a word I'd not call her beautiful, not even pretty in the accepted way. Pleasant enough kid, skinny as a waif. Yet there's something about her that tells you she could have a will like iron.'

'Ensnared him, I expect.' If there was no better grist for next term's mill of scandal, she'd have to make the most of some scheming friend of an ex-employee captivating the handsome squire. At twelve years old, anything smacked of romance – from the pure desires of Romeo and Juliet to the ambition of Scarlet O'Hara, to the letters in the women's magazines smuggled in by day pupils and pored over by her and her friends in the privacy of the dormitory. What they couldn't thoroughly understand, they imagined. On the brink of puberty, their hormones were in a state of turmoil, something that was both frustrating and exciting. For Form IIIB sex was absorbing, wonderful and full of promise. She turned to her father with a broad smile, pulling off her black velour hat and stretching her black-stockinged, plump legs.

'Let's stop in Deremouth, can we, Dad? Let's go and have tea at the Ivy Tearoom, then I shall really feel I'm home. Anyway I want to go into the depot and see Grandpa. He always comes home so late all the excitement will be over by the time he gets there. Perhaps he could come to the Ivy with us. Can we, Dad?'

'Your mother will be waiting. We ought to go straight home.' But he knew they wouldn't; Dee knew it too and took his hand to plant a loud kiss on it. 'We'll call and ask Dad if he's free.

79

But we mustn't hang about, Dee. Just ten minutes won't hurt.'
The words cleared their consciences. Even though inevitably a
visit to the depot then tea at the Ivy Tearoom would set them
back an hour, it didn't deter them. These first minutes, bringing
her back from the station, were always Matt's most precious.

Sidney Sullivan had secretly been hoping they'd stop on the
way, knowing Dee would be sure to suggest it. So, delighting in
their stolen few minutes, they all crossed the road from the depot
to the café. Inelegantly digging her strong white teeth into the
largest doughnut on the dish, Dee's happiness was complete. If
this happened every day she'd soon get bored, she'd miss the
company and the fun of school. But in her first hours, being
with her two favourite people was enough.

At Dunsford House, Christmas had had much the atmosphere of
a Sunday. Not that Sundays had been given to churchgoing, but
the programmes on the wireless had overtones of the Sabbath and
when Mrs Short changed into an afternoon dress, she always wore
her best. In the days Miss Sherwin had been there, rain or shine,
she and Anna had gone for a walk after dinner on Sundays. And
that was another thing that had set the day apart from the rest of
the week: Mondays to Saturdays each midday they ate lunch,
even though the evening meal was called supper and served at
six as a concession to her grandfather's digestion; once a week a
meal was graced with the name of 'dinner' and that was brought
to the table promptly at one o'clock each Sunday. Only Christmas
Day shared that routine, followed by the ritual gathering around
the wireless to listen to a programme linking up all parts of the
Empire before they got to their feet – something of a struggle
for her grandfather, but one he insisted on upholding – for the
National Anthem.

Dee hadn't been home more than a day before Anna realised that at Christmas things were done very differently at
Manningtor.

'We're going on our holly hunt,' Sam told her. 'Do you want
to come? You can if you like.'

Anna felt rather than saw Dee's frown.

'I'd love to,' she accepted with all the eagerness Sam expected.
She sensed Dee didn't want her but she looked on getting to know
the young members of her new family as a hurdle she had to get

over. Her only experience of people of their ages was that she had lived through that time herself. But how could she liken her background to theirs? Hence this feeling of uncertainty. At Dee's age what sort of thing had interested her? Certainly not those that would fill the mind of a girl brought up surrounded by classmates – and not only in class, for Thelma had said that Dee shared a dormitory with nine others. How dreadful – nowhere to be by herself; no solitude to follow her dreams. She remembered the stories she'd written at that age, sitting up in bed, letting her thoughts live amongst the characters who peopled her mind. All Dee would have would be girlish chatter. Sympathy prompted the smile she turned on the sturdy child. 'I really would love to come with you – as long as you don't mind someone extra. I expect you've always done it together?'

'Yes, we have,' Dee answered, concentrating on tying her shoelace. 'But if you want to, then of course you can. You'll need thick gloves, it's a scratchy job. And we walk a long way. Perhaps you're not keen on walking?' Was there a hint of hope in the question.

'Walk you two off your feet any day of the week,' Anna replied laughing. 'Where I came from, walking was a *must*. I'll get ready. Don't go without me.'

It was a week since the night she'd lost her baby, a week when she'd felt weak in body and spirit. Only *she* knew the effort it had taken for her not to give way to the waves of self-pity that assailed her without warning. When Sylvia had said she ought to carry straight on with her riding lessons, she had put on her jodhpurs and forced herself to walk to the stables with a spring in her step designed to hide the pain in her groin and the ache in her heart. Now her body was back to normal and she was determined that her spirit would be too; she'd make friends with Thelma and Matt's children – they belonged in her new family, she would know them for the rest of her life and soon the few years' difference between their ages and hers would count for nothing. So that was partly why she accepted Sam's invitation so readily.

As well as that, though, there was a feeling of suppressed excitement in her. She'd read books where families celebrated the Christmas Festival; she'd read about houses bedecked with greenery, about carol singers – and she'd heard those on the

81

wireless too; each Christmas Eve while her grandfather had been having his rest she had listened to the glorious voices from the Cambridge choir of King's College Chapel, the sound always giving her a strange hollow ache in her tummy even though she had no idea why. Losing herself in reading, she had come close to the spirit of Christmas, imagining the glow of warmth from great open fires banked with Yuletide logs. When she'd been very young Miss Sherwin had brought life to the legend of Santa Claus too – dear Miss Sherwin who'd made her hang her white sock from the bedpost and who'd sat with her to watch the excitement of taking out the small gifts: tangerine, nut, comb, crayons. For the child Anna, those moments early each Christmas morning had been touched with wonder. Now, as she put on her sheepskin gloves, she resolved that when she came home she'd write a really long letter to her faithful friend.

In the coach house Theo was tinkering with the engine of his Riley. Not that there was anything wrong with it. If there had been he would probably have taken it down the long lane towards Moorleigh and let the mechanics at the depot repair the fault. Theo's attention was superficial enough to be of the clean-hands variety – looking at the car came in the category of visiting a dear friend. Normally he would have been at the flying club, but today a veil of mist hung across the moorland.

'Hey,' he shouted when he saw the holly hunt expedition setting off. 'Can anyone come? Wait for me.'

'It's the holly hunt,' Dee called back. 'Usually it's just me and Sam – but Anna wanted to come.'

'Sounds like fun. Give me two minutes to get my wellingtons and I'll join you.'

'Suppose you might as well,' Dee shrugged. 'We shall be out for hours. When Anna gets tired and fed up you two can go home together.'

Theo grinned at Anna, oblivious of the sudden hopefulness that tingled in her arms and legs. 'What do you reckon? Are we going to be outdone by a pair of kids?'

'I told them,' Anna laughed, 'I can outwalk them any day of the week. True, isn't it?'

'The lady's invincible,' he told the young ones. Dee's sulky expression was lost on him in his anticipation of the morning ahead; collecting holly may be a prickly job, but it held promise of being a lot of fun.

Five minutes later they were striding down the long drive to the lane. Anna suspected he would have been just as delighted to be part of the expedition even had she not been with them. But she wouldn't let her thoughts go down that trail. How handsome he was, his almost Latin good looks enhanced by the brown duffel coat and university scarf. His own? He gave the impression of being totally disinterested in his past, all his attention given to making the most of the moment. The only thing he seriously cared about was Manningtor, or so it seemed to her. More than anything she wanted the thing he cared about mostly to be *her*, but she had no illusions. And she could bear to give pride of place to Manningtor – it was a sentiment she could understand and share. If she questioned him about a past that honestly seemed of no consequence to him, she might learn things she'd rather not hear. She made no comment about the ownership of the scarf, but instead she gazed on him with all the adulation of youthful hero worship and, like him, lived for the hour.

And just as Theo had watched the three checking they all had sticks, secateurs and sacks, so Thelma stood by the window to watch the quartet march purposefully down the drive.

'You'd think they were all of an age,' she smiled contentedly. 'Theo never alters does he? Married man or no, he's always ready for anything with the promise of pleasure.'

Kath left her fireside chair and came to her side. 'Who could guess that child to be a married woman? I swear from here she doesn't look a day older than Dee. Piecing together the snippets we can glean, I imagine childhood passed her by. She deserves some playtime.'

'Make no mistake, that's what she'll get with Theo. Now then, Mother, let's get that wool wound into balls. I've boxed up the things we've finished, but I'd really like us to finish that pram set to pretty some poor woman's baby for Christmas. Do you think we can manage it?' It had been Thelma's idea two or three years ago that they knitted for Deremouth Philanthropic Society. Until then Manningtor's local philanthropy had gone no further than inviting the carol singers into the house on Christmas

Eve and plying them with mulled wine and warm mince pies. A lovely idea though it was, Thelma soon found a more practical way of showing goodwill. The people on the estate had always had a Christmas hamper, but it was she who organised a party for the local children held in Moorleigh's small village hall. Tea, games, a conjuror, a present from the bran tub and a balloon to take home. When they'd been younger Sam and Dee had always been there for a party that mixed well-to-do and poor, with Thelma on hand to make sure everyone had a good time. The children from Manningtor had outgrown the occasion, but Thelma was still the mastermind, and still the pianist for the party games on the first Saturday after Christmas. Word of its success soon spread to Deremouth where the Philanthropic Society enlisted her help in setting the wheels in motion for something similar for children of the town. With no responsibility for the running of Manningtor, she had made a place for herself in the community. And from that had stemmed the knitting that went on for months beforehand in readiness for distribution in the appropriate packages. No town is without its poor. Thelma worked closely with the members of the Philanthropic Society, all of them local, and tried to ensure no needy person slipped through the net. When a new baby arrived in a home struggling to stretch a low wage, or perhaps with no wage at all, she made a note of it. Her book might show: 'No. 10 Tanners Row, Jenkins, Husband sells papers corner Station Approach, wife, children 1930, 1932, 1935, new baby boy June 1937', the latest addition ensuring that along with the annual grocery package and a toy or book for each of the others, there would be a knitted garment of the right size for the baby. That was Thelma's way. Locally she was labelled 'a truly good woman', 'a real Christian', and only seldom would come the rider: 'Easy for her, her life must be pretty comfortable.' As of course it was, married to even-tempered, undemanding Matthew.

The holly hunt was a great success and they came home with four sacks full of prickly, red-berried branches.

'We'll leave them in the shed until tomorrow,' Sam said.

'We shan't be here tomorrow, we're driving up to Wickley Cross,' Anna said, keen to get on with her first chance of decorating.

'Sam and I always do it by ourselves. It's *our* job. We know exactly how we do it.' Dee glared at her defiantly.

'A rotten job anyway,' Theo said cheerfully, her barbed retort just as surely lost on him as was Anna's disappointment that he showed no resentment at the way Dee had answered her.

The next day he and Anna set out early for their drive to Wickley Cross. The village high street looked just as she remembered with less than a fortnight to go before Christmas. A notice on the hoarding announced that Santa Claus and his toy-makers were in his grotto in McBean's Emporium in Brindley, where sixpence would ensure a child could have a private word with him and come away with a present wrapped in blue paper for a boy or pink for a girl. Nothing changed. She could still feel the magic of walking alone into the tiny enclosed cubbyhole, festooned with coloured lights and silver 'icicles', and still remember the embarrassment of not knowing what he was talking about when he'd said, 'Come along in, little girl, and give me your letter.' Letter? What letter? Ought she to have brought him a letter from someone? She'd stood there tongue-tied and miserable. 'No letter for Santa? How can I know what it is you want for Christmas if you don't write me a letter? Never mind, come and sit on my knee and tell me what you think about all these busy people.' At six years old she'd had no experience of sitting on anyone's lap, least of all a stranger's. The clockwork models of the toy-makers had nodded and hammered; the grotto which at first glance had had the wonder of fairyland, was oppressive and frightening. 'I expect they're very clever, but they don't actually make anything.' She could still feel the effort she had made to sound grown up and composed, just as she could still remember the man's dirty fingernails and the smell of something she didn't like on his breath. A glass of beer with his midday sandwich had left a lasting impression.

She found herself telling Theo about the visit as he stopped the car in front of the notice.

'I bet you were ready with a list of requests by the next year,' he laughed.

'I didn't go again. You see, by the next year I knew it was all just make-believe.'

'What difference does that make? Filling the youngsters'

stockings is all part of the fun. I'd be surprised if Sam considers himself too old to tie a hopeful item of hosiery to his bedpost.' Then, changing the subject, 'I'm just going across to the butcher. Do you want to do any shopping – see anyone? Or are you waiting in the car?'

'I'll come too,' she said, clambering out, excited to be back amongst shopkeepers she'd known all her life. The butcher raised his boater to her, something he'd never done before, surprising her with the sight of his shiny bald head.

'Hello, Mr Brooks.' Yet even as she greeted him with a beaming smile, she knew there was a divide between the girl she'd been and the girl she'd become. Only a few weeks earlier this had been her natural habitat; now she had become a visitor. She listened as Theo ordered and paid for a goose to be prepared for the oven and delivered to Heathfield Cottage on Christmas Eve; she felt herself swell with pride at his largesse.

'Oh, and the same again for Dunsford House,' Theo remembered as he started to put his wallet back into his inside pocket.

Anna knew it was meant kindly, knew she ought to be pleased. So why wasn't she? She felt herself swept into the same bracket as the people on the estate at Manningtor, or the employees at the coach station.

'Grandpa doesn't care for goose. You don't have to –'

'A nice joint of Scottish beef, that would be best.' George Brooks didn't mean to lose a sale.

'I leave it to you,' Theo agreed, passing another note across the counter.

'You didn't have to do that,' Anna said as they got back into the car, hearing the sulky tone in her voice. 'I'm not staff waiting for my Christmas bonus.'

'What? What's up, Anna?'

'If you don't know, I can't tell you.' And neither could she. Her jaw ached with the effort to hold it rigid. What was she to him? 'Don't even know you, properly *know* you.'

'What's all this about?' He might well ask her, but she heard the laughing tone of his voice. 'What's it got to do with a joint of Christmas beef?'

'If you don't know, I can't tell you,' she repeated, hating herself for behaviour she couldn't control.

'I'd have thought you'd have been glad to order it for your grandfather.'

'Wasn't me, was y –' The battle got harder.

This time Theo laughed outright. 'Same difference.'

But how could it be when all she'd ever been to him, all she *ever would be* to him, was an obligation? That's all I am, she gave her thoughts free rein, the outcome of a romp in the hay – in the scratchy field, not even warm, sweet-smelling hay. It's only his optimistic nature that lets him accept me and make me an agreeable playmate, yes, that and – and a means of satisfying his sexual needs. Lust, that's what Grandpa called it. She needed to hurt herself, to turn the knife, ashamed of the way she felt but powerless to help herself. Along the lane leading to Heathfield Cottage he drew the car to a halt and turned towards her.

'Is it coming back here, is that what's bothering you?'

'Of course not.'

'I think I understand. It's being back here where you were a free agent; it brings it home to you how different it all might have been. Especially now that the reason for your having to get married is gone. But Anna, we've been through all that. Can't we both pull together in making it work?'

'I do. That's not fair,' she croaked. 'I've tried.'

'Christ! I'm making a mess of this. You're doing well – and we get on – surely you agree that we get on? Tell me the honest truth: if you could, would you turn the clock back and have your freedom?'

She shook her head.

'There, then,' he said, his boyish smile back in place, his confidence restored, 'so that's all right. I'd thought we were doing rather well. Married six weeks and not a single row!' He was back on familiar ground; life was a laugh again. Obtuse, seeing things just from his own angle, but in that moment she was grateful. In a few minutes she'd be back at Dunsford House – an emotional scene must be avoided at all costs.

But first there was a visit to Heathfield Cottage and that went a long way to slotting them into the roles they tried to play. With no knowledge of the reason for their quick and quiet wedding (or if they'd had their suspicions, the Humphries were too loyal to the Sullivan family to voice them), they were received at the cottage as any recently married young couple would have been,

87

something that helped wipe away what had become perilously close to being a scene with more emotion than either of them could handle. Then on to Dunsford House.

'The old gentleman is staying in his room,' Amelia Short greeted them. 'This is always a bad time of year for him. And without you here to jolly him along' (hardly a true description!) 'he gets no further than his fireside chair in his room.'

'We'll go up and talk to him,' Theo said, sounding a good deal more enthusiastic than he felt.

'No –' Anna had quite recovered from her near lapse '– you can come in a few minutes. But first I want to see him by myself.'

How frail he looked. Had he always been like this and was it that only now, having been away, she was seeing clearly? His thin hands, resting on the arms on his chair, were blotched with the liver spots of age; the skin of the lids of his closed eyes hung in folds.

'Grandpa,' she said in a loud whisper, surprised at the surge of affection she felt at the sight of him, 'are you awake, Grandpa?'

'All your noise, of course I'm awake.'

Six weeks away must have changed her more than she'd imagined. At one time she would have felt irritated by his manner, now she recognised in him something that she'd become familiar with herself: a charade of pretence that hid her feelings.

'Theo wanted to come up, but I told him to wait. I wanted to see you first. I wanted to tell you about things, Grandpa.'

Immediately he was alert.

'Things? I was right. You're not happy, child?'

Uninvited, she kissed his cold brow, then dropped to her knees by his side just as she had done the day he'd had to give his consent to her marriage.

'I *am* happy, Grandpa.' And was it a lie? 'Honestly and truly, I love Theo.' Then, before he could cut in with anything she didn't want to hear, 'And his family are all friendly. You wouldn't think they would have been, after all they didn't know me when I was dumped on them. The house is beautiful – well, I told you in my letters.'

'So you don't have to waste your time thinking of anything back here. Is that what you're saying?'

Time had been when a remark like that would have served to make her see him as difficult and selfish. Now she knelt up and looked him straight in the eyes, her own two pools of affection.

'Grandpa, you really are a wicked old spoof,' she told him. 'You know jolly well how much you and all this means to me. You're my rock, you're what I've built on. Isn't that what families are for?'

His mouth trembled. 'Silly old fool I am,' he mumbled.

It was her opportunity. She rested her head against his knee, avoiding looking at him as he groped for his handkerchief.

'Things I always took for granted, I miss them all. The black looks Mrs Short used to give me when I argued with you about things we read in the newspaper – remember? The way we used to talk French on Tuesdays – remember?'

'But you've found what you want, Anna? I had your letter telling me there wasn't to be a baby. How does that leave you and Theo?' Memories of the way he'd been forced to give his consent cast its long shadow over both of them. 'Without that, would you have married?'

'Of course we would,' she answered a little too quickly. 'There will be other babies.' Her reward was the sound of his sigh, a sound not of anguish now but of thankfulness. He said nothing and in a minute she realised sleep had overtaken him. It seemed to draw a line under their unusually honest and emotional conversation and perhaps the charade of her assurance to her grandfather helped put some of her own misgivings behind her.

'I'm glad we came,' she said to Theo as, late in the afternoon, they headed westward. 'I don't quite know why, but it's been like laying a ghost. Fancy, after all the time I lived with Grandpa, it's only now I believe I've seen the person he really *is*.'

'A bit different from the last time I confronted him,' Theo replied, recalling the sudden strength in the frail old man when he'd been told about the child. 'I tell you, I wasn't looking forward to coming face to face with him again. But he was nice as pie. How did you bring that about?'

How much ought she to say?

'I told him how much I'd missed him. And it's true. It's as if I've moved on and from this distance I can see clearly.'

'Funny elf you are.' He gave her a quick smile. 'Feel in the glove compartment and you'll find some toffees.' Theo never travelled far without a supply of sweets and, for the time being, chewing put an end to conversation. As her jaw moved, the treacley taste was soothing. She realised that Theo had preferred not to go down the road her remark had pointed, whether she was homesick, whether in seeing her past clearly she regretted her present. And just as he avoided it, so did she. She heard the echo of what he'd said to her not much more than a week ago: 'This is where we're at, and we have to see we make it work.' Perhaps not his exact words, but certainly that was his sentiment.

'How far are we driving today?' she asked, her cheek bulging with toffee. 'Can we spend the night where we did last time?'

'No. We'll stay somewhere new. We shan't get as far as that tonight. Anyway, that place was no great shakes.'

She wished she hadn't suggested it. His causal words cast a shadow on her memories of the wonder and promise of their first night together.

'Cigarettes are in the glove compartment. Light me one, will you.'

No one at Dunsford House smoked, but she'd taken to it willingly with Theo. There was something companionable about drawing on a cigarette then passing it to him, just as there was in lighting one for herself. Outside the last of the daylight was fading, a cold rain starting to fall. She pulled the rug around her, drawing on the cigarette she held to her mouth. Swathed in smoke, they were contained in their own private world, or so she liked to think. Their overnight stop was very much more luxurious this time, but for Anna the surroundings counted for nothing.

Christmas at Manningtor held all the ingredients of her dreams. A house bedecked with greenery, the scent from the huge spruce tree in the great stone-flagged hall seeming to fill the house; carol singers, hot mince pies and mulled wine; the whole family together in Moorleigh church for Midnight Mass; Uncle Sidney carving the most enormous turkey; an afternoon walk in the crisp air that promised frost before nightfall. And through it all, Theo's enjoyment was infectious. Cheerfulness was second nature to him – Anna could almost pretend that this was the way he had planned his life.

On Boxing Day the family went hunting.

'Fancy you not being able to ride well enough,' Dee looked pityingly at Anna. 'You'll have to stay home with the oldies.'

'Bet you that when you come home for half term I shall be out there with you!'

'How much?' Dee accepted the bet.

'Half a crown to sixpence.'

'Done. An extra half crown will be useful.' But despite herself, Dee couldn't stop her face from smiling. Theo's wife was quite a sport – which made it much harder to dislike her and build the sort of character picture that would be a talking point at school.

'Save your pennies. I'll be riding out with you by half term.'

She believed it to be true. And under different circumstances so it might have been.

Chapter Five

It was seldom that Deremouth saw frost and that January of 1939 was no exception. The same couldn't be said for Manningtor Park, in distance less than four miles inland but known locally as 'above the snow line'. Frozen bird baths in the garden, frozen drinking troughs at Home Farm, if not commonplace, were not unknown. It was towards the end of the month when Daphne, recently given the responsibility of family breakfasts, brought her empty tray back down to the kitchen.

'Real brass monkeys it is this morning,' she told anyone who liked to listen. This was the sort of weather when the best place to be was down here in the semi-basement region where, winter or summer, the Aga never let the temperature fall. 'When I undrew the curtains, I tell you I was glad I didn't have to go out to earn my keep. Garden looks a picture, mind you, like something on a Christmas card – only what we got is frost not snow.'

'Before they venture out then,' Mrs Gibbons answered, 'one of you just take that drum of salt and see to the front steps.'

Between the front portico and the sloping lawns of the parkland the flight of stone steps led to the forecourt. The magnificent frontage added to the grandeur of what had, many years ago, been built by a Sullivan ancestor who had made a fortune in the wool trade, with the pretentious aim of letting himself be recognised as a man of substance.

As Mrs Gibbons spoke, plump and cheerful Gwen came indoors from the coach yard. She was junior to Daphne in the rank-conscious hierarchy of the kitchen. 'I'll nip up and do the salting in a tick, Mrs Gibbons,' she offered with her usual willingness, 'just as soon as I've put the cutlery round the table for our breakfast. No, second thoughts, I'd best let that wait till after. I just came a cropper when I took those cloths out to Grant. After last night's rain it's like a sheet of ice in the stable yard. We want it to have time to melt the ice before Mr Matt drives on it.'

'Get a move on then. We don't want any accidents. You fell down you say? Not hurt yourself, duckie?' Mrs Gibbons' word was law below stairs, unless she was overridden by Nicholls, the butler, and unquestioned supremo – but that didn't prevent her looking on the staff as hers to care for.

'I bounce pretty easy, Mrs Gibbons. I'll just take that salt – and this time I'm ready for it, I'll mind how I go.'

Shutting the lobby door behind her to keep the warmth in, young Gwen and her drum of salt went back into the icy morning air.

'No coat on, Gwen? Don't hang about too long out here.'

'Oh Mr Matt, sir, I was trying to get the salt down before you got the car out. Mind how you step, I just went down. Wasn't hurt, mind you, but you don't half feel a ninny sitting there. The rooks up in those trees seemed to think I'd done it just to make 'em laugh.'

'Give me the salt, Gwen, and tell Mrs Gibbons I'm finishing off for you. Hop back indoors before you freeze. I'll leave it in the garage.'

The girl's pink-cold, round face beamed her appreciation. 'Honest? It nips your fingers, blowed if it doesn't.' She handed over the large tub of salt and, still smiling, turned back to the lobby. What a dear he was. How many bosses would be out there before eight in the morning chucking handfuls of salt? And when she got back inside and told her tale, that was the general opinion. Neither Matt nor Thelma ever did anything to blot their copybook with the staff.

Upstairs, breakfast dealt with, Ethel Bryant, the cook, dolled out the porridge and they all took their places at the large scrubbed-wood table. Nicholls, poker-faced as always, sat at the head as befitted his position, Mrs Gibbons at the foot, Esme, Daphne and Gwen on one side in order of rank with Esme nearest to Nicholls. Facing Esme was Ethel, then Digby, the head gardener, and Grant, who was everyone's to command and who had only missed the job of scattering the salt because he'd been up a ladder with a cloth and a pail of hot water trying to thaw the waste-water pipe from the central bathroom. The warmth of the kitchen, the smooth creaminess of the porridge (made with an extra drop of milk to keep out the cold) cast its spell. This little band who lived in felt themselves to be luckier than the outside workers who came by foot or bicycle to Manningtor, either each day or in some cases no more than once or twice a week. On a morning like this the resident staff appreciated being where they were, indeed they were luckier and 'superior' to the casuals, as they thought of the outside helpers. Everywhere times were changing. When the house had been built it had needed a veritable army of domestics. Electric equipment had lightened the workload, and a good thing it had, for young people in these modern times saw opportunities outside, even girls of working homes preferred to stand behind shop counters or write in shorthand and use a typewriter – anything rather than learn to run a home. Mrs Gibbons blamed it on all that nonsense that came out of Hollywood, filling their heads with glitter and glamour.

Upstairs, breakfast was a movable feast, the family coming down whenever they were ready and taking it for granted that they would find something appetising when they lifted the lids of the chafing dishes. Usually Sidney was the first at the table, to be joined by Matt, the workers of the family. Sometimes Theo was ahead of any of them, for he had no routine and liked to view the morning and then decide how best to spend his day. A brisk but not too powerful wind and he'd go down to the Dere estuary where his boat was moored; a clear blue sky and he'd make for the flying club; fog or that persistent drizzle which all too often enfolded that part of Devon and he'd spend the day in the estate office. Since he'd taken over the running of the estate himself he'd worked alone in there, rather enjoying learning to put two fingers to work tapping out his correspondence. These days, though, the fun came from teaching Anna. Sometimes it surprised him just how much he enjoyed having her there with him. But, of course, he would think with satisfaction, what's so good is to know that she is honestly interested, she really cares about Manningtor. If she didn't, I wouldn't want her there, he decided quite firmly, it's not that I need her to help, there's nothing that one person can't manage. But I can feel her genuine interest. She's remarkably bright, especially considering she never went to school. More than bright, though, she cares; all the time her knowledge grows, I can tell so does her interest. No bad thing that they had had to get married when they did, he considered. Munching contentedly at his bacon and eggs he let his mind wander, not listening to the morning conversation of the others.

All in all, happy-go-lucky Theo was rather pleased with himself. He'd never yearned for a great, consuming romance so his present situation suited him remarkably well. He found being married to Anna rather satisfactory. Sometimes he would look back to his days of single freedom and think of the company he used to keep – some of them girls who he'd had no doubt had had hopes of becoming Mrs Theo Sullivan, girls he had made sure he soon discarded. Then there had been others who'd harboured no such aspirations and it had been from those that he'd taken his first lessons in sex, an art he'd practised to perfection! These carefree affairs had made life a very pleasant affair and when he'd talked to Anna of their duty and obligation, he'd had no intention of marriage changing anything. Yet at the moment he had no desire to look outside marriage for sexual gratification. Nearer the truth, looking back at those escapades he felt they had been no more than preparation for what was to follow. There wasn't one of those willing and eager girls with Anna's natural sensuality, he thought, not for the first time and yet always with surprise. They'd had a lot more experience, no doubt about that. And who would look at Anna and guess at the uninhibited passion he knew just how to release? She was like –

'Wake up, Theo.' Sidney laughed, looking at him across the breakfast table with affectionate humour. 'Where were you? You looked miles away, somewhere nice from your expression.'

'You don't imagine I'd waste my time on unpleasant thoughts,' he replied, smiling, 'and I wasn't miles away. Quite the reverse.'

He'd been no further away than the room he shared with Anna, and in time he'd been but a few hours back. Whatever he'd hoped for from a wife, he'd never expected anything as exciting as he found with her. Generous? No, *that* implied that she submitted passively. There was nothing passive about funny, childlike Anna. She was warm, passionate, demanding, unrestrained beyond his most optimistic dreams. Not just to

95

please him, oh no, he was sure it wasn't that. Funny thing the way life works out. When he'd first met her – a funny little elf, that's what he'd thought. He'd known from that first afternoon that she believed she'd fallen for him, but then she'd never known anyone else so it was no great compliment. And now? Of course she was in love with him. If she weren't she would act very differently, he was sure of that. So things had worked out pretty well. It was more than five weeks since she'd lost the baby and if she could get pregnant in ten minutes by the river, he'd be jolly surprised if it hadn't already happened again. She said it was too soon to be sure, but give it another few weeks and she would tell the others and this time she'd take no chances. Really he was remarkably lucky the way Fate had taken control. He wasn't in love with Anna – whatever being in love really meant – but she was a good sport, she was absolutely terrific to make love to, each day she cared more about Manningtor, the staff looked to her as mistress and Aunt Kath seemed to have accepted her. Nanny approved of her too, and he put a lot of store in her opinion.

For himself, he had no intention of letting anything as demanding as the emotion of love creep into his life. Perhaps in his subconscious was the memory of what his mother's death had done to his father; perhaps it was that that made it so impossible for him to allow himself to feel deep emotion. Anna's great company – again his thoughts cut him off from the others at the table – we have a lot of laughs together and making love with her is, well, look what just thinking about it's doing to me. She doesn't just *give*, that's what's so great, it's as if both of us are grasping at the same thing. Get a hold on yourself, think about something else, think about the leaking roof at Myrtle Cottage, make your mind up about what you're going to do this morning: flying or the office? I know the answer to that one: I'll let Anna go down and talk to old Mrs Chedzey at Myrtle Cottage, which will mean I can go to the club. Great morning for flying.

So his rambling thoughts carried him, planning how to squeeze every last drop of fun out of the coming day. That a part of his contentment with life came from his knowing that Anna had always been besotted with him wasn't to be wondered at. That was the way his life had been. Everyone had always loved good-tempered, cheerful Theo. He took it as his natural right.

By this time the meal had progressed; Matt stood up from the table.

'I'll go and bring the car to the front door, Dad. Don't rush putting your coat on, I'll let the engine run and warm up while I wait,' Matt said.

'I've finished eating,' Theo told his uncle after the door had closed on Matt. 'Stay in here in the warm while I bring your things. The hall is like an icebox, you wait by the fire until Matt brings the car round.'

It wasn't that Sidney Sullivan was dreadfully elderly, but a bout of pneumonia the previous winter had taken its toll. No one any longer took him for granted.

'Bless the boy, I think I will. As you get older, Theo, the winters get colder and the summers hotter. Yes, bring my coat and things, I'll spoil myself with no one watching and warm them in front of the fire.'

Theo was never happier than when he was doing someone an act of kindness. He came back with Sidney's astrakhan-lined overcoat, his scarf, gloves and bowler hat, and proceeded to hold the inside of the coat towards the hot coals.

'You're downstairs early this morning, Theo. Plans for the day?'

'I'm off up to the club. It promises to be the best possible kind of day for flying.'

His elderly uncle looked at him affectionately, even with a trace of envy.

'Make the most of it all while you can. The years rush by, each one quicker than the last. Seems to me like yesterday when I opened the depot down the lane, just one omnibus. Different world it was, all of us so full of hope after that dreadful war – at least all of us who were spared to have a future. It worries me, Theo, the way things are going. Peace in our time . . . in mine perhaps, as near the end as I am –'

'Rubbish Uncle Sidney, you've got ages –'

'No, no, no. That's another thing with getting old. It makes you look at things squarely. Three score years and ten, isn't that what the good book says? Things are different nowadays: comfortable lives, good food, we keep going longer. But I don't want to hear a lot of nonsense about years ahead of me. I'll take all that the Good Lord allows and be grateful. All I'm saying is, I may see peace in my time but I fear *you* and your generation won't. Do you trust Hitler? Open your eyes, lad, read the papers; open your ears, listen to those rallies on the wireless sometimes when we hear the cheering and shouting he stirs up; think of the arsenal he's building. And here, what about here in England? Peace in our time – do you honestly think the government is stupid enough to believe it? No, of course not. For years Winston Churchill has been warning them. Perhaps now at last they're using a bit of sense and building some weaponry.'

'For peace?' Theo said laughing, his head as deep in the sand as any ostrich.

'Ultimately war will come. Perhaps not for a few years, but don't be complacent. Germany, here, probably the world over, all feeling the threat. No country builds an arsenal of weapons just to leave them stockpiled.'

'Perhaps you're right, Uncle. But give us the chance and we'll show the great bully what we're made of!'

Nothing dented Theo's confidence. Sidney's eyes were moist with affection and fear as he looked at the cocksure nephew he loved like a son. There had been no need for Sidney to go to war, even when conscription had been brought in he'd been beyond the age to be called. But he could understand Theo's 'we'll show the great bully what we're made of'. Hadn't it been that that had sent him to enlist, offering his knowledge of vehicles to his country, swaggering with confidence in his uniform and never doubting he'd return to his wife and the son who was nearer the age the Army were taking into service than he was himself? Just look at Theo, such a dear boy, please God take care of him. He doesn't know the meaning of war, the smell of death, the deafening noise of guns, the loss of friends, the sickening fear in the pit of the stomach. Please God, take care of him, keep his world good.

'Ah, there's the car. Thank you, my boy,' Sidney muttered as he struggled to get his arms into the sleeves of the warmed coat Theo held for him. 'You just take care of that little wife of yours. Life's greatest lesson is: live each day. No one can be certain about tomorrow and years go by before you know it. Lucky fellow you are, head over heels she is.' What made him say it he had no idea, except that his thoughts of war and his fear for Theo and all those thousands of young men – young men on both sides of any quarrel, that was the wicked folly of it all – seemed to have knocked the stuffing out of him. Anna, now Anna would always be there for the boy. A good child, she'd be his rock. Coat on, scarf wrapped tightly around his once-stalwart neck, gloves buttoned and hat in hand, Sidney started out for his day's work. The conversation had upset him. All very well for him at his end of the scale, and Matt too, he was turned forty, he'd be safe out of whatever lay ahead; and so he deserved, he'd seen service in the last lot. Sam was fifteen, too young now but who could say when trouble would come?

Matt had salted the coach yard, already the ice was melting. But Gwen hadn't mentioned the front steps to him and neither had he thought about them. Pulling his mind away from the conversation with Theo, away from the memory of the frenzied cheering of the German youth rally he had heard when he'd been twiddling the turning knob on the wireless the previous evening, and which had kept him awake through the watches of the night, Sidney squared his shoulders as if in readiness for the day's work ahead and stepped briskly onto the top step.

Like all accidents, it happened in an instant. His spontaneous shout brought Kath to the window of their bedroom in the east wing, and Anna to the window of hers over the front door. While Theo rushed outside to help lift his uncle to his feet (as he thought) and Matt leapt from the car, half-dressed Kath pulled on her dressing gown and ran down the corridor. Always dignified, always correct, but in that moment she had no thought that her hair was in its nightly pigtail or that she was without her dentures. She hadn't moved at a speed like this for years.

'Careful how we move him,' Anna heard Matt call to Theo. 'We must get help.'

From below stairs came Mrs Gibbons; Anna met her as she too reached the open front door.

'Such a crash he must have gone! See, just lying there like there's no life in him!' It took a good deal to throw Lily Gibbons off course, but from the way she gripped her hands together, holding them to her ample chest, it was clear this time she was well and truly thrown.

Perhaps it was easier for Anna, for Sidney wasn't so closely interwoven into her life as he was the others. 'Who is his doctor? I'll phone for him to come. Have some blankets taken out to him, Mrs Gibbons, he must be kept warm. Perhaps hot water bottles.'

'That's it, Mrs Theo. I'll see to it right away. Dr Price is his name, I don't know his number but Molly Arkwright at the village exchange will put you through to him. I'll get the bottles to tuck inside the blankets. Poor dear soul.' Still talking to herself she bustled back across the hall to the back stairs. 'Please God no bones are broken. But at his age, it'll shake him up. I'll give that young Gwennie the sharp edge of my tongue not seeing to those front steps herself.'

For twenty minutes they had to wait for the doctor, whose instructions on the telephone were that on no account must they try and move the patient unless he was in a fit state to move himself, which he clearly wasn't. Two rubber hot water bottles were laid on him then covered with blankets; his front was kept warm but through his semi-consciousness he felt as though his back had turned to ice.

Opening his eyes he found Kath kneeling stiffly at his side, the bedtime Kath familiar only to him. It was the sight of her, cold, worried, frightened and dentureless more than the concern of the rest of the family gathered round that determined him to make a supreme effort to move. He reached his gloved hand towards her and felt it grasped in hers. Another effort on his part – if he bent his legs Matt and Theo would help him to his feet. The shock receding, he wasn't in great physical pain. So why wouldn't his legs move, why wouldn't they bend?

'Indoors, Kath . . . darling Kath.' Dear God what had he done? Why couldn't he move? 'For me, Kath . . . inside in the warm.' His voice seemed to have lost its power too. She mustn't be here when Dr Price arrived; he didn't want to watch her when she heard, not out here with all the others around them. For her sake he made another supreme effort, even to move his feet, to feel that he could wriggle his toes. Nothing. He could raise his arms, he could feel his shoulders, but it was as if from the waist down didn't belong to him; he couldn't even feel the cold from the ground.

Thelma had come outside as soon as she heard the commotion and by this time word had reached Sylvia and Francis and they, too, were waiting anxiously for the first sound of the doctor's car. When Kath's grip on Sidney's hand tightened he turned his head towards Anna. 'Good child . . . take her indoors . . . stay with her.' Even in his shocked state, he was surprised that it was Anna he'd turned to. Reason told him he should have called on dear, kind Thelma.

'We'd better do as he wants, Aunt Kath.'

When Kath felt Anna's arm round her and heard the quiet assurance in her voice, she still shook her head. But whether it was the way Anna took control or Sidney's agitated expression, something persuaded her to let herself be led indoors. Just as Sidney knew something was seriously wrong, so too did she.

'Dr Price will be here in a few minutes.' There was something hypnotically soothing in Anna's voice as Kath let herself be led back up the stairs and along the long gallery to her room in the east wing. 'I'll help you dress; we'll be as quick as we can so that you are ready to hear what he has to say.'

'Never mind dressing. Just want to be down there.' Kath fought her corner, but all the while she was letting Anna take off the quickly thrown-on dressing gown.

There was something heartrendingly vulnerable about habitu-ally dignified Kath in her underwear, even her face strangely old and sunken without her teeth to hold it in place. Unable to stop herself, Anna reached up to kiss the taller woman's lined cheek. 'We'll make Uncle Sidney proud, let him see how strong you are and know he can depend on you. You see to your teeth, I'll find you a warm dress to wear. It worried him to see you cold.'

All those years with her grandfather had taught Anna more than she'd realised. Don't fuss, don't show any fear, just be brisk, kind and efficient. It was the only way he would accept help from anyone, even from Potts, and her approach did the trick with Kath. Together they hurried, both keeping a watch for the doctor's arrival – both certain that they would hear nothing good, but neither of them daring to put their thoughts into words. Dressed and ready to face the world, Kath found the inner strength that had temporarily been lost. Through the last quarter of an hour she had barely been conscious of Anna, and had done as she'd been told with only one goal – to be ready to support Sidney. It was only afterwards, when she somehow had to face the memory of the accident and what had followed,

101

that she realised the gentle understanding and assurance Anna had shown.

Another hour and Sidney was in Deremouth, being lifted from the ambulance on the forecourt of the hospital. Following closely behind, Matt had brought his mother.

The sky had the clear brilliance of a crisp winter morning, perfect for flying. When Theo's car disappeared down the drive everyone, even Anna, supposed him to be going to the flying club. No one voiced what was in their minds, that they were surprised he would want to 'play at aeroplanes' as if today were the same as any other. After all, why should they be surprised? Hadn't he always followed his own devices, bent on every pleasure-seeking inclination? Anna felt a sense of disappointment in him, one she hated to admit to and yet couldn't put out of her mind. She found her imagination going constantly to the scene at the hospital even though she'd never been more conscious than today that she was an outsider. And where were Theo's thoughts? He was everyone's darling, probably spoilt all his life, she thought crossly. If it had been he who'd fallen, she asked herself, can you imagine Uncle Sidney carrying on as if nothing had happened? No, of course he wouldn't. Even *I* can't settle to anything. Today was making her realise that, although she'd met with no hostility when Theo had introduced her into the family, yet she wasn't one of them: Sylvia, Francis and Thelma were bound by common anxiety while she escaped to the estate office. But how hard it was to concentrate on Mrs Gibbons' monthly accounts.

At Manningtor that morning, only in the kitchen did life have any pretence of normality and even there it was forced, no one daring to voice an opinion and knowing it would take only one wrong word to upset Nicholls' icier-than-normal silence.

Sidney had been the younger son, never the heir, yet he had been constant through the years and was held in very real affection below stairs. With a business of his own to run, he'd still held the reins when his elder brother had been driven ever further downhill by grief that had ended with death; it had been Sidney who had borne the responsibilities of the estate, become like a father to the orphaned family, somehow managing to instil into fun-loving and easy-going Theo a deep love for his inheritance and a sense of duty that fitted uncomfortably with his general outlook on life.

So on that late January morning, as everyone waited for Matt and Kath to return from the hospital, Manningtor seemed to hold its breath.

Driving his car along the rutted track that followed the coast from Deremouth to Chalcombe, a distance of some five miles, Theo stopped at the highest point about midway between the two. He knew he ought to be at home waiting with the others, with Anna. What was it his uncle had said? 'You just take care of that little wife of yours.' Looking far out across the shimmering sea, he seemed to hear the familiar voice: 'Life's greatest lesson is, live each day. No one can be certain about tomorrow and years go by before you know it.' There had been something about her being head over heels too, but that had had less impact. Theo had never been short of love, or what passed as love. He had taken it for granted that his family delighted in indulging his every whim, just as he had that 'would-be sweethearts' and women with less rigid moral codes had refused him nothing. He'd always been aware what it was that had prevented him asking more than was wise from those who fell into the bracket of aspiring brides: his freedom had been precious. So why had he acted differently with Anna? It was a question that had come back to him time and again, but today it wasn't Anna he wanted to think of, nor any of the other league of beauties. It was his uncle. He couldn't stay at home with the others, watching, waiting, repeating their anxieties.

He'd never felt like this. Was his uncle going to die? Only here, on his own, could he let the question form. He'd lost both his parents, but he'd never felt like this. A thousand memories crowded his mind, a thousand memories that combined into the certainty of safety, of continuity. To lose his uncle would be like cutting out something of himself. 'Take care of that little wife of yours . . . years go by so quickly . . . no one can be sure of tomorrow.' When he'd said it, had he had some sort of premonition? Can't be sure of tomorrow . . . don't let him die . . . he's always been there . . . sometimes I've been bloody selfish, I know I have . . . make him know what he means to me . . . Christ what's the matter with me? Thank God they've got Matt, no good looking to me for help. Useless, bloody useless.

In the reversing mirror he caught sight of his face, his

eyes bloodshot with unshed tears. It was the last straw. With something akin to sadistic pleasure he watched his face crumple as loud and uncontrolled sobs shook him. After the ambulance had taken Sidney to the hospital Dr Price hadn't minced his words: there was little doubt the damage was to the spine leaving him paralysed from the waist.

'Never walk again,' Theo rasped, his voice as unfamiliar as his tears, 'he can't live like that . . . dear God don't make him endure a life like that . . . he couldn't . . . I know he couldn't, I couldn't either. But I don't have to. I'm just a weak coward, frightened of the pain of losing him. I'm like some damn-fool hysterical woman. Aunt Kath won't behave like it.' All this he spoke aloud, he couldn't stop himself; rather he needed to hear the anguish in his voice. 'Take care of Anna, you said. She's tough, not like me. Just look at me! Men don't cry. Feel sick. Oh God, what a bloody weakling I am. He's going to die, I know he is. Never be sure about tomorrow.'

The truth was that this was Theo's first real experience of the threat of losing someone he loved. When his mother had died he'd been five years old and had been brought up by Nanny Harknell; after that he'd learnt to dread his father's presence. He could still recall being told that he'd died in an accident. Something that had been stored all these years in his subconscious was his own feeling of relief – no more would he have to endure being the scapegoat for his father's hatred of the world and everything in it, no more would he have to be shouted at or beaten, knowing his punishment was unjust. Today, faced with the fear of losing his uncle, his mind cleared and he saw the child he had been. He remembered hiding himself in Dingley Wood, even then ashamed of the sensation of freedom and joy as he looked to a future without the threatening fear of his father returning home from one of his bouts in London or Paris, angry with life, angry with everything and everyone he used to love. If the memory had been forced to the depths of his mind all these years, today Theo welcomed the shame it brought him to remember. Was the aching pain he felt now his punishment?

He was never sure how long he sat in the car on the cliff top, frightened by emotion that was beyond all reason – shame for his behaviour as a child; shame that he was incapable of going home and sharing their vigil; shame that he was no more a man now

104

than he had been when he'd hidden himself in Dingley Wood. There had to be a bottom to his pit of misery and self-abasement; at some point he must have reached it. It wasn't so much that he fought to control his sobbing, rather he gloried in the pain of hearing himself. But nothing lasts for ever and gradually he was quiet, feeling weak and empty in the silence.

Habit made him run his pocket comb through his dishevelled hair, shaken by the sight of his reflection in the reversing mirror. He couldn't sit here, but he couldn't go home looking like this. Instead he got out of the car and started to walk along the empty track towards Chalcombe. Sometimes walkers might climb the slope from Deremouth, but seldom was there anyone walking at the Chalcombe end of the rough road. So near the sea there had been no morning frost and by now – what time was it, he wondered without sufficient interest to look at his watch – the sun was high in the brittle blue sky. No wonder he was cold, he'd left home without an overcoat. Instead of heading back to the shelter of the Riley, he strode on, quickening his pace, somehow glad of the discomfort of the cold air. By the time he reached Chalcombe, more than two miles on, his face was restored, the redness in his eyes was matched by the colour in his cheeks. The Lobster Pot was a welcome sight.

'Morning, Squire,' the landlord's greeting never varied, whether to the squire of Manningtor or the newspaper vendor from outside the railway halt made no difference. 'Parky out there this morning and no mistake. What'll it be?'

'A pint of brown ale, please,' Theo told him. 'And is there anything to eat? Bread and cheese?'

'No trouble at all. I'll get the missus to rustle up a good ploughman's for you. Take a seat by the fire and I'll bring your drink across.'

The friendly landlord, the warmth from the blazing log fire and the crusty bread and Cheddar cheese all helped to revive Theo's flagging spirit. The thought of lingering, following the first pint with a second, was tempting. Then his mind jumped back just as it had earlier and he remembered the little boy rushing away to Dingley Wood. Running away, that's what he'd been doing all the morning. Running away from what he didn't want to face. But that had been this morning. This afternoon he would do as his uncle would want.

105

Invigorated by good intentions, he left The Lobster Pot and strode back up the track from the one-time fishing village. Walking westwards, once he reached the cliff top he could see beyond Deremouth with its harbour, across the estuary to Otterton St Giles beyond. The healthy crispness of the cold morning air had been overtaken by a raw chill; the sun had already started its decent. Soon it would sink behind the trees of Downing Wood. Already, to remember the morning was like recalling a terrifying nightmare. Beer, bread and cheese and a brisk walk had built a protective barrier between him and the unfamiliar sensation of misery. In fact, by the time he drove into Deremouth his habitual confidence was back in place. Soon he'd go home, soon but not quite yet. Instead of driving right to the top of the hill to the junction with the main road, halfway up he took a turning to the right towards the red-brick building of the hospital.

Anna understood as well as any of them that presenting a composed front to the world was no guarantee of a spirit at peace.

'Mother's taking it splendidly,' Matt spoke to the room at large. 'Perhaps the older you get the easier it is to accept death. I tell you, I can't take it in, can't believe he's gone.' His light blue eyes turned from one to the other. He looked hurt, mystified.

'Thank goodness we're all here together,' Thelma took his hand in hers as they sat side by side on the sofa. 'So hard for you – you and he have always been closer than most fathers and sons – but Mother knows she can depend on you, she won't have to be worried. Imagine if you hadn't been with him in the business, there would have been so much to think about.'

'Until it happens, none of us have any experience of death to fall back on. There's lots to see to.' Francis knocked out his pipe against the fire dog and thrust it into his jacket pocket, a sure sign that he was ready for home and bed. 'If I can help, Matt, you know I'm there. But I don't want to push Theo out. Where in the world do you think he can have got to? He told us he was flying today, but even the bar at the club must be closed before this. I'm surprised he still went there, knowing about the accident.'

Anna heard the criticism in his voice as he expressed what

106

had been her own unspoken view. Immediately, though, she was on the defensive.

'He didn't go there. When it got late I telephoned and they said he hadn't been at all today.'

'You've been worried?' There was enough room in Thelma's kind heart to care about all of them. Still holding Matt's hand in hers she turned to Anna, quick to reassure her. 'We've learnt never to worry about darling Theo. I'm glad he didn't go off amusing himself at the club. I expect Dad's fall upset him. He ought to have gone to the hospital, it was thoughtless of us to leave him like we did.'

'If he'd wanted to go, he could have followed the ambulance the same as we did. Dad asked for him, you know. "The boy not here?" that's what he kept saying. Got really agitated, even though he couldn't move we could tell what a state he was getting in. Then,' Matt closed his eyes as if to shut out the scene he'd already described more than once, but felt he had to repeat as if that was the only way to make his mind accept what had happened, 'a gasp, a sort of stifled yell. Christ, but it haunts me.'

'Poor darling,' comforted his loyal and caring Thelma, 'you've had a dreadful day. But we must thank God you were with Mother, she didn't have to be alone with him when he went. They say a massive heart attack is a mercy for the one who is taken, but my goodness what a shock for those who are left. Let's put an end to this dreadful day, let's go to bed. Tomorrow you have a lot to see to. I hope Mother's sleeping. I crept to her door; if I'd heard any sound of tears I would have gone in to her. But it was quite quiet. Come on, dear, you need a good night's sleep too. In the morning, when we know the arrangements, we must contact the children. They'll both want to come home for the funeral. Poor Dee, it'll break her heart, she thought the world of her granddad.'

There was an end-of-the-day, closing down, atmosphere in the room. Sylvia and Francis stood up to leave.

'Don't wait up half the night for Brother Theo, Anna,' Sylvia advised. 'When there's something he doesn't want to face he's champion at running away from it. By this time you know Theo is a law unto himself.' Then with a mischievous wink that was as much out of character with her perfectly made-up face as it was out of keeping with the sobriety of the occasion, 'When you wake up in the morning you'll find he has crept home with his tail between his legs like all naughty dogs do.'

'Oh Sylvia, what a thing to say to her when she must be so worried,' Thelma remonstrated kindly, feeling the day had brought troubles enough without upsetting little Anna to round it off. 'Normally we wouldn't give it a thought if he suddenly disappeared – it's just that today of all days . . . We know just how fond of his uncle he was, just like we all were. Silly boy, he ought to have been with the family. All of us being together has been a comfort. You can tell that by the quick way Mother got off to sleep.'

During the morning while those left at home had waited together for news, Anna had felt herself an outsider. But never more so than now. Comfort in being together? Perhaps for them it was, but then they'd always had each other, or at least always had someone. Anna knew the value of solitude.

'When he does get home, Anna,' was Sylvia's parting shot, 'treat him kindly. Don't forget he doesn't know what's happened. You'll have to be the one to tell him.'

A minute later and the two couples had said their goodnights and gone their separate ways. For Anna it was a relief to be alone, only now could she concentrate on her own thoughts. She threw another log on the fire and sat in her favourite cross-legged position on the rug in front of it. All of them were sad about Uncle Sidney – and she was sad too, she told herself, sad because she'd never really got to know him and sad for the rest of them who loved him. But Theo? How much did his uncle mean to him? Why had he stayed out all day instead of wanting to know what had been happening at the hospital? How would he react when he knew that the fall had been followed by a heart attack and while he'd been amusing himself – not at the club, so where? – his uncle had died? She thought about her grandfather, a smile tugging at the corners of her mouth. All those years and they never came near to showing affection, yet now she was certain he loved her, just as he knew she loved him. But what if she'd never met Theo, what if she'd still been living at Dunsford House where emotions were secret, affection kept securely under wraps? What if her grandfather had suddenly died while they'd been living like that, not knowing how dear he was to her with his fragile body such a contradiction to his quick mind and indomitable spirit? Would it be like that for Theo with his uncle, or had they always understood each other?

An hour or so later, the log little more than a pile of ash, she put up the fireguard and went to bed. She wouldn't sleep, she would lay awake and listen for the sound of his car – please let him come soon.

As a child Anna had been taught – and supervised – by Miss Sherwin to kneel at her bedside, hands together, head bowed and make her nightly supplication. The governess would have grieved to see her training come to naught as her one-time pupil lay staring at the dark ceiling, bargaining with her Maker. Anna held nothing back, she bared her soul.

And please let him talk to me, came her silent plea, really talk to me. But he won't. Why should he? Today has shown me clearly enough that I'm not important to him. He hasn't given it a thought that his family must all know he doesn't see me as anyone special. Mistress of his home? He doesn't give me any more thought than – than – than if I were a prostitute he likes sleeping with. I was just a silly child with a head full of dreams, that's all I was when I fell in love with him. And now? Do I love him, the real *him*, or was I always in love with the person I wanted to believe he was? Where's my pride? Why do I stay here? I'll tell You why. It's because I haven't the willpower to leave him. Manningtor *matters* to me, I've only been here a few months but it's as if it's part of me. Imagine going away from here . . . You know what I wish? I wish I'd never met him. No, that's not true – You know it's not, it's just how I ought to feel if I had any pride. I want to be here, I feel so *right*. But he doesn't really think about me, only when I'm with him. Where can he have been all day today, running away from everyone? If he's miserable why couldn't he have talked to me? I'll tell You why: because I'm not important. If You'd wanted to You could have put it in his heart to love me, it could be so wonderful here, running Manningtor together, seeing our children grow up in this beautiful place, surrounded by love. 'Next time you're pregnant' was what he said. I expect he sees it as part of my 'job', expect he sees it as my 'job' to learn to look after Manningtor – part of my duty, not because I love it. He never tells me what he feels. I'm two weeks late, but would

109

that be because last time was when I lost my baby? Him and me – it's all such a sham, he treats me like a good-humoured playmate. Even when we make love I don't expect it's because I'm *me*.

She knew it was silly to cry, yet there was comfort in tears, comfort that within minutes lulled her into sleep.

She snuggled close to him, her half awake body ahead of her mind. Slowly memory stirred. He was home. Was he awake? Did he know what had happened? Where had he been all day? Questions crowded one after another as full consciousness returned. His family accepted that his behaviour was always unpredictable as he followed his own desires. But Anna suspected that the day's absence had been a way of escaping what he didn't want to accept. Wherever he'd fled, it hadn't been to *her* – that was the one thing that even in her first waking moments her mind shunned.

'You haven't been here . . . you won't know –'

'I've been to the hospital. I was too late.'

'Theo.' Her arms were warm round him. If the day had brought her disappointment in his behaviour, in that moment she was aware of nothing but aching love, a need to comfort him, a longing for him to let her into the secret places of his mind.

'Shut up.' There was no anger in the way he said it, only a need for silence. She pulled him towards her, surprised and yet thankful that there was at least this way of reaching out to him. For them lovemaking followed many roads. Sometimes it was a journey of sensual, uninhibited eroticism; sometimes it was an expression of youthful exuberance, joy, fun – something so dear to Theo. Tonight it was neither. Wordlessly he entered her. She longed for him to say her name, to give her a sign that it was *her* love he craved, *her* comfort he needed. But there was nothing personal in the quick, thrusting movements that brought him to an almost immediate climax and so to oblivion.

Winter nights are long – she had no idea how far this one had gone. Alone and lonely she lay by his side, hearing his deep even breathing, remembering the bargain she'd made with God. She remembered Mrs Humphries' firm belief that Fate mapped out the course we had to follow. By tomorrow perhaps there would be a sign. Never had Theo made love with the sort of

110

brutal force he had tonight. 'Shut up.' She heard his words again, spoken through tight lips. No pretence even of caring about her, nothing. She might have been *anyone*, anyone with a willing body. By morning Fate would surely give her a sign. Then it would be up to her. You can't make pacts with God, then not keep your word.

Please, I know I promised, but even if he doesn't love me like I do him, I don't know how I could bear to go away – from him . . . from Manningtor . . . from the life I've let myself dream about. If I'm pregnant I stay. Please don't tell me I'm not . . . help me to be all he wants . . . don't let . . .

But the prayer didn't get finished; Anna slept.

Family from far and wide congregated at Manningtor in readiness for the funeral. Some were Kath's relations, but mostly they were from scattered Sullivan branches. For Anna, this gathering was a new challenge. She was an outsider, a stranger, 'a child' by the standards of most of them, but it became important to her that she didn't fail Theo – or herself. Mrs Gibbons treated her with the same never-failing respect that she would if Theo had brought home a wife with the skills and experience needed to run an establishment like Manningtor. Yet beneath her unbending manner Anna never doubted very real kindness. So, confronted with an invasion of family, she sent for the housekeeper to discuss arrangements. After half an hour, hints from Mrs Gibbons had been dropped so subtly that Anna believed the ideas had been her own, and the three or four days of their stay were organised, bedrooms allocated and menus discussed. The reception following the funeral was to be on a much larger scale for Sidney Sullivan had been known and respected throughout the district. Representatives from companies dealt with by Sullivan's Coaches, owners of other automobile firms, all of them would drive from Moorleigh church back to the house.

Dee and Sam came home from school and Theo's younger sister, Alex was expected from the school on the western fringe of London, where she was sports mistress. This would be the first time Anna had met her, and it was something she viewed with uncertainty. Alex had been expected for Christmas but had written saying she was spending the holiday skiing with a friend. 'A pity I shan't meet Theo's bride, but Vicky and I

111

have so looked forward to this trip.' Anna hadn't understood the veiled whispering in the family – excluding Theo, who seemed removed from such things.

The cold weather held, log fires blazed in the grates of every living room, the largest logs of all in the great stone open fireplace of the hall. One on either side of it sat two Sullivan cousins, Augustus and Clifford.

'Pretty little filly young Theo has found himself. Poor show not inviting the family to the wedding, but the young these days aren't like they used to be. Different set of rules – or more likely from what I remember of the lad, no rules at all.' That was the opinion of Augustus who, like the Sullivan who had originally built Manningtor, made his fortune from wool on his sheep farms in Northumberland.

'Not what I would have expected to be his choice,' Clifford replied, stretching his legs towards the fire. 'But she'll do very well. Nothing flibbertigibbet about her, pint-sized though she is. For myself, I've always liked a woman with a bit more in the way of upholstery, you understand me. Nice little shape she is, but not much of a handful, eh, what? Young Matt – not so young I suppose now, but all of them boys to us, what? – he tells me she is getting a grasp of things on the estate too. Keen as mustard, that's what he says.'

'Humph. So what about our young squire? Hands his responsibilities to her and off he goes, I suppose. You know, Cliff, it's always amazed me. All of them, every one, even Sidney – God rest him – even him, they all think the sun shines out of that boy's arse. Put another splash in my glass, there's a good fellow, you can reach the tray. Thanks. Very pleasant, sitting here like this. Pity Sidney isn't with us, he'd have enjoyed it too. No –' he picked up the conversation at the point he'd interrupted it '– young Theo we were saying, nothing about him you can fault him on. Makes us all welcome, perfect host you might say. But at heart he's an idler. No stamina.'

'Cares well enough about this place. We're none of us perfect, Gus. Born with a silver spoon, that's been his trouble. Imagine having this place handed to you on a plate.'

'That, and Sidney to see the wheels turned smoothly.'

'Not just Sidney –' contentment was in every word as Clifford sipped his host's hospitality '– Matt has always been a second string to his bow. Now, there's a fine chap if ever I met one – his father all over again. Pity Sidney hadn't been the elder. Reliable, calm, nothing upsets Matt. Thank God Kath has him on hand.'

'Have you seen Alex yet? She drove herself from that school; I met her as she parked. What do you make of her?'

They looked at each other silently, weighing the question, weighing the answer.

'I always had a very soft spot for Alex,' Augustus said, 'a jolly kid, real tomboy. That was when she was a child.' He seemed to be going to say more, but changed his mind and took another large sip of the pale malt whisky. 'Perhaps we shouldn't be put off by the way she dresses. Funny lot, women, these days. Young ones, I mean.'

'See there, outside on the lawn.' As curious as any over-the-gate gossipers, they both craned their necks. 'The pair of them. Same age, so Thelma was saying. Not much else the same about them.'

The date of Anna's driving test had been fixed soon after Christmas and, still kept secret from the rest of the family, was looked forward to as much by Thelma as by her pupil. So they hadn't cancelled it when Sidney died. That's how it was that as the two elderly men watched, she climbed out of the car waving a piece of paper in her hand for the world to see and admire. Not that the world was watching or would have known what it was even if they had been.

Leaving Thelma to drive on to the coachyard, Anna cut across the grass towards the front steps just as a stranger strode round the corner of the building. At a quick glance she supposed it must be the son of one of the northern contingent, and her first impression was how like Theo the lad was. Hair just as dark, the same well-set shoulders and easy manner of walking.

'You must be Anna,' the stranger called, coming towards her with his hand outstretched, a youth looking so like Theo that Anna immediately liked what she saw. Except that the voice wasn't what she'd expected, it was almost effeminate. 'Where's Brother Theo? Taken refuge somewhere from the influx?'

'No knowing,' Anna laughed, covering her surprise. 'He'll turn up when it suits him. Yes, I'm Anna. And you're Alex.'

113

They sized each other up. Anna was tiny, Alex was surely almost as tall as Theo. Anna was better described as skinny than slim; Alex had broad shoulders, powerful hands, large feet that trod purposefully. No wonder in her light-grey slacks and jacket Anna had briefly mistaken her sex!

Different backgrounds, different experiences, different aspirations – Theo's wife and Theo's sister. Two things they had in common: they both adored him and he accepted each of them with his habitual casualness.

Chapter Six

How many facets were there to Theo's character? And what inspired his behaviour on the day of his uncle's funeral?

The wearing of black was an accepted custom and determined not to put a foot wrong in this, Anna's first public 'outing' as his wife, she had gone to Exeter with Thelma and bought what was required. Black did absolutely nothing for her, making her look smaller than ever, like a child playing at dressing up. The four-inch heels of her new shoes added a touch of dignity, mentally if nothing more.

In the plain black dress she turned to Theo, hoping against forlorn hope for his approval.

'I've never worn black before,' she told him, trying to will him to tell her he liked what he saw.

'Best you don't wear it again,' he laughed. 'But today is different.' Taking a small key from a box on his tallboy he lifted an oil painting of a Dartmoor scene from the wall, exposing the safe she'd had no idea had been hidden behind. 'I think today you must wear something of Mother's jewellery. She had other things besides these, pieces that were hers before my father married her. Sylvia has those. Some of these he bought for her, some belonged to his own mother. They were handed down to me. Today you'd better wear the pearls. Turn round so that I can fasten them.'

Standing with her back to him she watched their reflection in the long mirror. Six months ago if she could have looked ahead and seen this, her happiness would have been almost too much to bear. But then six months ago, foreseeing this, she would have believed it was part of the romantic love she'd yearned for. Perhaps the easy companionship she and Theo shared, that and the sensual wonder beyond anything she'd dreamed, were foundation enough for marriage; perhaps the sort of romantic love she'd imagined only existed in fiction. In the looking glass her wide eyes must have given away the secret uncertainty she couldn't overcome.

'What a funny elf she is,' Theo raised his brows enquiringly as he looked at her. 'I'm not taking what isn't mine to take, I promise you,' he laughed. 'My father was besotted with her; young as I was always knew. If he could he would have given her the earth; nothing was good enough let alone too good. So today, Anna, you may wear her pearls. There are earrings too, but elves don't have holes in their ears, it seems, so you'll have to be content with the necklace.'

'They're beautiful,' she breathed. To speak loudly might have broken the spell of the moment.

'Now let me look at you again. Incredible the difference they make.' Then, his face breaking into the smile that won him hearts wherever he went, 'Word will spread like wildfire at the wisdom I showed in my choice.'

A shame he had to say something so far from the truth of their situation.

'Didn't have much choice,' she mumbled, avoiding his eyes.

'We had no choice at all,' but still he smiled. 'But don't let's hark back on all that. We're rubbing along pretty well, I'd say. Come on, Anna, let me see a smile.' She nodded, making an effort to oblige. 'I say, are you all right in those heels? They make you look smashing, but how the devil you can walk on them I don't know.'

'They're very comfy, and I don't feel they're a bit too high. That's because I was so extravagant, they cost the earth. Thelma told me you have an account at Reid's, so that's where I got them. I could see she was a bit taken aback when she heard them tell me the price, but I wanted to make sure I dressed properly today. Was that all right?'

'Money well spent. And Anna, you don't have to ask me. Making your own clothes, wearing last year's fashions, all that sort of thing, that may have been good enough when you were a country girl at Wickley Cross, but you have a position to uphold here. And today you do Manningtor credit.' Insensitive, tactless, careless of her feelings, he ought to have known better.

'I'm no different just because I live here and get called

116

"madam". I'm *me* just like I was before.' Hurt and angry she wanted nothing more than the luxury of collapsing into the tears that threatened. To ward them off she purposely turned the knife in the wound he'd unintentionally inflicted. 'But whatever job a person takes, they have to dress right for it. So I bought posh clothes.'

'And quite right too.' He gave his hair a final touch with the pair of silver-backed brushes, seemingly oblivious there had been a change in the atmosphere. Only then did the smile vanish and for a second she caught a glimpse of the seldom seen serious side of his character. 'Uncle Sidney was held in great regard. I want today to be – to be – oh, I don't know – I want it to stand out as a tribute to all that he was. You didn't really get to know him. He was pretty special.' Then, his expression changing as if he'd drawn a curtain on that brief glimpse of his inner self, back came the habitual cheerful expression. 'Come on, then, best foot forward, high heels and all.'

A sad day for the family, a sad day for the staff, even for Sidney's friends and business associates who gathered together at Manningtor Park after the ceremony, but for Anna it was important beyond the occasion. A stranger to so many of those present, she was accepted without question as the young mistress of the house. Even Dee and Sam, home for forty-eight hours, viewed her with new respect. For Theo's sake – or perhaps more truthfully for her own sake because she knew that was what he wanted of her – she was glad. Sensing the role expected of her, she found herself playing the hostess with dignity in part owed to the solemnity of the occasion and, surely, in part to those gloriously comfortable, expensive, new shoes and the added inches they gave her. And something else invisibly and naturally happened on that day of Sidney's funeral: Kath slipped into a new role too, that of dowager.

'You did remarkably well,' Theo told Anna as they prepared to change for dinner. 'Seeing how you charmed all Uncle Sidney's old cronies, it was hard to believe you were the same kid I rescued when she sprawled off her bicycle!'

'You didn't rescue me, I was quite capable of cycling home.' Then, unable to stop herself, 'But I did do all right, didn't I?' She *had* to hear him say it again.

117

'I told you, I was proud of you.' Her cup of happiness threatened to run over.

'Unzip me, will you.' She turned her back to him, her heart pounding as she felt him unfasten the long zip, unhook her bra, then push everything from her to fall round her ankles. Leaning back against him, feeling the warmth of his hands, she forgot her new dignity, she forgot everything but the certainty of where they were heading. When he turned her towards him and dropped to his knees she guided his mouth, glorying in his arousal just as she knew he was in hers. This had been a day to heighten every emotion. Their move to the sheepskin hearthrug was spontaneous; the banked fire scorching their naked bodies. For neither of them was there anything but the urgency of the moment. Immediately, he entered her and in no time together they reached their climax.

'Weak as a kitten now,' he panted, his smile back in place. But she wasn't weak; she felt as strong as a lion.

An hour later they walked side by side down the shallow curving staircase, he in black tie and dinner jacket, she in a long, moss-green gown and, once more, wearing his mother's pearls. Today Theo's delight in knowing he was pleasing people had taken a new turn: Anna had been admired by young and old alike, admiration that reflected on *him*; he'd been aware of the general approval of his choice of a wife. Certainly he'd seen her anew, been aware of a cool serenity about her that in his subconscious he felt was due in part to the pearls. Perhaps that had been why as she'd done up the zip at the side of her dress, he'd once again taken the safe key from his tallboy, this time handing it to her.

'I think this should be yours. I'd look silly in baubles and beads.' Then, with his ever-ready smile, 'Like you said, they go with the job.'

Walking by his side into the drawing room where the family waited the call to dinner she recalled his words, tried to feel the pride she knew his trust deserved, tried to remember those glorious shared moments by the fire. Yet nudging her from the back of her mind was the scene she'd imagined when he'd told her about the jewellery, about how besotted his father had been with his mother. 'They go with the job' crushed her pride, took away her joy. Nothing was left but determination; and even *that* was double edged, determination not to let him guess at her hurt and determination that it wouldn't always be like this – one day he would be as 'besotted' as his father had been before him.

Only nine days after Sidney's funeral Anna celebrated her twenty-first birthday. In the present circumstances it was almost a non-event. Certainly the family all gave her gifts: from Thelma and Matt she had a gold watch, from Kath a silver trinket box, from Sylvia and Francis a miniature painting of Manningtor. Presents had never played a great part in previous birthdays, when invariably Mrs Short had made a special cake and bought her a box of hankies or a new purse. Each year her grandfather had given her a pound note to buy herself something (which had always seemed odd, as she'd never been kept short of money to buy anything she needed). Never had she had anything like the beautifully wrapped gifts Theo's family gave her. And on this special birthday the postman brought her a pen and pencil set from Mrs Short and from her grandfather the photograph of her parents he had always prized and kept in his bedroom. Now he'd had it re-framed and even written a note telling her to treasure it always.

Before any of that, though, her day started well. She woke to find Theo sitting up in bed, hissing her name urgently.

'Anna, wake up, Anna. Happy birthday. Wake up, don't waste it.'

In a second she too was sitting up. But if she expected him to thrust a package into her hand she was disappointed.

'Buck up and get dressed. We'll go out quietly before anyone else is about. It's already getting light.'

'Out? You mean we're going out for the day?' All hint of disappointment was gone.

'Don't ask questions, just obey your lord and master.' She could feel the suppressed excitement in his tone; it was infectious, no wonder she hurried. Little more than ten minutes later they were stealing down the wide stairway in a way quite unfitted to the master and mistress of the house. Like two conspirators they slid back the bolt of the heavy front door. 'Shut your eyes.' Still he talked in a stage whisper that made her bubble of excitement frighteningly large. Surely any second it must burst! Still she did as he said and let herself be guided out into the cold morning

119

air. Like a blind person she slid each foot forward until she felt the first step, although he was just behind her holding both elbows.

'Down here?' she asked.

'No, that's far enough. Now open your eyes and tell me what you think?'

'Whose is it? Did someone come last night?' But she knew no one who would drive a car like that, a red MG, its chrome gleaming in the early light.

'Happy birthday. It's your present. It's from *me*. *I* bought it for you. It's no use passing your driving test and not having your own car. You do like it, don't you?' Like a small child who'd been saving his pocket money, he watched her expression, not so much wanting thanks as wanting praise. He wasn't disappointed. Surely no elf's eyes had ever shone as hers did. 'Theo, it's the most wonderful present! I don't mean because it must have cost you such a lot of money, but because it's – it's – it's just perfect. And *you* chose it, *you* had the idea.'

He beamed with delight. This was even better than he'd imagined. 'Let's go for a spin. Here are your keys. I filled it with petrol yesterday before I brought it home. Nanny promised to keep you for tea so that I had time to get it in the coach house. Then I brought it round to the front after you'd gone up to bed. You *do* really like it? Tell me again. The colour's right? You wouldn't rather have had a black saloon like Thelma drives? No, of course you wouldn't. Well, I know I wouldn't.'

So she told him again just how perfect it was. Then under his surprisingly patient eye she drove them towards the moor, somehow the most perfect place to be on a crisp winter morning.

Coming of age was an important step in anyone's life, and in hers it meant that she had control of her parents' legacy. At one time she had imagined it would have given her the freedom to leave Wickley Cross, to go to London just as Dick Whittington had, to make a name for herself as a latter-day Brontë. Ambition still niggled in her mind, but now the longing for freedom had gone. To imagine being anywhere but Manningtor was impossible. Sometimes she wondered whether she had been here before in some previous life, for surely this was where her spirit belonged. And then there was the family, Theo's family, and yet they had accepted her without question. It didn't occur to her that, since they all lived in Theo's house they could hardly have acted differently. And perhaps, when he'd first brought a wife into the house, that had been the case. Since then she had settled into her place like a well-fitting piece of a jigsaw puzzle. Family life had been as unknown to her as had living in a house such as Manningtor, yet the feeling of déjà vu must have crafted the shape that fitted so snugly into the picture. Only one thing marred what could have been a perfect period in her life, something that cast a shadow she couldn't escape. It would have been perfect, it *could* have been perfect, if only Theo had sometimes spoken her name as he'd made love to her, fed her dreams that what they did wasn't only the outcome of sexual need. Friendship, sensual adventure that unfailingly led to sexual satisfaction, for him that was enough. For her, it couldn't be.

Being twenty-one gave her a new responsibility. Theo made arrangements for her to see his own accountant for advice, but the appointment made, she was on her own. A smart suit and four-inch heels might have given her the appearance of the inheritor of a fortune (albeit a small one in terms of Manningtor), but sitting facing the soberly dressed man who had such knowledge of investments at his fingertips, she felt more like the child who'd learnt to 'be seen and not heard' at Dunsford House.

Soon after that she told the family that she was pregnant. How different from last time! The prospect of a baby cemented her position in the house. It was important to her that her grandfather should be told just as soon. Since she'd left home she'd often sent him a letter, or sometimes a picture postcard, neither expecting nor receiving any reply except for the one brief note with her parents' picture and a very occasional note from Mrs Short. This time, by return post came an envelope in his shaky hand. 'Your news gives me great joy. My blessed Elizabeth's line goes on. Indeed, I appreciate all your letters, even those which receive no reply. I know I have your understanding. Your affectionate grandfather.' She folded it carefully back in its envelope and put it in her handkerchief drawer for safe keeping. That his affection for her was because she was her mother's daughter was something she had lived with all her life. Now, safe in her new life, it had no power to hurt.

*   *   *

121

The day Dee arrived home for half term was clear, bright and cold. Perfect for flying, in Theo's opinion, so by mid-morning he was at the flying club and wasn't likely to reappear until daylight was fading, leaving Anna to 'hold the fort' as he called it in the estate office. These days she was authorised to sign cheques, so she was busy paying the monthly accounts when Dee came to find her.

'You didn't come to say hello to me – didn't you hear Dad bring me? Aunt Sylvia came over from the farm. Hunt tomorrow.' Dee's eyes sparkled with mischievous challenge. Anna had no doubt it was the challenge of the hunt that had brought her to the office.

'I have my half crown ready for you,' Anna laughed.

'Chicken! So I was right! After all these weeks you ought to be good enough. The ground isn't icy or anything, you've no excuse.'

'I've the best excuse in the world. Didn't they tell you? I'm expecting a baby and Theo has made me promise not to ride. He doesn't trust me not to fall off!'

'Crumbs.' Dee looked at her with new interest before her expression changed and a note of sneering mockery crept into her voice as she mimicked no one in particular but all of them collectively, 'Tut, tut, don't talk about such things in front of the children! But you're skinny as anything. When will you start to get a bump? I feel cheaty taking your half crown – I mean, you're not chickening out because you're scared. Isn't Theo being a bit silly? If you didn't jump it wouldn't do any harm, would it?'

'Probably not. But this time next year I'll be out there with the best. Ten bob to a tanner.'

'You're on. Although I don't know why I'm taking you up on it, I don't think there's much risk of you having to pay me ten bob.' On her last visit Dee had taken a fiendish delight in mocking Anna, but no longer. It seemed that being pregnant with a child who, if male, would one day inherit Manningtor, put her above criticism.

So the weeks went by. March brought winds that set the daffodils dancing, then gales and hail storms that flattened them to the ground. There had been plenty of winters like

122

it in Wickley Cross, winters when Anna had donned a thick mackintosh and sou'wester and faced the elements rather than stay in a house that had been filled with gloom. Manningtor was different. Never before had she experienced the feeling of snug contentment that was part of the cold, blustery afternoons of that winter. It would have taken more than unpleasant weather to tie Theo to the house: his nature demanded that he be occupied, always following the mood of the moment. Even though there were few days suitable for flying, there was always something to do at the club. As a child he had been keen to watch and listen to what went on in the repair shop of the coach depot; as a student (for that university scarf Anna had wondered about was his own) he had studied engineering. But for Theo, studying at university, being genuinely interested, not even minding getting his hands dirty when occasion demanded, these things in no way tempted him to turn his knowledge into a routine job of work. He much preferred to amuse himself as the mood took him, whether with the maintenance engineer at the club or alone on the shore where his boat was in a dry mooring for the winter. Scraping barnacles from the bottom, painting on the anti-fouling, whistling happily as he worked by himself, that was an equally satisfactory way of passing a winter's day. Then there were the hours he spent with Anna in the estate office, taking personal pride in how well be had instructed her as he purposely did less himself, confident of her grasp on running the estate.

Often Anna spent her afternoons with Kath and Thelma in the drawing room. She wondered how it was that she could be so content to idle her time away; it must have had something to do with the sound of two pairs of knitting needles clicking merrily, and their obvious pleasure that the Philanthropic Society was put on hold as they concentrated on preparations for the promised new Sullivan, one of their own. Just as the new baby was imagined as 'one of them', there was no doubt that that was how they saw Anna.

For as long as she could remember, stories had built themselves in her mind. So, not surprisingly, with the experience of real rather than imagined emotion, she had found her writing to be superficial; she knew she wanted to do better. Already characters were living in her brain, a story was unfolding. Ahead of her was a lifetime of joys and sorrows – why should her path be different from any other? But since she'd met Theo she had experienced heights and depths previously unknown; now she would share the emotions of those she brought to life – she would write from the heart in a way a year ago would have been beyond her reach. And that was why she spent so many hours alone in the estate office, warmed by a coal fire in a small grate instead of by the roaring logs in the drawing room. In the past she had carried notebooks and fountain pen with her to some secluded spot; but no longer. The office typewriter became her friend and even though she made mistakes, crossed words out with x's and made good use of her typing eraser, she knew it was a skill she must learn, for no publisher would waste time reading her handwriting. That was something she'd never considered in the past, which must have been a sign that her focus on the future was becoming clearer. So, although she never neglected the work of the estate, many of the hours she spent there were her own.

'Hello. Letters?' Walking in on her unexpectedly, Theo's voice surprised her.

'No. Well, there is some post, a letter to Bill Giles about the roof at Clay Cottage, and a cheque I wrote for the farrier. Over there,' she nodded her head towards the open roll-top desk where she had put her finished work out of the way.

'Humph,' he nodded, glancing at the letter. 'What a clever lass she is. So what are you up to now?'

'Just practising,' she lied, taking the sheet of paper out of the typewriter and casually putting it in the drawer. 'See what I bought in Exeter the other day.' To distract his attention before he got too curious, she took a book from the drawer and passed it to him. *How to Type Perfectly – Without a Teacher.* 'You see, proper fingering too. Give me a month and I'll show you how fast I can do it. There weren't any mistakes in the letter, were there?'

He sat down and pulled his chair closer to the fire.

'It was fine. Nice in here, isn't it. The others are knitting away like the peasants around the guillotine.'

With the cover on the typewriter she came to kneel on the hearth rug.

'Yes, it's nice.' She gave a sigh that must surely have been

124

the human equivalent of a cat's purr. 'Where have you been?'
Not something she would usually have asked.

'Just here and there.'

'You didn't come home for lunch.'

He smiled, eyebrows raised quizzically. 'What's so strange?
I often don't.'

She wished she hadn't said it. Lulled by the cosy fireside
atmosphere she had let herself imagine him telling her where
he had been, what he had been doing; his casual answer only
emphasised how little of his life she shared. Hard on the heels
of that thought came another: she too had a life of her own, one
she shared with no one. So she gave no ground to self-pity;
instead she reached for the tongs and dropped another piece or
two of coal on the fire.

'You can reach the bell, Theo. Let's have our tea in here
shall we?'

'I was going to walk over to see Nanny. Never mind tea, we'll
both go. We'll have it there with her, she'll like that. Get your
coat and collect your post, we'll get rid of it on the way.'

If she thought of them as sharing two compartments of his
life, she knew from the way he spoke that the outing slotted
happily into the one of being easy companions. It wasn't what
she had wanted, it wasn't what she'd hoped for as she'd knelt
by his feet in front of the fire, but she knew better than to refuse.
It must be enough that he included her, took her presence for
granted.

And so winter gradually gave way to spring in that year of 1939.
Had she been living at Dunsford House she would have been
much more aware of the cloud that hung over Europe. There the
only newspapers had been those she'd cycled to the village to
collect; here at Manningtor no less than three were delivered each
morning: the *News Chronicle* for the staff (important to Nicholls,
who put it carefully to one side until the day's work was done,
then had first option, when he read anything that took his fancy
and did the 'Chaotic' before anyone else was allowed so much
as a glance), *The Times* and the *Daily Telegraph* for the house.
Yet Anna and her grandfather had always kept abreast of the
news, whether from the newspaper or the wireless bulletins. They
would read the leader article, voice their opinions, something

she'd never been frightened of doing. Yet here there was a feeling of isolation from the troubled world. The house ran smoothly, conversation in the drawing room seldom touched on subjects beyond the family, or occasionally some event in Deremouth or even more rarely in Exeter. Francis was a farmer, so the only changes to interest him were those created by the seasons; Matt may well have had a mind that stretched beyond the coach company but he was old-fashioned enough to believe that politics and national strife were subjects for men not women; Theo? Who could guess at what went on in his mind? Much the same now as when he'd been a boy, no doubt. Even to Anna, to read of Franco's troops taking Madrid and finally bringing an end to the civil war, and soon after that of the King of Iran's death in a car accident, was like viewing something through the wrong end of a telescope. 'Dear me, how sad,' was the only response she got when she read out to Kath and Thelma that rioters in Iran had killed the British Consul, believing he had instigated the car accident. Those things did but dull the edges of the real terror that was threatening. The homes and shops of German Jews were being attacked, anti-Semitic slogans painted on them, windows broken. Many pulled up roots and came to England, even more to America. But this could be no answer. Hatred was gathering apace and like a flame beneath a bubbling cauldron, one day, perhaps one day soon, it must boil over.

Anna imagined her grandfather at Dunsford House, listening, thinking, no one to discuss the situation with, for Potts was a kind enough man but his thoughts went no further than tending either his master's physical needs or his garden. At Manningtor it was so easy to hide from the world, to see no further than the never-failing change of season. The first rosebuds came into flower, Digby brought the early peas to the kitchen and, instead of carrying the teatray to the drawing room, Daphne brought it to where she'd set up a table in the shade of the elms. It was frighteningly tempting to pretend that happenings in Europe were far away and removed from meaningful life.

Anna said this to Theo one afternoon in early August when she found him tinkering with the engine of her car, checking the radiator didn't need topping up, making sure the plugs were clean – in fact, generally looking for work where none was necessary.

'You wouldn't think this was the same world as the one we read about in the newspapers. It's frightening, Theo –'

'Frightening? Here?'

'Not frightening in that way, just frightening that we can be living in a fool's paradise when there's so much misery. Do you suppose Fate keeps a record on us all and evens things out? Do we get an allocation of good and an allocation of bad?'

'That sounds more like Mrs Humphries than you,' he laughed, brushing the suggestion aside. But he couldn't brush aside her earlier comment so easily. Weighing her words, he looked at her, his brows drawn into a frown that made his thoughts hard to read. According to the date Dr Price had forecast, the baby was due in six weeks and two days. A tall woman could often carry a child, giving the impression that the procedure was effortless. Anna was different. Back view she appeared unchanged, her hips were no broader, her arms and legs still 'as thin as sticks' as Mrs Short used to say. Sideways she looked like a little girl with a mammoth balloon on her stomach – except that a balloon is light as air and, from the drawn appearance of her thin face, her burden was anything but. If she imagined Theo's frown to be based on anxiety about Europe's troubles, she was wrong. Not often was he touched as he was in that moment.

She never complains, he was thinking, but she looks really rough. Poor little Anna. Anyway what's the use in wasting sleep worrying about a war, nothing we can do about it.

'Do I think there's trouble ahead? Yes, Anna, I do. No use our not facing up to it. I never used to bother much about things that went on, you know, buried my head in the sand as happily as anyone. It was that dreadful morning, the day Uncle Sidney fell. Waiting for Matt to fetch the car to the door, he was talking to me, and opened my eyes to things I hadn't considered – didn't want to consider, more likely. He believed we were heading for another war, if not this year or next, some time soon. He believed it was inevitable.'

'It must be. An army like Germany has trained isn't for nothing. Austria, Czechoslovakia, yet there's still no sense of peace, no feeling that his boundaries are reached. Where is it going to lead?'

He wandered past her to the open door of the garage, and

was silent for so long that she almost thought he hadn't been listening to her.

'It's hard even to imagine what's going on, isn't it,' he said at last. 'Here at Manningtor amidst peace and beauty, we live in a world apart.'

She didn't purposely reach out to touch him, it just happened.

'Before the last war was over they brought in conscription. Suppose it happened again . . .' It was impossible to contemplate, that 'Mrs Humphries streak' in her wouldn't even let her finish the sentence lest it tempted fate.

'Conscription? Hey, hey, what sort of a chap do you think I am? I can fly an aeroplane. I'd be in there sorting Adolf out before you had time to miss me.'

Instinct carried her hands to her stomach, cradling the unborn child that leapt and struggled within her.

'We're just being gloomy,' she forced a note of brightness. 'Anyway –' her pale, thin face turned to him with that elfin smile '– I can't spare you. Who would look after my car if you weren't here?'

'I agree, we're getting too glum. Your car's fine, even the tyres didn't need me. Anyway, on a day like this, what am I doing here? I'm off down to the boat for a couple of hours. And don't get worrying about things we can't control, things that might never happen.'

His serious side had been taken over again by the ostrich. Giving her a friendly pat on the bottom, he told her he'd see her later and slammed down the bonnet of her MG, closing their conversation just as firmly. His mind had already jumped ahead to the estuary where his boat was moored.

After he'd driven away she walked across the stable yard towards the side door where she bumped into Dee coming from the other direction.

'I'm hot and sticky. Sweaty,' the girl laughed, then mimicking Thelma, 'Now Dee, that's not a word I like to hear a daughter of mine use.' Her face was shining and the short ends of hair that had escaped from her pigtail were sticking to her neck. 'Had a tremendous gallop, Sylvia and I went miles. She's a terrific horsewoman. Gosh, I'm about dead.'

Anna laughed. 'Dead's about the last thing you look.'

128

'Corpses don't sweat, you mean? I need a bath.'

'I didn't mean that, just that you look so healthy you make me feel like the one who's dead.'

'It must be jolly tiring carrying that great hump about. I said that to Mum yesterday,' she giggled. 'She tut-tutted like mad. Honestly, Anna, they never say a word about it if they think I can hear. Aren't people funny about things like being pregnant. When Nanny's Tibby had kittens we all knew how it happened, even Mum and Gran didn't get all tight-lipped if we mentioned it. But with a person instead of an animal they won't let me talk about it. *You* don't mind me talking, do you?'

'Of course I don't. It's about the most natural thing in the world, so why should we hide it?'

'Jess, at school, is an auntie. Her sister had a little boy during the Easter holidays. But Jess said she didn't go outside the house for the last month or so.'

'Was she ill?'

'No. Just hiding. And if Jess was there, it was just like they are here, no one mentioned there was a baby coming. You know what –' she guffawed '– I reckon they wanted her to believe the stork was going to shove it down the bedroom chimney. I say, Anna, does it move about in there? Does it kick?'

There was something refreshingly innocent about the clumsy schoolgirl's natural curiosity. Taking her hand Anna guided and held it against her stomach. Such a small action, yet both of them were aware of the importance of the moment. Here they were, sharing a moment that belonged to no one but the two of them, one that had special importance to Dee because she knew how thoroughly her mother would have disapproved. Anna had grown fond of kindly and unchanging Thelma, but she had no feeling of disloyalty as she saw Dee's expression of wonder. A small action it may have been but it was a giant stride. The difference between twenty-one years and thirteen might seem vast, but before many more had gone by, eight years would count for nothing.

'Phew . . . gosh . . . alive as anything. Oh Anna, isn't it the most exciting thing.'

Those minutes with Dee pushed Anna's gloomy thoughts of war to the recesses of her mind. But in that August of 1939, within days even those at Manningtor were being hurtled into a future too dreadful to contemplate. For Dee and Sam there was a spirit of heroism, even adventure, in the challenge that 'threatened'. For those who had lived with the memory of the last war emotions were a mixture of disbelief and horror. Anna had been the product of her father's brief leave after a shrapnel wound in 1917, being born early in 1918. If she'd still been at Wickley Cross she would undoubtedly have felt all the challenge, even the adventure. But now she listened to each news bulletin, dreading what must surely come. What was it Theo had said? If not this year or next, there could be no other end to the way Europe was shaping. And Theo was a flyer.

She'd been in bed no more than an hour or two when, as so often happened, she was woken by cramp. Unable to lie still, she eased her legs over the edge and, careful not to disturb the sleeping Theo, got to her feet. The night was warm, the wide-open window drew her. The child kicked and struggled as if it knew it was lying on a nerve and tried to move.

August is over, she told herself silently as she held the bedside clock so that what light there was from the sky let her see the time. Now it's September, a new month, and by the time it's over I shall have my baby. And what else might have happened? Don't think about it, even imagining it is tempting fate. If we have the baby, then surely that will make him really love me. For myself I don't care whether it's a boy or a girl – but for *him* please let me have a son. For *me* too, I suppose, because if it's a boy then surely, surely he will start to feel like his father did about his mother. And, forgetting about the baby, there's *him* too. Please don't take him away. You know what he says, he's a flyer, if there's war he'll be gone. Lots of women must be awake like I am, all pleading, all frightened. Not for myself, I'm not frightened for myself, honestly. But for him, I am. And for the way the world seems set to go mad. Why do politicians and – and – and leaders, not ordinary people but leaders – why don't they think first about *people*? If women ran the world we'd make a better job of it. Don't know what's going to happen . . . wish it could be like it used to be . . . don't know why I'm crying.

And that was the truth. She didn't know why hot tears were silently wetting her cheeks. Was it because she was overtired? Was it fear of the loss of a world she knew? Was it compassion for those who, according to newspapers, were suffering for no other reason than the race or religion to which they'd been born? Were all those things no more than an excuse while the truth was that she wept for a love she couldn't have?

Before many more hours had passed, the slim grasp the nation held on peace was slipping. The expressionless voice of the wireless newsreader told them that German troops had invaded Poland, Warsaw was being bombed. That was on Friday. By Sunday even the ostriches had had their heads pulled from the sand: war was declared, there was no turning back.

Above stairs and below, the atmosphere was the same. There was excitement mixed with fear for the unknown in Daphne's mind, just as there was in Esme's and Gwen's. They'd all heard tell of how women had come into their own during wartime. If it had happened before, so it would again. Already, in those first few hours, they forgot the companionship and contentment they'd shared in the busy kitchens; ahead of them was a life in the 'outside' world, even though they had no clear idea of exactly where they would fit in.

It was much the same for Sam and Dee. Usually two years' difference in age put a barrier between them but today that barrier was gone.

'They won't take me till I'm eighteen, I bet,' Sam grumbled. 'Do you reckon it'll last that long?'

'No, of course it won't. Our lot will soon sort Adolf out. I heard Theo say that the other day. He'll go in the Air Force I suppose. Dad's too old, they won't want him.'

'And Francis too. Anyway he's more use on a farm, I expect. Doesn't seem much of a contribution from Manningtor – just Theo. Gosh, I wish I could put my age forward. What do you reckon? People used to in the last war, I've read about them.'

'Perhaps they'll let men join up at seventeen,' she tried to cheer him, both of them delighting in the word 'men'. 'I wish I was your age, but I'm going to be just useless.'

'Oh, well, you're a girl. That's different. You can always help on Home Farm in the holidays if it makes you feel better. I say, there's Theo going out. I bet he's off to the flying club. Lucky devil, he is. He'll have a head start over most chaps: there can't be that many with the flying hours he's got under his belt.'

*   *   *

131

The next few days proved Sam right. On the Monday morning, when Theo disappeared without saying where he was going, no one thought anything of it. With the cloud too low for him to be attracted to the club, the breeze was just right for sailing so very likely he intended to have a few hours on the water. By lunchtime he hadn't come home – not unusual. By teatime there was still no sign of him – he must be really enjoying himself. They dressed for the evening meal and were congregated in the drawing room when they heard the roar of the engine as he came up the drive.

'We were about to have dinner without you,' Kath greeted him as he opened the drawing-room door, almost forgetting her dowager state, her tone making no secret of her dislike of unpunctuality.

'Sorry I'm late, Aunt Kath,' his smile showed anything but sorrow. 'I won't change if dinner's ready.'

'Good boy,' she forgave him just as she had all his life. 'I dare say you were enjoying yourself too much to consider the time, is that it?' What a darling he was.

'You could say that.' Then to the room at large and no one in particular, certainly not Anna, 'You don't need two guesses what I've been doing. I've signed on, I've enlisted in the Air Force. What do you think of that, then?'

Everyone was talking at once, everyone except Anna. The more fuss they all made of Theo, the more pleased with himself he appeared. He'd known his announcement would create a stir, but this was even better than he'd imagined. Watching them, Anna felt removed. If he'd got home while she was dressing, if he'd told her first – but it hadn't even occurred to him. No one noticed as her hand caressed the movement of his child. No one knew how as she watched him, uninvited, the words of the old nursery rhyme can into her head.

He put in his thumb and pulled out a plum,
saying 'What a good boy am I.'

As the thought filled her mind, so she was ashamed. He was brave, he was patriotic, he was answering the call of duty. In the midst of them all, she felt alone and lonely. His doting family gathered around him bombarding him with questions:

132

where would he be sent for officer training? How long would it be before he was given his commission? In the excited babble it was only Anna, standing outside their magic circle, who heard the shrill ring of the telephone bell in the small and seldom-used study.

Chapter Seven

'You'd better talk to Theo,' Anna said. 'Just a second, Alex, I'll fetch him. He's joined the Air Force, he's just been telling us.'

'Of course he has,' answered his unflappable young sister. 'It would be a jolly poor show if he expected to skulk at home. I'll talk to him when we've got things fixed. Anna, it's *you* who will be sharing the house, he won't even be there.' Theo's younger sister accepted his wife as mistress just as she'd grown up knowing Theo, junior in years to the others, was master.

'Even so –'

'Even so, nothing! Who's going to have the responsibility of the estate when he's serving? *You will.* So what do you say? Last week I saw train loads of youngsters going off with their labels on them – quite horrid, poor little devils. Don't know why we felt that just because we're not right in London our kids would be safe.'

'How many are there?' Anna felt she was being carried along on a tide too strong to fight.

'We're a small school.' Then, with a good-humoured laugh that Anna knew held a shade of mockery. 'Small and select, rearing young ladies of tomorrow – children of today's successful tradespeople with aspirations. Good kids, all of them. Forty-two boarders and thirty day girls, but if we evacuate the school we shall have to give the parents of the day pupils the option of upping their fees and letting them board. At a guess I'd say there would be above sixty plus staff. The rooms are big, they'd make good dormitories. So, what do you say?'

'They can't stay where they might be bombed.'

'Right. And Manningtor?'

134

'Can I ring you back – or get Theo to? I ought to see what Aunt Kath and the others think. The house is huge, but it will mean we give up some of the family space.' Silence. 'Alex?' There were rooms in the west wing which hadn't been used for years, rooms where the furniture was protected with dust sheets. Sleeping accommodation would be the least of the problems.

'When I was down for Uncle Sid's funeral, Theo told me you'd taken to things splendidly, and were already turning into a perfect keeper for the estate. What sort of a mistress can't make her own decisions? Children have to be protected as far as we are able – that's as much a duty as what Theo's doing rushing off to fly an aeroplane. By the way, talking about children, how's the newest Sullivan developing? What a time for the poor little brat to have to get acquainted with the world.'

'By the time he – or she –' added as a sop to Fate '– knows what's going on, it'll all be over. It must be, Alex.' Another silence; Alex didn't rush her. A world on the edge of disaster – tomorrow's future rested on today's children; there could be no one untouched by the announcement, even those who hadn't made a habit of reading the newspapers and listening to the wireless, who hadn't feared for years there could be only one end to the hatred and bitterness that gathered impetus. Neither Anna nor Alex voiced their thoughts, but through the ether they were in unison. After a minute it was Anna who broke the silence, her voice calm, her decision made. 'When will you come? I'll have to organise space – dormitories. I'll start first thing in the morning. Some of the furniture will have to go into store. You'll bring your own desks of course.'

'Desks, dining tables, beds, the lot. You're a scout, Anna!' came Alex's brisk acceptance, relieved that her hunch hadn't failed her and her sister-in-law was confirming her opinion that she wasn't one to make a drama when clear thinking was what was needed. Really Theo had shown a surprising lot of sense when he'd fallen for her. 'Now that we've got that settled, you'd better fetch that brother of mine so that I can give him my assurance that we shan't wreck the place. That and give him a pat on the back for not having to be told where his duty lay.'

'He's excited as anything.' Anna tried to sound proud. Of course she was proud. But why couldn't he have told her where he was going today? If he felt burning patriotism, why couldn't

135

he have let her know his thoughts? Or had he enlisted because he loved flying and he could never resist adventure? Only one thing was certain: neither *she* nor the baby had come into his scheme of things. He would miss Manningtor, for she had no doubt at all how deep a hold its roots had in his heart. But her? 'I'll go and get him for you. But, yes, Alex. Tell him I've said yes.' The decision did something to ease the hurts he so often unwittingly inflected. Having called him, she left the study, shutting the door behind her. What conversation passed between brother and sister she didn't know, but when he rejoined the family it was with a smile of satisfaction on his face.

'Listen to this! A chance for the rest of you to do your bit for the war effort!' he announced, like a conjuror pulling a rabbit from the hat. 'Alex is coming home – and not just Alex. I've told her Manningtor will make itself a safe haven for that school she's so wrapped up in. So when Mrs What's-It from the Billeting Office calls again you can tell her you are "full house".' From the way he beamed at Anna, she imagined he was waiting for her congratulations on *his* decision.

Even if the family saw it as *his* decision, he took no further interest and disappeared to the beach next morning intending to spend the day having a final sail, before arranging for his boat to be lifted onto dry land for the winter. That it might still be there when summer came again was something he wouldn't consider.

That same day Anna went into action.

'Do you want any help?' Dee's voice cut through her thoughts as she went from room to room in the west wing, trying to visualise how many beds each would take. Then without waiting for an answer, 'What a jammy lot they are. Fancy being sent to spend the war at Manningtor. Just my luck that I'm buried in deepest Shropshire. Dad says that'll be what they call a reception area. Safe as houses.'

'You're just the person I want. You sleep in a dormitory. How many beds do you think we can get in here?'

So they worked together, the age difference telescoping and the job turning into something akin to fun, despite the reason for it. Anna welcomed Dee, adamant that all the family should be involved in the alterations. But it was she who arranged for rooms to be cleared and the furniture to be taken into safe keeping at the depository in Deremouth for the duration of the war; it was she who decided that the upstairs saloon with its plaster-carved ceiling and Adam style fireplace should be given over to the school as an assembly room and the library as a dining room. The desk drawers in the seldom-used study next to the family drawing room were emptied so that the room could be made available to the teaching staff. The rooms at Manningtor were all vast and without turning any of the family from their usual accommodation there were unused bedrooms that, once cleared of existing furniture, would give space enough for their evacuees as dormitories, and three partitioned by Mr Hopkins, the local carpenter and joiner, into private cubicles for staff. The final choice of their use would be with Miss Henderson, the headmistress. In the servants' quarters were three bedrooms which hadn't been occupied since before the last war, rooms that would be taken by domestic staff who were coming with the school.

So while, in his usual way, Theo spent that day about his own affairs, Anna hardly had room in her thoughts to dwell either on his imminent departure or the baby's almost imminent arrival. There was a need on everyone's part to be fully occupied, to make changes that somehow involved them in the national situation.

Later in the week the furniture was moved out, furniture that was antique and valuable, each item carefully draped for protection. And by the following weekend, the carpenter and his helpers having worked from early mornings till dark, making sure everything was ready, four large removal vans trundled up the drive bringing beds, desks, blackboards and easels, boxes of books, cabinets, linen, school dining tables, cutlery, all the day-to-day trappings of Chiltern House School. Manningtor Park was braced for its new life. On the Monday, teaching staff and the schools' domestics arrived, met at Deremouth station by a Sullivan's Coach. The family's contribution was over: from now on all they had to do was keep out of the way as Alex and the rest of the staff erected beds, and decided how best to position desks and blackboards in their new surroundings.

Declaration of war had rekindled memories for all those old enough to have seen it before. Yet, even for those, in those days of September, as Manningtor was made ready for its new role, there was an underlying feeling of adventure. In the kitchen Daphne and Gwen saw the changes as evidence that they too were on the brink of an exciting change in their routine; Ethel Bryant eyed

Dolly Holbrook, the school cook, with a mixture of suspicion and cordiality, aware that it would be useful to have someone willing to take over the occasional evening meal so that she could cycle in to town to the pictures or spend an hour with a friend in the village, but ready to give the necessary rebuff if Dolly attempted to 'throw her weight about'.

Soon Theo would be gone. Eagerly each morning he looked through the post hoping for his instructions. And, just as eagerly, Anna noted each new twinge in the hope that it might herald the baby's arrival. Except for Dr Price's first visit she had seen nothing of him, but Nurse Radley, the Deremouth midwife who served the Moorleigh area, had called every month or so. She was a powerfully built woman, almost six foot tall, with broad shoulders, ample bosom, large hands and feet and a voice that knew only one volume – loud. If Theo ever happened to be home when she was seen pedalling up the drive, he immediately vanished. There were few people who didn't immediately fall under his spell, but instinct told him that Jessica Radley was one of those few.

'Let's see how well we're doing, Mrs Sullivan; upstairs we go.' With energy as abundant as her size, she led the way up the shallow stairs and into a small spare room that had been made ready for Anna's confinement. It was the fourteenth of the month. The next day Theo would be gone, the one after that all those empty rooms would be filled with Alex's influx. And two days later still, Dee would be on a train heading north, Dee who watched her every movement looking for some sign (even though she had no idea what!) that the birth was starting to happen. 'Let's get our clothes off and lie on the bed.' A bubble of laughter rose in Anna at the picture the midwife's words conjured up. Whether Nurse Radley spoke with the royal 'we' or whether it was intended to give her patient a feeling that the battle ahead was something they shared, remained unclear. Unquestioning, Anna did as she was told.

'Ah-ha,' Jessica swooped on her, 'but this begins to look like business, oh yessee, yessee, dropped nicely.' She nodded her head sagely, then blowing on her hands and rubbing them together just to make sure they were warm, she proceeded to prod 'the hump'. 'Beautiful, just beautiful. Position just right, head engaged, no problems here. No backaches or anything?'

'I feel fine,' Anna assured her, so cheered by the nurse's expression of satisfaction that she wouldn't admit to anything less. 'You mean the baby is ready to come? It's so important, Nurse Radley.'

'So it must be. I hear you've a school-load of children to be evacuated here at the Hall. We can do without a lot of inquisitive children round us when we go into action, yessee, that we can.'

'I didn't mean because of them. It's my husband. He's had his joining instructions. He goes tomorrow. I've been dashing round, doing everything I can, to make the baby start. Does that help, do you think?'

'This little one will come when it's ready. Joined up already, has he, the young squire? My word, but that gives a good example. I remember in the last war how men rushed off in those first weeks. I had a young man then,' then with a sniff as if to show how thoroughly she had put the past far behind her, she went on, 'I was young myself, mark you, only just finished my training. He went off in that first fortnight. Proud as punch I remember I was, yessee, so I was. Ah well, we all learnt a lesson with what came after those early weeks. Now then, that's me done. Give Mr Sullivan my good wishes –' then, for a second dropping her usual good-natured, brusque manner '– and don't you start worrying about him because he's out of sight. He'll be in better hands than ours, you have to learn to trust.'

'Is that what you did?' Anna wished she could have recalled her words, for the young man Nurse Radley spoke of was no longer in her life.

For a brief moment the powerful shoulders seemed to droop and the nurse hesitated before she answered. 'It was a hard lesson to learn. Yes,' and she sat on the edge of the bed, a sure sign that she'd been knocked off balance. 'I did trust, we both did, Billy and me. He was a truly *good* young man, better than ever I'd been. Used to go regular as clockwork to the chapel on the corner, even if it was my Sunday off; nothing stopped him. Now me, I was just run of the mill. But Billy, he was a real God-fearing young chap. So we both trusted. That's what I found so hard to accept. I was angry, I felt that that God he put such store in had let us down when, like so many more, word came to his people that he'd

139

been killed. It was a bad time – you lose your faith and you lose everything. Black days they were.' The long pauses told Anna more than her words. 'Then I had a visit from a friend of his and it was from him I learnt that for Billy's sake I had to be grateful. Not for mine, mind you, but for his. Any road, I was no saint, I didn't deserve special favours. He was an infantryman, fighting there in those dreadful trenches. This friend saw it happen. Billy was in a raiding party sent out over the line; it was a hand grenade that killed him. Happened in a second, he couldn't have known.'

'How awful for him – for you too.'

'It's a funny thing, Mrs Sullivan, it was talking to his friend, having a picture in my mind of what Billy's end had been, that took away the anger. Can't really find the right words – haven't talked about it for years – but I'd known from the letters that he was half crazed with fear and disgust. Half crazed, did I say? Worse. He wouldn't be the first to lose his reason in that hell. Then it was all over for him. For the first time I was able to go down on my knees – didn't even know what it was I wanted to say. But I felt calm, at peace. And, tell you another thing, it was that peace that brought Billy back to me.' For a moment there was silence, an easy silence. 'Don't always know what it is we're called to put up with, but come what may, if we lose our faith then life's a sorry business.' She appeared to realise she'd said more than she ought to a girl in Anna's circumstances. 'Things will be better this time, there will never be that sort of carnage again. And you wait till word gets round the village that Mr Sullivan's off in the Army.'

'No, Theo is a flyer,' Anna couldn't keep the pride from her voice. 'He's flown for ages.'

'Well, we must keep our pecker up, my dear. Safer up there in an aeroplane than down on the ground, I dare say. And, as for this baby, it might be in a rush, it might not. Certainly the head's come down well, but I've known many a little rascal to stay like that and keep its mother waiting. We'll just have to see. Better get our clothes back on. You'll find they'll give your husband time off to come and see his new baby, you may be sure. Now, if you need me I'll be on my bike and here before you can say knife, but more likely I'll be riding over again a week today. Your date isn't yet, and these little creatures get themselves all ready but that doesn't mean you can push them out to suit your own convenience. Dear me, no. You may think you're the boss, and once it arrives that's what you will be. But over this, you have to let nature take its course.' While she talked Anna had been struggling awkwardly back into her clothes. The nurse watched her. Take away that hump and she looked nothing but a child. Let's hope she didn't have many more days to wait. Her man going away, too. Not that he'd be much use hanging around here getting himself into a stew. For one thing was certain, with a tiny frame like that, young Mrs Sullivan had a battle ahead of her, poor little soul. 'Now then, my dear, like I say, I'll come again this time next week and if you haven't got any nearer by then I'll give you a good dose of castor oil. Lubrication, when everything's set to go, that and follow it with a good piping hot bath. Nothing better to make it get a move on.'

'Castor oil?'

'Not as nasty as it sounds. I always top it up with water, slips down before you can say knife, with the water chasing it. You'll hardly know you've had it. I'll be off, then. Now that you're up here, you just lie back on that bed and give yourself an hour's rest.' Clearly she meant to see Anna settled first, then with a cheery, 'That's the way. An hour's shut-eye is what you need,' off she went.

A minute or so later Anna was peeping out from the side of the window watching her well-meaning carer propel herself towards the open gates, head down, case strapped on the luggage rack. That was just before three o'clock. By the time the sound of the chimes of the hour rang out, she was swallowing the water that chased a large dose of castor oil. Nurse Radley hadn't said how much to take, but it was no use doing things by halves!

The bathroom was filled with steam. Half-submerged in water almost too hot to bear Anna looked at her naked body and was put in mind of a lobster, its shell turning red as it boiled. If the castor oil wasn't shifting the baby, it was telling her that the last thing she felt fit for was sitting at the dinner table with the family. Theo's last evening – by this time tomorrow he would be swallowed up in a life she couldn't even imagine – only a few more hours – come on, baby, come on. Awful pain but so would anyone have after all that castor oil – it *must* be more than just that, it *must be* – come on, baby, she said you were ready, please try and come now, tonight. With all her might she strained in an effort to turn

141

the unpleasantness of an overdose of oil into something she would recognise as different.

'Anna, Anna,' and a quiet tapping on the bathroom door. 'It's me, Thelma. Are you all right, dear? I heard you running the water ages ago when I came in from my round.' Like a mother hen Thelma kept an eye on her.

'Yes, I'm fine. Well, no. Actually I've got a bit of a tummy upset. I thought a hot bath might make me feel better.'

'Oh, what a pity. Theo's last evening too and Ethel is preparing such a special dinner, all his favourite things.'

But by the time the gong sounded and, determined to uphold tradition in the face of every changing circumstance, the family filed into the dining room, Nurse Radley had already been summoned and Anna was beginning the longest night of her life. Looking back on it, pain clouded her memory. Kindly Thelma had been her only opportunity to prepare herself in the preceding months but, gentle and caring, she had always emphasised the wonder of 'when you hold the little darling'. So, what started as a battle against time, one Anna fought with all her might, gradually became overtaken by a fog of searing pain. After what seemed like eternity, hardly aware of what was happening, she felt something held across her mouth and nose. Was she dying? The question was half-formed and fading, fading. Later (how much later?) she heard the cry of a baby, then she felt herself drifting, without the strength or the will to clutch at consciousness.

'You're awake,' faithful Thelma's voice came to her out of the mists. 'What a time you had, poor darling. But it's all over now. He's perfect. Let me sit you up then I'll get him out of his crib for you to hold.'

'Theo? Where's Theo?'

'He saw the baby before he had to leave.'

'Gone?' It was as if the world had gone on without her while she'd defied agony beyond anything she'd imagined and fought to give her baby life. 'Theo . . . gone . . . didn't know . . .'

'Such a shame he couldn't wait, dear. He and some friend from the flying club were travelling together. We tried to wake you, but I think you were still hardly conscious. Do you remember how when the delivery came they had to give you a whiff of

142

chloroform and put you right out? But he's, oh Anna, he's the prettiest little darling.' Thelma beamed with such pride she might almost have taken a hand in the affair herself. 'When Nurse Radley was tidying you afterwards you seemed to be back with us, yet I doubt if you even remember it now. As soon as she laid you back comfortably you drifted off. Nanny's moved into the nursery rooms. Poor Nanny, she was quite weepy when Theo left; she's always thought the world of him. But he'll be home soon. War or no war, I'm sure when he explains that his wife has just had a baby – well, of course they'll let him have some time at home.'

'He saw Christopher? That's what he's to be called. Theo chose his name. But I didn't want you told, in case it tempted fate and it wasn't a boy after all.'

'If it had been a girl you would have been just as thrilled. That's one of nature's little tricks.' Pulling her chair close to the bedside, Thelma took out her knitting needles and a new ball of pale blue wool. 'Now we know it's a boy, I'm going to make this into a pram set. Such a delicate blue, I thought. I bought it back in the summer.' Then, in a voice that implied they shared a secret joke, 'I didn't tell you I had it – in case it tempted Fate. Not that a little girl wouldn't have been a treasure, but I know what having a son meant to Theo.' Between them hung the unspoken reminder of the perils of war. 'But hark at me! Talking about sitting here and knitting, when you haven't even seen your son. I'll come back up presently, but first I'll tell Nanny you're awake. You don't want us all in here while you make his acquaintance.' Ramming her empty needles into the ball of wool, Thelma got up inelegantly from the low boudoir chair, smoothed her ruffled skirt, stooped down unexpectedly and dropped a kiss on Anna's brow, and bustled from the room – or as near to bustled as her portly frame allowed.

He was perfection in miniature. Anna heard the door close on Nanny and, left alone with her son, gazed down at him through an unexpected mist of mindless tears.

'Our little boy,' she mouthed almost silently, 'that's who you are.' Part of Theo and part of me. You've got blue eyes. We haven't. Little Christopher. Are you staring at me? Are you seeing me? Did you look at him like that? Daddy. I've never thought of

143

Theo as being Daddy. I wish I'd seen him, Christopher. I wish we could have had a moment for the three of us. But he'll come home soon. Then everything will be like I dreamed. I'm so thankful, so grateful, that you're a boy. Not for *my sake*, but because Theo so wanted it. Little Christopher, you know what? You're such a wee scrap of a person, but he truly *loves* you. Perhaps he'll never feel like that about me. But you're important, you're his tomorrow's man. Let's try and make it different, shall we? You and me? Let's *will* him to fall in love with me. After all, I've given him what he wanted, I've given him a son. But you're more than that. You're *my* little boy, you've been with me for months. You darling, darling little man. I do thank You, God, with all my heart. And please, just because I'm feeling like that about my baby, that doesn't mean I'm not caring that Theo has gone. He was so excited about enlisting; it seemed to shine out of him. I wonder if he ever talks to God like I do. I hope he does. But if he's been so wrapped up in all the excitement of being made a hero that he hasn't, please God don't think badly of him. Life's always been so easy for him – except for that time after his mother died. I remember what Nanny told me about the hard time he had when his father was miserable. But Theo doesn't talk about miserable times, he likes everyone to be happy. And I *am*. Happy and so grateful for our baby. Christopher, I'll be a good mother . . . so thankful. I wonder if everyone feels like this when they first hold their baby. Like what? Sort of weak and aching – nothing to do with all the hurting – filled with wonder and a bit frightened. This tiny person looks to *me*. Newborn like he is now, he is utterly pure. No grown-up is without sin, yet it has to be up to *me* to guide him, to teach him the difference between right and wrong, meanness and generosity, truth and lies. I'm so grateful. Please God always take care of Theo and make him proud of what I do.

'Now then, Anna child, and what do you think of our fine young man?' Nanny spoke as she came back into the room. 'Reckoned I'd given you time enough to say how-do-you-do to each other. My, but he's a bonny little lad. Now I'll tell you what you and me will do. Nurse Radley's gone off home for a sleep – earned it too, the struggle you gave her and Dr Price – but she'll be back later on to see you're going on right. Before then, let's see if we can't give our young man an idea of taking the breast.

Nothing in it for him yet and, until there is, what he needs is just plain boiled water to flush out his system. The sooner he gets acquainted with the feel of the nipple, the easier he'll take to it.' As she talked she was busy unbuttoning one shoulder of Anna's maternity nightgown, exposing the small, barely shaped breast. 'Dear me, you look nought but a child. Give you a day or two and the milk'll come in, or so 'tis to be hoped, then you might look a scrap more promising for the poor wee man. 'Tis to be hoped we don't have to go out buying bottles. All the others have thrived on the breast, all but poor little Alex. Losing her dear mother like she did there was no choice. Not the same though. I may be old-fashioned, but for healthy teeth and strong bones, nature's way is best. Why else would our Maker have sorted it out the way He has? That's it, move it into his mouth. Won't suck yet, but he'll learn. Just see the way he's staring at you. Doesn't see you, of course, not see properly. His eyes wander. I was brought up on a farm, you know. To this day I never cease to wonder at the way the newborn calves learn, on their feet and suckling in no time. There, little one, that's it, smack your lips.' As if he was aware of all the attention, the baby let his head fall backwards and his eyes wander to some unknown spot on the ceiling, then he sneezed. Nothing funny in it, yet both Anna and Nanny laughed. Why Nanny found it funny Anna didn't question, but for herself, she clutched at anything to laugh at, anything that would take away an unfamiliar emotion that was almost too much to bear.

Term wasn't due to begin until the 21st of the month, later than usual due to the move. Days before that the classrooms and dormitories were ready. Feeling slightly put out that their own lives were to continue unchanged by the events of war, Sam and Dee had both returned to school. It was arranged that Alex should travel by rail to meet the Chiltern House pupils on Maidenhead Station, so on Wednesday the 20th a complete carriage was reserved to bring Manningtor's visitors to Deremouth. From there the journey was completed courtesy of Sullivan's Coaches.

A new baby, a houseful of girls full of good intentions, all eager to write home with descriptions of their 'unschool-like' surroundings – at Manningtor it seemed the old order had given way to the new.

'The poor children have had quite enough upheaval and dis-appointment,' Thelma was saying as Anna joined the family gathered to wait for the dinner gong at the beginning of November. It would take more than war to disrupt the routine at Manningtor. 'It's a nonsense to suppose that it would throw the country into danger to have a bonfire and a few fireworks.'

'Rules are rules.' Francis, who'd just dropped in with Sylvia as they so often did, said with a humourless laugh, 'Can't you just imagine Bert Morton's delighted "Put that flamin' fire out!"' He mimicked the West Country dialect. '"What do you think you're doing, guiding Adolf in?"' Moorleigh's Chief Warden took his duties more than seriously: an evening never went by when each house or cottage wasn't scrutinised to make sure no glint of light escaped round the edge of a curtain; he even pedalled out to Manningtor, for to catch 'the big house' breaking the law would be worth at least two of those small ones clustered round the green. Manningtor, or at second best, the vicarage – they were his goals. 'I tell you what we could do,' Francis went on as the idea struck him. 'I could turn the tractor and all the other gear out of the implement barn just for the one night. No chance of a bonfire, but with those doors closed and lamps burning there'd be warmth enough. The kids could sit on straw bales and what about if they got a load of potatoes and sweet corn cooked in the house and taken out there. Not the same as fireworks, but this year nothing's the same for them. By the light of lanterns they would make something special of it. Perhaps they could have a sing-song. I'll have a word with Alex later on, see what she thinks.'

Anna saw him through new eyes. She'd lived at Manningtor for a year but despite the amount of time he spent there, Francis had remained an unknown. A quiet man, clearly he adored his lovely Sylvia, but beyond that his interest had always seemed to be in the land. Yet he was prepared to go to all the trouble of preparing the old stone barn with its heavy wooden doors for the schoolchildren who had taken over so much of the house.

'If it's a sing-song you have in mind, what about that old piano accordion of yours?' Sylvia urged.

'Haven't touched it for years.' Some of his confidence in the success of the following week's 5th November rituals dimmed.

146

'Playing would be like riding a bicycle, Francis,' Thelma encouraged. 'Once you've done it it would come back in no time.'

Strange how now, even after living amongst them for a year, there were moments like this when they bonded together and Anna was still aware of being outside the orbit. From the tone of their voices it seemed the family was warming to the subject, their enthusiasm evident. Perhaps, in those first months of war, with the promise of nothing but increasing austerity, anything that hinted at change was attractive. Only Anna noticed that Matt contributed nothing to the conversation, his face set in a fixed and unnatural smile. Perhaps, for her, fear was never beneath the surface for, watching him, she had a premonition of disaster. Was he even listening to the others? Or was he waiting to drop some sort of bad news? Theo – no, not Theo, please not Theo. Reason told her that a flying accident was no more likely while he trained in an Air Force plane than when he used to 'show off' looping the loop in the local skies. But these days reason could so easily be silenced.

The gong sounded, Thelma helped Kath from the deep chair, sherry glasses were put down and they started towards the door.

'Just a second, there's something I want all of you to hear,' Matt's voice halted them. Something serious, why else would he sound like this? Anna was frightened to breathe; she knew the moment was important, it was one they would remember. 'It's something I've been thinking about for weeks. You know that back in the spring I took on a working manager. No expectation of war then, of course, but Millward is a good man, capable, responsible.'

'He's not leaving you, dear?' Thelma's face was a picture of concern.

'Not a bit of it. No. That's what I want to tell you. He's older than I am, coming up to fifty. Last time, I only got in at the end. This time I believe I have something to offer. Anyway, that's what I've done. I've volunteered for the Army.'

'But why? You're doing a useful job of work.' This from his mother.

Anna had never been more conscious of what the year had done to Kath as one after another of those she loved, those who'd been entwined into the structure of her days, had gone. And now Matt,

147

the son who had modelled himself on his father, who had seemed as enduring as Manningtor itself. To say there was a tremor in her voice would be to deny the hold she always kept on her emotions. No, it wasn't there to be heard, yet all of them, not only Anna, knew the effort she made to hold it back.

'Millward won't fail the firm, Mother. For weeks I've been thinking of this – ever since Theo did the right thing and joined up.'

'But this man is an employee, no matter how reliable,' Thelma clutched at the nearest straw. 'How would your father feel to see you entrusting to a stranger what has always been a family business?'

'Father served in the last war – and not because he was of an age to be conscripted . . . Of all people he would understand that I can't – *can't* – spend my time organising local bus routes, ferrying women and shopping baskets. Thelma, my dear, no one is irreplaceable. With or without me there will be changes in the coach business. So far the petrol ration is adequate. But for how long? Millward will find he has to trim the business to suit the fuel we're allowed. If the war lasts, rationing will be tightened; if it doesn't, then I'll soon be home. As for me, if I can run a coach company then surely I ought to be able to do the same with Army vehicles? Don't you see I *have* to do something. I'm not old and decrepit yet. It's different for you, Francis – if there's one breed the country depends on it's you farmers, even if it's taken a war to make the government realise it.'

Thelma's face was pink with emotion. Almost shyly she came towards him and took his hand. 'We're all very proud,' she told him simply. 'And we must hang on to the thought that at your age surely they won't send you overseas. There must be plenty of younger men for that.'

For a second his expression changed. For her to speak of pride, that gave him what he wanted to hear. It was those last words, the expectation that he was too old to be sent abroad, that knocked him off his pedestal. Young Theo was 'cock-o'-the-walk', each day adding to his flying hours at Cranwell. By the time he came home on leave he would be a dashing young officer with wings emblazoned over his tunic pocket. Placid, dependable Matt would have been appalled if anyone had accused him of being jealous of his young cousin; but, for all that, he was determined to

148

prove that being older didn't mean he was less use. Indeed his experience was worth more to the country that the confidence of untried youth.

In silence they filed into the dining room. Just as it always had been, the table was laid with gleaming silverware and tonight the two extra places were a sign that Francis and Sylvia were staying. Although there had been fear of food rationing, so far it hadn't materialised. The war was only two months old and although some of the young men had joined the forces, although many city children were still living in the safe country surroundings where they'd been evacuated at the beginning of September, although the streets were dark and the windows heavily curtained, the expression 'phoney war' was being bandied about. If food rationing followed, people blithely supposed it would be on the generous lines of present-day petrol coupons. Even the thought of Matt following Theo's example didn't cast too black a cloud on the household: it wouldn't be for long, and how proud they would be of the example he was setting. A phoney war was a relatively comfortable affair.

'Perhaps they won't send for you until after Christmas. Perhaps it will all fizzle out before you have to go,' Thelma said as, clad in a long-sleeved, winter nightgown, she stood in front of her bedroom mirror and treated her hair to its nightly hundred stokes of the brush. 'If you go before, poor little Dee will be heartbroken.' In the reflection she watched him as he tied the cord of his pyjamas, trying to imagine her life without him and utterly failing. 'Damn Adolf Hitler, damn him.' The words slipped out even as she thought them, frightening her by their unusual intensity and sending stinging and just as unfamiliar tears to her blue eyes.

'Hey, come on, love. We'll get by. The more people who show their colours the quicker it'll all be over. And what was that you said about being proud, eh?'

'If you want to make yourself a hero, of course I'm proud. But it's just not fair, Matt. All over the country there must be couples talking like this, people who were secure in the lives they'd made. Nearly twenty years, always we've been together.'

'So we will be again, love. And I'm not gone yet.' He drew her plump body into his arms.

149

'Too cold to stand out here.' She gave him a reassuring smile designed to tell him she'd recovered her momentary loss of control.

'Humph,' he moved his chin against her prematurely greying hair. 'Warmer in bed.'

Pushing the hot water bottle to one side, she willingly cuddled close to him, pulling the covers around their chins. Then, with her back warmed by his stomach she drew the hot water bottle in her arms. Could there be any greater comfort than this?

'You don't want that thing.' He moved it further away, his hands caressing her ample but still flannelette-covered breast. 'Not tonight.'

His meaning was clear. Turning onto her back she surreptitiously moved her fingers against the pocket of his pyjamas making sure that he had come to bed prepared for the lovemaking she recognised he wanted. Satisfied that he had, she undid the cord of his trousers, pushed them down, then wriggled her flannelette nightwear to her waist. Dear Matt. She drew him to her. How much would she miss this when he was gone? she wondered as she held him gently. Oh but she'd miss everything: she was frightened to imagine the emptiness of days when she wouldn't know that on the dot of half past twelve he'd be home for lunch and just as punctually at half past six she'd hear him driving his Rover to the coach yard and garage it for the night. In between she always filled her hours contentedly; perhaps she would hardly think about him if she were quite honest; yet, however she organised her days, she geared her plans to fit *his* timetable, to the sound of his tread in the hall and the knowledge that he was home. Dear Matt, he was like a second self. He's got heavier over the years, or is it because I have that the weight of him makes me so short of breath? That was as near as she'd let herself come to acknowledging that she hoped he wouldn't take too long. He's breathing faster now, yes, he's almost there. Dear Matt. How much shall I miss all this? In a way, quite a lot. It's like him telling me he needs me. And I need him. Imagine getting into this big bed and having nothing to cuddle up to but a hot water bottle. Even these newfangled rubber ones are miserable, and you wake up in the morning to find them cold. What is it he says? Like having a dead dog in the bed.

'Don't drift off to sleep without your trousers back on, dear. You don't want to get a cold back.'

150

Two minutes later, trousers on and cord tied, flannelette pulled well down, they were back in their 'sleeping position'. Oh but she'd miss everything, everything about their life together. For twenty years this was how she'd ended her days, she wouldn't let herself think of how it would so soon be.

Occasionally Theo spoke to them on the phone. Nothing about him changed and, just as he always had, he found satisfaction in giving pleasure, in hearing from their voices just how much his call meant to them. So he blithely talked as the minutes melted away, feeding more money into the machine at three-minute intervals when the sound of the pips warned him his time was running out. He chattered to Kath, to Thelma, to Matt (Theo's enthusiasm and his belief that wherever there was a fighting zone men of Matt's experience would be nothing short of a Godsend, doing much to soothe the wound of Thelma's trust in Matt's being too old), to Nanny, to Anna, to Francis and Sylvia, to Alex, in fact to anyone who was on hand, seemingly as happy to talk to one as another. Their delight in hearing from him was apparent, it was what prompted him to bring a pile of shilling pieces to the phone. That he failed to pick up the vibes of Anna's hurt when never once did he just *ask* for her, or when so often it was Nanny who gave him Christo's progress reports, wasn't entirely due to an insensitive nature. Rather it was because like an alcoholic craves drink, so Theo craved praise and affection; he always had. And, more than that, each and every one of them was part of Manningtor and, despite his thriving on the challenge of his new surroundings, the link that held him to Manningtor never weakened.

'I wish I was there to give a hand, I could play my mouth organ,' he said when Matt told him the plans for the 5th November celebration. 'Get them to make a huge pot of soup too and carry it across to the barn, that'll keep the kids warm. I say, what a lark! You two chaps have got stamina enough to carry it from the kitchen. I can just see it.' Something in his tone told Matt that he wasn't a stranger to nostalgia for the Park.

'But things are going well on your course, old chap?' Matt steered the conversation back onto safer ground. 'Won't be long now before you are given the all clear to join a squadron.'

'Don't get me wrong, I know war's a bugger,' came Theo's

151

cheerful reply. 'But – well, you'll see for yourself – this is the life, Matt! A lot of chaps, a lot of laughs, hours of flying. Tell me, is Anna keeping on top of things at home? She always sounds fine if I ask her, but she's not just putting on a show so that I don't get worried? Once you've gone she won't have anyone to turn to.'

'Believe me, she hasn't had need of me. Not once. Of course, running the house is less of a responsibility since the school came and anyway the others are always here for her. But as for the estate, she has meetings with Ken Briggs about the woodlands, she deals with instructions for repairs, she knows all the tenants, there's no end to the glowing reports I hear. She spends hours in the office each day. And it can't be that she's driven off her feet: I think she does it because she enjoys the responsibility.'

He believed what he said. But it was only half the truth. A year at Manningtor, a year of marriage to Theo, a year in which she'd been weighed down by disappointment and failure when she'd lost the baby that had brought her here in the first place, a year that had taken Theo away leaving her with responsibilities that at one time would have seemed impossible and then given her Christopher and a love that was beyond the need of words – all these things had touched depths of understanding she'd never dreamed. She'd believed she'd always felt the joys and sorrows of the characters she created as furiously she'd scribbled, but that had been in her daydreaming years. Now she was like a prisoner whose chains had been cut. With each week, almost with each day, her fingers moved with more accuracy on the keys of the office typewriter and as the silent words came into her head, so they found their way onto the page. She didn't question why it was that, just as she always had, she set her stories in a century long gone, an age when the Brontë sisters had created their own way of escaping the narrow confines of the Haworth rectory. Quite naturally her imagination carried her to a time she'd always seen as an era rich with emotion and romance. She wrote of love and jealousy, of loneliness and death, of joy and trust, of faithlessness and anguish. Alone in the estate office she lost herself in the world known only to her. And because of that, in some inexplicable way, she was able to concentrate her other hours on the demands of Manningtor.

Only one thing shone through brighter than all else – and that was her simple and complete love for Christopher. Every four hours through the day she went to the nursery. Nanny looked after him, bathed him, changed him, when no one was watching she even rocked him in her arms and sang to him just as she used to Theo and Alex and Lance and Sylvia before them. But there was nothing and no one who could share Anna's moments with her son. His eyes focused on her now; they had changed to a brown as dark as his father's. He would stare at her unblinkingly, sucking hard at her nipple as if he drew to the depth of her soul. Weak with love, aching with longing that was nameless and almost too much to bear, memories would crowd her mind. Out of her joyous hours with Theo had come this miracle of love. Holding him, adoring him, feeling the hard pull of his rosebud lips, her own mouth felt dry, her heart beat hard, the empty longing in her groin an exquisite agony. Later, back at her desk, frustrations still drove her. Her thoughts held no barrier of censorship but, censorship or no, she had clung to her sensual longing as being precious and personal. Sexual starvation found an emotional outlet as she worked. She had no realistic thoughts of ever seeing her writing in print, only a driving need to live in the people she brought to life.

How much did she miss Theo? Even though his days had more often than not been spent somewhere else, she'd drawn strength and enthusiasm from knowing that he was proud of the interest she took in the estate. It put her in mind of when she'd learnt to drive the car, how thrilled she'd been to hear Thelma's words of praise. But until she'd passed her test and gone out on the road alone, until she'd accidentally driven with the handbrake on, until unseen she'd stalled the engine at a junction, she hadn't started to be a real driver. So it was with Manningtor. While Theo had been there she had looked on herself as a helper, someone who would write letters, pay bills, visit tenants, but always defer to him before her decisions became actions. Now she was on her own, but never frightened by the responsibility; on the contrary, she drew strength from it. Theo had answered the country's call, and before the year was out, Matt had gone too; Daphne no longer worked in the kitchen, instead she was training to be a cook in the ATS; Alex had war work in caring for the next generation; Francis had taken on three Land Army girls to replace two farm labourers, one now in uniform and the other earning more money at the boatbuilders' yard in Deremouth; and Anna's contribution was

153

caring for Manningtor, making sure its standards were maintained and she didn't fail the trust Theo had shown in her. Yet thinking along those lines, she knew that for her looking after the estate was more than just war work, much more.

So how much did she miss Theo in those early days of the war? She missed the carefree joy of being in his company; she missed his unchanging good humour; she missed his sensual need of her and the never failing miracle of his loving. She remembered the waif-like girl she'd been in the beginning, the gradual change in her body as the months had gone on. Frightened to hurt the baby with his weight they had experimented until they found a position that satisfied them all, him, her and the baby too. Now there was nothing, nothing but memories and an unfulfilled need. Was it the same for him? Theo had never been used to not getting what he wanted when he wanted it.

How would I feel if I found he was with other women? I don't know. I ought to mind, and I suppose I would. But he was never like me. For him there had been women before, but they hadn't meant anything to him; he'd not been in love. And what about with me? By now he would have forgotten I even existed if he hadn't made me pregnant. But what about him and other women up there in Lincolnshire? He's talked about going out locally, about dances and what he calls 'larks'; he'd never be the sort of man who could turn on or off according to convenience. So how much do I care? It may be wicked of me, but honestly not all that much. I mean, I hate to think of him actually making love to someone else. I don't want to let myself imagine it, but of one thing I'm truly a hundred per cent sure: it wouldn't alter him, it wouldn't really touch him. Soon he'll get leave, he'll come home, he'll be just the same, my playmate, my love mate.

So she tried to slot her feelings safely and neatly into a compartment marked 'Waiting for Theo'. When she undid the compartment and let them free it was Christmas, and he had ten days' leave. By that time Matt had gone too, a man with years of experience but who still had to undergo officer training before he could be commissioned and become a useful cog in the war machine. For ten days they were both home, a Christmas that seemed unreal. Dee and Sam still went on the holly hunt, this year leading a bevy of schoolgirls who were to spend their first

Christmas away from home for, term or holiday, for the time being Manningtor was their home.

With no transport at Dunsford House, other than Anna's own bicycle, the long and rutted lane to Wickley Cross had meant that no one had attended the annual midnight service. Like other Christmas traditions in so many households, it had passed Anna by. This year was different. By eleven o'clock the contingent from Manningtor Park set out, a long crocodile of girls in their uniform dark-red capes with hoods, accompanied by teachers just as they had been throughout the term each Sunday morning. But this outing was different. There wasn't one of them who wasn't homesick and yet there was a feeling of magic abroad, being together, looking at the starry sky, touched by its wonder as only the young can be. So was Anna, perhaps, not quite as adult as she imagined? For her too the sound of their footsteps, the eerie shadows thrown by the shaded lamp held by Alex who walked at the head of the column, the nearness of Theo, the miracle of knowing Christo was at home safely watched over by Nanny, the unacknowledged fear of what changes the future might bring, all these gave her an awareness that knew no words. Behind them came Sylvia and Francis, two land girls who hadn't gone home for Christmas, then most of the staff. On they walked, their footsteps sounding like an advancing army. The dimly shaded lights of Matt's car cast a feeble beam; it was the constant blast of his horn that warned them to crowd onto the grassy verge. Matt would have preferred to walk, but he knew it was too much for his mother so he and Thelma were bringing her by car. The tail lights disappeared and the walkers reassembled. Left, right, left, right – Anna's hand reached for Theo's. Did he feel the wonder of the night too?

'All right?' She knew he was smiling even though it was too dark to see.

'So all right, I could walk all night.'

'Don't you believe it,' he laughed softly. 'Santa would wonder where you'd got to if you weren't safely tucked up when he came.'

Never had Manningtor Park been so well represented. Even tightly packed together on the long pews they more than half filled the church.

Strangely the walk home seemed further, the stars less bright.

155

Already it was Christmas Day. Then, in what looking back on it seemed like a blink of an eye, it was over. Dank January took over. It needed a stout heart to 'keep the flag flying', as Matt said when on the first day of the New Year they came to the end of ten days into which so much normality had been packed that never a moment had been truly normal.

It was in April when Anna read through her finished work, then bundled up the typed pages and locked them in a filing cabinet. Putting the key away and looking at the empty roller of the typewriter she had a feeling of loss. For months 'her people' had been waiting for her. It was too soon to put them from her mind and draw others together; just as after losing someone one loves, time must be allowed for grieving, so now she was in a void.

From the window she could see Christopher's pram in the spring sunshine. Too early in the season for wasps, but Nanny had covered it with its protecting net so that Tibbles, her tabby cat, wouldn't decide the pillow was a comfortable place to curl up. The sight, combined with the empty feeling of loss, was irresistible.

Five minutes later, having told Nanny not to worry about a missing pram, as proud as any young mother could be, she turned out of the gate with the intention of walking to the village. She was about halfway there when she saw the stranger coming towards her. A tall man, well built, something indefinably different about his style of dress setting him apart from anyone local.

As they drew nearer she was conscious that he was watching her closely. Her mind jumped to veiled warnings of spies, people who pretended to be what they weren't. Careless Talk Costs Lives, the noticeboards in Deremouth were a constant reminder. While his pace slowed, hers quickened.

Chapter Eight

'Sister Anna! Forgive me if I'm wrong – but I'm not, am I?'

Her scurrying pace was halted, even though half-formed fears lurked. He must have been making enquiries about her – how else could he know her name?

'I'm afraid you're wrong. I'm not a sister of any kind.'

'But you *are* Anna? Theo's wife.'

Her doubts vanished. She found herself looking at him closely, conscious of a strange feeling of déjà vu. Hard on the heels of that came the realisation of the resemblance between this man and Theo. Both had the same dark eyes and thick lashes, both had the same olive complexion, although he hadn't the perfect symmetry of Theo's handsome features. He was larger built too. Yet in her mind there was no doubt that he must be part of the family.

'Are you a relation – a cousin or something?' But surely if he were he would have been at Uncle Sidney's funeral. Amongst so many elderly relatives, he was hardly a person she would have forgotten.

'Something, but not a cousin. Didn't I call you sister Anna? I'm Sylvia's brother, home from the big US of A to join in the fight. Today's a surprise, I haven't told anyone I'm coming, not Sylvia, not even Nanny. I hope you'll find me a place to lay my weary head for a few days. In fact, I shall be in a right hole if you turn me away. I've already been into the recruitment office in Southampton –' then with an utterly Theo-like grin '– and assured them their troubles are over, I'm right with them. I gave them Manningtor Park as my address.' Finally, with a complete change of expression, he added, '*Your* house, Anna. You don't mind? I ought to have done the right thing, visited

157

first and asked permission of Theo's wife. But the truth is, when I think of England I think of Manningtor as home.'

'Of course it's your home. Sylvia's never suggested you might be coming back to join up. She'll be thrilled. Lance? Isn't that what they call you? I've never known a Lance.'

'Nor yet a Lancelot, I'll bet. Lance does me fine. Mother had Spanish roots, but she loved all things English. Even King Arthur and his Round Table.'

'Lancelot is a beautiful name, its full of chivalry. I was reared on King Arthur too.'

'So, little sister, we have good grounding for friendship. Are you going anywhere special with this young son of yours?'

'No,' she shook her head then added with a laugh, 'I expect I just thought if I pushed him to the village I'd be sure to meet people who wanted to see him and admire him.'

Lance gave the sleeping child his full attention. 'He looks to me a very fine fellow. I've not been an uncle before. Won't just *my* admiration do? We could walk back to the Park together. Do you think he'd have any objection if I rested my case across his buggy? I'll push him for you if you like.' A most unusual offer! A grown man to push a pram! That was something even Theo had never done on the brief occasions he'd been home, proud though he was of his son. In that he was no different from other young fathers. It was an era when there was a clear, firm division of male and female responsibilities, and pushing the pram was not far short of cooking the meals or doing the ironing. As they walked back up the lane she had the chance to study Lance Franklyn; she realised now that his resemblance to Theo came from their mother. All she had known about him was that he was ten years or so older than Theo and, that he lived in America where he'd married a local girl.

'How did you know I was called Anna? And how did you guess that's who I was?'

'I cheated,' he laughed. 'I've seen your picture. Sylvia sent me a snap of you and Theo. Granted it was taken when you first came to Manningtor, but add to that this young fellow in his buggy and who else could it be on such an unfrequented lane? But in fact it was more than the picture. Nanny writes often, you know. She tells me all about things at home. The others write sometimes, but it's Nanny who is my real link.'

158

'I expect she writes to Theo too. Nanny's a dear.'

'Indeed she is.'

Her mind leapt to her grandfather. So often he would use such an expression: 'Indeed I am', 'that is indeed the case', or simply 'Indeed', his manner of speaking the single word in reply to some comment or other of hers clearly telling her that her opinion wasn't worthy of consideration. But Lance's 'Indeed she is' was quite different. Something in the way he said it reminded her of the years he'd spent in the United States. And that was strange, for he spoke with no trace of an accent.

'Well?' he asked, the question in his voice making her realise how hard she'd been staring at him.

Thankful he couldn't read her mind and know her sudden confusion, she took possession of herself and answered with friendly assurance.

'Well enough. I was trying to decide why it is you so remind me of Theo. Except that you're both dark you aren't really very much alike. Yet you *are*.' Then, laughing, 'I don't usually stare at strangers. It's just that you seem familiar.'

'Let's take that as a good sign, shall we? Tell me, sister Anna, have you any other brothers?'

'No. Grandpa is the only family I have – well, he was until Theo brought me here. But now of course I have loads. Lance, you've been gone a long time. Nothing stays the same. You know that Theo and Matt are away, but it's more than that. I expect everyone will seem changed – even I can see how Aunt Kath has aged since Uncle Sidney died. And the house – it's full of children who all sound as if they wear size nine shoes, but they're great fun and I think they're happy at Manningtor.'

'Nothing is the same anywhere. After I docked yesterday I found a recruitment centre first of all. By the time I'd done that and arranged for transport of my luggage – that's on its way to Manningtor too, OK?' and hardly waiting for her nod, 'I found there were no trains to the west. So I went to London. Your trains are eerie once it gets dark. Blinds pulled down and only a spooky blue light bulb in the compartment, not bright enough to read the newspaper. Newspaper? Is that what it was? Jut one double sheet, four pages. Back in the States we think we know about how things are here, but you can't know till you're part of it.'

'You make us sound horribly deprived. And we're not, not a

159

bit. In a funny sort of way I think people welcome the fact that we have to tighten our belts and can't live like we used to, especially those with someone in the forces. I'd hate to live in comfort and luxury with Theo away. So I'm glad the Government has brought in food rationing, it sort of eases my conscience that I'm being so useless. Not that I have to worry about eking the ration out, and Ethel does wonders, you'd hardly know the difference. Francis has three women workers – Women's Land Army they call it, did you know? – and the Ministry of Agriculture is making him dig up a lot of his grazing land so that it can be put down to cereals.' Suddenly aware of how much she'd been talking – and all about themselves – she glanced at him as he pushed the pram, wanting to ask about *his* life and realising how little she knew about him. 'I've talked enough, now tell me about what it's like in America. Your family must be thinking of you and wondering how you're getting on.' It was a lead for him to tell her something about his background, for she didn't want him to suspect he was talked of so seldom that she knew nothing but the bare facts.

'Maybe.' One word that drew a firm line under any further questions.

'Are you going into the Army like Matt?'

'Not on your life, I'm not. For one thing, if I did join the Army I would hardly be like Matt. I had a letter from dear old Thelma, proud as a peacock, telling me that as soon as he was given his commission he started up the stairway to success. And so he should. Depots can't be that different whether they house a fleet of coaches to take women to the shops or lorries to take men to the line. No, for me it has to be flying. I've flown for years, a bit like Theo at the local club I dare say. So the Royal Air Force will have the benefit of my enthusiastic support. Theo and me both, with the two of us knocking hell out of the enemy, this war can't last long!' His laugh was full of confidence. No wonder she felt so at home with him: he was more like Theo by the minute.

'Is it the same in America as here? Lots of men who join up have their jobs held open for them – some even have their salaries made up if what the services pay is less than they were earning. But I suppose, with America not at war it doesn't work like that for you?'

It was his turn to study her. Was she just a natural chatterbox, talking easily and naturally to any stranger? Something told him

160

she wasn't. Of course it was years since he'd seen Theo, eight years to be precise. But even at that age his young half brother had shown signs of being every woman's darling. Yet he'd married a funny little scrap like this. Funny? No, just unexpected. What eyes, though – huge, with their dark smudges of lashes, eyes that were a mirror to her thoughts. A funny little face, high cheekbones, pointed chin. And look at her hands (his glance went to the one that rested on the end of the pram handle as he pushed), so slender, like a child's. Not a bit what he would have expected for the man Theo showed promise of becoming.

'It was different for me.' But he didn't explain why it was different and, curious though she was, she could hardly ask. 'Did Theo appoint a bailiff before he went?' he turned the subject on its head again.

'No. Just me. He trained me, so I'm much more use than some outsider would be. We can do without that at Manningtor.'

Ah-ha, so there was more to his little sister than met the eye.

'And you enjoy doing it? Or is it a labour of love for Theo?'

'I've never divided the two in my mind. Of course I do it for Theo, but – even that's not the real truth. I do it for Manningtor. I do it for myself. Wouldn't you, if you were living there?'

And again that one word, 'Maybe.'

They walked on in silence, a comfortable silence. She'd been told nothing more about his life in America; and he seemed uncurious about how she came to be mistress of the place he thought of as home.

'Wow,' he breathed as they turned off the lane and into the drive, the house coming into view at the top of the rise. 'Just the same. Nothing ever changes Manningtor.'

'Maybe.' She stole his expression, wondering whether the influx of sixty-five girls would change his opinion.

It was Thelma who saw him first, recognising him even though they were only halfway up the drive. It could hardly be said that she ran to meet them, for running was beyond her capabilities and had been for almost as many years as he'd been away and she'd been steadily and comfortably expanding. But moving with speed that showed her delight, she blundered down the drive to meet them.

And so he was taken back into the bosom of the family, even Nanny thrown off balance by the excitement of his return.

It was chance that made Theo ring them that lunch time. Nearest to the hall, Thelma answered it, calling to Anna as soon as she recognised his voice.

'It's Theo for you, Anna,' then as Anna ran down the stairs from the nursery where she'd been spooning a mess of mashed food into Christopher's mouth so that Nanny could be part of the excitement in the drawing room, 'You'll never guess who's here, Theo. Out of the blue he came. Lance. He's come home to join up. Here's Anna.'

'Hello, I was with Christo.'

'Anna, I've not much small change so I can't waste time. Give Lance a shout for me.'

So as he fed his shillings into the slot, all Anna heard of his call was odd sentences of an animated conversation about the joys of flying. It was unfair of her to feel resentful of the 'returning hero' as none too kindly she thought of Lance; it was unfair of her to forget what an easy companion he'd been as they'd walked home together. If she were honest, she knew all that. But it hurt less to lay the blame on him rather than accept that Theo never phoned home simply because it was *her* he wanted, simply because he was as lonely for her as she was for him.

Young men were being trained to fly, but Lance had a head start. Within days he received instructions to attend for a medical examination. After that there was nothing but to wait for joining instructions, something that soon followed.

During that short waiting period there was one weekend when both Theo and Matt managed to get home. A family reunion, strengthened by shared memories and now with a new member of the clan who at seven and a half months old was already firmly established. After a year and a half, despite the way she handled the running of the estate and Theo's obvious pride in her capabilities, Anna knew she would always stand just outside the magic orbit.

She'd taken great pains with her appearance for Theo's short stay. A visit to Deremouth, where her hair had been razor cut encouraging its natural inclination to wave; delight that she was slim and unchanged from the days before she'd had to share her body with Christopher; out-of-character hours spent trying on clothes in the privacy of her bedroom, deciding what she'd be

162

wearing when he arrived, what to wear for dinner in the evening (enhanced by what she still thought of as 'his mother's pearls'). A word of praise would wipe out all the disappointments of the weeks he'd been away, temporarily make her forget how often he made her aware that she was no more important to him than any other family member, never the one he specifically asked for when he phoned. To him she was just part of Manningtor, someone he could comfortably take for granted, someone who would be the same whether or not he paid her any attention. They must all be as aware of it as she was herself. Pride determined her to make an effort with her appearance.

That weekend Matt was home in time for dinner on the Friday evening; Theo wasn't expected until later. After a sunny day there was a chill in the evening air and Gwen had lit the fire in the drawing room. Coal was short, but home-grown logs gave out a lovely warmth and sent shadows to dance on the ceiling away from the light of a single standard lamp. Anna was tempted to go up to the bedroom where, with open curtains and no light, she could watch for the first sign of the car's dimmed lights. By nine o'clock temptation got too much for her and, expecting that no one would notice her going, she slipped out of the room and climbed the stairs.

'She's anxious that he's late, I expect,' Thelma said, safe in her own contentment. Dear Matt looked quite handsome in his uniform. It had been the same at Christmas; when he'd first arrived she'd felt quite shy. Silly of her. Dear Matt, underneath he was still the same. After all, she'd never expected to be part of his work with the coaches so how could it make any difference to them that now his days were filled with thoughts of Army vehicles. Such a shame he couldn't have been stationed somewhere close by, but he really looked remarkably well. Younger somehow. But then uniform did that to a man. How nice it would be later to have him all to herself, to cuddle up to him, warm and secure. Secure? As if his being away could ever change that. And look at the way her own days had altered in this last year helping with the WVS. And then there were the first aid classes she took with the girls from the school. A year ago she wouldn't have had that sort of knowledge. Of course, she mustn't let him feel that she'd moved on without him, for that wouldn't be true. But it did one good to know one was useful. And she really did enjoy organising things and seeing they worked. Later on, when they were upstairs and all by themselves, she would tell him about it all. She looked forward to that, sure that he would be as proud of her as she was of him.

Their conversation drifted over her as her thoughts wandered. '. . . still only sixteen,' his words broke into her reverie. 'Let's hope this lot's over before another year's through. He won't wait to be called, that was plain from the way he wrote.'

Sam! Oh no, please God, not Sam. He's just a child. War is for grown-ups. Sixteen now – at seventeen and a half he could volunteer. No, not Sam, please, hurt me how You like, make anything bad You choose happen to *me*, but don't hurt my Sam.

Upstairs Anna shivered. She'd dressed with such excitement, knowing she looked her best in a fitting green dress, the pearls and high-heeled shoes. Theo's pride in her at his uncle's funeral had made a lasting impression. But now, watching for the first sign of the shielded lights of the Riley as it turned in at the gates, some of the anticipation gave way to a nameless, numbed fright. No wonder she shivered. Going to the wardrobe she pulled a thick jacket from its hanger and slipped her arms into the sleeves. So another ten minutes passed.

Her thoughts wandered along the gallery to the nursery, the pull of the sleeping baby too much to resist. She needed the warmth of looking at him and loving him, knowing full well that at this time of the evening he was never awake. Another hour or so and it might be a different story. He was no more perfect than any other baby: some nights he slept, some nights he was fractious. The difference was between her and the average young mother, for it was Nanny whose nights were sometimes disturbed. Soundlessly she opened her bedroom door and crept along the long gallery hung with portraits of family members long dead – probably part of far-off generations who had risen from nothing to build the first Sullivan fortune and meant their success to be remembered. Passing them without a glance Anna crept into the nursery at the start of the west wing. From one of the dormitories came the sound of hushed talking. Half an hour past lights out, but girls in the upper class considered the night still young and usually spent the last hour or two of their day in the close harmony of their own torchlit world. The confidences exchanged and the dreams shared were of far greater importance to them than the compulsory revision period that had preceded supper. The nursery looked towards Home Farm – although like every other room in the house, the window was curtained to thwart even a glimmer of light's escape. In fact the flame from the single nightlight that floated in a dish of water would have been hard pressed to excite even Warden Morton on his nightly pilgrimage of hope.

Nanny had put the baby into his cot wrapped in the accepted way, arms to his side and cocooned in a shawl.

How can you sleep so sweetly, tied up like a parcel? Anna asked silently as she leant over the cot, drawn to him by a love like nothing she'd ever anticipated. These moments alone with him were precious beyond words. And just as she so often did, silently she spoke her thoughts to him. He's not come yet, she shared her disappointment not needing to explain that the 'he' was Theo . . . I've been watching. When we talked about having you – making it work and all that – long ago, when Theo married me – oh I know it wasn't actually *you*, that's what people might think, but it *was*. For me it's become like that now. But that's silly. As soon as I lost the *you* that didn't happen, we wanted me to get pregnant again with the *you* that did. You're really why I'm here, you know that? Of course you know it, I've told you lots of times. He sort of loves me, I think, because of *you*. Tonight he's going to be home.

Leaning nearer and, too lightly to disturb him, she touched his tightly wrapped shoulder.

I'm so lucky, her silent monologue went on, this time to herself, not to the sleeping baby. Theo's coming home, and look at Christo, thank You, thank You for making things like they are for me. Well, no. With Theo away nothing can ever be perfect. But think what must it be like to be in France, supposing we lived there with no channel between us and the fighting. There must be tiny babies just like Christo – how can their mothers bear it? Please help them, keep them safe, make them strong. Imagine having no sea around them to keep them safe. Invasion – some scare-mongers talk about Hitler trying to invade here. Barbed wire on the beaches, lookout towers, but none of that seems real enough to make me believe it might happen. They'd be beaten back before they could land. But France wasn't surrounded by sea to keep it safe . . . and think of Denmark and Norway. Please help the poor people there, give them courage, don't let anything hurt the babies. It's too dreadful to contemplate. And Theo, supposing Theo gets sent overseas. But he won't. Bombers fly from this country. Theo taking a plane to drop bombs on people – people like you and me, Christo. He wouldn't purposely hurt anyone, you know how he is, he loves to do things to please.

If an inner honesty reminded her that giving pleasure to others stemmed from his own need to see their appreciation and to hear their praise, she loved him far too well to admit it.

'So this is where you're hiding.' In a 'mustn't disturb the baby' whisper, Nanny spoke as she came quietly into the room. 'Didn't you hear him come?'

'You mean Theo's home? But I was in our room until –' Until how long ago? Lost in thoughts, lost in adoring wonder, how long had she been with Christo?

'I just looked in to check the wee man. I wonder you didn't wake him leaning over him like you were. Ten minutes or more Theo's been home. Fancy, you never heard the commotion and excitement.'

'He must have wondered wherever I was.' Subconsciously Anna tried to will that to have been the case.

''Midst all the hullabaloo, I doubt it. My word though, he looks fine. The two of them in uniform and before long instead of two it'll be three. Breaks my heart to think the state we've made of the world – for all the fine promises.' A sniff, her way of drawing a line under that train of thought and following another. 'Why, child, you'll get chilblains, going around on these floors in your stockinged feet.' A warning snort from Christopher gave notice that he was becoming aware of his surroundings. 'Sshhh,' to Anna as if she'd been doing all the talking.

Escaping the room and with no thought of chilblains, Anna ran down the wide, shallow stairs, pulling off her coat as she went, then dropping it on a chair in the hall – a hall she longer saw as vast and overwhelming but simply as part of home.

'I didn't hear the car!' She burst into the drawing room, where her voice was drowned in the buzz of conversation. At the centre of it all was Theo. They were drawn to him as if by a magnet. Each time Anna saw him she was struck afresh as if she were looking at him for the first time. It was something indefinable,

166

something more than handsome features. He thrived on adulation and, despite Matt being home for no more than a seventy-two-hour leave and Lance being with them for the first time in years, yet it was he who was the centre of attention. Just for a second Anna was irritated by their undisguised and possessive excitement as they feasted their eyes on him – but only for a second before joy, adoration, hero-worship, perhaps a combination of all three, left room for nothing else.

Thelma was the first to notice her.

'Where were you, dear? Theo was just coming to find you. I'm afraid we sidetracked him with all the excitement.'

True or false? Knowing sensitive Thelma as well as she did, Anna wasn't prepared to look for the answer.

'How's the elf?' Theo beamed at her. 'Don't grow any taller, do you?' So he might have greeted his young sister – except that in his case his young sister was certainly no elf. Standing close by his side, Alex looked from one to the other, her expression inscrutable.

'I forgot to go back for my shoes,' Anna half explained her stockinged feet.

'And I thought you'd be at the head of the red carpet waiting for me.' His teasing expression told her – told all of them – as clearly as any words that he knew just how her day had been geared towards the moment of his coming. With the exception of Alex, the family smiled on him.

Alex was an enigma to Anna. Always friendly when their paths crossed, which was surprisingly infrequently, she lived amongst the staff of the school and was seldom with the family, treating her old home as she would have any other establishment large enough and generous enough to house the children of Chiltern House. Sometimes Anna suspected that she was less happy with her relatives than with her working colleagues, always wary, ready and confident to rebuff criticism. But tonight she brushed all thoughts of Theo's sister aside. Only *he* mattered. Just his presence amongst them made the talk more animated, heightened their awareness of the special importance of the evening.

'I was with Christo.' Saying it took away the feeling of inadequacy that had held her apart from the family and made her just a girl too overjoyed on hearing he was home even to remember to go back to her room for her shoes! Again she was

167

bending over the baby's tiny, sleeping form; again she seemed to smell the sweet powdery fragrance of him. When *he* gave her that beaming smile that showed the four milk teeth that had just appeared, it wasn't because she was the girl Theo had brought home as his wife, it was because she was *her*, the centre of his world.

'Is he awake?' Theo asked hopefully.

'No. And if he were, Nanny wouldn't thank us to get him excited at this time of evening.' Purposely she said 'us' as if that claimed him, pulled him into their own magic circle and reminded him that he was more than 'the young rascal' as he was so often affectionately called by the family and Nanny.

Matt, Kath, Thelma, Sylvia and Francis probably didn't realise how patently obvious was their look of indulgent fondness; to them he was the much-loved child grown to be a much-loved man. But Anna sensed that she wasn't the only one to have noticed it. Lance missed nothing, so she avoided meeting his gaze lest it told her that he read her thoughts and knew that she resented coming second best. As for Alex, who knew what went on in her mind? Her expression was aloof. But one thing Anna was sure, even though she had no concrete evidence: Alex's love for Theo was possessive, jealous that anyone might usurp the place she'd always held in his affection as they'd grown up with no real parents. Yet she'd never been hostile, so how was it Anna detected an undercurrent?

'You ought to have something on your feet, dear,' Thelma urged. 'Away from the fireside the floor is enough to give you chilblains. Why don't you run up and get your shoes?'

With all her might Anna willed Theo to hold out his arm to draw her to where he stood in front of the burning logs, the others either seated or standing round him. He probably didn't even hear what Thelma said, let alone detect the silent message Anna was sending him. What chance had she against the 'life in the services talk' that already lifted the returning heroes onto a plane outside the realms of reach? And when she went out of the room she knew he didn't even notice. Upstairs she sat on the edge of the bed, slipping her feet into her shoes and letting her mind run riot with thoughts of how different it would have been had he not been heir to Manningtor – and the family that went with it. Most people would consider her invested legacy a fortune. So it was, even if it would soon have been swallowed up if she'd been responsible for the upkeep of an estate like this. Enough though to have enabled them to buy their own home, somewhere perhaps not even as grand as Dunsford House. It would have been their own and he would have come home this evening just to her and Christo. All her life she indulged in daydreams, and here was one that had enough substance to soften her mouth into a smile. Downstairs he belonged to the family; her time would come.

And so it did. He'd not been home since Christmas, a time when he'd felt himself slightly ousted by the demands of his young son. Now her body was her own again, as slim and straight as when he'd first known her. Willing, passionate, sensual, she was all those things just as he'd known she would be. In the intimacy of those hours of night she clung to every waking second, wanting to capture it, hold on to it to relive when he'd gone. For her, the hold the family had on him had no power to diminish the wonder of those hours; for him it ceased to exist as soon as he was alone with her. But then, hadn't that always been his way? Accepting every gift life offered, glorying in the moment, abandoning himself to every hedonistic delight, every thrill of adventure, and always his satisfaction made complete by the knowledge that his presence was responsible for someone else's obvious pleasure.

Next day he crammed every moment full. He galloped on the moor with Sylvia, he rode round the estate with Anna, openly proud of the way she was managing. Finding Kath alone by a fire that to everyone else was unnecessary on a sunny April day, he sat with her and reminisced, looking at faded photographs. Then he went to the farm to listen while Francis talked to him about the changes made under new Ministry rules. This was *home*, the very air he breathed here was like no other. Contentment cleared his mind of things he didn't want to remember.

That first morning he went to talk to Nanny

'No use pretending it's me you've come to talk to,' she greeted him when he found her in the nursery dressing Christopher after his morning bath. 'It's this wee man. And quite right too. Just wait

169

while I pin his nappy, then slip him into his pram suit, and you can hold him for yourself.' Quickly and efficiently she finished dressing her tiny charge. 'My word, but what a handsome young man he is in his new togs. Mrs Matt made him this rig-out, but your Anna said he wasn't to wear it till you came home. Now then, while I empty the bath water you and him just get yourselves acquainted. And where is your little Anna? Most days she's here to see him go down for his morning sleep.'

'I've no idea, Nanny. I've not seen her since breakfast. I went riding with Sylvia.'

He took his young son in his arms, holding him high across his shoulder.

'Not like that, boy. It's a baby you're holding, not a sack of tatties. That's the way, now keep your hand firm on the top of his back, make sure you don't let his head loll. Best keep your chin against him, makes the wee man feel safe.' Then, carrying the small bath carefully so that she didn't slop the water, she turned her back on them. Her manner was brusque, there was nothing to hint that she wanted these next moments to be special for her darling Theo.

His own son, flesh of his flesh, one of these days he'll grow up to be the owner of this place. One of these days, but not yet, not for many many years, please God. Bring him home safe from the beastly war. Not going the way we'd all hoped. Hoped? Took it for granted, more likely. Once the British Lion roared it would put an end to all the troubles in Europe, that's what we believed. Well, we were wrong. Oh, we'll get there in the end, but it's not going to be a walkover. Thank God for that strip of ocean, it's giving the country time to get its act in order. But what about the poor boys out there in France. Please dear God don't let anything happen to Theo, don't take him away from us all. Bless the boy, in there with his little Christo. And Lance, before you can say knife he'll be in that blue uniform too. Dear boy, fancy coming home all those miles to fight for his country. Because that's what it is, this will always be his country – live out there as long as he likes. Not changed a jot. He might have come back sounding like a Yankee, but not Lance. Keep Lance safe too. And Mr Matt. Is this what everyone is saying, us and the women out in Germany too? Are we all asking You to take care of our own? Oh, damn all men and their stupid, intolerant ways. Put a few more women

170

in charge of things and the world wouldn't get in this state. I wonder where young Anna's hiding herself. You'd think with the boy home she would be with him. Jealous of the time he gives to the family I dare say. Silly girl. She ought to know him better. Our dear Theo will divide himself up making sure no one is left out, yes that's the way it's always been. And each one of them will feel – feel warmed by being with him. Like a flame he draws them. And Anna too. I'll just take a peak and see if he and the boy are getting acquainted – won't let him hear me.

Clearly they were. Only for a moment did Nanny indulge in letting herself watch through the crack of the not quite closed door. Theo had changed Christopher's position and was holding him lying against the crook of one arm, a position the baby seemed to enjoy if the way he kicked his legs was any indication. A beaming smile, his mouth open wide and his trembling tongue protruding. Nanny felt a sting of tears as she watched and perhaps the effect on Theo wasn't very different, for he hoisted the warm, wool-clad bundle back against his shoulder, rubbing his cheek against the downy head. Perhaps it was loving him so dearly that gave her her perception: why couldn't the silly boy – dear, silly boy – give little Anna the love she deserved?

With only two full days at home Theo had so much to pack into each hour. It was as if he divided himself into sections, one for each member of the family, believing he did it because his being with them was important to them; taking family for granted, he wasn't even aware how much he depended on their never-failing affection. His love for Manningtor was something quite different. Standing at the bottom of the sloping lawn, he looked at the great house, willingly letting himself be filled with pride that *he* was its custodian; one day it would pass to Christopher and on through generations to come. Never had the thought struck him so forcibly as it did during that weekend in the spring of 1940. It was out of character for Theo to let his mind dwell on the serious side of life, but in that moment (and, in truth, more often than he would admit) he was haunted by a reality he couldn't escape. Would his luck hold? Each debriefing following a bombing sortie someone would have failed to return. What was ahead? Before he could pull it back, his imagination had carried him to a world that had become hideously familiar: the cockpit of his loaded bomber, a plane that

171

comprised the whole world for him and his crew for those hours of shared, unspoken and unspeakable terror. The horror of what they were doing was as inescapable as the knowledge that they had no choice. And always, as beneath them they saw the havoc and knew it spelt disaster and death, was the thought of home. Theo had never been a praying man: school chapel, visits to the village church at Christmas and Easter, in a life where every plum fell into his lap he'd felt no need for an Almighty. But that had been in the carefree, fun days when his world had been young. He was ashamed of his fervent prayers that Manningtor and everyone in it would be unhurt. And never had he asked it more sincerely than as he stood alone looking at the centre of his universe. But there was Lance! Thankfully he pulled his thoughts onto happier ground.

'What about a drive out to the club?' he called. It was the first thought that came to him, his lifeline to sanity.

Home for just those same seventy-two hours, Matt used his time differently. He spent most of the Saturday with the men at the coach company, only in the evening relaxing at home. Not for him time spent alone with any one of them, not even Thelma. It was almost as if he'd never been away – he slotted comfortably into his allotted place just as they expected, for Matt had always been a placid man, his presence giving any gathering an atmosphere of unexciting stability.

Anna tried to will Theo to want her with him: 'I'm going to check the boat, are you coming?' or 'I'm going to look in at the club for an hour, why not come with me?' To imagine him simply saying, 'Let's get away from the others, let's be by ourselves' was beyond even her wildest dreams. In truth, no matter how hard she concentrated on putting the thoughts into his head, no such invitations came. When he went to the boat he waited until after school lessons finished so that Alex could go with him; when he went to the flying club he took Lance. If any of them were reading her thoughts, Anna had an uncomfortable feeling that it was Lance. She believed that although he was one of the family yet, like her, he remained on the edge. They welcomed him warmly, they went out of their way to see the years he'd spent away didn't leave him feeling excluded. Perhaps it was their warm hospitality that emphasised the fact he'd grown apart from them. No one smothered Matt with consideration and cordiality,

172

it wasn't necessary. As for Theo, there was nothing unusual in the way they all claimed his company. Only the nights belonged to Anna, hours of intimate loving. It was impossible to ignore the suspicion that nudged her as, her passion unleashed, all control was lost. Was he doing this to please her, was it because he needed the assurance that he had the power to lift her to such sublime ecstasy? No, no, she told herself, it's the same for him too. It has to be, it has to be. Only afterwards, trying to hold on to memories that would live with her when he was gone and she was alone, did some of the joy leave her. You could no more hold Theo than you could hold a moonbeam.

She was thinking something on those lines as she watched him striding down the drive with Alex. They'd not said they were going out. She'd been up in the nursery collecting Christo, imagining pushing him to the village with Theo on the Sunday afternoon. Now here she was, the baby in her arms, the sunshine beckoning her outside and Theo gone.

Impossible to hold Theo, impossible to hold back the precious hours of the weekend. By Monday afternoon he and Matt had both gone. By evening it was as if the weekend had never happened. Yet, had they but known it, it was a brief time encapsulated in all their memories, something that was never to be repeated.

They were no different from any other family during that first full year of war. Each news bulletin was listened to on the wireless, their resolve strengthening even though they felt powerless. Patriotism had always been accepted without the need for flag waving; yet now it took on a new outward show. Those who had flagpoles, as did Manningtor Park, flew the Union Jack; perhaps it was a sign of national unity or perhaps they did it in a show of faith for Matt, Theo and by the end of May, for Lance too.

So much happened in the country over the months of that summer. Neville Chamberlain stood down as Prime Minister and was replaced by Winston Churchill. No wonder families gathered around their wireless sets, his words adding steel to their determination. When France fell and the bedraggled remnants of the British Expeditionary Force were brought home in that armada of little boats, instead of feeling defeated the blood of the people was up: '. . . fight in the air . . . fight on the land . . . fight on the

173

beaches . . . we will never surrender.' The words rang in every house and in every heart. That phoney war of the first few months was over.

By the middle of June German troops entered Paris and, in Manningtor just as all across the country, the family listened to the news that France had made a desperate appeal to America. Two days later, the appeal declined, they heard the bald statement that France had asked for an armistice.

'So they've given in.' Kath sat very straight as Thelma reached to turn off the wireless.

'Poor souls,' Thelma's kindly blue eyes were defused with tears. 'Poor dear souls. Mother, how must they feel tonight? People like us, people with husbands at the front, with children –' then remembering Anna – 'with tiny babies like little Christopher.'

Frightened to go down that road, Anna allowed no doubts to muddy her thinking. 'Well, now we know where we stand. There's only one way to give France back to its own people, *we* have to do it.' Words, just words. What was *she* doing, half looking after her own baby, overseeing a well-staffed estate that if she were honest didn't take more than a few hours a day, pouring out her loneliness in another book to follow the others and be locked away in the office drawer? What help was any of that towards winning the war? Sylvia worked as hard as any land girl on the farm, for by that time most of the men with the strength of youth had either joined up or else found better paid work with Deremouth's boat builders; Thelma gave hours of each day to the WVS, visited the houses where the evacuees were living and worked for the Philanthropic Society. Now that petrol was short, she often travelled on her bicycle. Thelma was certainly doing *her* bit for the war effort.

With France out of the war, England was next on Hitler's list. Each day that precise voice on the wireless told them of air attacks, bald announcements of how many enemy planes had been shot down, how many British ones had been lost.

'Thank God Theo doesn't fly one of those fighters.' Who was Thelma trying to cheer, especially when Lance was attached to a fighter station?

Nonetheless Anna clutched at her words, trying not to be irritated by their stupidity. A fighter or a bomber . . . imagine

174

being fired at in a plane laden with explosives . . . no, don't imagine it, please God keep him safe. And I do nothing. I must do *something*, I must think of *something*. If I took a job in the dock I should be failing Manningtor, and that I'll never, never do. Even Aunt Kath knits khaki mittens.

It was what she read in the paper about the Spitfire drive that decided her. Being married to the serving squire of Manningtor had its advantages: it ensured that when she telephoned Deremouth Town Hall and asked to speak to the Town Clerk her call was put straight through to him. And so it was that before August was out there was erected on the west-facing side of the tower of the Town Hall a wooden column painted as if it were a ladder. On it was charted the progress made by the community in the 'Spitfire Fund'. The Town Council took credit for organising the fund, but that didn't trouble Anna in the least. Perhaps without her, and after many committee meetings and discussions, the end result might have been the same; but *she* knew she had been responsible. And that was only the beginning. She visited all the schools in the district (starting of course with Chiltern House!), found she enjoyed talking to the assembled children and, more important, even from the poorest home each Monday morning they would all bring their 'Spitfire Money' to morning assembly. Some might bring as much as a shilling, some as little as a penny, but 'doing their bit' was as important to one as another. She hoped the young men who took the Spitfires up in the air knew the loyal trust of those who depended on them.

It was November, a day when the fine rain seemed not to fall from above but to sweep horizontally across the country from the south-west in the way Devon knows so well. The unemotional voice of the BBC announced the bare facts of the air raids that were designed to bring the country to its knees: 'Heavy raids last night on the towns of . . .' and then the number of aircraft brought down. London, Plymouth, Liverpool and so many more; Deremouth with its boatyard amongst them. Locally, bombs may have been unloaded haphazardly from a plane returning from a raid on Plymouth or, more likely, gone astray from their Deremouth target. Either way, there was a crater on the banks of the Dere, another just inland of the main Exeter road and a third just beyond Home Farm. The drone of heavily loaded aircraft was familiar north and south, east and west. If it was intended to break the spirit of the people, it was certainly not succeeding. But then what attacks ever have? If the country's original confidence had bordered on arrogance, now it gave way to anger. Yet arrogance, anger, grief, anxiety, on that November afternoon, the predominant mood must surely have been depression. Who could fight it when daylight had scarcely pierced the gloom, when the wind was catching at the fallen leaves and carrying them on that same horizontal flight as it did the never-ending rain?

It wasn't quite half past three yet already it was too dark for Thelma to see to work at her sewing machine. Yesterday she'd called on Ethel Miller at her cottage in the village to enquire after a little Londoner whose mother had been killed. Ethel's husband was a merchant seaman and 'making two ends meet' wasn't easy. Thelma had found her turning the cuffs of a thoroughly worn-out but spotlessly white blouse belonging to her evacuee lodger.

'Give me something the right size,' Thelma had told her, 'no matter how worn out. I just want it for a pattern. I believe I can find something in the cupboard to make up a blouse or two for the poor mite.' So here she was in what was known as 'the workroom' at Manningtor, setting in the sleeves of Creation No.1. The double sheet would allow for two, or more likely three, blouses and the remnants of the material would make good clean rags. Screwing up her eyes, and thinking not for the first time that she ought to see about getting spectacles for close work, she was perhaps the only person in the house not depressed by the gloom outside.

I'll just see to the blackout, then I can put the light on. Fancy half past three and having to put up the blackout. Still, I mean to get this done before I have to tidy myself up for dinner. My word, but how things change. Tidy up for dinner. Wash my hands and brush my hair and put on a different cardigan, that's about all it will amount to. Funny really, because we have plenty of clothes hanging in our wardrobes. It's as if to dress like we used to would be saying that for us nothing was changed.

For just a matter of seconds she stood in front of the window, the cord of the heavy blind in her hand. Then she was back in control. Who would have expected Matt to be the one to be sent abroad? At his age he could have stayed safely at home; instead all there had been was one week's embarkation leave and since then – silence. If he'd been sent to North Africa (keep him safe, please, I beg You keep him safe) surely there would have been a letter home by now. How long could it possibly take to get to North Africa? But if the troopship had been torpedoed – no, don't think of it, don't give it a chance. Tomorrow there might be a letter. Funny how much they missed his phone calls. He always used to phone so regularly each Tuesday and Saturday evening. Not for a long talk, that wasn't necessary, but just to make sure they were all right. Now, naughty Theo, sometimes he'd ring two or three times in a week, then they'd hear nothing for a fortnight or more. But then Theo was different, bless his heart.

Whose car was that coming up the drive? There was no logic in imagining it might be Matt. From there her mind jumped to Theo just as, although she didn't know it, Anna's did from the window of the estate office below. Of the two women, Thelma overcame her disappointment the quicker. Lance! How lovely. But not quite lovely enough to distract her from her sewing. With the blackout in place and the light on she continued to pin and tack the sleeves in place determined that the next day she would cycle down to Ethel Miller's cottage with at least one finished article.

Anna watched Lance get out of his car and climb the steps to the portico, then she picked up the telephone and put a call through to the farm office, imagining Sylvia's pleasure and trying to fight down her own disappointment that it was the wrong man wearing that blue uniform with the wings blazoned over his breast pocket.

It hadn't been estate work keeping her at her typewriter but somehow his arrival made it hard for her to lose herself in the unfolding joys and sorrows she hammered out – and often crossed out too when her mind worked faster than her fingers – on the keyboard. So she locked her work in the drawer and went to join the others in the drawing room.

'Here's Anna, come to hear the good news,' Kath greeted her entry.

'Hello Lance. Promotion?' But that wasn't fair. Theo had joined up six months before him.

'They push us up the ladder quickly these days,' he laughed. 'But the news is my new posting.'

If only Theo had drawn this plum of a posting only seven miles inland from Manningtor. That his bomber base was miles away in Lincolnshire made Anna's expected smile of pleasure hard to hold in place.

When a letter finally arrived from Matt he could only hint at the circuitous route he had taken to North Africa. Small wonder Thelma had waited weeks for news. And, of course, when she did hear, she learnt nothing of his day-to-day life. Everywhere the hoardings blazoned reminders that 'Careless Talk Costs Lives', so it was hardly likely anything of use to the enemy could be sent through the post.

One day far into the future they might all look back on that winter like a kaleidoscope of images impressed for ever on their memories. That letter from Matt, coming after so many weeks of silence, was something they'd remember; the level west lawn turned into a hockey pitch where their gym-slipped guests showed varying degrees of expertise – one or two with an eye for the ball, a few who flittered uselessly out of harm's way with an eye only to their own blossoming femininity, while the bulk charged with neither grace nor skill; the pride that went far beyond Anna and touched the whole household when Christopher took his first steps; the highlights of Theo's brief visits, days so different from the increasing drabness that try as they might, it was futile to see them as part of a normal existence; watching for the post; listening for the telephone; the relief of Lance's casual visits that in some inexplicable way saved their day-to-day living from being completely set apart from the war that was relayed three times a day, at one o'clock, six o'clock and at nine, in the authoritative voice of the BBC.

The snowdrops had flowered and died, the daffodils were being flattened by a furious March wind on a day when, home for the Easter holidays, Sam came in search of Anna.

'Oh, sorry. You're busy.' He pulled back from the half-open door as if his moment of bravery had gone and he wanted to escape. 'We none of us ever offer to give you a hand. Dad always asks how you're coping and I always tell him you're OK, but I don't really know.'

'There's not as much to do these days, and we're lucky having staff who've been on the estate for decades and won't get called up. It's funny how the war seems to have made everything else run at slow speed as if no one wants to throw a spanner in the works. The rents come in on time, no one reports minor jobs that need doing. I bet when the war's over they'll all think of things, but for the moment I feel pretty useless.'

'That's just it, Anna.' Confidence restored, he came into the room and shut the door. 'It's a rotten feeling, isn't it? That's what I wanted to talk to you about.'

Right from the start she and Sam had been in tune. Now, before he started to explain, she knew just what he was going to tell her.

'You're old enough to join up. And you want to. Is that it?'

'I knew *you*'d understand. Not just me – a lot of the chaps from school. We've been in the OTC for ages. Of course, some are cleverer, they'll stay at school till after the summer exams.' She believed that even though he'd come to her for support, his mind was already made up. 'I wrote and told Dad at the beginning of last term, but he says I ought to wait till I'm called. I know what he's thinking. He's hoping it'll be over by that time. He says I have a duty not to worry Mum. But Anna, that's not fair. He never thought about how Mum would feel when he went marching off like some bloomin' hero. I'm seventeen and half. There's no point in my staying at school to take my Matric. I probably wouldn't pass, anyway, and I'm never going to university. I'm not the brainy sort and he knows it. If it hadn't been for the war he would have let me leave after my School Cert. And go into the company. Lots of the chaps are joining up.'

'You want me to say I agree with you,' she mused. 'If I were in your place I'd feel just the same; if I were in his, thousands of miles away and wanting home to stay unchanged, I can understand why he doesn't want you to do it.' Of course he wanted to be seen as a man, not to be left behind while those 'other chaps' marched off to find glory. But Thelma? It hurt too much for Anna even to try and imagine how *she* would feel if this were sixteen years on and it were Christo wanting to prove himself a man already. How could she expect Sam to understand what she only half understood herself? 'And have you talked to your mother?' He shook his head miserably, imagining the silent hurt he'd see in her blue eyes. 'That's what you must do, Sam. Let her see that you realise and care what it will mean to her, don't make her pretend. And, Sam, don't tell her you've talked to me or anyone else – except your father – first.'

He went in search of Thelma while his courage held. That was another picture on Anna's kaleidoscope of memories, one even more vivid than the look of pride on his boyish face when, not many weeks later, he appeared in his khaki uniform, a white band on his forage cap, soon to be removed, when he gained the first pip on his shoulder. By that time Anna had been at Manningtor more than two and a half years, long enough to have taken away her first fears of responsibility. Yet still she knew she was her own person, always just beyond the rim of the circle of this family who'd shown her nothing but kindness.

Somewhere, out there in an unknown future, was *her* world. The days of Theo's leaves might be filled with a heady and unreal excitement, and the nights with a wonder of sensuality, yet even in those brief periods she was aware that she was playing a role. Surely everyone has a niche, a place where body and soul come together and find peace. That's what she believed sincerely and what, each time Theo came home, she longed to capture. Yet always it eluded her.

Chapter Nine

By the end of 1941 Britain no longer stood alone. In June Germany had invaded Russia; in December, when Japan bombed the American fleet in Pearl Harbour, the United States, too, entered the fray. But there was no glimmer of hope that the end was in sight; at Manningtor, as at any home where the arrival of the postman set the mood for the day, habit and routine had become a protection against the constant anxiety.

By the summer of 1942 Christo had his world at his small feet. A combination of both parents, his hair was the same chestnut brown as his mother's, his eyes as dark and long lashed as his father's. Neatly made, he was light on his feet and quick in his movements. And his temperament? His background was much the same as his father's had been, surrounded by love and attention. And his reaction to it was much the same too. Instinct told him that he could give pleasure with a show of affection, and seeing that pleasure never failed to fill him with a warm, happy feeling.

By showering devotion on him, Thelma tried to hide her ever-present anxieties for the two people who meant more to her than all else, and hide her own guilt that she had no power to love Dee as she did Sam. Dee had come first with Matt, Sam with her. One thing Christopher had definitely inherited from Theo: instinct taught him how to wheedle his way into everyone's affection.

'Me tum to see oo,' he would lisp to Kath as she sat in the summertime shade of the horse-chestnut tree. 'Me tum to talk wiv oo.'

Oh you darling, you precious little Theo-all-over-again, the old lady would hold her hand to him. It would be all he needed, just that small sign that his coming had made her happy. So Christopher Theodore Sullivan would beam with pleasure, lower his small bottom to the grass so that he leant against her bony leg and sigh with contentment. But only for a moment. By then something else would attract him. Perhaps it would be the sight of Sylvia, holding out the hope that if he told her 'Me tum too, me on horsey' he might be taken to the stable and lifted to sit on docile Dilly's back; perhaps it would be Thelma pedalling home from some good cause or other; perhaps it would be his mother drawn by the sight of him or perhaps he'd hear the jangle of the end-of-lessons bell telling him his friends – oh, so many of them! – would be expecting him. And his ears were always tuned for another sound too: that of a car engine. Being with women and girls was fine, he took them all for granted just as he did their attentive devotion. But what he really liked best of all was when those men came. He supposed that the one who carried him on his shoulders was more important than the others, but from his almost entirely female empire he hadn't come to understand why the Daddy one was more special than the one who came most – Lance, they called him. In fact he wasn't quite sure about the one they all expected him to want to be with. He didn't understand yet about jealousy, but if he'd been a cat his feline fur would have stood in a ridge on his back when his mother was with the one called Daddy. Then there was another man who came sometimes, one who wore different-coloured clothes. Colours were still on the perimeter of Christo's understanding. He knew the blues and greens and reds in the books Anna showed him; he even realised that although the Air Force uniform was nothing like the colour of the sky in those books yet it was still blue. Khaki was beyond him; it was just a funny colour that looked nice on the jolly man who wore it. And how proud Sam would have been to know that from the eyes of a not-yet-three-year old he fitted comfortably into the bracket of 'the men'.

So summer gave way to autumn, another winter stretched ahead. The war was in its third year.

Hearing the shrill note of the telephone bell, Anna ran down the stairs to the hall. It was nearly eleven o'clock at night so it could only be Theo. She wouldn't listen to that other thought, that it could be one of his squadron, someone returned from a raid. Theo had told her about that list – planes out and planes in, each ticked off as it arrived – or – no, don't even imagine.

'Theo? Hello,' she gasped, gripping the received hard.

'No, Miss Anna – Mrs Sullivan – I've ridden to the Cross to the phone.' She recognised Potts' voice. Disappointment that it wasn't Theo was immediately overtaken and she was back at Dunsford House where Potts had always managed to 'do the things Grandpa couldn't manage', as she'd told Theo in what seemed like another life.

'What's happened? Is it Grandpa?' Stupid question. Of course it was Grandpa, what else could take Potts to the village at this time on a cold November night?

'He'd been a bit off colour, you know how the dark days always pull him down. What with that and never a bit of news to cheer him, never a thing to lift one day from another.' She heard the criticism in his voice. 'Seems like there's no end, he'd say. I wished he'd give the wireless a rest, but never missed a bulletin. I don't have to tell you.'

Yes, she knew just how he would be. But that couldn't be the reason for phoning at this time of night.

'He's ill, Potts?'

'That's what I'm here to tell you. Fainted right off, he did, it must have been about six o'clock it happened. Oh, drat it, there go the pips.' The telephonist's voice, as impersonal as any BBC newsreader's, informed him his time was up and he would have to insert more shillings if he didn't want to be cut off. Then the sound of the money being fed in. 'That's better.' And despite his reason for phoning, Anna smiled at his obvious satisfaction. In the days she'd lived at Dunsford, ready and willing to act as errand girl for the needs of the household, for Potts to have cycled to the village at any time would have been a feat in itself, but to have made the bumpy journey at night and with the added responsibility of wrestling with something as outside his realm as a public telephone, gave him reason to be pleased with himself. 'Second time I've done this ride this evening, Miss Anna. First was to fetch the doctor and now to get you to come.'

'Is Grandpa in pain? What's wrong?'

'If you ask me he's just plain tired of living. All these years . . .' More than anything else it was the sudden break in

183

Potts' voice that touched Anna. As long as she could remember, the kindly man had been there in the background, a shadowy figure whose life revolved around being one jump ahead of her grandfather in seeing what was needed. 'Mrs Short says for you to get here quick as you can if you want to be in time to catch him. But she says – and you'll understand, Miss Anna – she says you mustn't come if it means bringing the little lad; you know how children about him worry the master.'

Indeed, she knew.

'I'll leave Christo with Nanny, he'll be much happier here.' How clearly she remembered her own childhood, feeling a greater resentment now than ever she had at the time. Yet was that fair? 'Tell Grandpa I'll come on the first train I can get tomorrow. And, Potts, give him my love.'

'Too late for it to matter. For weeks he's been right down . . . could have done with it then . . .' Again the pips, then the line went dead.

'Hello . . . hello . . . are you still there?' She put the receiver back on its stand, but still she stood lost in thought.

'Something's wrong?' It was Lance's voice. Wearing his heavy flying jacket, a long scarf wound round his neck, he came into the hall from the passage that led out to the coach yard.

'It's Grandpa – ill. Lance, he must be more than just ill. Grandpa's dying.'

'First train tomorrow, I heard you say. We could be there by that time if I drove you.'

'You can't do that. It's not just down the road, Lance, it's miles away in Berkshire. You wouldn't get back for duty –'

'I'm on seventy-two hours' leave. I've come home for it. I came as soon as I got debriefed instead of waiting until morning, wanted to get away. That's all right, isn't it?' She took Lance so much for granted that she seldom really looked at him. She looked now and realised what a strain he lived under. The West Country was suffering its share of raids, so there was little rest for the fighters who fought to keep the bombers from its cost. 'Listen, sister Anna, my petrol tank is almost full, enough to get us there. Bring your coupons so that we can get some on the way back. You do get an allowance, don't you?'

'Yes I do, for the estate.'

'That's settled, then. Better not disturb Nanny, but tell Thelma.

184

We can be on the road in ten minutes if you get your skates on.'

Hardly realising what she was doing she reached up and kissed his chin, a kiss befitting a sister's gratitude. Then she turned to run back up the stairs, her mind leaping ahead, deciding on the few essentials she would need to take. Thelma had gone to her room more than an hour before – she'd be sound asleep so there was no alternative but to wake her. Surprisingly the light was still on in her bedroom and her prompt 'Come in' to Anna's knock found her sitting up reading through a bundle of letters.

'You mustn't worry about a thing, dear. You know Christo will be looked after and loved. Oh dear, if only it could have been Theo who'd walked in with seventy-two hours' leave and could go with you.'

Loyalty silenced Anna's thought that with the prospect of seventy-two hours of freedom Theo would have had no wish to spend it journeying to Dunsford House and the bedside of someone who, even though neither had ever put it into words, they both knew hadn't forgiven him for the reason for their marriage.

So she and Lance set out.

'Here, wrap this blanket around you and try and have a sleep. Your grandfather will need you to be wide awake when we get there.'

How easy he was to be with, she thought, snuggling down under the blanket and obediently closing her eyes. Yet, sleep was miles away. Once they were past Exeter the empty road was shrouded in a blanket of fog, the November night in keeping with the nature of their journey. In the darkness she imagined rather than saw how Lance peered through the gloom, looking straight ahead and concentrating on the few misty yards ahead that were lit by the narrow beam from headlights which, to conform to regulations, were partially covered. After a day that must have seen action – for he'd spoken of leaving the base after debriefing – the last thing he'd needed must have been a long night drive. Yet he gave no hint that he expected gratitude; indeed, she felt that this was a joint mission. Keeping very still, knowing he believed her to be asleep, Anna watched him or came as near to watching him as was possible now that her eyes had adjusted to the dark. Just once he turned his head her way, but instinct made her close her eyes.

It was as they came through Newbury that a policeman waved them down.

'Sorry to stop you, sir, but I need to check your identity cards.' Then, after peering at them by the light of his torch, 'All seems in order. May I ask where you're going at this time of night? Something I have to check, you understand, sir.'

Satisfied, he finally sent them on their way. But by that time Anna gave up all thought of sleep, genuine or assumed.

'In a way it's rather comforting,' she said as they left the constable wandering down the empty street. 'I mean, it's gives you a feeling of all belonging.' She knew what she meant, but for a moment she wished she'd kept her thought to herself. Lance would probably think her stupid!

'That's because we are all belonging,' he answered. 'If we were fifth columnists we should feel quite differently. I think we must turn off this road soon, we need to be further north. I looked for Brindley on the map while I was waiting for you. Isn't that where you once told me you used to cycle to market?'

'Fancy your remembering that.' When he didn't answer she wriggled comfortably into her seat, the rug pulled up to her shoulders, thinking not for the first time what an easy companion he was. 'Lance, you must feel rotten being so far from home – from Jenny and the boys. When Theo gets a seventy-two-hour leave he comes home –'

'Reckon that's how I feel about Manningtor. But, yes, sure I miss the others.'

'What would you be doing now if you were there?'

'Midway through the evening – maybe on my way home. More likely still working.'

'A partner in the business and working through the evening? We could pretty well set our clock by Matt: he drives into the yard at six-fifteen come sun or ice – or rather he *did* until he went into the Army. I never thought he'd volunteer. When we heard Mr Chamberlain tell us we were at war I looked at Theo and knew the way his mind was working, I knew he would want to fly. But Matt – none of us expected him to go. Did Jenny know too, without having to be told?'

'I guess she probably did.' Such an English voice, or so she'd

186

always thought. Yet, strangely, when he talked of his home a change crept into it, not so much in pronunciation as intonation. She peered through the darkness at him, in vain trying to read his expression.

'I think if I'd been American I'd have been angry. It wasn't *their* war.'

'More or less what she said. I think the boys understood why I had to come.' She detected the pride in his voice, even the hint of a smile at the mention of them.

'Tell me about them. Phil and Barney.'

'They're great lads. Typical of their age, I guess; at least typical of their age back there. Guess it's different here, at any rate it was different when I was their age and at boarding school. I find the American way of child-rearing something again. Baseball, that's where their hearts lie – unless they get the chance to see a cowboy movie. Jenny's brother is a professional player, and that raises him to only one notch down from Roy Rogers. Me, a mere architect, what chance do I have?'

She laughed, not taking his words seriously and again noticing the subtle change in his so-English voice when he talked of his home in America. 'I bet they boast about you like mad to their friends.'

'Maybe. Sit where you are. This looks like a sizeable village, I'm going to check where we are. I can't help feeling that in the event of invasion reading the road signs would be the last thing on the enemy's mind, but taking them away works wonders for confusing travelling nationals.'

She watched him walk away, at least she watched his dark form, then by the light of the small torch he took from his pocket she saw him beam the light onto the sign over a shop. Had a local resident possessing an over-active imagination removed the blackout and seen him, his presence might have struck terror. There were those all too ready to jump to conclusions: a spy dropped by parachute, a fifth columnist on his way to some secret assignation or, especially as he was wearing his flying jacket, one of an advance party of invaders dropped into their midst. Fortunately the night was cold so the village was safely tucked in, windows well shrouded.

'Hold your side of the map, Anna, let's pinpoint our position.

187

It's just gone four o'clock, we've not done too badly, we must be nearly there.'

And so they were. It wasn't long before she recognised the high street of Brindley. The road used to be so familiar to her that she could have travelled it with her eyes closed. Perhaps she still could and yet she felt removed.

'Four years ago this was my home; all my life I'd known nothing else. Every bend is familiar but I don't feel it's part of me. Ought going home to be like that, Lance?'

'You're not going home, Anna, that's the answer. Once Manningtor casts its spell nowhere else can ever be home.'

She nodded. And there in the dark, going towards Wickley Cross and finally the rutted mile or so down the lane to Dunsford House, she found herself telling him how it was she and Theo had first met; how she'd lived every hour of that summer watching for him, praying for him to come back; how willing she'd been for him to make love to her; and finally what she'd not spoken of for years, how it was that she'd become his wife.

'The way of many a great love, Anna,' he told her, for some reason reaching out his hand to take hers.

'Fate took a hand. I'd never ridden before – I'd never done *anything* before – and I was learning. I got thrown. And I lost the baby even before we'd told anyone I was pregnant. But it seems a lifetime ago. Now there's Christo – and Manningtor.'

And Theo, he added silently.

They came to the top of the rise that brought them to the gate of Dunsford House.

If Anna had felt removed from the familiar roads of her childhood, it was nothing compared with the dreamlike quality of her old home. It was the ever-faithful Potts who heard a car draw up outside and went to the dark landing to pull the curtain to one side and look out. Only seconds later Mrs Short followed him down to the front door. Tall, austere, ruffled by nothing, that's how Anna remembered her. Tonight she looked old, her hair in two thin pigtails, the cord of her woollen dressing gown tied around a waist that surely hadn't been so thin, her felt slippers somehow out of character.

'Why, who's this then? Your husband not brought you?'

'This is his brother, Lance. Lance, Mrs Short and Potts. They look after Grandpa.'

'Someone has to.' There was criticism in Mrs Short's retort. 'Poor dear gentleman, never a moment's trouble. But with a busy life, I dare say all you can spare time for is an occasional note when your conscience stirs you.'

'How is he, Mrs Short? What happened?' Lance noticed, just as more than four years ago Theo had, that Anna took no offence at Mrs Short's words.

'What happened? What happens to any man, neglected by family, wearied with the years. As he says, three score years and ten is our allotted time and he's been kept waiting to go to his Maker for more than three score and thirty. Poor dear soul. Nothing of him. Appetite of a sparrow. I'd better put the kettle onto the gas stove and make a cup of tea. Nothing better to give you – the only drop of anything we've been able to get is kept for your grandfather. A sip of brandy helps him sleep. Best you go back up to him, Potts, we daren't leave him, not tonight, not when the angels are so near to taking him.' Turning her back she brushed away a tear that escaped onto her lined cheek.

'No, Potts, you and Mrs Short take Lance through to the kitchen, it'll be the warmest place. I'm going up to see Grandpa.'

To her own ears her voice sounded normal, to Lance's the instructions nothing unusual. Yet Mrs Short and Potts looked at each other, saying nothing but understanding each other's thoughts: just hark at little Anna giving instructions! There was an unfamiliar note of authority in her voice; here was a young woman used to making decisions.

The bedroom was warm and airless, the fire hadn't been allowed to die down for days, the occasional handful of lavender thrown on it serving as an air purifier.

'Grandpa,' Anna leant over the frail old man. His face was ashen, his eyes sunk into his skull. The bedcovers were pulled up to his chest, but his arms were outside, his hands cold to her touch. Large brown blotches were on the backs of the skin that hung in loose folds over the bones. But it was his thin wrists that touched her most; she encircled one with her thumb and middle finger. Why did his breathing sound like that, each shallow gasp a loud unearthly rattle?

189

'Are you awake,' she whispered. His eyes were open but his soul seemed to be somewhere else. 'I've come home to you.' Home? Even as she said it, she realised again just how far from the truth it had become. But perhaps it was those last words that penetrated. How many times through her adolescence had he gazed at her, glorying in her likeness to her mother, glorying in it and yet resenting it as a constant reminder of the pain of losing her? He'd told himself she'd never had Elizabeth's sense of fun, nor yet her confidence. Now those words 'I've come home to you' cut through his feeble and wandering mind. With his lips falling open a cry escaped him, but not of pain. His thin face had been void of expression yet in that instant a change came over him: joy, rapture, something beyond her understanding possessed him. He opened his mouth to speak, but whether his mind was too confused for him to form the words or whether he wanted nothing but to feast his eyes on the miracle before him Anna didn't know. She should have come more often.

'I didn't know –' she started to say, as if to make excuses for giving herself so wholeheartedly to Manningtor and to Theo's world. But before the words were out, she realised just how confused he had become.

'Liz, my darling Liz . . .' He tried to raise his hand and touch Anna's face, but he hadn't the strength. She stooped and laid her face close to his. He was dying. Perhaps it was an illusion in his mind that made him see her as his beloved Liz, but in those last minutes of his life she believed he saw beyond the veil.

They were living through abnormal times, the phrase 'the war effort' was in everyday usage and efforts were frequently made to accommodate commitments to it. Cuthbert Hamilton died in the early hours of Tuesday morning. While patients waited in Dr Giles' surgery at Wickley Cross, he was already at the house writing out the death certificate. From there on, while Mrs Short shed tears of genuine sadness mixed with those of fear for her own future and Potts set about seeing 'the old gentleman's' room was in apple pie order for him to be carried from it for the last time, Lance set off for Brindley giving the impression of being far more confident of what had to be done than he felt. It was still only the morning of Tuesday.

'This is supposed to be three days' holiday for you,' Anna said

190

when, on returning, he told her the funeral was to be on Friday, the speed a sure proof of willingness to help that ever-present 'war effort'. 'Even if you go home now you'll have lost your first day completely. But you've had nothing but a couple of hours sleep.'

'Neither have you. That cat nap in the car doesn't count. One thing I've learnt over these last years is not to depend on regular nights' sleep. You ask Theo, he'd tell you the same. What are you doing?' He came to stand behind where she was sitting at her grandfather's writing desk.

'I never knew Grandpa kept all these.' She waved her hand over the pile of letters she'd taken from a drawer she'd unlocked for the first time. 'It must be every word my mother ever wrote to him, right from when she was a child and staying with some aunt in Cornwall. Everything. And the faded pictures. See.' She passed him one showing her grandfather, plainly in a photographer's studio, a pedestal bearing an aspidistra by his chair and on his knee a small, elfin child.

'That can't be you, she looks too young and the clothes are wrong. So it's your mother? But Anna, you must have been her image.'

'To look at.' Her mind was back down the years, how often she'd believed she heard resentment in his ageing voice when told her, 'Don't know what your mother would have made of you. My Liz loved to dance, she loved to laugh and have fun.' Always it had been a criticism of her and her isolated life. The small child in the photograph was gazing up at him; Anna could imagine the twinkle in her dark eyes. 'She was his whole world. I always knew that. That's what was so cruel,' she spoke more to herself than to Lance. 'As if losing her wasn't enough, he had me planted on him, a constant reminder. She really loved him, I can tell that from the way she wrote. Not gushy loving words, but letters that tried to include him in every small thing. Then he got me. I looked like her, but when I was small I was quite scared. Not so much scared of him, as scared of letting him be reminded that I was here. Yet I never really understood why. I could have made his life so different if I'd learnt to love him like she did.'

'Maybe you're loving him now and he knows it.' Lance laid a hand on her thin shoulder.

191

Perhaps over-tiredness had something to do with it, or perhaps it was the atmosphere of the house where Mrs Short made sure her face was void of expression as if in that way she could disguise her reddened, swollen eyelids and where Potts continually whistled tunelessly through his teeth in an attempt to sound cheerful. Or perhaps it was something in Lance's quietly spoken words. Whatever the reason she knew the moment would stay with her. Yet almost as she thought it, there came another image to chase it away. Supposing Theo had been here with her, supposing she'd said to him what she had to Lance. No, don't suppose it, she told herself. The two are so different: Theo likes nothing better than to do something to give pleasure (don't go down the road of questioning why), but he'd hate dealing with death, so I don't want to picture him here; Lance is relaxed, kind, dependable. Am I saying that Theo isn't? No of course I'm not. Theo is different, Theo is my love, he is the centre of my life. Then, putting an end to any wayward thoughts, she bundled the letters back in the drawer. If for that one brief moment Lance had escaped his allotted place in her scheme of things, he was soon slotted back where he belonged.

'Later I'll light a bonfire,' she said. 'These were meant just for Grandpa, I don't want them left around. Now, Lance, about you and your leave.' It seemed that, the letters disposed of, she was about to deal with *him*.

'Hold on! I phoned the base from the village, had a word with the C.O. I don't need to be back until Sunday morning. You've a lot to do here, an extra pair of hands might come in useful. Is there any family you have to tell?'

'One or two distant cousins of Grandpa's, pretty well as old as he was. I found the names in his address book so I've written notes to them. There's no rush for them, they wouldn't expect to come to the funeral. A Christmas card once a year, that was all the contact between them. It was losing my mother that must have changed his life – I never remember him being happy. It all might have been so different if my parents had lived.'

'Indeed it would have been different. This would never have been your home. You wouldn't have met Theo. And I wouldn't have had a sister Anna.'

192

She found herself smiling. 'I dare say it's wicked and selfish of me, but I'm glad things went the way they did.'

'It isn't decent, turning a person's house upside down with him not even in his grave. His own granddaughter, wouldn't you think she'd respect his memory more? Did you see the load of his clothes she put into the back of the car this morning to take to Brindley to the casual ward? The master's clothes to go on the backs of vagrants and ne'er-do-wells.' Then, needing to vent her anger on someone or something tangible rather than simply on absent Anna, 'For goodness sake, Andrew Potts, if you must keep on with that stupid whistling, put a bit of tune in it.'

'Habit, don't hear myself,' Potts answered, unruffled by her carping manner. 'Had any thoughts about what you'll be doing now the old gent's gone? There's no chance Miss Anna will keep this place. Plenty of work about these days; we may not be spring chicken but thanks to friend Adolf we'll have no trouble earning a crust. Maybe a better buttered one than we got here too. Times have changed. A man can pick up good money with factory work.'

'Don't say a word against the wages you got here. I dare say times have changed and the poor dear soul might not have kept abreast, but we lived well, better than you will in a cheap bed-sit and bringing home a bulging pay packet from some factory.'

'Can't deny I shall miss your cooking,' he said and gave another tuneless whistle while he made up his mind to take her further into his confidence. 'When I cycled to the village to telephone for Miss Anna I dropped a letter into the post to my brother up in Coventry. I told him the old gent looked to be at the end of the road and soon I'd have to look for another place. You'll have noticed I had a letter this morning. Must have written as soon as he got mine. He tells me I could earn good money in his neck of the wood. And, listen to this: until I find somewhere I can stay in their spare room. Sue, his missus, she's a good lass, happy-go-lucky sort that one extra in the house won't ruffle her feathers.' Amelia Short's stony expression gave him no idea how the certainty of his future only made her more aware of her own position. For over forty years this had been her job. And this house, hadn't it been *she* who had had the vision to see how those workers' cottages could

193

be transformed; hadn't it been *she* who had chosen the name Dunsford House?

Could put all I possess in a couple of suitcases, she told herself silently. Every ornament, every last teaspoon in this place, has felt as if it were my own. But what have I? Nothing. That's the true fact, nothing but my few clothes and a bit of money in the Post Office that I've managed to put by me through the years. Yet I must have known this would happen. You're a fool, Amelia Short. Young Anna, hard as nails she is. Look at the way she burnt all those papers the poor old gentleman had cherished all those years. Gone in a puff of smoke. And never a tear, oh dear me no. Keen to be off back to this great place in Devon. And that chap she's with, she says he's her brother-in-law. If he is, why hasn't he got the same name as that bounder she had to marry? Well, like it or not, it's time I washed my hands of the lot of it here. Though, even with plenty of work about, who'll give a job to an old girl my age, God only knows. Next month I'll be seventy. There'll be a few bob a week pension from the Government, that and what I've managed to save will have to see me out. Oh just hark at that stupid Andrew Potts, if he doesn't stop his silly whistle I'll . . . I'll . . .

But in fact she'd do nothing. Her blank expression was a mirror to her mind, empty of hope.

One thing of importance Anna found in her grandfather's writing desk was an envelope, yellowed with time, her grandfather's writing on the envelope firm and strong. 'To be opened in the event of my death.' With Lance at her side she took the paper knife and neatly slit it open to take out the single sheet. The date on it was August 1921, only a month after tragedy had robbed him of his daughter. The brief note read: 'On this date I have deposited my Last Will and Testament for safe keeping with my solicitors, Higgs, Houghton and Chown of Brindley.' Then his signature.

It was Thursday morning, the day before his funeral.

'It's no use waiting until after tomorrow,' Anna said. 'On Saturday we must go home. Lance, there's so much to sort out here. I want to talk to the solicitor, ask him to arrange for the place to be sold. Even a furniture auction would be difficult here, so far from the road. Perhaps I'll have to get auctioneers to collect everything.'

'The drawers will have to be sorted, there must be personal things you won't want to go under the hammer. Then there's Mrs Short and Potts, you'll want to suggest they might want something of your grandfather's.'

'I'll talk to them both. They've worked for Grandpa for years – Mrs Short wasn't much older than I am now when she came to him.' Already the future was taking shape in her mind. When she went in search of them she knew exactly what she intended.

'You've both been with Grandpa a long time. This won't be easy for either of you. But you mustn't worry, I shall find places for you at Manningtor. On Saturday when we go home, both of you must come too. I shall talk to the solicitor this afternoon and instruct him to arrange for the auctioneers to dispose of things here.'

'A kind thought, Miss Anna, but not for me,' Potts told her. 'Got myself a place to go to up with my brother.'

'I'm glad, Potts. But you, Mrs Short, you'll come to Manningtor.' She didn't mean it to sound like an order, but immediately she'd spoken she realised her approach had been tactless.

Standing even taller and straighter than usual the housekeeper looked down at her.

'This Manningtor you set such store in, you might have gone off there gladly enough when that young husband of yours had no choice but to accept his responsibilities, but you needn't think I'm going to follow along. Poor old woman, seen her best years, now like a broken-down horse put out to grass, you think I'll be grateful for a bit of pasture to graze in. Well, my girl, just you think again.' Both Anna and Potts looked at her as if she were a stranger. Never had they heard her voice rise like this, nor seen the muscles of her face work as she lost all attempt to hold back her hysterical crying. 'He's been my life, never even loved my own family like I loved him. And *you* –' her bony finger pointed at Anna '– what do you care? Nothing. Burn his things, dress any old vagrant in his clothes, put everything that made his home under the hammer for any Tom, Dick and Harry to sift through looking for a bargain. And you think, for the sake of a bed and a crust, I'd spend what time's left to me serving you!'

It wasn't fear that made Anna's heart feel like a drum beating in her chest and her mouth suddenly dry. Yet she was unnerved,

195

out of her depth in seeing Mrs Short, always unemotional and unchanging, behaving in a way so out of character. Hearing the commotion Lance came into the kitchen.

'I guess everyone's overwrought.' He spoke quietly yet with a hint of the years he'd spent on the far side of the Atlantic. 'Whatever Anna has suggested, Mrs Short, she will have done out of consideration for you. Don't you think we might try to pull together?'

Anna looked at him and knew that, like so much else that had happened over these last few days, the memory would last. Hardly aware of what she did she reached her hand towards him and felt it taken in his. Mrs Short noticed the action, that was clear from her sneering expression. But even contempt couldn't override her utter misery.

'I don't want kindness, I don't want charity. Always earned my way. Wish I could have gone the same as the dear master.'

Nothing came near to consoling her and her mind was made up. She'd pack her things and leave Dunsford House. Where she went or what she did was her own business. And while Anna listened to the tirade, her mind was made up too: she would insist that Mrs Short was made to accept a gratuity.

Keen to take Anna away from the scene, Lance suggested they should have their lunch in Brindley before seeing the solicitor. So, taking the death certificate and the letter they'd found in the bureau, thankfully they drove away up the bumpy lane. Leaning over the gate of Heathfield Cottage was Mrs Humphries.

'Stop the car, Lance. You remember Mr and Mrs Humphries.' He didn't, but he slowed down as they approached anyway. 'I was coming to see you as soon as I could,' Anna called as they came alongside.

'Why, it's Mrs Theo. Oh, he's not with you . . .' They both heard the disappointment in her voice.

'You've heard about Grandpa? That's why I've come. You remember Theo's brother Lance.'

'Can't say I do. How do you do, sir.' Then, back to Anna. 'How is the boy? We get a picture postcard from him once in a while. Bless him, he doesn't forget. Yes, I heard Mr Hamilton had been taken, they were talking about it in the butcher's. The funeral is to be tomorrow, I hear. So, he'll be coming, Theo will be here with you for that?'

That brought home to her something to which she'd not given any thought: she'd not even written to Theo with news of her grandfather's death. Lance had told Thelma by telephone from the village so he would have heard if he'd happened to speak to anyone at Manningtor. But over these last days she'd hardly spared him a thought.

'I don't think he'll be able to get leave, Mrs Humphries. Too busy winning the war for us,' she added with a laugh, subconsciously trying to lift her feeling of guilt. 'I wish we could stay and see Mr Humphries too. Is he well? We have to be in Brindley for appointments.' Again guilt reared its head that she could put a lunch outing with Lance before spending time with people Theo cared about. (Cared? Yes, of course he did, why else would he have taken time to see them settled in the cottage, why else would he send them postcards?) 'Tomorrow is the funeral and the next morning we have to leave, Lance has to be back on duty.'

'We shall be at the funeral. Not that we knew your grandfather, but Amelia and I get along very well. I want her to know we feel for her.'

And so they went on to Brindley.

'Where do you recommend?' Lance asked her as he opened the car door for her.

'I only know The Copper Kettle. That's where I always used to buy my lunch even when I cycled all the way on my fairy bike.'

'And you'd like to go there?'

Suddenly she knew she wouldn't. This had nothing to do with the little girl who'd grown up knowing the market town so well. Today she was a different person. Was that normal – to be loath to bridge the time between past and present?

'Let's go somewhere different, somewhere neither of us have ever been before.' Somehow that would make a memory free from the shadow of her yesterdays. The Red Lion, an ancient coaching inn at the far end of the High Street, fitted the bill perfectly, its sparkling white damask table linen as far removed from The Copper Kettle's red check as its attentive waiters were from the tea shop's Peggy Grimble, who knew most of her customers and enjoyed a gossip with them all. Not that Anna had ever risen to those heights of familiarity, for in the eyes of

197

the never-young waitress she had always occupied her allotted slot of 'funny old-fashioned little girl, ordering her lunch as if there was nothing unusual in a child eating out by herself'. So as the years had gone on Anna had still been seen as that same child showing the sort of quiet self-assurance that put a curb on Peggy's naturally busy tongue.

Was it wicked to be having such a good time? With her grandfather's funeral not over, with Theo miles way and leading a life he avoided talking to her about, had she any right to this fluttering, excited feeling? Her gaze met Lance's, and right or wrong, there was no way of hiding the tell-tale message in her tawny brown eyes.

'Is it because of Grandpa, or is it the war that makes one feel guilty – ashamed – of enjoying things?'

She could almost feel him turning the question in his mind.

'The way we live perhaps makes every emotion more vivid. Do you believe your grandfather would rest more easily if he thought you were miserable? Of course he wouldn't.'

'So it can't be Grandpa.'

'This ought to have been Theo with you.'

'No. He would have hated dealing with death.' She remembered the day Sidney had died, but loyalty silenced her.

'Death at a great old age is a luxury these days.' At his seriously spoken words, whether as a result of guilt that during so much misery she should have this unaccountable sense of elation, or from the knowledge that it was too fragile to hold, her imagination ran amok. She seemed to hear the drone of loaded planes overhead, planes perhaps setting off to drop their load of havoc and carnage or flying overhead on their way to Bristol or the industrial Midlands; over Germany, Theo in the pilot's seat, Theo surrounded by bursting shells from the enemy barrage; the wail of the siren in Moorleigh sounding like the harbinger of destruction; the glow in the sky from the fires of Exeter or Plymouth; the memory of a 'dogfight' in the sky above Manningtor and the unearthly thud as a burning plane hit the ground; Lance in the pilot's seat of a Spitfire swooping with the grace of a bird. Terror and destruction everywhere.

'It's as if all the joy, all the misery, the loneliness, the moments of treats like coming here today, all of it is heightened.' Her wide eyes seemed to plead. 'But it won't always be like this. One day we'll all be normal, you'll be home with your own family, Theo will be back looking after Manningtor –'

'Sure, sister Anna.' He agreed, with that smile that never failed to remind her of Theo. And that's what she had to hang onto: it was because he was Theo's brother, so much like him, that being with him made her feel like this. Theo was her world, of course he was. Anyway, he'd be glad to know that she was getting on well with Lance. Getting on well – she took the menu the waiter passed to her, realising that for all the attentive service and elegant trappings food shortages affected The Red Lion as surely as they did The Copper Kettle.

The visit to the offices of Higgs, Houghton and Chown proved disappointing. The too-old-to-fight head clerk heard the reason for their visit, murmured all the right things when he was told of Cuthbert Hamilton's death.

'I fear there is no one in the building to deal with the matter of our client's Will. You understand it is outside my domain to convey its contents.'

'But that's stupid.'

'Mr Higgs, I believe, has dealt with Mr Hamilton's affairs but he is away for a few days –' she might not have spoken, or the clerk might have been stone deaf for all the notice he took of her interruption '– Mr Houghton is unfortunately ill and Mr Chown is away from the office with a client until late in the afternoon. May I suggest you leave the papers with me and I will explain the urgency and ask him to dictate a letter to you on his return.'

'I must be gone by Saturday and there are things I have to arrange.'

'Indeed madam, you have my word.'

So they had to leave it at that.

Just as Anna came downstairs on the Friday morning there was the clatter of the letterbox and two envelopes dropped onto the floor. Identical envelopes, one addressed to her and the second to Mrs Short. They'd expected to drive back to Manningtor on the Saturday so that Lance could return to his station that same evening. But all that was changed.

The committal was over, the gravediggers shovelling the earth back into place almost before they closed the gates of the churchyard.

Mrs Short tugged at Anna's sleeve. 'All those things I said to you yesterday, I behaved badly, that much I know. Now I feel ashamed. The poor dear master, he was your grandfather, your flesh and blood —'

'You don't know how pleased I am, Mrs Short. I didn't really want Dunsford House to be sold to strangers.'

'Yes, but to cut you out like this. Supposing you'd been hard pushed for a pound and he'd seen fit to leave it all to me. You were just a wee thing when he made the Will it seems. I remember those days, you don't. Demented with grief, he was. Wouldn't have you brought near him, all you were was a reminder that your mother had put another man before him. It wasn't healthy the way he loved her. Perhaps the good Lord knew what He was at when He took her. Was like that all your early years, wouldn't have you at his table, ready to complain if he heard you at play. A good man, I never loved a living soul like I did him; was only grief that got between him and living. Different later on, he came to like – love? – no it wasn't liking nor yet love he felt for you, but he saw you as your own person, that much I'm sure. Remember how he raged when he knew what you and Mr Sullivan had been up to. Brought it all back to him, that's what the real trouble was. Just besotted with her, he was. And when she went he turned to me. For a while I thought he really cared – like that, you understand. Nothing harder to understand than men. Some things I can't talk to you about, not to you, not to anyone. But I know why it was he made his Will the way he did. And the way he worded it '. . . if she's still with me'. Covering himself, you see. Wasn't like an open cheque. If I'd gone off and got myself work somewhere else, or found another man – likely thing! – then I suppose he would have had to think again.' All the time she'd talked she'd seemed to be in a hurry to say what had to be said, but never once had she let herself look Anna in the eyes. Now she did. 'At least you'll never be short of a bob. I dare say that's what made me say the spiteful things I did yesterday. There was me, a few pounds in the Post Office and all I possessed to be carried in a couple of suitcases; and there was you, a well-to-do husband even if you did go over the traces to catch him, all your mother and father left, and on top of that you'd get Dunsford. Was me found its name, you know. My mother was a Dunsford before

200

she married my father. Now all that's done. Me, Amelia Short, lady of means.' Then to the driver of the official car, patiently waiting for her with the door held open, 'Shan't keep you but a jiff. I need to have a quick word with my friend. We shall go right by her house; I'll just offer her a lift.'

Anna felt a laugh bubbling up inside her, a laugh quite out of place with the solemnity of the occasion. And, Anna forgotten, Amelia hurried towards Tessa Humphries.

Anna's sudden desire to laugh may not have been in keeping with the solemnity of the occasion, but it perfectly fitted her mood of freedom.

'We don't need to go back to the house,' she told Lance. 'Let's not hang about.'

'Are you sure that's what you want?'

'I've never been surer. I put our things in the boot before we left this morning, but I didn't say anything – just in case when the time came I wanted one more look at things. But I don't.' As Mrs Short ushered her friend to the funeral car, Anna went to say her farewells.

'You mean because of how things are? But you know you're most welcome at the house.' And again Anna clenched her teeth to repress that bubble of laughter.

Two minutes later, even before the stately Daimler had driven off carrying Dunsford House's owner with her first guests, Anna and Lance had already left Wickley Cross behind them. Darkness fell early; the fog was dense, making the journey slow.

'Friday night. We hadn't expected to go home until tomorrow. What do you say to putting up somewhere and waiting for daylight? If you're desperate to get home, we'll go straight on, but this isn't getting any clearer.'

Anna tried to believe that it was to spare Lance the strain of a night drive in such conditions that made her agree so willingly. Perhaps she just didn't try hard enough. With the fog so dense they probably passed off-the-road hotels without being aware, for when they finally found somewhere bearing the sign The Green Man Hotel they'd already been on the road four hours and had covered less than the first hundred miles. On a clear day it would have been no more than early dusk, but on that November Friday night was coming early. They were shown to two single rooms, one at each end of a long corridor where the

201

uneven and squeaky floorboards were evidence of the age of the building.

'It's only five o'clock. We shan't eat for hours. How do you like the idea of some fresh air?' Lance suggested.

'I like it very much. Did you notice the lounge? It looked as though no one ever shared it with the aspidistra!'

Somehow the idea of exploring unknown and pretty well unseen territory together suited her mood. And how easy it was to link arms as they found their way along the narrow pavement. Even since the morning post she'd had this feeling of freedom, almost rebirth, as if the door of her past had been thrown open and she'd flown free. Peering at him through the all-too-early dank evening light, she wondered where his thoughts were. In America with Jenny and the boys? Her arm gripped his more tightly and was answered by his hand finding hers.

'All right, sister Anna?'

'Fine, thanks.' No sister could have sounded more cheerfully natural. He mustn't guess at the sudden burst of realisation just how all right she was. She wished they could have walked for ever, walked into the night, walked off the edge of the world. But this was crazy. She loved Theo – more than that she was in love with Theo.

You know your trouble, she told herself. It's weeks since he was home. You want him to make love to you – Theo, I mean. Like you get hungry for food, you get hungry for sex. Is that what you want with Lance? She gave him a quick glance as if she were frightened he might be following her thoughts. I don't know what I want with Lance. It's just that I've never felt like this before, so right, as if he's part of me. So is it just that I want to make love? No, I won't even imagine what it would be like. With Theo it's perfect, always it's wonderful. I just want Theo. So why do I feel like this with Lance? No one can be in love with two people. Think of all the books I've read, great romances. Always there's just one person, one who is utterly right. No, don't think of that. Think of Theo. Please send him home soon. Perhaps what I need is a reminder of how wonderful it is with him.

'You're very quiet?'

'Sorry,' she said with forced brightness. 'You aren't saying much either. I was just thinking.'

202

He stopped walking, turning her to face him and raising her chin. Could they really see each other or did they only imagine the message.

'All these months I've been coming to Manningtor. Anna – oh hell, what am I saying? Come on, let's go back to that funny hotel. If we're lucky they may have enough hot water for a bath before dinner. Damn this war.'

Three short words, seemingly apropos of nothing. But turning back the way they'd come, fingers tightly linked, neither had the will to delve further.

Chapter Ten

That overnight stay on the way back to Manningtor drew a line under the past even though the doors of their two separate rooms remained firmly closed. Morning light helped, as they tried to keep their thoughts on home, on the routine the war had imposed.

And so the weeks went by. Theo and Lance both came home whenever they had time and fuel, the family's delight at Theo's appearance only exceeded by his own at being at his beloved Manningtor. Lance had said that to him it would always be home, but he knew and Anna knew too that it wasn't the therapy of his surroundings that drew him. It was seldom the brothers were home at the same time. Even at Christmas their paths didn't cross: Theo arrived on Christmas Eve and left in the early hours of Boxing Day; Lance arrived that same afternoon. The demands of the service made no concession to the festival. Anna avoided facing her confused emotions, frightened to admit that she dreaded being with the two of them, seeing them together, filling the role expected of wife and sister-in-law.

It was a Thursday afternoon at the end of the first week in January, daylight fading early and made worse by the condensation that misted the windows on the inside and sleety rain that ran down the outside. For months Anna had worked (worked? To her it was escapism, never work) on the story of a family in wartime. Today she finished reading it through. It was finished. The outline she'd planned had been very different. This was the first time she had peopled her book with characters recognisable in the present. In the days she used to scribble into her notebooks, whether in the winter isolation of her room in Dunsford House where she would wrap herself in her thick dressing gown for warmth or the summer solitude of the surrounding fields, all she'd known of life had come from reading great romances of the past. Now, though, the Milford family were born: James and Penny, happily married and with two children, the future seeming unruffled until war divides them. It's the story of loneliness when James is posted to North Africa, of Penny's battle with the everyday cares and restrictions, a background familiar to women up and down the country. When the first Americans arrive in England and are stationed nearby everything in Penny's war-drab life runs out of control. With characteristic generosity, an abundance of the kind of food that has become no more than a memory in its host country, they give a children's party. That's where she meets Barrie O'Neill, an American sergeant. It's a story of love, loneliness, a will to hold fast to the past while the present is sweeping her along on a tide she can't fight. Desperately lonely, she longs for love. Images of James become shadowy. When his parents take the children on holiday she sees it as a sign: what harm can it do anyone for her to clutch at the chance of happiness with Barrie? As a lover he possesses her body and soul; during that brief period she is lifted out of her normal life, even her conscience doesn't trouble her. But with the children home again there is no escaping the truth of the situation. Aware of atmosphere as children can be, they become fractious, filled with anger and misery. Wounded in North Africa, James is sent home on leave to convalesce. The old ties are gone, they have become like strangers to each other. When she tells him about Barrie he sees himself as being magnanimous when he says he is prepared to overlook her unfaithfulness, he even admits to having behaved in much the same way during their separation. But for her his casual acceptance makes it impossible for them to hope to restore their relationship. Anger, hurt, grief, all those things she could have taken as no more than she deserved, could have given her love for him rebirth; but casual acceptance and the assumption that they can carry on a normal married life as if what she'd done hadn't been important to her makes her future with him impossible. So the wheel of divorce is set in motion. And with it comes the shattering of the children's world and her own gradual realisation that because of what she's done to them her happiness with Barrie is destroyed. There is no happy ending, no way of straightening the tangle. It wasn't the route Anna had planned, she'd planned Barrie's to be no more than a secondary role, a temptation to be overcome, leading to a glorious ending with a happy family.

Stacking up the pile of typed sheets ready to tie them and lock them away with those that had gone before, she didn't hear anyone come into the room.

'You look very engrossed.'

Like a thief caught with her fingers in the till she turned at Lance's voice.

'Not really. It's nothing.' But it was. It was a mirror to her inner self. And this was Lance, nearer to her than any other being. 'It's a story. I wrote it. No one knows. It's what I often do when they think I'm dealing with estate things. Don't know why I'm telling you.'

'I do.'

'Years ago, when I first came to Manningtor, I told Thelma that I used to try and write. But I've never mentioned it since so I expect she thinks I just did it because I didn't have anyone to talk to in those days.' She talked fast, feeling uncomfortably out of her depth with the situation.

'What are you going to do with it?'

'Lock it in the bottom drawer of the filing cabinet with the others. They're just rubbish, I expect. That's why I don't tell anyone. Well, not till you. No one else. I suppose I trust you not to laugh.'

'May I read it? Please, Anna.'

Her hold on the stack of papers tightened. It would be like looking at her soul. But why should that matter? This was Lance. Wordlessly she nodded, finishing tying up the bundle then passing it to him. It was another of those milestone moments – she felt she was giving him part of herself.

'My blessed Anna,' he spoke quietly as he took it from her. Such happiness flooded through her; she knew he understood what she was sharing.

Before they joined the family he pushed the tied bundle carefully under his flying jacket and took it out to his car in the wet coachyard. It wasn't mentioned again, and yet it was there between them as they talked to Aunt Kath, binding them ever closer.

Next time he came he brought it back, but not before he'd taken things into his own hands. An old school friend of his had moved to live in America at much the same time as he had himself. Not that they often met, but their roots were strong and they'd never lost touch. He remembered there was a brother, considerably older, and the director of a publishing house. What are friends for if not to help each other? If Anna had written to the firm out of the blue it's unlikely she would have aroused any interest. Paper was in short supply, no publisher was going to risk taking a chance on an unknown author unless the work was seen as saleable.

Briefly Lance told her what he had done.

'I was tempted to put your name on it and send it. But I didn't. I just wondered about the name – Anna Sullivan, Manningtor Park. I couldn't do it without asking you.'

Despite excitement that made it difficult to think straight, Anna saw his point.

'When I first started to try and write I was Anna Bartlett. That's who I'll be.'

Lance wrote a personal letter to go with the manuscript, making sure that it got into the right hands. Then, as excited as children wrapping their surprise Christmas presents, they parcelled it up. In their ignorance they expected that a week, or perhaps a fortnight, would bring her a letter of acceptance, and by bedtime in her certainty she seemed to see the bound book. That was in the middle of January 1943. When the weeks turned into months and no word came, hope faded with the dream.

Every available acre had had to be put to the plough: food production was the first priority of the countryside. Still the sheep and cattle grazed, but no longer were they turned from one field to another. In this, Home Farm was no different from any other. On the northern edge of the estate was Blackmore Wood and it was there that on a morning in late spring Anna was with Ken Briggs, the forester. The business side of the estate had been her first introduction to its timber production and she was aware how much was brought into Manningtor's coffers from the sale of wood. For almost three years she had held the overall responsibility for the Park, but she never ceased to be aware how much she still had to learn. On that morning they had been marking beech trees for felling and she set off for home feeling thoroughly pleased with herself. She had learnt a lot, listening while Ken Briggs explained his reason for each one chosen, at first tentatively but gradually with more confidence, and encouraged by the forester, making her own suggestions. Once or twice he explained why it would be better to leave a tree standing although she'd thought it could be marked, but mostly by the end of their tour of inspection she had followed his way of thinking so that she could judge the tree's age, its condition and, most importantly, whether its removal would enhance the light and give those around it better scope.

These days there wasn't petrol enough to drive unnecessarily and, in any case, Anna had grown into her role and now travelled the estate on the ever faithfully Dilly.

'You can leave me to see to Dilly if you like,' Sylvia called, seeing her ride into the stable yard. 'Theo's home. You'd only just left when he arrived. He's home until Tuesday.'

That was Saturday morning.

'Thanks Sylvie, I'll leave Dilly with you then.' Her face showed all the expected eagerness. And of course she was eager; yet behind that first rush of excitement was a niggle of disapproval. How like him not to hint at the chance that he might have the weekend at home! She knew exactly why he hadn't mentioned it when he'd phoned on Thursday: he'd wanted to see their faces when he walked in unexpectedly. The idea that if they'd known he was coming they would have had the extra pleasure of looking forward wouldn't have occurred to him – he'd wanted to share their thrill of surprise at his arrival. The family must all have recognised that he'd kept his visit secret because he wanted to see the pleasure on their faces; only Anna was irritated by his characteristic behaviour and even she wasn't prepared to acknowledge the shadow it cast. Hurrying from the stables towards the house, she held a strict rein on her errant thoughts. Darling Theo, where will he be? In the nursery? In the drawing room with Aunt Kath? With Alex? Perhaps he'll see me coming, perhaps he'll come out and meet me. That's what she willed him to do, but telepathy couldn't have been his strong point.

In the drawing room she found Kath and Thelma but there was no sign of Theo; he must be with Nanny and Christo.

'I'm back,' she announced unnecessarily. 'Sylvie says Theo's here. He must be with Christo?'

I'm glad. It's Christo who binds us, makes us a proper family.

But what am I saying? It's not true, she told herself, we're bound because Theo is what my life is all about – of course it is. Don't even think about – and so firmly did she hold her racing thoughts that even in her mind she wouldn't say Lance's name. She started back to the door on her way to the nursery where Christo would be having his lunch, imagining Theo there, helping to guide his baby fork.

'No, you won't find him there,' Thelma stopped her. 'We told him where you were, but I expect he thought it would be no use looking for you, if you and Briggs were walking through the woods he knew he'd never find you. He's walked into the village with Alex and the girls. You know how they love having him with them when he comes home. You remember they always take their sweet coupons along Saturday mornings to see how far they can make them stretch. He couldn't get out of that uniform quickly enough and how nice it was to see him in ordinary things, like old times.'

'Can't you just picture them all arriving at that little shop.' Kath laughed. 'Alex says she makes them keep in their crocodile and wait outside; she only lets them in six at a time. Such trade it must bring. Wouldn't you think Mrs – Mrs –?' But the name of the owner of Moorfield's paper shop, where the shelves behind the counter housed jars of sweets, eluded her. 'Wouldn't you think with all the custom the school brings her she'd give them all a few sweets extra? But Alex said she weighs them out to the last chocolate bean.'

'So she must, Mother. She can only restock against the coupons she hands in. Oh, how I do hate this war,' said with such force and quite out of character for placid, kindly Thelma. Matronly-looking and always managing to convey the impression that her clothes had been made for someone else, she was dressed in her WVS uniform suit of green. These days they seldom saw her in anything else, as she gave hours of each day to its work in the community. Sometimes she'd be behind the tea urn in Deremouth Hospital, sometimes she'd be visiting the elderly, sometimes she'd be at the local school teaching first aid. And when she wasn't working for the WVS she found plenty else to do. She supposed that the hours Anna spent in the estate office must be her way of staying close to Theo; similarly she kept her 'motherly eye' on the staff at Sullivan's Coaches, always writing to Matt with up-to-date news of his staff and their families. Her talents were many, her enthusiasm seemingly endless.

'You've heard from Matt?' Anna changed the subject, recognising the light blue of the air mail lettercard on the arm of Thelma's chair. She knew it was more than a fortnight since the last had come.

'Just a short letter. He can tell me so little. I do hope he's not too uncomfortable out there. He says he finds the heat trying. Like me, I expect, he carries too much weight to take easily to a hot climate. Oh dear, I just wish it would all be over. Seeing dear Theo walk in on us so unexpectedly this morning seemed to bring it home how all our lives have changed. Oh, we're lucky, I know I ought not to complain.'

'You never complain, my dear,' Kath was quick to reassure her. 'Matt, poor boy, I dare say at his age it's harder on him than the young ones. I had a note from him, too, Anna. No news, but all we ask is that we know he's safe. It's easy for us to write, we can tell him every little detail.'

'That's the trouble, Mother,' Thelma's round face was unusually solemn, 'he must hate not to be able to describe his life to us. Sometimes when I write, as you say telling him every little detail of our lives here, I wonder whether I'm being kind. Perhaps it just rubs salt in the wound, makes him yearn for the old familiar things. Poor Matt. Such a man of habit, we could have put our clocks right by his movements.' Then, with fresh determination, 'Still, we have to keep our spirits up or he might read between the lines. I shall write to him this afternoon and tell him what a surprise Theo gave us. And Lance, is he managing to get home at all this weekend? I hope so. The boys need to be together sometimes. Even in the Air Force' (for apparently Thelma considered the Army, boosted by the services of Matt and Sam, to be of superior importance) 'and stationed in England, they must need to feel the bond of family.' She had herself in hand again; for Matt's sake she had to stay strong. If he could put up with the dreadfulness then she mustn't fail him here in the comfort of his home. How she hated even to imagine him part of the dreadful fighting there must have been out there in the desert these last weeks. But he's safe – he was safe when he wrote this – thank God. Please, I beg You, please always take care of him. When the fighting ends in the desert, and the news tells us it's going well, surely it must soon be over, then perhaps he'll be sent home, perhaps they'll let him finish out the war in England. He's done enough. Surely he ought to come home. Nothing in her sweet smile hinted at her fervent plea. 'Did you have a good morning with Briggs, dear?'

'Yes, it was interesting. I wonder how long Theo will be.' And well she might wonder. Alex and the girls returned, but it seemed Theo had met an old friend from the club, like him home on leave, so they'd dropped in at The Flying Pig to have a beer together. The family had lunch without him. Then she went into the office to write up the notes she'd made in Blackmore Wood, the number of trees to be felled and sold. Just like an ordinary day, so how could she be expected to hold her excitement at fever pitch when he didn't even bother to put her before some friend from the club?

'That's where you're hiding!' Despite herself, at the sound of his voice that old, familiar feeling overcame all other.

'Me, hiding?' But there was a teasing note in her voice. It was impossible to be resentful. In a second she got up from her chair at the desk and was somehow only inches from him, her face raised to his.

'And how's the elf? Don't you ever stop work, woman?' he laughed, drawing her into his arms. All the old magic was there. 'And now,' he said, releasing her, 'bring me up to date. How are things going?' No longer did he ask 'Are you coping?' He drew a second chair to the desk.

Together they went through the events of the past weeks. Did she imagine it or could she really sense that as Manningtor claimed him, so he relaxed? Relaxed from what? He'd never given any hint of being tense or strained. Fun-loving, yes; over-exuberant, often, especially when he was organising games to involve their evacuees; making no secret of the fact that amongst his flying colleagues he found many with a will equal to his own to squeeze every bit of pleasure from life at the air base. Looking at him as he read through her neatly kept lists – income from rents, outgoings on necessary repairs, wages, everything clear and concise – her mind was pulled in many directions: pride in knowing he could find no fault; pleasure at being with him; the ever-present knowledge that something was missing in their relationship; the image she wouldn't let take hold, an image of Lance; and today, something she'd never detected before,

211

something about Theo that was different. Surely those lines around his eyes were new, and she'd never noticed the restless movement of his fingers nor the way even as he concentrated on what he read he bit the corner of his mouth, unconscious that he was doing it. She'd detected nervous movements like this in Lance but until now never in Theo.

'It's time you had a proper leave,' she voiced her thoughts aloud.

'Sounds as though you must be missing me.' His smile was as immediate and confident as ever it had been. 'But, leave, you say. They'd never manage without me.' Just as he intended, she supposed she must have imagined his uncharacteristic tenseness.

An hour or so later, when Lance arrived, she left the two of them to kick a ball with Christo. Thelma was in the morning room writing letters: her weekly one to Dee, who would soon be home for half term; her weekly one to Sam stationed in Kent; and her twice weekly one to Matt. Nothing was allowed to throw her regular routine off course. Kath was in her room having her afternoon rest. Anna was alone in the drawing room, watching the ball game from the window.

I could have stayed and been part of it. That's what I ought to have done. No one could believe I have anything pressing to do in the house. So did they guess why I was running away? I ought to be ashamed, I *am* ashamed. Why can't Theo be enough for me? There, I've admitted it. I do love him, truly I do. If I didn't, how could I look ahead to tonight and want us to make love like I do? I couldn't. Yes, and he's fun to be with, he loves Manningtor, he's proud as Punch of Christo, and even if he never actually fell in love with me that doesn't mean anything. Theo could probably never fall in love with anyone – he just loves the whole of life. So why can't that be enough for me? Lance – he *knows* me, not just the me I show but the me that is deeper, more private. He's never talked to me about his marriage, except for the boys; but that's not because he doesn't want to share things that are private and precious. I know, I absolutely *know*, that something is lacking for him too. Lacking? For Theo and me? No. No, of course it isn't. How can I let myself even *think* . . . Anyway, if Lance's marriage wasn't happy he'd talk to me about it – there's nothing he couldn't say to me, I know that and he knows it too. But if he knows me so well, knows even the way

212

my mind works, does he know too that I can't bear to look ahead to when he won't be here any longer?

'My word, but you *were* in a dream world,' Alex's voice broke into her wandering thoughts.

'I was watching Christo. He's got a mighty kick, come and see.' Why was she never thoroughly comfortable with Alex?

'He's a great lad. With Lance and Theo here, I wonder you're not out there too.'

'Boys' games,' Anna's laugh was designed as a smokescreen. 'It's tough on a little boy to be brought up in a house of women. Let's hope it won't be for much longer.'

'Hope is all there is to live on. Things still look pretty bleak. But, for all that, we have been hearing from quite a few of the girls' parents that they want their children home. Things have been much quieter and Thelma says most of the local evacuees have gone back. Let's hope we're not all counting our chickens. Anyway, that's what I came down to tell everyone. We've just been talking it over – "we" meaning the teaching staff – and we've decided that when this term finishes we'll go back where we belong. We'll advertise locally that we shall be back for the start of a new school year.'

'Are you sure it's safe? Just because for a while it's been quieter, that doesn't mean it'll last. It's only because Russia is bearing the brunt.'

'No one can say what's safe and what isn't. Anyway, we can't spend the entire war holed up. Not that we haven't been grateful. You've no idea how proud I was to be able to bring them home here to Manningtor. Anyway, I'm not going to waste Saturday afternoon in here chattering, I'm going outside to join in the game with Theo. He's more than ready for being taken off flying again for a break. He's had enough of this damned war.'

'You mean he said that?'

'Don't be daft, of course he didn't. I expect I know him better than you do. I can tell.' And with that she went.

Alex had never been hostile towards Anna yet there was something in her manner that prevented a close relationship. That she adored Theo was apparent; sometimes Anna suspected the root cause of the barrier between them was jealousy that he had a wife. Watching the footballers, listening to Christo's screeches of excitement now Alex was part of the game, Anna let therself be tempted to join in. Often she and Lance had played like this with Christopher, occasions when in delighting in the little boy's enjoyment they had both been aware that the moments were important. Yet on that afternoon she couldn't look at him for fear of meeting his gaze and reading in it a reflection of her own confusion.

'I came home to relax,' Theo laughed as he gave the ball a final kick and watched Christo stumbling after it. 'How about coming down to the quay and checking the boat with me, Lance? It's not in the water of course, but I like to make sure it's OK.' It seemed it didn't enter Theo's head to put the suggestion to Anna. She supposed he considered she'd 'had her turn' in the office; in the way he shared himself around, the next hour or so belonged to Lance.

'And me,' Alex attached herself to them. On Saturday afternoons she was free, just as free as were the pupils who amused themselves as they liked around the estate, some of them helping on Home Farm, others offering with youthful enthusiasm to muck out the stables, clean the chicken houses and collect eggs or help in the kitchen garden. Almost three years at Manningtor – for some of them term time and holiday time too – had turned them into country girls. Of course there were fewer of them now than had come during the first days of the war. Three years had seen the top two classes leave school; when this term ended another year of students would be gone. Now the youngest was twelve, Chiltern House School was shrinking. That was a possible reason for the staff deciding it was time to leave Devon: a few more years and they would have no one to teach.

'Are you coming, Anna?' It was Lance who suggested it.

She shook her head. Then, aware of the way Christopher was listening and watching from one to the other, and even more aware from his expression that a storm was about to break, she rushed on, 'I promised Dilly I'd bring Christo to see her. Bring your ball, Christo, we'll put it back in the shed on our way to the stable.'

'Gotta go see Dilly,' he explained to the other three as if in apology for not being free to accompany them, all interest in their outing forgotten.

'Better not waste our fuel,' Theo said. 'We'll cycle, how's that?'

214

The young squire, as he was known locally, cycled through Moorleigh, calling greetings to people who must have seen him around all his days. 'Hello, Mrs Andrews, how's your son?' he slowed down to ask an overalled woman who was clipping her front hedge. Then hearing that her pride and joy had been promoted to Leading Aircraftsman, he called, 'Well done. Remember me to him,' and pedalled hard to catch up with the other two.

'Good to see you home, sir,' called Bert Higgins, one of Sullivan's drivers.

'Thanks. You well, Higgins?'

'My boy, Derek, he's off in the Navy next week.'

'Gosh, he's old enough for that? Makes me feel ancient. Give him my good wishes, tell him steady on splicing the main brace.'

And again a furious pedal towards where the other two were waiting. Thus ever it had been with Theo, a cheerful word for everyone and somehow his presence making the sun seem to shine that bit brighter.

It was his idea that they put the war behind them and dress for dinner that evening. He found the idea of dressing no differently for dinner than they had for lunch depressing; and one thing he shied from was a mood of depression, his or anyone else's. So that evening he donned his black tie, Anna a full-length pre-war gown of peacock blue, four-inch heels on shoes which could still be bought without using precious clothes coupons. Seldom did she use the jewellery that was locked in the safe, but seldom was there an evening like this. So she selected the rope of pearls and slipped them over her head, as she did so remembering the first time Theo had opened the safe and brought them out for her to wear. How important it had been to her to know he was proud of her, how pathetically she yearned for some sign from him. As the memory rose to the forefront of her mind, it was immediately pushed out by the realisation of how much had changed in these last years. That day of Sidney's funeral had been the first time she'd stood tall – or tall by her standards – in high-heeled shoes and, in a way, the fact that she now wore them with the same comfort as she would sandals seemed to symbolise far more than a change in the way she dressed. Then, Manningtor had been awesome, she'd still been conscious of the responsibility of being seen as its mistress; now it was home, there could be nowhere she would rather be. From dealing with the tenants of the meanest cottage on the estate to overseeing the running of the house, a role that had begun as her side of the bargain she and Theo had made, it had become her life. Still she had so much to learn, but all the while Manningtor's hold on her grew stronger.

'You look very elegant,' Theo's voice broke into her thoughts.

'And why not?' she laughed. 'Tonight seems to be turning into a celebration. Sylvia and Francis are coming, Alex too. Francis produced two chickens for the occasion.'

'Jolly good. Not often Lance and I are both here. Pity about Matt.'

'And Sam. That's what Thelma must think but she never says so.'

'Lance comes over often, I suppose?'

She nodded. 'Pretty often. Well, naturally he does.' She heard her answer as defensive, but that was probably in her imagination for it was apparent he hadn't noticed. 'He says even after being away so long he still thinks of Manningtor as home.'

Theo smiled, well pleased. 'That's the way of it. Once it gets a hold on you, go to the ends of the earth but you'll never be free.' Then seeing what looked to be a shiver, 'What's up? Surely you can't be cold?'

'No. Just a goose walked over my grave. Theo . . .' She needed some sort of assurance, she needed the goose to be chased away. Turning to him she raised her hands to his shoulders, slipping them round his neck.

'Don't tempt me,' he laughed, moving his hand down her narrow waist. 'What is there about you that does this to me? Nothing but a pint-sized elf, but just look at me.' So sure of himself, so happy with the evidence of his virility. 'Down, boy!' He was adept at laughing his way out of moments with no other way of escape, whether of sickening fear or, as now, of sexual desire. Somewhere a bedroom door closed, there was the sound of footsteps Anna recognised. Lance on his way downstairs. Her thoughts were a tangle of confusion. If only they hadn't to go down and join the family, join Lance. If only they could shut the door on the world and find each other in the never-failing miracle of lovemaking. But they couldn't. Even their pre-war dinner attire

216

was a mockery, as much part of the charade as the evening ahead of them.

'How was the boat?' she asked, pulling away from him, in an effort to restore their former status quo. 'Alex keeps an eye on it, I think. I expect she told you.'

'She's a good scout. She tells me they're moving back to base during the summer holidays. The old house's war work's almost over. Can you cope with getting it back to normal?'

'Of course. Every piece was carefully marked which room it came from and, even if I can't remember, I'm sure Thelma and Aunt Kath can. Come on, Theo, they'll be waiting for us downstairs.'

'Lead on.'

So side by side, elegant beyond what had become normality, they walked down the wide, shallow stairs. Tonight everyone at Manningtor was determined to show the world – or at least confirm to themselves and each other – that gracious living was no more than temporarily on hold; the old ways would return. Only Lance, with the gold band of Squadron Leader on his cuff, brought home to them the make-believe of their determined effort.

Next morning Alex excused herself from the church crocodile and went riding with Theo.

Lance found Anna, 'helped' by Christopher, cutting flowers for the house.

'Anna, I've told Aunt Kath I can't stay all day.'

'No, Lance! You're only pretending you have to be back early.' What was it he read in those tell-tale wide eyes? Fear? Worry? 'Don't run away.'

'There's nowhere to run to, Anna, nowhere to escape. I've known it for weeks. Christ, I've no right to talk to you like this. Theo's wife. My sister-in-law, damn it.'

'Lance, I may be those things, but most of all I'm *me*. No. there's no way of escaping, not for either of us. I know it and you know it. There's no future in what we want. Theo, Jenny, whoever we were married to, there's no future in what has happened to us.'

'Mumma,' Christo tugged at the skirt of her print dress, 'we doing flowers,' he reminded her. 'We got to fill up that.' He indicated the partly filled trug she'd put on the grass.

217

'You sort out the flowers we've cut, try and put them into colours, pink ones together, yellow ones together. See if you can do that for me.'

'P'raps.' With a sigh he tipped the cut flowers onto the grass, knelt with his legs apart, feet spreadeagled and his bottom on the ground as only small children can, and set about his task. Colours needed a lot of concentration and he was only just learning about them.

'You see?' Anna said to Lance, knowing his mind would have moved with hers onto the responsibility and love they had for their children. 'For Theo's sake, stay today, Lance. I've got things to do. Why don't the two of you play tennis; Theo always insists that the court is marked up each year. I believe he'd have it done as one in the eye for Hitler even if the school weren't here to use it.' It was just something to say, something sane and normal that would put the brakes on where their conversation was heading.

'He's my kid brother. I used to play with him and look after him when he was Christo's age and younger. Now all I can think is that he's married to you, *you*, like part of my very being. If I were just in love with you, if it were no more than that I want to sleep with you – and God knows, I do – that I suppose I could learn to live with. But it's more than that, it's as if –'

'As if we are two parts of one whole,' hardly above a whisper, she finished the sentence for him. 'I know, Lance. I've known for a long time.'

'Done – Mumma, tum on, flowers all smart.' And so they were: pink ones in one line and yellows in another. Anna saw them through a haze of tears.

Turning to Lance she didn't try to hide how she felt.

'Promise me you'll come back as soon as you've got a free day. Lance, we're not hurting anyone. We both know where our futures lie.' Please God, please, please, let him have a future. Keep him safe. Keep both of them safe. Don't make something dreadful happen as punishment because this has happened to us. Anyway, how can love be a sin?'

'I'll come, my blessed Anna. I haven't the willpower to stay away.' Then, his voice taking on a firmer tone, 'As you say, we know where our futures lie. Sometimes I'm filled with shame – and I know you are – that I can't control what has happened. Can't even try.'

218

She nodded, not trusting her voice and aware that Christo had sensed something he didn't understand and wasn't comfortable with the atmosphere.

'I get ball,' he said hopefully to Lance. 'I have game wiv you – boys' game,' he added the words he'd heard his father use to him.

'Not today, Christo. You help Mummy with the flowers. I have to go. We'll have a game next time, shall we?'

That satisfied Christo, whose main reason for the suggestion had been to put an end to the funny feeling he'd had in his tummy when he'd stood by himself watching the two of them talking and making him feel left out. Now he sighed contentedly as he bundled the flowers back onto the base of the trug, forgetful of the colour separation that had absorbed him, and watched Lance turn back to the house. If he was surprised to find himself lifted into Anna's arms, it was a more than pleasant surprise. She hugged him close, burying her face in the warm sweetness of his neck, willingly drowning in the pure love that swamped her. Delighted, he wrapped his arms and legs round her, threw back his head and laughed from sheer joy.

A minute later they heard Lance start his car in the coach yard.

'Unca Lance going home,' the little boy announced, sitting upright in her arms so that he could wave as the car disappeared down the drive. He and Anna went back to their flowers; only for her the summer sunshine seemed to have lost its golden brilliance.

So the weekend passed. It was the small hours of Tuesday morning. By breakfast time Theo would no longer be the relaxed young squire of Manningtor, he would once again be Squadron Leader Sullivan, ready to return to that other life where he was popular, fearless, fun-loving, the right man in the right place. But how little one person ever knows another.

'I'm awake,' he heard Anna whisper, very quietly so as not to disturb him if he were still sleeping.

'Anna.' The way he said that one word was strangely unfamiliar, or did she imagine it? This wouldn't be the first time they'd come together in the early hours, starting one day as they'd ended the last. It was what she wanted, it was the one way to focus her mind. Letting him know just how awake she was she reached her hand to caress him, her first reaction one of shocked surprise. If his voice had sounded different, so was the unresponsive state of his body.

'Couldn't you sleep?' she whispered companionably, not wanting him to realise what she had expected.

'Can't tell you. Christ, Anna, don't know how much more of it I can stand. You don't know. Thank God you don't have to know. Night after night. So bloody frightened. And the poor devils down there, people, women, children.' The first tight croak in his voice had lost the battle: Theo was crying, almost silently he was sobbing.

'Tell me, Theo, tell me, darling,' she whispered, holding him close, feeling the wet warmth of his tears.

'Can't. It's me, just me. The crew get in that bloody plane, they joke and laugh, they don't know how my gut is in knots, how I'm sweating with funk. What a hero you're married to.'

'Yes, I am. If you weren't frightened you wouldn't be half the hero. I bet one thing, I bet when they laugh and joke, so do you.'

'Too bloody right, I do. Anything but think. Just talking about it, knowing it'll happen again tomorrow – Anna, help me.'

'Darling Theo, the only help I can be is to pray for you. And I do. Always I do. Nurse Radley – remember Nurse Radley, the midwife you used to hide away from – she told me that.'

'What would she know?'

'More than us perhaps. She had a sweetheart in the last war.'

'*Miss* Radley. Much good her prayers did him.'

Anna had to think quickly. 'They never married. She'd just qualified. I suppose marriage isn't for every woman, some follow careers.' Not very clever of her to have made an example of Nurse Randall's prayerful sweetheart. 'Darling, we have to keep faith, hang on and believe it'll soon be over. Every time I hear the sound of bombers I think of you; I imagine the pilots all with families, all hating what they are doing as they rain hell and havoc. Poor Exeter – even Chalcombe had what they called a stick of incendiaries last week.' As she talked she could tell from his breathing that the storm was passing.

After a while, his voice almost steady again, he said quietly, 'The chaps in the crew, all the leg-pulling. Yes, you're right, I

220

carry on just the same as they do. If I didn't they'd see me for what I am.'

'Every one of you must feel the same, Theo. Leg-pulling is a smokescreen. You've blinded me with it all this time.'

'Now you know. Now you know just what I am.' He took her hand in his and moved it on his neck, then his chest. He was wet with sweat, clammy and cold; even the sheet he lay on was damp. She could feel the fast hammering of his heart. 'Even talking about it does this to me.' Again she heard the warning rasp in his voice. 'You know what? Sometimes when we've been flying through flak, trying to avoid it, waiting for a hit that would explode the petrol tank, I've almost longed for it to happen. Just to end it, anything to end it. It's not just me. I'm responsible to get the chaps home, they depend on me. Can't go on like it, oh Christ, there's no way out.' She knew the battle he had to hold his control. 'The only thing that keeps me sane is to remember Manningtor. Searchlights, ack-ack, the glow of fire on the ground, I try and black it all out. Sometimes it's what happens. Perhaps I'm going mad. I see the house, the sloping lawns, I see Christopher kicking his ball and I swear I hear him laugh.'

And me? Am I part of the picture? She didn't ask. Perhaps she was afraid of his answer, or even more afraid of acknowledging that whether or not she was there in his head as he escaped the hell round him had lost its power to hurt her. She was ashamed. Fidelity goes far beyond physical faithfulness. 'Two parts of one whole' – wasn't that what she'd told Lance?

She needed to help Theo hold his devils at bay. And in doing that she might forget her own guilt? Her hands caressed his unnaturally cold, clammy body; she moved onto him; in the dawn light she could see his face. Until that moment she'd thought of him as unchanging, handsome and debonair, the same now as when she'd fallen in love with him. Just as handsome – to the world, just as debonair – but barely recovered, he looked more haggard, his closed eyelids pink. She moved her naked body against his as she straddled him. He might look back on her words and be comforted, but she knew only one way to put everything else from his mind.

Neither of them spoke. The only sound was from outside, the clamour of the dawn chorus in tune with the urgency of what they did. Theo's night had been long, lonely and full of terror. Desperately he wanted to escape his ghosts. For them, lovemaking followed many avenues, all of them explored to the full, all of them journeys of excitement and wonder. In those next few moments, though, there was nothing but a driving urgency. Then it was over and, physically and mentally exhausted, Theo slept. Only Anna lay awake as the summer sun rose.

How well had she ever known him, known what lay beneath his never-failing cheerfulness, his 'goodwill to all men'? How long had he been tormented by unspeakable fear, isolated by his own feeling of failure? He condemned himself, saw himself as a coward. But lying wide awake by his side, Anna knew the failure to be hers. If she'd ever honestly loved him, not just been in love with the facade he chose to show, then wouldn't she have understood what he'd been suffering? Of course she would.

She wanted to think just of *them*, Theo and herself. But her mind took a sideways leap. She was with Lance. Never once had he talked to her of the perils he faced, the loneliness of terror as fighter planes soared and swooped in their battles to defend. Kill or be killed, the will to survive, that sick fear that must surely turn each man in on himself. Sometimes when Lance had come to Manningtor she'd known of the aerial 'dogfights' or the fighters' mission to stave off marauding bombers. She'd heard Aunt Kath say to him, 'You look tired, dear,' and so he had. But she'd known without a word that tiredness had its roots in fear, loathing for seeing death fall out of the skies, sickness of his spirit. He'd never talked about it, but neither had he put on a show of bravado. The thought that fear and cowardice went hand in hand had never been part of the equation.

Pushing him firmly into the background, she turned her thoughts again to Theo. She felt that what had happened that night had given her her first glimpse of the real man. She ought to rejoice that when he could be silent no longer, it was to her he turned. And, of course, she did. Yet there was no running away from her disappointment that he could be so ashamed that anything lay beneath the jolly, bantering personality he'd let nothing knock off course. Did being ashamed of fear make him more of a man? No. His tears, his sweating terror, these and his garbled confession, his gut-knotting funk as he'd seen it, these things filled him with shame, set him apart from his crew and his family. Why couldn't he have been man enough to know that he wasn't alone in how he felt? Of course she loved him – again she told herself so. And what about what he called his 'funk'? It was more than fear for his own person, that she never doubted. It was horror of the whole situation. Yet the night made a stranger of him. Instead of drawing her closer, it seemed to set her apart. And that was *her* fault. That fun-loving, handsome young god she'd fallen in love with was all she'd ever known. And when she'd prayed so earnestly for him to feel the same about her, how much had she honestly understood about a deep, meaningful relationship?

Think of Thelma and Matt: she let her thoughts go off at another tangent. No one could look on them as romantic, yet they are like one being; they know each other so well they must be able to read each other's minds. What they possess is true gold, which turns mere 'romance' into dross. No, don't think about Lance. Once let him creep into your mind and there's no hope left. Two halves of one whole. Matt and Thelma, they're the perfect couple. And you and Theo will grow more and more like them. Surely tonight is a start.

She wanted to reach out and touch him, to reassure herself. But she knew she must let him sleep. A glance at the clock told her it was nearly six – already the sun was casting its pale golden ray through the gap in the half-undrawn blackout curtains. Except for the occasional chirrup, the birds had finished their morning performance. Careful not to wake Theo, she slid out of bed and crept across the room to open her wardrobe. A quarter of an hour later, she rode out of the stable yard. There was nothing like an early morning ride to fill her heart with thankfulness, her head with sanity and her lungs with pure fresh air.

By the time she joined the family at the breakfast table Theo was already there, his smile back in place and his brave face put on with his uniform. Less than an hour later he'd gone; the memory of the night might have been a dream.

It was during lunch that the youngest member of the domestic staff, a bottle blonde of sixteen who rejoiced in the name of Gloria, brought the second delivery of post.

'Excuse me, m'am,' she said to Anna, who, due to her being the wife of the wonderful Theo, was always given due respect and to spare, 'the post has just come. I brought it through cos I recognised the air mail. For you, Mrs Sullivan.' She put Matt's letter in Thelma's outstretched hand. 'Then there's this one too, m'am.' A parchment envelope, the address typed, was laid by Anna's plate. Her heart was racing as she took her dessert knife and ripped it open. But the news hardly had time to register. What could be wrong? Surely the air mail must have been in Matt's writing – that had been apparent by Thelma's eagerness.

Never graceful, but they'd never seen her move like this. Pushing her chair back from the table, oblivious of Kath's 'What is it, my dear?' Thelma stumbled from the room.

Chapter Eleven

'My poor Matt,' Kath spoke her thoughts, spoke to herself rather than to Anna. 'Don't let him be gone, dear God, don't take him too.'

'It can't be that, Aunt Kath,' Anna made sure her voice was strong, she had to sound positive, more certain of her facts than she was. 'It wasn't a telegram, it was a letter. Perhaps he's been posted somewhere else, still overseas. She'd been so hoping he'd soon get home.' She said the first thing that came into her head, anything that might take away Kath's look of naked fear.

Visibly Kath took herself in hand. Her mind jumped back to the day Sidney had died and she recalled how through the haze of her misery Anna had been her support.

'Yes,' she made her voice firm, 'that's what it'll be. Thelma has listened to every word of news; we could read how her mind was turning as the troops gained control in the desert. If anything serious had happened, even if he's been wounded – oh dear, my poor Matt, it's not fair, it's not right.' Then, another effort and she went on, 'Anything serious and it would have been an official notification. Go up and see her, dear. I've never known Thelma behave like it.' Her eyes closed, her lips moved; this time it was no more than a silent, heartfelt plea.

'Thelma,' Anna called softly as she tapped the bedroom door, 'are you in there? May I come in?' She dreaded what she might hear, for no matter what reasons she'd tried to find in her effort to help Kath, in her heart she knew (just as Kath knew too) that gentle and stoic Thelma wouldn't break easily.

The voice that answered her was restrained, expressionless,

225

strangely cold. 'Come in. I do apologise, I ought to have considered Mother's feelings.' Dry-eyed, her face a mask to hide behind, she stood in the middle of the large bedroom, her hands gripped together as though she needed *something* to cling to. On the tallboy behind her were photographs: Matt and her on their wedding day, the two of them with the children when Sam and Dee had been riding in the local gymkhana, Matt in the uniform of an army major just before he embarked for North Africa, widely smiling Sam bursting with pride on the day he received his commission. Anna took in the scene, instinct moving her hands towards Thelma, who had been the first to befriend her at Manningtor.

'Who was it from? Is Matt hurt? What's the matter, Thelma?'

'From Matt –'

'Oh, thank goodness. Poor Aunt Kath was so frightened. Is he going to be sent somewhere else when you'd so hoped he'd come home?'

'I said I'm sorry. I behaved badly. Yes, he's not coming home.'

'So you've still got to battle on. Thelma, I'm terribly sorry. There must be scores of younger men –'

It was that that broke Thelma's icy reserve.

'Too old? Matt's not too old. Oh no,' she croaked, her voice rising out of control. 'Comfortable, set in his ways, wanting the old routine. Is that what you thought? No, not Matt. I'll tell you what he wants: he wants me to divorce him.'

'I don't believe it! Why, you and Matt . . . Thelma, another letter will come . . . everyone gets bad moments, perhaps he'd had too much to drink, perhaps he wrote it when he wasn't himself, perhaps –'

'Here, read the *bloody* thing.' She thrust the single sheet of thin paper into Anna's hands, then slumped on the edge of the bed. As much as the sudden sound of her blubbering crying, it was her language that told its story. Anna read the few brief paragraphs. Fallen in love – but this was *Matt*, kind, honest, easy-going, middle-aged-before-his-time Matt. Pamela, he called the nurse who seemed to fill his mind – and his bed too; he was uncharacteristically outspoken about that and about the joy he found in the wondrous Pamela. Anna felt she shouldn't be reading what had been meant for Thelma alone. As completely as any adolescent, Matt had lost his heart.

226

'It'll be a nine-days' wonder,' Anna heard herself say, 'no one's life is normal today, not his, not ours.'

'Never said those things to me,' Thelma blurted out. 'Can't face my future without her – you read what he said – everything I've ever wanted . . . not *me*, oh no, not good old Thelma, always waiting when I go home, comfortable as an old pair of slippers.' In her misery she rocked backwards and forwards, her knees spread inelegantly wide apart and her hands hanging limp between them. Her wailing was like a cry of pain.

Desperately wanting to give comfort, instinct sent Anna to kneel in front of her, moving closer between her thick legs, holding her round the waist and rocking with her.

'Don't know what to do, Anna,' wept Thelma, gripping her so that her head was cushioned against the ample and matronly bosom. 'And the children, what about the children? What'll I tell the children? That all these years I've failed him? Never loved me like he does this – this – oh I don't know. Is he bad, or is it just that I was never right for him? Thought I was, thought we were like one person. Poor Mother. It's not fair. He ought to have thought of Mother and of the children. It's not just *me*, I don't count, not to him anyway.'

'Yes you do, of course you do.'

'Oh yes, poor old Thelma.' She loosed her grip and Anna raised her head. For the first time they looked directly at each other. Thelma's round face was blotchy, her lids so swollen her eyes were almost closed. 'If he was bored with me, if the sort of comfortable love – huh, love I call it! – if what we had, left him wanting more, why couldn't he have told me. I would have done anything he wanted. I mean – if it was the bed thing like he seems so excited about – you know – oh Anna, don't know what to do. Perhaps the children see me as boring like he must have.'

'Stop it, Thelma!' Perhaps speaking sharply might cut through her despair. 'You're the least boring person. You're pure gold and he's not worth – not worth –' she dug deep for the most belittling thing she could say '– not worth the drippings of your nose!' The words hung between them, out of place in the emotional misery. But as fresh tears rolled down Thelma's cheeks she no longer bellowed in her misery, it was as if the fight had gone out of her. She even forced herself to smile (or perhaps she smiled in spite of herself) at Anna's choice of words. Groping for her crumpled

227

and wet handkerchief, she tried to mop her face. 'Must look a sight. Don't let Mother come up, Anna. I'll have to tell her, just don't know how. So much to think about, don't know what to do.' Again she said it, looking around the room as if she expected it to give her clear directions. 'See a solicitor . . . look for somewhere to go . . . and the children . . . have to tell the children . . . a home for the children . . .'

'None of that will alter, Thelma.'

'You mean they'll go on living here?' More mopping and sniffing as she fought to keep her mind focused. 'Yes, it's always been their home. Just visit me.' Her trembling breath tore at Anna's heart. How she wished she could tell Matt face to face what she thought of him!

Still kneeling she pulled herself to her full height, willing Thelma to meet her eyes.

'Of course Manningtor is their home, just as it's *your* home and mine too.'

'And Matt's. He'll bring her here like he did me. I'm only here because I'm Matt's wife.'

'You're jumping too far ahead. Don't rush into anything, Thelma. Another day or two and you may hear again. All right, Matt might have been having a fling with this woman – he won't be the first man to find comfort with another woman, away from home all this time. He probably wrote his letter in a glow of – of – of sexual gratification –'

'Don't! It's too revolting. Making love has never been like that, not for us. It wasn't that I didn't want us to do it, but to write about it, to make it so clear that all these years he'd never found what he wanted, it's cruel.' As cruel as beating a faithful dog, was Anna's silent opinion, but Thelma was hurt enough without her adding to it. 'I never refused him, not once in all our years. Why couldn't he have told me, he always went off to sleep as contented as a babe. That's what I thought.'

'It's this war, Thelma –' and Anna tried to sound convincing '– living apart, all of us doing things we wouldn't have done – you with the WVS and goodness knows what else, me with the estate, Matt in a life alien to anything he's ever known, Theo dropping bombs on people like us just because they are on the other side.'

'And Lance. All this time away from his own family.' Anna

228

gave her a sharp glance. Were her words a warning? Probably not, for glancing at her watch and making a visible effort, she went on, 'It's getting late, I must wash my face and get tidy. I promised to take old Mrs Cardew to the hospital. Poor old soul, she's in dreadful trouble with her arthritis; she could never manage to climb onto a bus. Whatever must I look like?'

Instinct again was Anna's guide as she leant forward and kissed Thelma's damp cheek.

'To me you look lovely. But then we're mates,' she added with a grin, partly to hide her own confusion at such a show of affection and partly to put them onto a more cheerful footing. 'To the rest of the world you might not look so hot. So I'm going to close the curtains and leave you to have a sleep. Mrs Cardew is the mother of Bill Cardew, the baker in Moorleigh, isn't she? What time are you due to pick her up? I'll take her instead, I'll say you've got an upset tummy, how's that?'

'What about fuel? I was using my allowance from the WVS.'

'I can manage. Lately I've been going everywhere either on my bike or on Dilly, so there's some in my tank. Close your eyes and try and block out all your worries. Whatever they are, Thelma, however things work out . . .' What was she trying to say? 'Just that you're not on your own, nor ever will be.' And of that she was determined even though she saw no way out, for, as Thelma had said, Matt was a Sullivan: Manningtor had always been his home. 'And Thelma, about Aunt Kath. I'll tell her you rushed off because you hadn't been feeling well, bilious or something, and trying to eat was the last straw. Suddenly you had to make a bolt for it. I'll say you're feeling better but are trying to have a sleep.'

'Anna, you're a saint. I know I have to face her, but with my face like this – and everything – I'd only make a fool of myself again. Mrs Cardew's appointment is at half-past three.'

'I'll get her there, don't worry. Aunt Kath might like to drive in with me, then when we've brought Mrs Cardew home we'll have a chance to talk. I'll explain things. Easier for her in the car, at least I feel it might be.'

'Won't be easy wherever it is. Not for her and not for you to do the telling.'

'Nor for any of us. But we'll all hang together.' Then with what Theo would have called 'her elfin grin', 'You concentrate on your bilious attack.'

This time when Thelma smiled some of the old warmth was in her expression. Perhaps it was put there by Anna's assurance that 'we'll all hang together'.

Usually, but not always, Kath rested in the afternoon. On this occasion, though, she suspected that Anna had invited her because she needed support in taking old Edith Cardew to the hospital. And Edith would be much happier with someone of her own generation there. Thelma was different – no one considered age with regard to Thelma. So the outing went according to plan. While their passenger was with the doctor, Anna and Kath drank weak and tasteless tea bought from the WVS trolley. They were recognised by Thelma's green-uniformed colleague who showed concern on hearing she was unwell. A passing nurse overheard and came with enquiries and messages of sympathy. Thelma spent many hours each week at the hospital, and she was as well liked there as she was everywhere else where she gave her time with warmth and kindness. As the afternoon wore on Anna became ever angrier; to treat her as Matt had was like taking from an innocent child. Yes, she let her imagination follow that road, a child who offers a bag of sweets to share with a friend only to have the whole lot snatched. Was it just because in this Pamela creature he had discovered previously unknown adventure in sex? Thelma called it lovemaking, saw it as a gentle, caring way of letting him use her, doubtless always in the dark and beneath the bed covers. No doubt Pamela took him on an exploration of sensual wonder. But if it was all new to him, whose fault was that? Anna's mind went back to her early days with Theo. She'd known nothing, only that she wanted to follow her instinct. It had been he who'd led the way, he who'd taught her there were so many aspects: lovemaking could be fun, it could be hungry passion (even lust – yes, that too, glorious, animal lust), it could be tender. Whatever avenue they took it always carried them to the same deeply fulfilling journey's end, sometimes to lie weak and helpless with laughter, sometimes her cheeks would be wet with tears of happiness that knew no words. But never did boredom or duty come into the picture. Dear Thelma, how dare Matt lay the blame at *her* door alone!

When she helped Mrs Cardew up the step into her son's bakery Anna knew the hardest part of her afternoon was still ahead.

'We could ride just to the edge of the moor if you like, Aunt Kath. I've scrimped on my petrol this month so we have

230

enough.' Away from home it might be easier to say what had to be said.

'You're spoiling me, dear. I thought looking at poor Edith Cardew, I ought never to complain. She was married the week before Sidney and I, all of us here in the little church down the hill. They had a hard time, any baker's life must be hard, up before the dawn chorus to get the bread in the oven. She used to look after the shop while he went off with his horse and delivery wagon. There can't be much of a living in loaves of bread or a few cakes either. Her boy, the one who runs the bakery now, was born about the same time as Matt. Then just when he was old enough to be a real help in the business, Edith lost her husband Claud, on the wagon. And now look at her, every step a battle. What an unfair thing life can be. I lost my darling Sidney, but we had good years and he was fit until his last hour, thank God. Surrounded by comfort and love, that's been my lot. Poor Edith.'

They had come to where the tree-lined lane gave way to open countryside; ahead of them lay the moor. As soon as she reached a patch firm and clear enough for parking she pulled off the narrow road and switched off the engine.

'Just look at it,' Kath murmured. 'God knew what He was about when He made the moor, that's what Sidney used to say.'

'Aunt Kath, I want you to listen.'

'News? What is it, another baby?'

Anna shook her head. 'We'll make do with just Christo until after the war.' However was she going to tell her? However was she going to talk at all when her mouth was suddenly so dry? 'It's not about me. I told Thelma I'd tell –'

'Thelma! More than just a bilious attack? That's it, isn't it. Why couldn't she tell me? I may be old but that doesn't mean I have to be sheltered from the truth. What does she think is wrong with her?'

'That letter –'

'So something is wrong with Matt? I knew it. I knew it.'

'No, Aunt Kath, Matt's not ill. He tells her he never knew there was such happiness as he's found.'

Kath's lips parted, she looked at Anna in disbelief.

'You mean there's another woman?'

Anna nodded. 'It was a bolt from the blue. We all thought there hadn't been much post because it hadn't been getting through. It's a nurse serving out there, someone he calls Pamela –'

'Pamela!' Such contempt in her voice! This was no elderly dowager needing protection from the truth. Her eyes blazed anger. 'What in the world is the matter with the stupid boy? If I had him here I'd make him see sense. Well, and so I will on paper. How dare he! How dare he let some – some – some tart of a woman do this to his life. Pamela!' She seemed to spit the word.

'Thelma is distraught. He has asked her to go to a solicitor, to file for divorce on grounds of his adultery, he'll give her details –'

'Can't believe he can be so silly,' she seemed to slump. 'If only Sidney were here, he'd write to him, he'd tell him where his duty lies.'

'Thelma is too good for that, she's worth more than being a duty.' What memories the word brought alive: duty, obligation. This was no time to dwell on her own situation, but in that second she realised just how far her position had changed since that summer four years ago. In truth, until Kath had talked of duty, those early months had receded over a far horizon. When had it happened without her even noticing?

'She must be sensible. She mustn't rush into anything they'll both regret. Matt has never been impetuous, but a scheming woman, ready and willing, he's not the first man to be tempted. Too long away from home, that's the sadness. Perhaps the best thing is for Thelma to write to him with understanding, be prepared to forgive and put the incident behind them. Go to a solicitor, you say? If she's silly enough to let hurt pride send her rushing to a solicitor, she might be bringing nothing but unhappiness on all of them – Matt, the children, as well as herself. No, she wouldn't do that. Once she's thought about it she'll come to see that at her age she needs the security of a home and family.'

Anna had been prepared for a tirade of angry disappointment at Matt's action; she'd assumed Kath's wholehearted support and understanding would be for Thelma. She saw though that come what may, Kath was Matt's mother and maternity was the strongest instinct left to her. Perhaps, in any circumstances, for a woman it was the strongest. Thinking of little Christo, pure and as void of wickedness or deceit as any child of his age, who one day would be a man – whatever the circumstances he would know her own loyalty would never waver.

'Thelma won't lose the children, why should she? And her home is Manningtor.'

It was Kath's turn to be surprised.

'Oh dear, what have we done to deserve a worry like this?' Kath's assumption that the whole thing could be worked out if only it were handled carefully, melted. She sounded as elderly as she looked, old and defeated. Instinctively Anna took her hand, shocked that on such a glorious day it could been so cold.

'I offered to talk to you because she was in such a state. He's been her whole life.'

'And so he must continue to be. He's a good boy, never been an hour's worry to me. I suppose he's been to bed with this woman; all this talk of the joy she's given him, you may be sure it's not holding hands in the cinema.'

'Yes, he says Thelma has grounds to divorce him for adultery.'

Kath's mouth set in an unfamiliarly hard line. 'She mustn't be so selfish and stupid. He's not the first man to have fallen for temptation when he's without his wife for as long as he has been. It's not Matt who's to blame, it's circumstances, it's this dreadful inhuman war. I'll have a talk to Thelma when we get home, I'll make her see that it would never have happened but for being sent out there to that soulless desert, desolate, lonely – and more frightening than the dear boy would ever have let himself hint at.' It seemed Matt was the hero of the day and Thelma void of understanding. 'Better start up the engine, dear, and we'll go home. I'll have a talk to her. If she won't listen to reason I'll point out to her that it's no piece of cake for a woman of her age to face life alone. I know Theo is very good; with Matt away he wouldn't dream of hurrying her to find somewhere of her own, but a day of reckoning would have to come if she insisted on going through with breaking up their family. She'd have to find somewhere else before this wicked war ends. She couldn't still be at Manningtor when he comes home. She's always been a good wife and mother. Oh dear, oh dear, I never thought something like this would threaten to upset the house.'

In silence they drove towards Manningtor and were turning in at the gate when another thought struck Kath. 'This Pamela woman, a nurse you say. She may be a very nice person, Matt has never been the sort to chase after loose women. He must know what he's doing if he's planning to marry her and bring her to live at Manningtor. I don't know how Sam and Dee would feel. Oh dear. Oh how I hate this war and what it does to our lives.'

'Nice or horrid, he can hardly decide her home is to be Manningtor, Aunt Kath.' Anna said no more, but between them in the silence hung the reminder that lay behind the words: it was *she* who was mistress of Manningtor and, until Theo came home, it was up to her who was brought to the house.

'Put me down here,' Kath said as they came towards the front steps. 'I shall go straight upstairs and see Thelma. Poor girl. It's a hard blow for her to take. I'm glad you told me instead of letting me hear it from her, it's given me time to think how best to advise her.'

'None of us can do that, Aunt Kath. Matt isn't some hot-headed lad. Don't you think he has been fighting this for weeks, months perhaps, while all the time she has been worrying about why she doesn't hear, and why he can tell her so little.'

'So far from home, no one to talk to. He's always been a person to like order in his life. And that's what she has to remember. If, just for the moment he believes he is in love with this nurse, then it has to be up to Thelma to hang on, to give him time to cool down. That's what I shall tell her. Do nothing . . . wait.'

A few minutes later, Kath upstairs setting out the rules she expected Thelma to obey, Anna came along the corridor from the side entrance and into the great hall. Hearing her step on the marble floor, Mrs Gibbons signalled her with relief. 'Just a minute,' she spoke into the instrument of the telephone on the wall outside the study door. 'Here's Mrs Sullivan now, you can speak to her yourself if you hold.' Then, to Anna, holding her hand over the mouthpiece, 'It's the school. Something about Dee. Trouble, you may be sure.'

'Anna Sullivan here. My housekeeper tells me you're calling about Dee. I'm so sorry I can't fetch her mother to speak to you but –'

'Dee told me about her illness. The poor child really concerned me. That's why I agreed to her coming home.'

'Dee coming home?'

'Her train is due to arrive in Deremouth at six-twenty. I ensured she had sufficient money for a taxi from the station, but I wanted to lay your fears to rest. She is coming with my sanction.'

'You say she was very upset?'

'Indeed, that was what alerted a member of the staff to come to speak to me. It seems she had received a letter this morning telling her of her mother's sudden illness. I dare say it was you who wrote to her, Mrs Sullivan?'

'Yes, that's right.' Now, why did I say that? Anna asked herself. Then, a second lie making the first more plausible, 'Perhaps it wasn't as sudden as we thought. Her mother isn't the kind to complain. However, we are all hoping and praying the tests will prove negative. And thank you for sending her home. While she is so worried she wouldn't concentrate on her work, so it's much better that she's here than waiting and watching for letters. I really ought to have suggested it myself. I feel I've let her down.'

'Dear me, no, Mrs Sullivan. I'm sure you did what you considered best for her. All children react differently; there are those who need to be protected and to send them home to a sick parent would be a hindrance to everyone. But Dee isn't one of those. Whatever the situation she would wish to be there carrying her share of the burden of anxiety.'

Anna tried to cling on to hope, but it was impossible not to imagine the letter Dee must have received from her adoring father. Always his champion, already in her young mind she must be looking to her mother in an effort to find an excuse for his disloyalty. And today Thelma was in no state to face her criticism. Anna's decision was immediate. She would go to Deremouth and meet Dee's train; whatever the girl had to say could be said to her first; exactly how she would be able to defuse the situation she didn't know, she simply trusted that inspiration would come.

With Kath upstairs, the drawing room was empty and the first thing Anna noticed as she went in was that parchment envelope, lying just as she'd left it when she followed Thelma upstairs. The contents of it had seemed unreal even as she'd read it, and the afternoon that followed had put the whole thing so far to the back of her mind that now she had to take the single sheet of paper from the envelope to make sure the whole thing hadn't been a dream.

A glance at the clock told her she had twenty minutes before

235

she needed to leave for the station, time enough to do what she wanted.

> *Dear Lance,*
>
> *It's really happened! Your friend (his brother, I mean) has written to me. He likes what I've written and wants me to go to London to see him. He even apologises for having taken so long to read it. Doesn't he know how grateful I am that he bothered at all? And he didn't say it's nonsense, he talks about publishing it! Can't believe it! Thank you a million times, Lance. Apart from that, oh I just wish you were here. Can't write about it – but come soon. I know you only went back yesterday but it seems a lifetime ago and not only because I miss you.*

Her writing was fast and untidy, but she thrust the letter into its envelope, addressed it and put it in her pocket. It would go out on the evening collection if she posted it in Deremouth. Then, the exciting development in her own life once more overtaken by Thelma's troubles, she went upstairs to where Kath was fighting Matt's corner in the way she saw best, and told them about the telephone call from the school.

Only as she drove down the hill towards Moorleigh did she have 'thinking time' for herself. Edward Crighton, director of Hibbert Mills, a well-known and respected publishing house, had written personally to her. Well, she corrected herself with an unfailing streak of honesty, he'd dictated and signed the letter. Of course that wasn't because her work was wonderful, she was quick to stamp on hope before it rose out of hand; it was because he'd been approached by Lance. Lance. Like a needle sticking in the groove of a gramophone record, the image of him, the echo of his voice, the certainty of how right it was for them to be together, these things went round and round in her brain. Was she wicked? Was she any different from Matt, whom she was so quick to condemn? Was she any more faithful? Physically she was – but surely what really mattered was what went on in your heart and mind. Yet how could it be wicked to feel as she did for Lance, when it was something she'd had no power to prevent? Round and round went her thoughts, repeating themselves, time and again covering the same ground.

Then, as if she'd given the arm on the turntable a tap, her thoughts raced ahead.

Remember the day I first met Theo, remember how I took one look at him and after that couldn't stop thinking of him, dreaming of him. It wasn't a bit like that with Lance. I liked him because he was Theo's brother, or that's what I honestly thought. Liked? Is that the difference? Did I ever really *like* Theo, or was I so head over heels in love with him that I was blind, dazzled? Liked? Liked Lance? Yes, I did. I still do. But when liking and loving go together I feel *consumed*, I want to share everything that I am with him. And I want us to make love together, I want to share with him that blindingly wonderful moment that sweeps my mind clean of everything else. It's like that with Theo, when that happens I make myself believe he's everything I want; I almost make myself believe that it's the same for him with me. Perhaps just for those seconds it is. But he doesn't really *love* me, not love me with this certainty I have about Lance. And Lance? He never talks about Jenny, never tries to make me believe he's a misunderstood husband. Yet I know, I *positively know* that he and I have something more important, stronger, something neither of us can escape.

There was very little traffic on the road, certainly more bicycles than cars in days when most private vehicles had had to be laid up for the duration. Doctors, people whose work made travelling beyond the limits of public transport essential, people occupied in agriculture, others given medical certificates confirming their need, these were the few who were still driving. Anna's petrol allowance was small, so she usually travelled either on Dilly or on her old 'iron steed'; today had been an exception. On the almost empty roads she reached Deremouth while her thoughts followed a journey of their own, although with Lance at the forefront of her mind she didn't forget to draw up at the post office and send his letter on its way. The one thing unchanged by the war was the postal service; tomorrow morning it would arrive at the RAF station . . .

Dee's train had stopped at Exeter St Davids, so when it hissed and jolted to a standstill at Deremouth Station the platform was suddenly full as passengers spilled out. At that time of day there were returning workers, combined with shoppers and, almost last to alight, Dee. At the sight of her Anna's mind cleared

237

of everything but the reason for her coming. The unflattering summer uniform looked out of place on the sixteen-year-old. Always heavily built, she must surely tower over her form-mates at school. Five foot ten in height, broad-shouldered, her heavy bosom accentuated by the green girdle knotted round her thick waist, knee-high fawn socks emphasising her tree-trunk legs, a lightweight gym tunic of fawn under which she wore her uniform apple-green blouse and two-tone green necktie, the whole ensemble topped by Panama hat. And how cruel that a girl with size nine feet should have to wear school sandals. Suddenly filled with affection for her, Anna waved furiously to attract her attention. Poor Dee, how let down she'd been; Matt had been the centre of her universe. As the girl came towards her, her pale face and pink, swollen eyelids left Anna in no doubt at what the news had done to her. It would serve Matt right to see it for himself! The child had almost worshipped him. He must have known. If he'd spared a thought for anything more than indulging his own pleasures he would have realised her hurt.

'They phoned and told me your train time,' she greeted Dee, her voice holding nothing except welcome and pretending not to notice the swollen eyelids.

'Why didn't Mum come?'

'She's very upset, Dee. They said at school you told them she was ill.'

'I wasn't going to tell them the real reason. I wasn't going to have the teachers all mulling Dad over, blaming him for things they know nothing about. So I said I'd had this letter saying Mum was ill.' The way her mouth turned down at the corners, the way she seemed to breathe down her nose, the criticism in her tone, these all should have warned Anna that she had misjudged Dee's reaction. But they didn't.

'I'm glad you've come,' she tried to sound reassuring, 'this has really knocked the ground from under her feet. Perhaps it's a temporary madness, Dee. Try not to feel too badly towards him –'

'I suppose you're all ganging up on Dad? Well, I'm not.'

'Good. I know it's tough on you, but Dee, anger would only make you bitter. All we can any of us do is take a day at a time, give her all the support we can. Things will work out. Just let her feel you love her.'

'And what about him?' Getting into the waiting car, Dee

238

slammed the door with more force than necessary. 'I've written to him; I posted my letter on the way to the station; I've told him that I understand. Don't care what you think, don't care what any of you think – not Gran, not Mum, not even Sam. If Dad's gone soft on someone he's met out there, then you know what I think?' In silence Anna waited; if she'd spoken Dee wouldn't have listened. 'I think it's Mum's fault. It doesn't happen to every man who goes off abroad. Look at Lance, he isn't desperate for a girlfriend. Don't expect Theo is while he's away, either. Neither would Dad have been if Mum had been different, if she'd been *fun* sometimes, instead of always such a – such a – a righteous do-gooder. You know what I think?' Again a reply wasn't needed. 'I think he's never had any joy. Work or home, nothing ever changed. I suppose you're not expected to think like that about your parents – no good asking you, you never had any – but Anna, she couldn't always have been like she is now or why would he have married her? Always clicking away with her knitting needles, or rushing around sorting out other people's lives, looking after –' and here her voice changed in an attempt to mimic Thelma '"– looking after those who are less fortunate". She never throws her hat over the windmill. Dad and me, we have fun together, or we *did have* until he went way. We laughed about things, we both knew we were doing it behind her back, that was what made it so special. She's like all these people intent on doing good works, she's boring.' There was venom in her tone.

'Dee, you only say that because of what's happened. She's a dear. She was my first friend at Manningtor.'

'Bet she was. She can never leave a lame duck to find its own way back to the pond.' But guilt was nudging the back of Dee's conscience, Anna knew it from the croak in her voice. 'Dad and me had secrets, he liked that as much as I did. We always had fun. He says this woman, Pamela he calls her, he says being with her makes him feel free. That's how he used to feel when he was with me, I know he did.' In her ungainly way she was digging into the pocket in her fawn knickers to find her handkerchief, 'Now he's got *her*. When he comes home he won't want things to be like they used to be for us, for him and me. Was me who made him feel free then, playing truant from boring routine. He'll have *her*. And you know what I think?' By now she was blubbering, talking more to herself than to Anna and it wasn't easy to follow all she said, her words interspersed with gulps and snorts. 'I bet she's not boring in bed, that's what I think.' Anna suspected she said it not because she understood what she was implying but simply because she knew how embarrassed her mother would have been to hear her. 'Unfaithful . . . asked your mother for a divorce . . . that's what he said. Being unfaithful means that he's slept – all that – I may still be at school but I know about things, we talk about it – and he'll have done that, with Pamela.'

'It's the war, Dee. Separation puts an unnatural strain –'

''Tisn't the war,' Dee hiccupped, 'it's everything. Just want him to come home. I'll learn to share him with her if she really loves him and makes him happy.' The crumpled handkerchief came into use, an enormous blow, followed by a facial mopping up as she took a grip on herself. 'Been thinking about it, and I've made a sort of pact with God. If He brings Dad home soon – and they've got the Germans pretty well licked in North Africa, I know because I read the paper every day in the library at school – and I've prayed really hard for him to be sent back to England – well, if that's what happens and he brings Pamela home things might not be all bad. She could cheer the place up.'

'Don't talk like that to your mother. Promise me, Dee.'

'Not promising anyone anything. And I'll tell you something else: I'm *never* going to get married.'

'You'll change your mind one of these days.' Anna tried to bring a more cheerful note. They were already in Moorleigh; a few more minutes and they'd be home.

'Shan't. Anyway, I was telling you about the pact I've made. If Dad comes home from North Africa, even if he's head over heels about Pamela, I won't be horrid to her. He'll have enough to put up with from the rest of you, all blaming him and looking on him as some sort of sinner, and Mum being all martyred.' It seemed her imagination had led her into a maze with no exit for any of them. 'It's a sin to hate, that's what we're told. It isn't a sin to love.'

'Then it's a pity he didn't hang on to the love he had for your mother.' She didn't repeat what she'd said to Kath, that Matt wouldn't be bringing a new wife to Manningtor. Dee had suffered enough for one day. And there was something else even more important, words she clung on to: it's not a sin to love.

Putting Dee down by the front steps, she drove to the coach yard. Then, the car away, she avoided the family and went up to the nursery, drawn by the thought of Christo. Perhaps she'd be in time to see him in his bath. She knew the beaming smile that would light his face when she appeared, she knew how he would hold his arms out so that she could steady him to climb to the rim of the bath and then spring, warm and wet into her arms. It wasn't just Christo who drew her to the nursery, it was Nanny too, dear kind Nanny, full of common sense and wisdom.

Thelma surprised everyone by the action she took.

It was mid-week, two days after Matt's letter had knocked the chocks from under her, that she announced she was cycling to Deremouth, saying only that she wanted to call at the coach depot to enquire after the sick wife of one of the drivers.

'I would suggest you might ride in with me,' she said to Dee, 'but if Duke says she is well enough for a visitor, I shall call at the hospital and see her. I don't expect you'd want to do that.' Her tone was flat, giving no hint whether she would welcome Dee's company for the ride.

'Too right I wouldn't,' Dee answered in the ungracious way she knew so well. 'Don't know why you fuss about these people. I bet if you were ill they wouldn't care tuppence.'

'I dare say you're right.'

'Well anyway, even if you weren't on one of your *boring* –' the word said with such emphasis '– missions of kindness, you can count me out.' Every now and then Dee gave her mother a furtive look as if she were testing just how far she could go, just how gruff and ill-mannered she could be and get away with it. It turned the knife in her and hurt to hear herself, opening the wound even further that she seemed to have no power even to annoy. Yet she couldn't control the way she behaved, she needed the pain.

'Then, while I'm out I think, Dee, you should get your things together. You have exams ahead of you this term and you can't waste your time doing nothing here. This illness you invented for me can't go on indefinitely. If I can pull through it, then it's quite time you did. I shall call at the station for a ticket and find the train time for tomorrow morning.'

241

Dee shrugged her broad shoulders. 'I don't care one way or the other.'

She dropped the book she had been idly glancing at and went out of the room. Upstairs she turned the key in the lock of her bedroom door. Not that anyone would want to follow me, she told herself. Why should they? They don't care where I go: here, school, anywhere. If I were old enough I'd join up like Sam did. Had Dad written to Sam too? There hadn't been a letter from him, so probably not. No, Dad wanted *me* to understand, that's what was important. Dad and me, we're different, we always have been. And we still will be. Oh damn his pretty nurse, what did You want to let him go and fall in love for? What about *me*? I expect he was bored with Mum and all her good works – not surprised, even You must see that always being good to every Tom, Dick and Harry sort of sets her apart from ordinary people. If You're so great and powerful what did You let it happen for? It's not fair. It's bloody, *bloody, bloody* not fair. Sam's all right, he and Mum have always been buddies. But me and Dad, don't You care that it'll be all spoilt? Can't be the same with him doting on his pretty Pamela?

At that point she could have won the battle to hold back her tears, but instead she watched, fascinated, as her podgy face contorted.

Look at me! I hate You, yes I do, I *hate* You. First You took Grandpa; he was part of our gang, me, Grandpa and Dad. Now You've taken Dad – 'cos You *have* taken him – it can't be like it was. If You'd wanted, You could have stopped it happening.

Four people sat down to an evening meal of vegetable soup, almost meatless rissoles backed up by a variety of home-grown vegetables, then rice pudding. No wonder dressing for dinner had become a thing of the past. Conversation was forced, indeed there probably would have been no attempt made but for the fact that Kath was determined not to let anyone guess at the anguish she was suffering. Thelma told them no more about her trip to Deremouth except that Mrs Duke had appeared pleased to have a visitor. As for Anna, in her imagination she was showing Lance the letter from Edward Crighton. It didn't enter her head that while she shared her excitement with him, she had always hidden her writing from Theo. The one thing all three had in common as the meal progressed was annoyance that Dee should make no effort to help the atmosphere. Just once Thelma was about to tell her to behave like an adult, not a spoilt child, but the words died before they were spoken. She couldn't cope with an argument, better to say nothing; better to live through the minutes, let time tick away. Don't think of today, don't remember the afternoon, don't think of tomorrow, don't imagine next year, or the year after.

The next day Dee was taken to the station. There was no through train, so this time she would have to change trains at Wolverhampton. In the meantime there were four or five stops; her pile of hard-boiled egg sandwiches and her *Picturegoer* magazine would be hard pushed to keep her going for so long.

'Good luck for your exams,' Thelma tried to sound as if it had always been she who had seen Dee off, as if this day were normal. 'We shall see you at the end of term.'

Dee's smile was as forced as her own, her mouth turning up, her eyes empty of all emotion. So it wasn't to be wondered that Thelma had no suspicion of what was in the girl's mind.

Chapter Twelve

Coming from the stables Anna could hear the voices of the girls. With their classroom day over they were making the most of the hour before the bell summoned them to tea and, from his sudden squeak of excitement, it seemed Christo was with them. This morning a bill had come from Greg Hoskins, the local roofer, for work he'd done on the roof of one of the estate cottages. Anna hated unpaid bills but before she wrote the cheque she'd wanted to make sure the tenant was happy with the work. In fact she was pretty sure that this particular tenant, elderly and cantankerous Arthur Mills, would have been chasing her with a complaint if last week's storm had found a weak spot. Her real reason for riding out to see him had been her need to be occupied, anything that would bring normality into a mind that was alive with excitement, impatient for a word from Lance telling her when he would be free. For all her determination, it took more willpower than she could muster to hold her thoughts in check, to prevent herself imagining the two of them in London together. As soon as he told her when he could be free she would make the appointment. To the accompaniment of the clip-clop of Dilly's hooves she had given up the battle – what harm could there be in dreaming? No tenant seeing the squire's young wife – and what a credit she was, shouldering his responsibilities while he served his country – would have suspected the journey her imagination was taking her as she'd ridden by, giving her usual friendly greeting.

The sound of Christo's happy shriek broke through her daydreams and drew her, like a magnet, to the sloping lawns in front of the house. How good the children were to him. A game of leapfrog was in progress, something too advanced for a not-quite-four-year-old. But Christopher wasn't a 'man' to accept defeat and his friends encouraged his efforts. As they lined up to leap – at varying heights according to their ability, the one being leapt over bent lower or stood taller. When it came to Christo's turn she crouched to the ground; the fourteen-year-old following him had her hands ready to grab him if he fell, and over he clambered.

'Well done! Christo did it!' And, just like his father, he beamed his pleasure at them before running to the back of the queue ready for another turn.

'Bring that other chair, child,' Nanny greeted Anna. Just as in Nanny Harknell's eyes her charges remained unchanged by the years, so Anna was put into the same bracket. Having grown up used to Mrs Short, Anna hadn't considered there was anything unusual in the long-time Nanny's manner. In fact, had Nanny Harknell liked her less there would have been a barrier of formality. Only the best was good enough for that darling scamp Theo and, remembering some of the red-lipped floosies he'd frightened them all with, she never failed to thank her Maker for guiding the boy into seeing a bit of common sense when it came to making his choice.

'What are we going to do with him when his friends have gone?' Anna laughed, watching Christo.

'Lot of nonsense taking them back if you want my opinion. This war hasn't done with us yet. Nor any sign that it's likely to be.'

'They came as children, town children. Some of them are as old as Dee.'

'Poor child. Breaks one's heart that parents could do it to a girl.'

'Oh, come on, Nanny. She hardly went out of her way to make things easier for Thelma.'

'Unhappiness is like an illness. If she had come home stricken with flu we shouldn't have expected her to be a ray of sunshine. But she didn't. She came home stricken with grief, the rock she built on turned to clay.'

'She would have been better to stay at school. It's only put a rift between her and her mother,' Anna said, knowing very well that once Nanny took her stand nothing would move her from it. And wasn't she right? Matt had put his own happiness before his family's; Thelma had wrapped herself in an armoury of that loving kindness she made her defence, holding everyone away, even Dee – or more truthfully, especially Dee. No parent had the right, no parent had the right, no parent – round and round it went in Anna's brain as she watched Christo's innocent joy. And Lance's boys, in peaceful America where they could have no conception of the heightened emotions of loneliness and separation.

Nanny rolled away her knitting, a sleeve of a cardigan that grew only a row or two at a time simply giving her something to do with her hands while she kept her eye on Christo. The garment had started out to be last Christmas's present to her cousin but, never mind, next Christmas would do just as well or even better, for wool was even harder to come by now than it had been twelve months ago. Lily Gibbons had told her she'd seen a card in the window of the haberdasher's in Deremouth saying they would have a delivery last week, but who had the time to queue up waiting for the shop to open? Certainly not Lily, nor her either. This war was far from done and, if anyone wanted *her* opinion, it was wicked to take those poor girls back to their London suburb when they could have the freedom and safety of Manningtor.

'Time for your tea, Christopher,' she called in a not-to-be-argued-with voice. 'You may have the turn you're queuing for, then come straight back to me.'

His only answer was to smile beguilingly, instinct telling him that was the way to melt her heart. His turn came, he rolled over the bent figure, looked to his friends for their never-failing approval.

'That's it then, time to go in.' Nanny stood up.

'Just one more time.' How huge those dark eyes were as, with no hint of a grizzle, he clung to hope. 'Just one more, then no more. All right?' Had his plea been made to Anna she knew she wouldn't have been able to refuse him, but Nanny was made of sterner stuff.

'No, lad. We had a bargain and we have to stick to the rules. You had your last turn.' Out came his bottom lip, his small body stiffened. 'Careful now.' She raised a finger, a reminder that he was on dangerous ground, then with a hand that wasn't to be gainsaid she took his in a firm but kindly grasp. 'Men don't make scenes,' she told him in a quietly controlled voice, 'so say goodbye to your friends.'

246

'We're stopping now anyway, Christo,' Christine Murphy, one of those who'd been at Manningtor since she was only nine, came to his rescue. 'It's time we got scrubbed up for tea too. We'll go on tomorrow, shall we?'

His smile was back in place. 'I'll go high tomorrow,' he yelled as he retreated, his hand in Nanny's and turning so that he was running almost backwards and only just managing not to fall over his own feet. 'High as the moon I'll jump tomorrow.'

Another minute and they had all gone; Anna was alone in the silence of the sloping parkland, only her thoughts for company. She lay on the grass, her face upturned towards the clear early summer sky, her eyes closed. The familiar sound of the engine might have been no more than part of her daydream, but it was enough to make her scramble to her feet. Even before she saw him, she knew. Lance had come. Thinking of nothing except that he was here, she started to run towards the house just as he parked on the forecourt. Then, sure he'd seen her, she stopped running as suddenly as she'd started, standing still and waiting, knowing that he would cross the grass to meet her.

There in the shadow of the great house, Theo's house, like two actors they greeted each other, Theo's wife and Theo's half-brother. Never had they been more aware of the situation than they were on that sunny teatime in May.

'Well done, Anna,' and so he would have said it had they been in the midst of the family. 'I can't pretend to be surprised, Crighton would have been a fool had he turned it down.' Then, his role forgotten, 'Anna –' he held both hands towards her '– things have happened, I had to see you.'

'Happened? You mean our going to London?'

'More. Oh yes, we'll go to London. No one can take that from us. I'm here for fourteen days – I mean, I am if you'll have me.'

It was like a miracle; her thoughts went no further than that. In those fourteen days they would go together to see the publisher, but in those first moments even the reason for her trip wasn't important. Fourteen days became all eternity.

'It's embarkation leave.'

Nothing had prepared her for this. It was as if his brief statement had knocked the air from her lungs, taken away her power of thought even. Wordlessly they looked at each other, just pawns in the game, powerless to fight.

247

'Let's walk. Just for a while, Lance. Somewhere – don't want to go inside.' Later she would have to play her part in the charade, but not yet. A minute ago when he'd told her he was at Manningtor for fourteen days, she had known joy that blotted out all else. Now, fourteen days became a sentence to be lived through, each hour bringing them nearer to – to what? Her imagination refused to carry her beyond the abyss of despair and show her a future where he would have no part. Yet there was something else deeply submerged in her consciousness, a voice she tried not to hear. It was the voice of shame. Manningtor, its great edifice standing proudly at the summit of the sloping parkland; even in bright sunlight it seemed to cast its shadow on her. Theo put all his trust in her. 'This is where we're at – we have to make it work.' That had been his belief at every crisis point they'd reached. Always his maxim, he expected it to be hers. But nothing had ever given her this feeling of bleak defeat.

Neither of them considered they might have been watched from anyone indoors, and if they had they wouldn't have cared. Gripping each other's hands they turned towards the gate leading to the track separating the grounds of Manningtor from the land belonging to Home Farm. Anna's mind was empty of coherent thought, so it must have been instinct that taught her to lie when Sylvia called out to them.

'Were you coming to see us? Hello, Lance, time off again?'

'You have me underfoot for a couple of weeks,' he managed the sort of tone expected of him. 'Embarkation leave.'

'Oh Lord, that's rotten. I wonder where they'll send you. We've come to take it for granted you'd be based in England. Were you on the way to the farm to tell us?'

'No.' That's when Anna's instinct took over. 'He's coming with me to see that Mr Mills is satisfied with the work on his roof. If you see Aunt Kath, tell her Lance is here but I waylaid him.'

'Old Arthur Mills? I thought that's where you went this afternoon on Dilly?'

'It was,' Anna laughed, 'only to find he was out. Probably hadn't got home from the Bottle and Glass, I ought to have realised I'd be too early for him.' What was the matter with her that she couldn't just say 'It's too nice to be indoors, we're going for a walk'? Perhaps it was easier to lie than to face ever half a truth.

'Don't worry, I'll pop across and tell Aunt Kath, she can do with something to cheer her up. Is Thelma back from seeing Dee off yet?'

'I expect she's gone into the depot.'

So, hands no longer linked, they walked purposefully on their fictitious mission.

'I thought half term was over? Why was Dee home?'

'She came home because Matt has kicked the bottom out of her world. He wants Thelma to divorce him. Matt is trying to cling to his disappearing youth; it seems he's fallen for a beautiful nurse – Pretty Pamela as poor Dee calls her.' Her scathing tone condemned not only Matt, but herself and Lance too. 'People *don't think*, that's the trouble. Matt, you, me, all the others who try to snatch at some sort of transitory happiness and devil take everyone else.'

'Don't, darling Anna.' Her hand was back in his again, his hold on it tight. 'Don't try and pretend that's all it is.'

If only the corners of her mouth wouldn't quiver, if only she could sound as strong as she knew she had to be.

'That's all it can be, Lance. You know what I've been thinking – planning – since I had that letter from Mr Crighton? I've been dreaming of you and me in London together, not just going to see him but – *being* together, two days, perhaps three, two nights. There's been nothing else in my mind, no future, no, and no past either. Just that. See what sort of a person I am? Isn't that what happens in wartime, men away from home, women behaving like slags, no certainty in anyone's life.' She needed to denigrate emotions too powerful for her to overcome; she needed to hurt herself and him too. 'Does Pretty Pamela know what she's done to Thelma and the family? And Matt, sober, kindly Matt, as moonstruck as some callow youth. Breaks your heart to see Aunt Kath, she tries to defend him but deep down I know her life is as broken as Thelma's and Dee's – Sam's too, I'm sure. And all I've been dreaming about is being with *you*. Does that make me any different, any better?' When had she started to cry? She hardly realised she was, as the barely comprehensible words poured out. Clinging to his hand she plunged blindly on along the track.

She could feel the way he was looking at her but she kept her face away from him.

By that time they'd reached the point where there was a

fork in the track: to the left it branched between the fields of Home Farm and to the right it continued towards a group of cottages, one of them where Arthur Mills lived. In between there was a sparsely treed copse that ultimately broadened out to the beginning of Dingley Wood. Rhododendron bushes were growing wild amongst the hazelnut trees and gnarled beeches. It was an area of no economic value, an area left to the vagaries of nature. As they turned off the track they welcomed the isolation of their surroundings. When Anna had first discovered it she had believed it to belong to her alone. But the truth was it was here that generations before her had come to escape, to lick their wounds when things had gone wrong. Certainly it was here that Theo had hidden to hide his tears and misery when he'd been the butt of his father's bitterness and anger.

'I love this place,' she said, making an effort to control her previous outburst.

'And I love you, my blessed Anna. Yes, you're right, no one is an island. We can't live in isolation from others – Theo, Christopher, Jenny, my boys. But what I feel for you isn't what you call "falling in love", it's something deeper than all that, it's as if without you I'm only half alive. Is that wartime madness? No. Dear God, no. Anna, say something, Anna.'

'You know without my saying it. Now you're going away – feel as if something is being torn out of me. If God's listening to me, He'll be calling me wicked. I fell in love with Theo, dear Theo. But it was a child's love. I used to pray he'd make love to me, pray he'd want me. I fell in love with him with all that I *was* – but I was a *child*. He hasn't changed, he deserves something so much more than I can give him.'

'And he deserves more from a brother than the way I've used him. Yet, Anna, Theo doesn't come into it, Jenny doesn't come into it.' For a moment they were silent, she leaning against him, he rubbing his chin against her short hair. Did she imagine it or did he pull himself to stand straighter before he spoke again? 'I asked for a posting. They told me I was due to be grounded and I'd been recommended to go to a training station as a flying instructor. What I thought about it seemed to carry no weight. Why ground an experienced fighter pilot?'

'You asked? Is that what you said? You asked to be sent away?'

250

'I imagined they'd send me to another fighter station, somewhere out of reach of you, of coming here at every opportunity. Do you think it's the way I wanted it? Darling, you know, we both know, we're fanning the flames of the sort of fire that will destroy Theo, Jenny, the children, so ultimately us too. Seeing you like I do, knowing what we want is what we can't have . . . Anna, say something.'

Slight, slim to the point of thinness, she could have been a young lad in her jodhpurs.

'Can't think straight. Wish we could just stop living – now, this minute, here together. But we can't. We'll go on for years and years, we'll pretend, we'll have to. We'll make ourselves forget. Can't bear –' Her words were lost as his mouth found hers.

To the girls of Chiltern House School the handsome squire of Manningtor Park was looked on as little short of a god. He ranked with such heroes as Clark Gable, Errol Flynn, David Niven, Ronald Colman, the screen idols who tempted them to part with their pocket money for the weekly purchase of *Picturegoer*. At thirteen, Christine Murphy was as star struck as any and, to her, Theo was heroism made manifest.

Getting scrubbed up for tea had been a ruse to placate Christo, but with the game over the girls had broken up into groups. To outsiders the expression 'Walking round' might have sounded staid and sober, but to the pupils of Chiltern House 'Let's walk round together' was an invitation to share secrets, to talk out of earshot of friend and foe alike. But Christine had always been something of a loner, happier to lose herself in the realms of fantasy with a book, or in dreams she shared with no one.

So it was that she was alone in the one-time bedroom, now a dormitory for five, when she heard the crunch of tyres on gravel as a car swept round the bend at the top of the drive. Could it be *him*? Theo took pride of place above all others in her secret fantasies. Hope was immediately followed by disappointment as she saw Lance. That might have been the end of her interest except for something in the way Anna was coming to meet him, something in the way they stood as they talked, something in the way they turned from the house and started to walk. Forgetting that she'd come up to the bedroom to finish an article she'd been reading in *Picturegoer*, Christine hurried downstairs and out of the side

251

door into the coach yard. Where were they going? And why did she have this strange feeling that it was up to her to follow them? With Theo miles away, it had to be up to *her* to see he wasn't being cheated. It was happening all the time, she'd even heard a whisper that there was going to be a divorce between the Mrs Sullivan they called Thelma and her kindly middle-aged husband. That was horrid for Dee, because even though she looked like a grown-up she wasn't any older than some of the girls in the Fifth Form. Here Christine pulled her imagination up sharply, frightened to think of it happening in her own family where her father was in the Navy and her mother working in the National Fire Service in London. In some complicated way which she didn't attempt to unravel, it was on account of her own family that she felt she had to see Theo wasn't being cheated. Wartime you couldn't trust anyone, she'd heard people say so more than once. Perhaps they'd been referring to the notices reminding that Careless Talk Costs Lives – for there was always the chance that amongst friends and neighbours some might be fifth columnists – and perhaps it was because away from home it was all too easy to forget to be loyal to the family. Anyway, they could rely on Christine, she would see no one had a chance to betray perfect Theo.

While Anna and Lance talked to Sylvia, Christine kept a watching brief. Only when they were well on their way along the lane did she attempt to follow at a safe distance, walking silently on the grass verge and with an excuse ready that she was looking for a four-leaf clover if they should realise they were being followed. Nowhere on the estate was out of bounds to the girls. When the couple moved into the shelter of the copse tailing them wasn't so easy; there was no grass to walk on so they would be bound to hear her. She took the left-hand fork and followed the track that skirted Home Farm. It was soon apparent that Anna and Lance hadn't come to the copse because it led anywhere, but simply for the sake of privacy. Crouching in the ditch, Christine watched. If only they'd come a bit closer she might hear what was being said. Why was Anna crying? What they were saying must have been really important, even Lance seemed upset. Perhaps something had happened to Theo! Was that what Lance was telling her? At thirteen drama was the essence of life for Christine; at the thought of her beloved hero being shot down she clenched her hands together as if in prayer; she rocked backwards and forwards on her knees; silently she moaned, she knew she did, she could hear herself in her mind. In those seconds she honestly believed that what she was enduring was genuinely devastating grief even though she had only assumed the reason for it. Anna might have understood her suffering and her need to suffer, for was it so very different from her own original romantic adoration of Theo? Then, just as suddenly as in the child's imagination Theo had met with disaster, so the situation altered and all her previous suspicions crowded back, relief vying with anger. Most of the films she saw ended with the hero and the heroine in each other's arms, their kisses so long that she wondered they could breathe. But there was something different in what she was watching, it made her think of starving people snatching at food. In films the couple stood erect, arms round each other, the only difference between their kisses and ordinary ones was that they lasted longer. Fascinated, she watched the two in the copse, her ears straining to no avail. Their hands were moving on each other, even their faces, as if they wanted to *eat* each other. It was disgusting, she told herself. Wonderful but disgusting. Bet none of the others know that that's the way real people kiss, that it's not like they do it in the pictures. For a moment she forgot the reason for her mission.

Still clinging to each other, Anna and Lance were slowly moving on into the copse, going out of sight. Christine got up from her crouched position, her mind alive with what she had seen and the implication behind it. She must go back to school. If she'd been watching anyone else she would have wanted to rush back to share what she'd seen, but loyalty to Theo meant that she must keep it to herself. She'd keep her eyes open. Then what? Usually Lance only stayed a few hours, sometimes a single night. Yes, what she'd do would be keep her secret for the time being – he'd be sure to be gone at the latest by tomorrow and this evening they'd be with the family. Perhaps she ought to tell Anna what she'd seen, say it like a warning? No, warning her would be tantamount to condoning her disloyalty. She'd wait and watch, then if she thought they were still carrying on like it, she would send an anonymous letter to Theo, pretending she was someone from the village.

Satisfied that in her he had a trusty champion, she walked back down the track to tea.

*　　*　　*

253

The time had come for Anna to tell Thelma and Kath about her writing. It was something that, after that one occasion when first she'd come to Manningtor, she and Thelma had never mentioned. She supposed that if Thelma even remembered how she'd shared her secret, by now she would have put the thought aside as just something she'd done to fill her lonely hours before she came there.

'I have some news for you,' she announced into the silence of dinner.

Immediately they were lifted out of their own dark thoughts, at any rate Thelma and Kath were. As for Lance, his thoughts had already been with her and in any case he knew exactly what she was going to tell them; he even had his own suggestion ready to drop into the conversation at the right moment.

'Are you sure, dear? Oh, isn't this just the tonic we need?' Kath immediately jumped to the wrong conclusion.

Thelma's blue eyes swam with tears for no reason but that a new baby for Anna seemed to emphasise her own miserable position.

'Thelma, I told you ages ago that I liked to write, so long ago that you've probably forgotten.'

'To write? Yes, I remember. I remember how proud I was that you knew you could confide in me. But – where's the connection?'

'You know I taught myself to type. Well, half the time that's what I've been doing – even a novice like me couldn't have made a full time job out of running the estate with all the shortages of the present day. When I had a book all typed up I wrote to a publisher,' not the exact truth, but near enough. 'To be truthful I didn't expect to get anywhere. But this publishing house wants to publish my work, I'm going up to London to discuss it with them.'

If her intention had been to shake Kath and Thelma out of the doldrums, then she'd been successful.

'My dear, how proud Theo must be. Fancy and even *he* hadn't given a hint,' Kath's smile reached her eyes for the first time for days.

'I hope he'll be proud. I haven't told him yet. As I said, I didn't expect a publisher to be interested.'

'All this time and you've kept it from him. I can't imagine

having a secret . . .' Thelma's voice trailed into silence.

'I'll tell him now of course. I just thought he would read what I wrote and make fun of it.'

'That happened to me,' Thelma said as if in Anna's defence, 'the first time I tried my hand at making a skirt. I suppose it was pretty awful – and I know Matt didn't mean it unkindly – but I wished I'd just kept it hidden. And that was only a skirt. A book must have so much of yourself in it. I can see why you were shy of sharing it with anyone. But Theo would never hurt a soul, not purposely.'

'Well, I didn't tell him anyway. I wasn't prepared to risk it. If he rings up this evening I shall tell him then. And he needn't worry about the name, I shall call myself Anna Bartlett, that's who I was when I started writing.'

'Ring the bell, Lance dear. I think this deserves a bottle of something better than our nightly jug of water.'

'I had news for you this evening too,' Thelma said. The room seemed to hold its breath. Had Matt changed his mind? Had he realised he couldn't do this to his family? 'I didn't say anything while Dee was here; I thought it kinder not to. Yesterday my main reason for going to Deremouth was to see the solicitor. I left Matt's letter with him. If he wants more evidence he will contact Matt himself. He says that he should have no difficulty in bringing the case to court.' None of them liked to look at her, they could tell from her expressionless tone what a battle she was having to hang on to her control.

'And *I* have news for you too. It seems you're the only one left out, Aunt Kath,' Lance tried to lighten the conversation. 'This fourteen days' leave, it's embarkation. I don't know where I'll be sent, but you've no idea how much it has meant to me to have had time at home these last years.'

When the bell was answered Anna gave the order for champagne to be brought up from the cellar. A drink associated with joy and celebration, yet on that evening despite Edward Crighton's letter there was little joy in any of their hearts.

'How well do you know London, dear?' Kath asked her, swimming neatly into the net Lance had held in readiness.

'Not a bit. In fact I've never been there. But I have the address, so I'll take a cab from the station. And I'm sure it won't be hard to find a hotel. Poor London is hardly likely to be brimming with tourists even though Chiltern House says it's safe to return.'

'I feel responsible,' Kath's brows knit in a worried frown. 'If only you weren't so committed, Thelma, you could have travelled with her. Theo will be uneasy letting the child go off on her own.'

'Aunt Kath, I'm *not* a child.'

'Indeed you're not,' Lance's laugh sounded natural to their ears even if not to his own. 'You're an up-and-coming authoress, a wife and mother, capable mistress of an estate. You have the respect of all of us.' His over-exaggerated manner made Kath smile. 'Never doubt Anna's ability, Aunt Kath. However, before I get shipped off overseas I'd been promising myself a day or two in town. All the time I've been over here and not once have I looked up any of my old haunts from the time I worked there.'

'But of course, my dear. We've been selfish in taking it for granted you'd spend your free time here. You must have friends in London.'

'By now my contemporaries will all be in uniform, I expect. But I'd like to walk the streets of London again. I can stay at the club, but of course I can't take a guest.'

'I'm quite capable of finding a hotel,' Anna put in. 'There's no need for you to time your trip just to suit me.' Her performance would allay suspicion, even if there were any.

'Sister Anna, I won't get in your way, I promise you. We'll travel up together; to please Aunt Kath I'll see you booked into a suitable hotel; I'll make sure you have your appointment to talk to this man, Edward Crighton did you call him? We'll decide on our time of return and travel back together. How's that, Aunt Kath?'

Kath's mind was set at rest; Thelma's empty smile was supposed to carry the same message; Lance uncorked the champagne, fortunately cold from the cellar. Only Anna felt a blanket of cloud dulling her excitement. Tomorrow she would be miles way, she and Lance would be living a dream that had no connection with day-to-day reality. When they came home to Manningtor the others would be eager to hear about their trips, trips in the plural, time spent separately. They were embarking on a mission of lies. She looked across the table at him; for one mad moment she wanted to tell the truth, to build a future on the truth that filled her every thought but, even as she imagined the scene, her thoughts were brought back to earth by the shrill sound of the telephone. They all knew it would be Theo.

'Listen, Theo – don't say anything, just listen, or all your change will be gone before I can tell you. I've written a book, a publisher has read it.'

'A book, did you say? You, Elf, written a book? Does he think it's any good?'

'And why shouldn't it be? You needn't sound so surprised. I knew you wouldn't think I could do it, that's why I didn't tell you.' Before he could speak again she rushed on to tell him that she was going to London the next day. Then, hating herself more by the minute, 'Lance has come home on fourteen days' embarkation leave. Naturally he wants to look people up in London as he may not get back to England again. Anyway Aunt Kath is fussing about me going on my own. So we're travelling together. He'll go to the RAF club, but Aunt Kath has made him promise he'll see me into some safely respectable hotel first.'

'I bet she has,' Theo said laughing. 'Give him a shout, Anna, I must have a word with him. I wonder where they're shipping him off to. Italy seems to be where all the fun is now.'

'What you do is important, Theo,' she said, detecting a note of envy in his voice. His war had been spent on a bomber base in England, his prospects more of the same. 'Lots of people say it's the raids that will bring victory. Lance has been taken off combative flying, he's apparently going to be an instructor.'

'So they're hardly likely to be wanting him in Italy. Go and get him or my change will be gone. And, Elf, have a smashing time in London. Oh, and congratulations. I never suspected I'd married such talent.'

'Ring me after the weekend, I'll be home by then and I'll tell you all about it.'

'. . . all about it,' the words echoed. To deceive Theo was like deceiving a child – he had implicit faith in the goodness of them all. It was less than a week ago when, in hushed tones, she'd told him about the letter Matt had written. The silence had been so long that she'd wondered if the line had gone dead. 'Theo? Are you still there?' 'The stupid sod,' she'd heard the cold anger in his voice. 'Listen to me, Anna. I don't know what Thelma will do, but one thing I want to make clear. You understand me? Manningtor

257

is Thelma's home. If he's fool enough to break up his family, then at least we're all there for them. You understand?'

'I'd already made that clear.' And if he'd been surprised to hear her speak with such authority he'd given no hint of it.

And, in Theo's eyes, wouldn't what she was doing make her the one fool enough to break a family, Lance earning himself the contempt of those two short words, 'The sod'? Even now she ought to draw back, she ought to make it clear that she meant to go to London by herself. While Lance talked to Theo she retreated to the nursery. Nanny wouldn't thank her if she woke Christo, but she needed to look at his sleeping innocence. Beyond those moments she didn't attempt to plan. In her heart she knew she hadn't the strength to fight. And was it so wicked? She asked herself as she stood gazing down at her small son, asleep on his back with his hands raised as if in a position of surrender.

Theo is pleased we're going together, Lance and me. 'Have a smashing time,' he'd said. Hearing him, I could almost *see* him, his eyes full of laughter at the thought of us having fun together. But it's not fun I want. Fun is something Theo and I have together. Yes, we do. Always we have fun. And it's not as if sleeping with him isn't the most wonderful, more than wonderful, thing. But most of the time I see us as children at play. Lance is a man. Remember when Grandpa died, I knew even then that I could never love anyone like I do Lance. I *wanted* him to read what I'd written, I want him to know all that I am. And Theo? No, things that matter, really deep down matter, I wouldn't talk about to Theo. Is that fair? 'This is where we're at . . .' as he said whenever they hit a bumpy patch, determined to look for a silver lining to every cloud. We run well in harness together, his life and my life, separate, never quite meeting – except in bed. Yet, think of what he told me about being frightened – would he have said that to anyone else? No, don't think of what he said, just keep your mind on the Theo everyone loves: good-humoured, ready for anything that promised to be what he called 'a lark'. If he knew about Lance and me, I doubt if it would bother him. When he's home he spends just as much time with Alex as he does with me. I might as well be another sister – except that we wouldn't sleep together.

Looking down at Christo she was suddenly frightened. Matt was 'a stupid sod' 'fool enough to break up his family'. But

258

it's not like that for me, honestly it isn't. Yes, I love Lance with all my heart I love him, but You can't grudge us those few hours together. Can You? Let me have *that*, let our short time be complete and perfect, something that nothing can ever take away from us. It can be no more, we both know that. He's got Jenny and the boys; I've got my darling Christo – and Theo, good, dear, kind, Theo. You helped me find a way to marry him when I used to beg and beg You. So I'll keep my side of the bargain. Just let Lance and me have this brief interlude, something perfect and complete. I won't let You down, I promise You.

She kissed her fingers then touched them against Christo's dark hair, waiting long enough to be sure that although he snorted he didn't wake. Then, almost silently, she crept out of the room and closed the door.

By half-past nine the next morning they were alone in a first-class compartment, the train gathering speed as Deremouth was left behind. Anna remembered her silent plea the previous evening and sent up an equally silent 'thank you', for surely it must have been a sign that her pact had been agreed when Lance announced to the family that Theo was delighted Anna was to have company and had suggested that they ought to stay longer, make the most of what looked like being his last trip to London. Temptation had nudged at Anna, temptation she'd seen in the guise of the devil. But she'd been deaf and blind to it. Her pact had been for a brief interlude, complete and perfect; to try to take more would be to break her promise.

Not really the moment to imagine how different the journey would have been if opposite her Theo had been sitting instead of Lance. The journey would have had the excitement of an 'outing', chatter would have been spontaneous. She and Lance said very little, but the silence brought to her mind those words 'peace which passeth understanding'.

Taunton, Westbury – places that had been no more than names to her – then Reading where Miss Sherwin taught. The blue skies of the previous day had given way to a covering of sullen grey, a background to the barrage balloons that put her in mind of elephants in Christo's picture books. This journey was like nothing that had happened to her before. Yesterday she'd tried

259

to look ahead, she'd built pictures in her mind quite different from the truth.

'About twenty minutes and we should be in Paddington,' he told her. 'I've been watching you, you've been miles away. Sister Anna – is that how you want it to be? Is that what's going on in your mind?'

In a second she was across the narrow strip between the long seats where they'd sat facing each other. Clumsily – if anyone as trim and elfinlike could ever be clumsy – she hurled herself onto his knee, burying her face against his neck.

'No. I think I'd die if this was snatched away from us now. It's just that I hadn't known what it would be like – any of it – the places we've been through, being here with you, no one but *us* –'

'And?'

'If I were a holy sort of person I'd be on my knees saying thank You for letting me have this time –'

'For letting *us* have this time,' he corrected her.

'Somewhere I've heard or read an expression: "Time out of time". Until today I didn't know what it meant. Two nights and three days, time to remember for always.'

The train sneaked its way between the smoke-blackened buildings, hissing and swaying as it lost speed. Anna's first visit to London, ahead of her her introduction to the director of Hibbert Mills – in no more than minutes she would find herself swallowed up in the bustle of a city such as she'd never known; her heart was bursting with joy, not for London, not for Edward Crighton, not for hope of success, but for the wonder of the gift of two nights and three days.

At the end of lessons the girls changed into play clothes and, despite the overcast sky, gravitated to the garden as they always did.

'We play jump over, like yesterday?' Christo had been watching for them and made a beeline for Christine Murphy. 'You said we'd do that game.'

A promise was a promise, so half a dozen thirteen-year-olds lined up ready. Yesterday it had been warm enough for Nanny to be sitting outside with her knitting; today she watched from the nursery. She'd let the lad have ten minutes, then she'd go down

260

for him. That's what she intended, until she saw Alex wandering across the lawn in their direction. Perhaps there was something planned for the girls. Nanny decided she'd better go down and see what was happening, as they wouldn't want to take Christo out without permission – and he wouldn't be a ray of sunshine if they cluttered off without him.

'Hello Nanny,' Alex greeted her. 'Our lad's growing up, have you ever seen such determination?'

'His father all over again,' Nanny nodded her approval. There was nothing she liked better than to hear one of her charges praised – and she still thought of all of them as her charges, irrespective of age or station.

'Theo is missing so much.' While they talked they'd moved near to the children, near enough that at the sound of Theo's name they held Christine's attention. 'And Anna, where's Anna today? Out somewhere with Lance?' Said so innocently, after all, what more natural than that they should spend their time together? Or so her expression was designed to imply.

'You've not heard the excitement? Mrs Matt told me about it this morning. It seems Mrs Theo has written a book – a proper book. She's gone up to London to talk to some publisher. Lance has gone to keep an eye on things, after all the child has never so much as been to London before. A lucky thing he was on leave.'

'Just for the day?'

'Dear me, no. He wanted to spend a few days in the city anyway – you remember how he worked there before he upped sticks and went to America. Be away two or three days, so Mrs Matt said.'

'Does Theo know?'

'Bless you, yes,' Nanny laughed. It had always been the same with Alex, there was no one as important to her as Theo. 'He told Lance to see she had a good time – if there's a good time to be had in London these days. Kind of him to offer to keep an eye on her, what with seeing the city for the first time and having business talks about this book, my word but she'd have been overwhelmed.'

'Why didn't Thelma go instead? A change would have been good for her.'

'Poor dear soul, I could weep for her, that I could. And much

261

good that would do her. Best thing she can do is keep busy. And if that's the way Mr Matt is behaving, then the sooner she puts him out of her life the better. Poor girl. Isn't it always the same, Alex child, you find someone true gold like she is and they get taken for granted, used badly. Poor Dee, the girl's a great bundle of misery. And he pretended to be so fond of his little girl.'

'Where are Lance and Anna staying, do you know?' Such an artless question.

'He's going to find her somewhere in a nice, quiet, respectable hotel, then he'll go to his club, that's what Mrs Matt told me.'

'Hardly keeping an eye on her.'

'Oh I'm sure he'll see to it that she sees some of the sights – she can't be all the time with this publisher Johnny.'

So engrossed had Christine been that her turn had come around without her noticing.

'Wake up, Chrissy!' came shouts from behind. Even though she had no 'best walk-round-with-me friend', none of them disliked her; they accepted her as being something of an oddity, a dreamer. Coming to with a start, she rushed forward and leapt neatly, then bent down tensing herself for the weight of clumsy Monica Deering, who followed her in the line. Her mind was racing, memories of what she'd watched chased by images of what might be happening now, *now*, this very minute while her adored hero was risking his life for his country. At thirteen she saw life as black or white. She heard Nanny's familiar, 'This is your last jump, Christo, then it's time for us to go in.' The game had been for his benefit, so everyone was happy to put an end to it. They wandered off in groups, all except her.

Daily, Christo grew more like his father. He hated to see anyone left out, not having fun. So, giving her his most beguiling smile, he held his hand towards her.

'Coming wiv us, wiv me and the others.'

If she'd needed a sign, then surely this must be it. Not that the company she sought was Christo and Nanny's, but Alex had turned back towards the house with them. Sentences were forming themselves in Christine's mind; what she had to do was important, Fate had given her this responsibility. None of the others had been by the copse yesterday, none of the others had noticed what was being said as they waited their turn to leap.

*   *   *

262

From the public telephone on Paddington Station, Anna put her call through to Hibbert Mills, asking to speak to Mr Crighton. The nearest she could get was to his secretary, who told her that he was out of the office for a few days. There was nothing helpful in her manner, but with his letter in her hand Anna wasn't prepared to be brushed off.

'Perhaps you'd care to call again, say next week?'

'By then I shan't be in London. My name is Anna Sullivan and I have a letter from him asking me to see him.'

'I'm so sorry, Mrs Sullivan, I didn't realise. Yes, I remember. Will you be able to keep an appointment the day after tomorrow? I'm expecting him back then and if we can fix a time I'll call him and let him know you're coming.'

Just for a moment Anna saw herself in the corner of the field near Dunsford House, living the joys and heartaches she created as she scribbled. Where was reality? With a past that had become no more than a fading dream? With a present that had no place anywhere but in the fast-disappearing hours? Had she been able to see Edward Crighton straight away, perhaps even that same afternoon, then the days ahead might have become clouded by guilt. Instead she emerged from the call box with a feeling of freedom. These two precious days belonged just to Lance and her; they had to encapsulate a lifetime's living, make memories that would stay with them as long as they lived. And if she'd looked for a sign that the bargain she'd made with God had been approved, then surely this was His way of telling her.

When he signed the hotel register as Squadron Leader and Mrs her only feeling was excitement. Unpacking and hanging their clothes side by side was all part of the wonder.

'We'll eat in tonight,' Lance told her. 'We'll dance – then every time you hear the band on the wireless you can remember.'

'I shall always remember.'

Just once she had to wrestle with the thought of Theo. It was when they were dressing to go down to dinner or, more accurately, she was dressing. There had been moments like that at Manningtor when Theo had been on leave. She didn't want to remember. This evening there was no interlude of lovemaking; it was as if both of them were saving what they wanted most until there was nothing except themselves and the night.

'I hope I manage all right,' she laughed as she turned her back

263

for him to zip her dress. 'I've never been to a dance. Miss Sherwin – she was my governess, carer, like both parents rolled into one really – she used to wind up the gramophone and guide me round the floor while Grandpa was upstairs having his nap sometimes. She said it was a social necessity, but it never has been for me. We waltzed, foxtrotted, she even taught me the Gay Gordons but it was a bit useless with only the two of us.'

'My guess would be that the floor will be so crowded we'll manage no more than a shuffle.' Which turned out to be the case. The glory of it was being held close against him, rocking gently in his arms in time to the music. This was London, the familiar rhythm she heard so often on the wireless from this very band, was *real*. Yet there was no reality, she was living a dream. So she thought when she woke next morning. Lance was her lover, Lance was her love. Manningtor, everything that comprised day-to-day living was a million miles away.

It was only as they were standing on Westminster Bridge, the sun high in the sky, that she was brought down to earth at least momentarily.

'Hey, gee, man, what a stroke of luck! In all London, imagine meeting up with *you*.' Unmistakably American, even before they turned and she saw his uniform she felt a stab of shock. Lance's other life had caught up with them.

'Herbie Hislop, I do declare!' She even detected a trace of America in his own tone as he greeted this voice from his past. 'Let me introduce my sister-in-law, Anna Sullivan. Sister Anna, meet Herbie, a colleague from back home.'

'How exciting,' Anna played her part. 'Half a world away from home and you meet on Westminster Bridge. Lance, I'm not going to hang around, you know I said I had shopping to do. Then I'll go back to my hotel. This evening we have to meet friends, Mr Hislop, so keep him sober, won't you. You come for me when you're ready, Lance, you know where to find me.' It wasn't the first time she'd congratulated herself on her acting skills.

By their second night the future was coming up over the horizon. Dancing held no romantic wonder, even the thought of the next day's interview with Edward Crighton had no power. In a hotel such as theirs, despite wartime deprivations, every effort was made to produce meals that at least gave a pretence of haute

264

cuisine. The efforts were wasted on the couple who sat far away from the central dance floor.

'I wish to God I'd waited to be drafted,' Lance said, 'come over in the Army like Herbie and the rest. Sure, I would have met you, Theo's wife,' the words said with elaborate clarity as if he was compelled to torture himself, 'of course I would. But it would never have been like this. I might have been based in Berkshire like he is, too far to have grown used to letting thoughts of you rule my mind.' Silence. There was nothing she could say. 'It's the same for you, Anna, my blessed Anna.' She nodded, the sting of all-too-ready tears burning her eyes. Sister Anna, blessed Anna, how could she bear it when he was gone? 'You know what I want above all else, God forgive me? I want us to make a fresh start. Anna, listen to me. We'll find somewhere to make a home, here in England. We belong together. One day when this war ends I'll come back to you. I feel a heel, and so I should, for Theo is my brother. But that can't alter anything for us. Not Theo, not Jenny, not the youngsters. Love is a God-given gift, surely it is, Anna.' He was pressing her to speak, to say something, anything.

'It's what I want more than I thought I could want anything.' She seemed to stand outside herself, hearing her answer. That night was to have been their last together. Suddenly that misty, shapeless future had a meaning.

It was more than twenty-four hours since Christine Murphy had eavesdropped on the conversation between Alex and Nanny; to be precise, in those moments as Anna and Lance saw nothing of the bumpy road ahead, only the vision of their goal, twenty-eight hours had gone by since the child had carried out what she honestly believed to be her duty. Alex had listened to her in silence, her expression giving nothing away.

'Don't want to cause trouble, Miss Sullivan.' Relief that her tale was out coupled with fear that she was creating trouble that might rebound on herself, Christine had started to cry. 'It's just that – well she shouldn't be acting like that with him, not when he's married to someone else. She shouldn't, should she? Perhaps it didn't mean anything, he seems to have gone away again.' Ah now, hadn't that been a stroke of genius, not giving any idea that she knew they'd gone off together? Feeling more in charge of the situation she'd wiped her eyes hard with the backs of her hands.

265

'I expect I've just been silly. Perhaps grown-ups expect to behave like that, sort of greedy. Urgh! Was horrid.'

'I expect they were upset,' Alex had been careful to sound untroubled. 'Lance had just brought the news that he's to be sent overseas.'

'Good, I'm glad. Not fair, Mr Sullivan being away and *him* being like that with her.'

'You did right to tell me, Chrissy. Don't talk about it to the others, they might jump to the wrong conclusions. We'll keep it to ourselves, but I'm sure that must have been what had upset her.'

Yet if she'd really been so sure, if she hadn't already had suspicions of her own, why had she put a call through to Theo's base asking to speak to him urgently?

'What's up, Alex. No trouble at home?'

'No, it's not that. At least, not like you mean.' She blurted out her story, hiding nothing, loyalty to the brother she adored her driving force. Had she thought about it calmly, put herself in his place, she might have acted differently. 'Theo?' She spoke into the silence, 'Theo, are you still there?'

'I am. But I shouldn't be. I was just going in to tonight's briefing when you called.' His voice sounded different; she was suddenly afraid of what she'd done. Yet surely he ought to know. To be silent would be to condone.

'Of course, Anna doesn't know London, that's why Aunt Kath was so keen for him to go with her,' Alex rushed on, trying to calm the storm that must surely break. 'Theo, did I do right to tell you? If they do the dirty on you I'll kill them, I swear I will.'

'Of course you did right,' came the laughing reply. 'You're a good kid.' So he had called her so many times over the many years as she'd championed him so faithfully. 'I knew they were going together – this chap she has to see at Hibbert Mills is some connection of a friend of Lance. Don't let that school kid spread yarns like that, knock it on the head if you really want to do me a favour.'

'Oh I will. Gladly.' Thankful to put the whole thing behind her and, like Christine, glad that she had done what was surely her duty, Alex wished him 'Happy landings' and rang off leaving Theo to join the crews waiting to hear what the night expected of them.

*   *   *

266

Beneath him was death and destruction, to his right the sudden explosion as the fuel tank of one of his squadron burst into flames. This was hell, the hell he returned to night after night.

No more, please God no more. She knew what I was like. Just a rotten, yellow-livered coward. She knew – I told her – that's why she's done it. Who wants a coward? Christ, help me, help me, can't You. Sweating like a pig, icy cold and sweating like a pig. That's the sort of man I am. Shaking, can hardly hold the stick. Those poor buggers depend on me getting them home. Elf, my elf, that's what I thought she was. Someone moaning . . . Christ, it's me. Want to cry like a stupid girl, want to cry like I did that night with her. That's why she stopped loving me, she saw what a coward I am. Help me, help me get the boys home.

Still the bright flack lit the night sky, but each mile was one nearer home.

Chapter Thirteen

They took a taxi to the offices of Hibbert Mills, arriving exactly five minutes before the agreed time. Such a small thing, yet in Anna's eyes it added even greater credence to her view of Lance's ability. Suppose she'd been in London on her own, she would have had no idea how long the drive would take, would have gone far too early simply to be sure of not keeping the great man waiting and then would have had to wander up and down the neighbouring streets with excitement turning to fright. It was good of Edward Crighton to see her, she kept telling herself; if Lance hadn't been a friend of his brother he would never have bothered. That was her defence against disappointment, so she kept it at the forefront of her mind as Lance paid the driver.

'Here we go.' He took her arm in a firm grasp as he guided her into the building. 'I'll leave you to talk with him on your own, but first I'll just make sure he's there all right.'

'He'll want to see you anyway, he'll want to hear about his brother.'

'Then I'm not the one to tell him. I've been in England three years; America might be on another planet the way I feel right now.'

'It's us on another planet. And Lance, I want you there with me.'

'You mustn't be scared. You're at the beginning of something important; you don't think he'd waste time meeting you if he didn't believe that.'

Her eyes smiled into his, her mouth turned up at the corners as if she hugged to herself some secret joy. Theo would have seen it as the smile of his elf. Her eyes were always a mirror to her thoughts and in an instant her expression changed – she was as serious as these unbelievable moments allowed.

'I want you to be there when Mr Crighton sees me. While I wrote, all the people, the characters, they were just *mine*. Then you knew them too. Whatever happens now, Lance, we have to share it all.' All this spoken in no more than urgent whispers as the receptionist briskly led the way.

'Mrs Sullivan,' Edward Crighton stood up to greet her. If she expected the normal courtesy of a smile, this was her first disappointment. 'And you must be Franklyn,' he turned to Lance. 'Under the circumstances I'm glad you are with her.'

'Circumstances?' In the same second Lance and Anna said the word. Was he warning her not to raise her expectations?

'I take it your family didn't know how to contact you, except by calling these offices. Someone telephoned yesterday. This is the message my secretary left on my desk.' Anna took the note he passed to her, holding it so that both she and Lance could read it.

Telephone message for Anna Sullivan due to see you 11 a.m. tomorrow. Her husband's plane failed to return to base. Please ask her to telephone home.

'I'm desperately sorry. I think you and I, Franklyn, had better leave Mrs Sullivan to make her phone call.'

Anna's brain understood the words as she heard Edward Crighton's kindly voice, felt the tight grip of Lance's hand on her shoulder as she slumped into the chair in front of the large desk.

'Shall I stay?' His question held all the intimacy of the past hours, his gently spoken words filling her with self-hatred.

'No,' she rasped. 'Both go.'

'Anna . . . ?'

'Don't you see?' With eyes filled with terror she turned to him. 'It's because of *me*. I broke my word. I made a pact and I broke my word.'

Edward was looking from one to the other, not even half understanding. Then, alone, he went out of the room.

'If anyone's to be punished it should be *me*, not Theo.' Anna drummed her clenched fists on the desk. 'Just two days, two days

269

to last for the rest of my life, that's what I begged, that was the bargain I made. Then I cheated, I wanted more. But why did He have to punish Theo?'

'He?'

'God. Whoever that is. He must be mean and wicked to spite Theo because I couldn't keep my side of the bargain.'

Lance dropped to his knees in front of her, willing her to meet his gaze. 'Blessed Anna, perhaps His answer isn't as you see it now. If He willed this dreadful thing, then it must be a sign that it's right for us to be together.'

She hadn't listened. 'Theo dead. He loved life so much – until now, until this hellish, hateful war that was tearing him to bits. And what good was I? No good, no good, no bloody *bloody* good. He only ever wanted just for people to be happy, he never hurt a soul . . .' Now her words were lost as the tears came. 'Isn't fair,' she sobbed. 'This is where we're at, that's what he always said. Now look where we're at. And where is he? Gone, dead, never going to laugh, never going to see Christo. And us,' with a huge sniff she rubbed the palms of her hands across her eyes, 'we can't do it, Lance. Not now.'

'What I just said –'

'*No!*' she almost yelled the one word. 'Want to go home to Manningtor. Get Mr Crighton in, I'll tell him I'll agree to anything – or nothing. None of it matters. At least I can look after Manningtor, I can do that for him. And Christo, poor little Christo.'

'Do you want me to phone them?' He got up from his knees, reaching for the telephone.

'Doesn't matter. If you want to. I just want to go home.' The whites of her tawny eyes were bloodshot – in that moment not even her greatest admirer could have found anything attractive in the pale-faced, waif-like creature. She seemed to have lost the will to make an effort, she looked defeated. Lance talked to – Thelma? Aunt Kath? Alex? Anna wasn't interested enough to care nor yet to listen. It wasn't until she heard him say that they would be home by late afternoon that his words penetrated her misery.

'*No!*' she said as he replaced the earpiece on its hook. 'Lance, I'm going home by myself.' He didn't argue, only told her that he would see her safely onto the train and phone them again to say what time she would be in Deremouth. Then, leaving her by herself, he went in search of Edward Crighton. If she supposed anything, a feat which needed more coherent thought than she seemed capable of pulling together, it must have been that at some stage she would get a letter from the publishing firm. As they left the building her only wish was to get away, away from London and the time capsule of joy that had been hers, away from Lance and the reminder of her own weakness, away from herself.

'Are you saying you don't want me to come to Manningtor before I go overseas?'

'Don't ask me what I *want*. How can we be there together, you and sister Anna in Theo's house, with Theo's family? We didn't think of that last night, did we? Just leapfrogged to some Utopian time and place with no war.' As if the impact of her sudden thought defied her power of movement, she stood still, pulling her arm from his grasp. 'Failed to return –' there was a threat of hysteria in her laugh '– as if he'd lost the way, gone off on a joyride like he used to from the club. Failed to return. Why do planes fail to return? *You* should know, you shoot them out of the sky, see them nosedive to the ground.'

'Anna darling, don't –'

'Would it have been like that? Or would it have burst into flames? Theo trapped in a furnace. How long would he have known? When a plane burns what happens to the bodies? Is that how it would have been? Or did he get smashed like a broken doll when the plane hit the ground? Or drowned in the Channel because he couldn't get out of the cockpit, the water coming in, getting deeper? We'll never know.' She felt the ground was shifting under her, only the support of Lance's arm preventing her cotton-wool legs giving way.

'Anna, talking like this isn't helping Theo. And do you think I feel any less guilty? Theo's my kid brother and, God help me, I've stolen his wife. If one of us should be beating our chest, then it's me. If he were alive it would be different.'

'But he's not. He's dead, *dead, dead*.'

Round and round the conversation went while like a zombie she let him propel her into movement again. She had no idea where they were, no interest either, where he was guiding her. Finally they crossed the road and entered the park, stepping over the low brick wall which had been the base for iron railings until,

271

like pots, saucepans and garden railings up and down the country, they'd been taken in the drive for metal for munitions. They sat on the first bench they came to, his hand crushing hers in its grip.

'Last night we knew where we were going,' he told her, keeping his voice steady, careful not to give emotion a chance. 'None of it would have been easy, divorce is an admission of failure; but we knew it had to be. Are you listening?'

'Oh yes, I hear what you say. And yes, if we could have followed the path we planned I know we would have found the end of our rainbow. At least, last night I knew it. But last night I didn't know about Theo.'

'It was already all over for Theo even if we didn't know it. He didn't come into it, neither did Jenny.'

'That's just it, can't you see? We didn't consider anyone but ourselves, not even last night. Happiness could only have come from knowing your Jenny wasn't heartbroken, your boys didn't miss having a dad.' Here her voice croaked, her throat felt as if it had closed up. 'Christo didn't need me and Theo still looked on life as the same sort of lark he always had. We were just blind and senseless to believe we could get way with it. I can't do it, Lance,' higher and higher her voice went until it was a barely audible squeak, 'I can't. My poor little boy, no father, no mother –'

'We never suggested you should leave Christo behind.'

Open-mouthed, she looked at him. 'You thought I could take him away from Theo, not let him grow up in Manningtor? Just so that you and I could – could –'

Her words were silenced as he drew her into his arms. They didn't even notice how interesting a passing woman with a Pekinese found the spectacle; as Lance's mouth covered hers, Anna clung to him as though he were her only hold on life.

'I shall phone you in a day or two, Anna, that'll give you breathing space by yourself to think. What was it you told me Theo said, "This is where we're at"? You belittle him, you know, if you think he wouldn't want you to find happiness.'

'Shut up, Lance. Don't want to talk about it. Got to pick up my things from the hotel and get to the station. Perhaps I can be home before Christo goes to bed.'

This wasn't the time to argue.

*   *   *

272

When she started towards the exit at Deremouth Station she recognised Thelma waiting for her.

'Lance phoned to tell us the time to expect your train.' Unnecessary words, for how else would she have known? Her heart was heavy with pity for the girl who looked such a child and yet who, Thelma knew, had a will of steel. At least, that was the impression they'd formed at Manningtor as she'd wrestled with the responsibilities of the estate. But that had been when she'd known she had Theo behind her. Feeling inadequate, Thelma pulled Anna towards her in a bear-like hug.

'Have you got your ticket ready?'

'Sorry, I forgot.' Anna dug into her handbag to get it, thankful to be with Thelma and yet wanting not to talk, not to think. Where would Lance be now? Perhaps he'd have gone to the club in Piccadilly, the club where the family thought he'd been staying. Imagine it there, the place crowded with men in Air Force uniform. Theo had told her about it; he'd gone there sometimes when he'd had time enough to go to London but not to get to Manningtor. A great laugh there with the chaps, that's what he'd said. Only once had he lost his grip on the carefree face he showed the world, only once and yet it lay like a cloud over all her other memories.

'I begged a can of petrol from the depot,' Thelma whispered as they came through the ticket office to Station Square. 'I've never done such a thing before but these last few days – oh Anna, oh Anna, if only there were something I could say that would help.' Ever since Matt's letter, Thelma's face had worn either a set and cheerless smile or else been void of expression at all, one as much a mask as the other. How, otherwise, would she have got through the hours of each day in a pretence that nothing had changed? The news about Theo had almost been her undoing. Her efforts to console Kath had threatened to thaw the wall of ice she'd fought so hard to build. Then there was Alex! It had torn her heart to see Alex almost demented and saying the strangest things. It didn't surprise her that Anna didn't answer: she was well enough acquainted with misery of the soul to understand the hardest thing to talk about was the one that was always at the front of your mind.

Getting into the car they both slammed the doors.

'Did Christo miss me?' To hear her, Anna might simply have

273

been on a shopping trip. That was Thelma's reaction to the over-bright question, then she recalled something that had been overlooked since the call from the bomber station.

'Your book? What did the publisher say?'

Anna shrugged. 'He gave me the message about the phone call. Just wanted to come home. Expect he'll write.'

'Yes, I'm sure he will. And when's Lance coming?'

'Dunno . . .' Anna's answer was lost in a high-pitched squeak, before she squared her jaw and visibly got a grip on her control. 'Did Dee get back to school all right?' Silly question, but even a silly question was better than silence.

'She must have or I would have heard. Anna – I don't know why I'm bothering you with *my* affairs – not now, I mean.' Something in the way she spoke made Anna turn to look at her. Dear frumpy Thelma, so full of care for other people, taken for granted by all of them.

'Have you had more news? Another letter from Matt?' If she had, it clearly hadn't been good news. Instinctively Anna took the hand that rested on the gear stick, waiting for the moment when Thelma brought herself to start the journey home.

'It wasn't from him, not from Matt. Anna, why couldn't he have written to me himself? But perhaps it was as well it wasn't from him, Mother would have seen his writing and I'd have had to tell her. It was from the solicitor. Matt had written telling him he'd instructed an agent to sell the business. How's she going to feel about that? Matt had always seemed to care about it. We thought it was as important to him as it had been to his father. He always hoped that one day Sam would want to join him. Not now though. Does he think Sam will never . . . No, he can't think that. It's as if he's turning himself into a different person.' Then, realising how she'd let her words tumble out, she pulled herself up short. 'Oh Anna, as if any of that matters. You'll think I don't care about darling Theo –'

'It's all such a mess,' Anna felt herself taken in Thelma's loving hold and sunk her head to be cradled against the warm, soft breast. 'Wish it'd been me, me not him,' she wept. 'But even then, even though it's true and I *do* wish it, I'm *rotten*. I couldn't have the courage to wish I could change places with what he must have faced; I could never have faced the sort of hell he'd been living through. All that and then to *burn*. That's what happens, isn't

274

it, when a plane is shot, the petrol catches fire. I can see his face. He'd be so frightened, I can see . . .' The words were lost. Anna's outburst must have released a safety valve, for as she grew quieter she seemed to have found a new calm. As if she were holding a hurt child, Thelma rocked her gently. It was then, through the thinning mist of her own misery, Anna thought of Matt and the tender love he was casting aside. And only one step from that was another thought: Thelma had been telling her about the business, looking to her for understanding. And what had she done? Thought just of herself and her own conscience-stricken misery.

'He's crazy – Matt, I mean. He's got a good manager, so at least he ought to hang on to it until after the war. Who'd pay out good money for a coach business today?'

'He wants to get rid of all his ties. It's cruel. I know where I stand with him, he's made that clear. But why can't he consider Mother? One thing after another hits her. She used to be so full of – of certainty. First she lost Dad, then everything changed with the war – Matt, Theo, Sam gone, Manningtor full of women and children.'

'It's the same everywhere.'

'Not the same. Matt doesn't want to come back – now Theo. That leaves Sam. When's it all going to stop?'

This is where we're at, came the echo of Theo's voice. Tomorrow would come, whatever it threw at them they would have to accept. She wished she could say that to Thelma, but it wasn't life that had thrown her own particular misery at her (life? God? Is there a difference? Yes, there must be – one doesn't make bargains with life), it was Matt, the one person she had trusted completely.

'A day at a time,' Anna tried to sound wiser than she felt, 'that's all we can handle.' Surprised at her sudden rush of affection, she raised Thelma's hand and kissed it. 'Come on, let's go home.'

Was it Anna's imagination or was there an aura of silence in the house?

Since Thelma's world had been knocked awry she had discovered the therapy of activity and, partly in an effort to protect Kath, as soon as she'd heard that Theo's plane had been lost she had taken it on herself to go in search of Alex, knowing how the girl had worshipped her big brother. There could be no way of softening the blow, so she'd been prepared to comfort in the only way she knew; but Alex's incomprehensible near-hysteria had left her powerless. Next she had summoned Mrs Gibbons – the staff must all be told. Then, the household taken care of, she had dialled Directory Enquiries and found the telephone number of Hibbert Mills. Keeping her mind firmly on her tasks, she hadn't been aware that the pupils were being marshalled into the one-time music salon used now as their assembly room, nor did she consider the devastation in young hearts as they heard their hero was gone. A warning had followed the headmistress's announcement: bearing in mind the grief in the house, she expected her pupils to conduct themselves quietly, no ball games, no shouting. If they were in the garden it must be simply to walk and talk, keeping their voices low. Such instructions were unnecessary. The emotion of dealing with death was a new experience to most of them – even those who had believed themselves in love with their handsome host found a macabre satisfaction in the drama of their grief. Tip-toeing in the house, walking sedately in the garden, these things seemed to involve them in adult mourning.

After only minutes in the house Anna was aware of a change in the atmosphere, but she dug no deeper. In fact it was Christo's natural cheerfulness, so like Theo's, that brought home to her most vividly what had happened. As soon as she went into the nursery he shrieked with surprised delight, his beaming smile innocent of tragedy. Hugging the warm little body to her, feeling herself gripped by arms and legs, seeing the familiar way he held back his head and laughed just as he always did, she ached with tenderness. Poor little boy, poor little man, he had no father and didn't even know what had been stripped from him.

'Did he miss me, Nanny?' What a stupid thing to say when Nanny's lined face told its own story.

'I dare say he did. Poor wee man.' Then, both knowing better than to go down that road, 'I just promised him a nice boiled egg for his supper. Straight from the nest. Sylvia brought them over from the farm. That and some soldiers, eh, lad? That's his favourite.'

'Sounds good, Christo,' Anna's eager anticipation held just the right note. Did the child's presence make it easier or harder? She and Nanny played their parts well, for he was oblivious of any undercurrent. The only thing that had disappointed him had been that his friends wouldn't play the leaping game any more. He'd asked them in the nicest way he knew, eyes big and pleading, yesterday and today, but they'd just said he could come for a walk with them instead. That was better than nothing, of course, but he was at a loss to understand why his pleading had fallen on deaf ears. Perhaps tomorrow? Hope was never far beneath the surface.

'Have you seen Alex?' Nanny asked anxiously.

'No. Poor Alex. I will.'

'She's in a right pother. Blames herself as far as I could follow. Well, not just herself. I dare say unhappy like she is, she needs to hit out. Tread carefully, child.'

Once Christo was sitting at the nursery table focusing on dipping his soldiers, Anna left them. She'd faced Kath, she'd faced Thelma, but she dreaded talking to Alex. There was something so wholehearted in the girl's adoration for Theo. No sweetheart had ever usurped his place as the most important person in her life and it was that that made Anna see herself as a traitor. How Alex would despise her if she knew the truth.

'I'm home, Alex. May I come in?' she called quietly as she tapped on the bedroom door, then took no reply as permission. 'Nanny said I'd find you here.'

'He's with you? Lance?'

Anna shook her head. 'I wanted to come back on my own.' Wanted? Oh, but what I wanted was to spend the rest of my life with him, every day to be like those first glorious hours before we got brought back to earth. Back to earth – that's what happened to Theo, back to earth in a burning plane, back to earth because the engines had failed, which had it been? Then, pulling her mind into line, Alex's appearance registered on her, eyes that even bloodshot and half closed by swollen lids didn't hide their hate.

'It was because of *you*. You're a filthy lying bitch, that's what you are. You thought I didn't know how you were cheating him. That's why I had to tell him.'

'Tell him what?' Anna leant back against the closed door, the walls of the room seeming to crowd in on her.

'You and Lance. I told him what was going on between you and Lance. I want to tell everyone, I want the whole world to

277

know what you are. That's what you deserve. But I can't.' Tears came so easily, she'd been drowning in them.

'If that's what you think, then tell them. If you're right, then I shan't care. And if you're wrong it can't hurt.'

'Don't care about *you*. You're Theo's wife – widow, *widow*, I suppose you're glad – Theo's wife, lying, cheating him while all the time he trusted you. You think I'd let people remember him as someone betrayed by a slut like you – you and his own brother. But I shouldn't have told him, not when he was on his way to be briefed. Not that Theo was ever scared. No, he was too brave for that. But he must have been angry, that would have meant he wasn't thinking quickly enough. That's how it happened, so if I hadn't said anything he would have brought the plane home like he always did. All this time, always he's landed safely, nothing has ever upset him. He was getting tired, I knew that. *You* hadn't noticed, you were too busy watching out for lover boy to come and keep you happy.'

'Shut up, Alex. You don't know anything about us.'

''Course I do. What about in the wood? I know about in the wood. And in London.' The sneer in her voice was full of venom. 'How kind of him to see you were looked after in London. Looked after to your satisfaction? And while he was in your bed – you can't tell me he wasn't – where was Theo? Not that you would care.'

'Shut up, I tell you. There was nothing you could tell Theo that he didn't know.' Oh but there was. Theo had trusted her, he had trusted Lance, he had been glad they were going to be together. Never had Anna felt so low; surely she could sink no further, or so she thought. Reason might have told her that what she said next was aimed at helping Alex. Perhaps it was or perhaps she was prompted by that same devil who had tempted her to break her silent promise that if she could have that brief and perfect interlude she would ask for nothing more. Even worse, perhaps it was a loophole to allay Alex's well-founded suspicions. 'It was Theo who persuaded Lance to come with me. You're imagining things because you're unhappy.'

'Liar! You were kissing in the woods. Christine saw you. She was upset, that's why she told me. You can't deny that.'

So a child had been spying. Relief flooded through her. 'Why should I deny I kissed him? Alex, he's Theo's brother, we've been

278

friends for ages. He'd just heard he was being posted overseas, we're family, you, him, me, Theo –'

'*Was*, Theo *was*,' Alex sobbed helplessly. 'So I was wrong, that's what you're saying. I don't care now one way or another. You can sleep with who you like, it can't hurt Theo any more. If I was wrong, what I did was even worse. I told him about you and Lance in the wood, I told him –'

'If that's what you thought why couldn't you have talked to *us* instead of sneaking to Theo?'

'Wanted to hurt you.'

Anna sat next to her on the side of the bed. A cheat, a slut, a filthy lying bitch, the words mocked her as she put her arm around Alex's shoulder. 'You did what you did because you loved him,' she heard her words as syrupy. A few moments ago she'd thought her self-esteem could sink no lower; now she knew she'd been wrong.

No matter how difficult a funeral, no matter how it wrings every drop of emotion from one, it does present a blank page on which the future must be etched. 'Failed to return' leaves an enigma: there is no way to move on.

Somehow, each acting out a part in an effort to hide their misery from each other, they got through the next weeks. What a charade it was when Lance came to collect the luggage he'd brought with him for a fortnight's embarkation leave. Smiles from haggard Kath, gentle kindness from Thelma, who packed more good work into her time than there were hours in the day and unnatural cheerfulness from sister Anna.

It was the morning of his last day when he tracked her down in the stables, where she was watching the horse dentist filing Dilly's teeth.

'Don't you wish we'd been made like that?' she greeted him, her over-bright tone defying anything less.

'Very useful,' he agreed, 'until the rot sets in. Not so good when the only answer is an extraction. Isn't that so?' Bring the dentist into the conversation, keep it moving smoothly.

'That it is,' came the answer, while the great file kept up a steady backward and forward movement and Dilly, mouth clamped wide open, appeared unmoved by the whole procedure. 'Major operation that would be. Can't pull a tooth like you can for us lot, oh no, nasty business it is for a horse, proper surgery, cutting right through the side of the face. This old girl needn't worry herself – set of choppers like she has don't look like giving a problem. She's a good-natured old lady, isn't she, stands as good as gold.'

'Knows it's no good kicking against the pricks, I expect,' Anna answered, and Lance knew it wasn't only Dilly she meant. 'Are you just off?' she asked him.

'More or less. I've brought you a message from the house. Aunt Kath wants you apparently.'

Anna walked right into the trap and it wasn't until they were clear of the stable yard that he took her arm to steer her towards the summerhouse, more than half expecting her to pull away. But she couldn't.

'You said Aunt Kath –'

'I lied. Anna, I couldn't say goodbye to you in there. Blessed Anna, it can't be goodbye. One day all this will be behind us, we'll be free to follow that road we set out for ourselves. I don't know where I'm being sent, but even if I'm away for the rest of the war, I shall be sent back to England to be demobbed.'

'Don't make plans, Lance. Don't make bargains and tempt fate.'

'Just tell me it's what you want. For one precious moment forget everything but us, you and me. Tell me the truth.'

'I've no right to want it. But I do, I can't bear to think of my life dragging on without you.'

In the semi-darkness of the shuttered and seldom-used old summerhouse they clung to each other.

'You'll never be without me, you'll be in my heart wherever I go.'

She nodded. 'I know. So will you in mine. Go and say goodbye to the others, leave me in here.' She watched him cross the sloping lawn to the house, then she sank down to sit on a rickety bamboo chair, her eyes tight shut as if that way the image of him would be locked into her memory. It was only then that she realised she'd not told him about the letter she'd received from Edward Crighton and the offer he'd made her which only weeks ago would have filled her whole mind.

*   *   *

So the early days of summer passed. The wheels of divorce started to turn, the coach business was put on the market at a time of such tight restrictions that only a fool would buy it for anything but a fraction of what would be its post-war worth. Then, as if to prove there was no end to Thelma's worries, a letter from the school told her of the staff's grave concern over Dee. She showed no interest in her work, her behaviour was impossible and it was with great regret and out of duty to the rest of their pupils that they were asking for her to be removed at the end of term. By that time she would have taken her School Certificate but it was evident that her chances of passing it were negligible.

'Now there's just Sam.' Thelma's eyes were two pools of despair as she took the letter back from Anna.

'Sam never changes,' Anna said the first thing that came into her head, anything to take that look off Thelma's face. 'Soon he'll be home.'

'Don't say it,' Thelma rasped, 'I'm never going to take anything for granted again. And now this,' looking again at the letter. 'What am I going to do with her?'

'Ask Matt. It's *his* fault.' Not a constructive suggestion, she regretted it as soon as it was spoken.

Thelma had brought her troubles to Anna in the estate office. Now, looking at the letter as if she expected some magic change in it, she sunk into the armchair by the empty fireplace.

'His fault,' she repeated. 'No, nothing is as simple as that, Anna. I've thought and thought, remembering all the years I believed were everything we wanted. For me they were. You see, that's why it must be *my* fault too. All that time, was he bored? I'm ordinary, I'm comfortable with order and routine. I'd no idea . . . It didn't just start when I got his letter, not even when he met his wretched Pamela. It's only if there's a void that anything can fill it.' Anna desperately wanted to bring out some profound words to help her, but what was there she could say? If there's no void, then nothing will fill it. Had it been so different for her? If Theo had loved her right from the beginning, if marriage hadn't been a necessity, would that have kept her romantic dreams alive? Would Lance never have been more than Theo's brother and so hers too? 'Say something, Anna. What am I going to do about Dee?'

'You know what I think? I think you should write to her – not tell her about the letter you've just had. Bare your soul to her,

281

write to her that you need her, that you want her here at home and don't want her to go away to school next term. Sort of – oh, I don't know – throw yourself on her mercy to help you; tell her how alone you feel, tell her that if she wants to stay at school after her School Certificate it would be wonderful if she'd agree to a day school, cycle into Deremouth each day. Most of all, Thelma, I think Dee just wants to know she's needed. Matt always made so much of her. Whatever you say, what's happened to Dee *is* his fault.'

'If I did that, perhaps she'd find she could talk to me about it. Talking helps. You know something, Anna, it was a good day for me when Theo fell in love with you. This –' holding up the letter '– coming out of the blue on top of everything else seemed to knock all the common sense out of me. Couldn't even start to unravel the mess. But I'll do as you say – and I'll write to the headmistress at the same time. I won't tell her about Matt, just that with my husband and son serving overseas I feel the need to have Dee at home and had intended to give notice that she'd not be returning next term. If Dee wants to tell them the real reason for what ails her, that's up to her; but she won't, she'd rather they thought the worst of her.'

And did it really matter so much that two days later an ungainly sixteen-year-old was seen striding up the drive, her school Panama hat discarded in a litter bin en route? Through the following few hours Manningtor seemed to breathe a sigh of hope and relief, it was a step towards a new future. But, of course, to take a step one must have a vision of the road ahead. All Dee knew was that she had no intention of going back to school, not even in Deremouth. In another year she would be old enough to join the ATS; she kept that comforting thought at the back of her mind. In the meantime, when Francis suggested she should work for him on the farm – and Sylvia that she should take charge of the stables – something of the old sparkle came to life.

It was July when a letter from Lance, tactfully addressed to Mrs T. Sullivan and family, told them that he had been sent to a training base in Canada. Apparently Jenny had been delighted by the posting and had asked her mother to move in to look after things at home while she flew up to see him.

282

And while I was busy training tomorrow's flyers, guess
what she spent her time doing? Finding a school for the
boys and arranging a house to rent for herself. If you look
for speed and efficiency, look no further than a woman. It
was something I guess I just hadn't considered possible.
Anyway, they are packing up at home and will take over the
new residence just about when you get this letter. Whoever
would have expected I'd do service in Alberta? The beautiful
Dartmoor wilderness seems like a dream. But Manningtor?
Wherever I go, however long I'm away from it, forever it
will be home. One day I'll see you all again.

It was an unsatisfactory letter. As she started to read she thought
the veiled message was that his overseas interlude was over, he
was back where he belonged with Jenny. And yet what was the
coded message when he wrote of Manningtor, of one day coming
back? She didn't know. Lance had gone from her life like a dream
vanishes on waking.

As soon as term ended, confident that the raids were a thing
of the past, with the exception of Alex the staff and pupils
returned to Chiltern House. Four years at Manningtor had left
lasting changes in the children, but those had been years to see
changes in everyone.

'Another week and you'll have the old house back in place,'
Alex said as they all stood at the head of the steps watching the
two Sullivan coaches carry away the girls who had become so
much part of their lives. 'I said I'd follow on in a few days, but
I can stay until you get things straight again. When have you
arranged for the furniture to come back, Anna? The old place
won't know itself.'

'Nothing will come back until the war ends.'

'But once we've gone, that's crazy. All that empty space is
depressing. I'll be glad to get away. We have to make a new
start, Anna, we can't just go on in limbo.' One last wave as the
second coach turned out of the gate, then together the two of them
went down the steps to the forecourt and the lawn beyond, where
Christo was threatening a tantrum because his friends had gone
somewhere without him.

'If I brought the furniture back it would be like tempting fate.
How do we know there will be no more raids? You must have

somewhere to come to if you need it. Never take anything for granted.'

'Oh hell, isn't life a *bugger*?' Bugger or not, taken by surprise by the unexpectedness of her outburst, Anna found herself laughing as she slipped her arm through Alex's. 'Just look at us,' she chuckled, 'like a couple of those girls "walking round".'

'A time for girlie confidences, that's what they did it for. Anna, I've never said how sorry I was about – you know.'

'Talking to Theo? I told you at the time, that wouldn't have upset him. Anyway, there wasn't a jealous thought in Theo's head.'

'I know. You made me see that it wasn't because of what I told him that it happened. No, what I mean is – I've never told you how rotten I felt about thinking things like that about you and Lance.'

'Forget it, Alex.' If only she could follow her own advice, forget the miracle of love that had happened, forget her own shame and guilt, not give room in her imagination for that base in Canada with its nearby accommodation for Jenny and his sons. 'Come on, let's go and help Nanny sort Christo out. We shall all miss the girls in the house, but as for him, he'll be devastated with no friends to watch out for every teatime.'

'He'll have to set his sights on Dee. What do you reckon will happen when Matt comes back? Imagine him here with his sexy bit. Can't you just imagine her, everything that dear old Thelma isn't. Why do people have to make such a bloody mess of their lives. Sex! Thank God I can do without it.'

'I don't know why everyone is concerned about Matt bringing his new woman to Manningtor. You all seem to forget that until Christo grows up, it's up to *me*. And I promise you, this pretty Pam may be a saint for all I know, but she's not coming here. This is Thelma's home, hers and Dee's and Sam's.'

'Well done. Do you believe that when a person dies they still know about the ones they love?'

'What?' Anna hadn't kept up with Alex's thoughts.

'Theo, do you reckon he can read your thoughts, do you reckon he knows what a good job you're doing here? I hope he does. Manningtor meant a heck of a lot to him, you know.'

'Yes, I do know. About the only time he was a hundred per cent serious was when he talked about Manningtor.'

'Poor old Anna,' came Alex's gruff comment. Why was it this sister of Theo's had more power than anyone to bring to Anna's mind so much she tried to forget?

Christopher's summer ended with his taking a huge stride forward. Although he was only four Anna decided he should start school. Feeling himself to be almost a man already, each morning he dressed himself (with Nanny's help with buttons and laces) in a grey suit, its short trousers to his knees and his tall grey socks with a red stripe at the top pulled so there was almost no leg showing. In normal circumstances his first suit would have been a size smaller, but clothes coupons were scarce, so his uniform had been bought to last. On his head he wore a red cap and on his back he carried a satchel, more for effect than necessity. If Thelma had official need to take the car to Deremouth she would take him at the same time; if not and Anna had petrol enough and could conjure up an excuse, then she took him; there was even the occasional trip with Sylvia in the pony and trap; but mostly he was strapped onto the seat behind the saddle of Anna's bicycle. He enjoyed the variations as it gave him a great feeling of responsibility that, come what may, wet or fine, warm or cold, he had to find some means of doing the journey. Baby days were over. Even so, best of all he liked it at teatime when he came home and Nanny was waiting for him with nursery tea. She was a wonderful listener who never tired of hearing the tales of how his day had been; she encouraged him to form his first letters and she listened to his first halting reading: 'Rover is a dog. The dog sat on the mat. Tabby is a cat.' So it had been with one child after another. They had been the building blocks of her life and gave her her faith in the future.

'Folk might say I've had no life of my own,' she said to Anna as they picked the last of the Blenheim apples on an afternoon of Indian summer, 'looking after other people's children, loving them like my own.'

'And so they love you, Nanny. I knew that even before I met you.'

'Bless the boy. I loved them all, but of them all it was Theo who wormed his way right deep into my heart. And your Christo, sometimes it's like seeing Theo all over again. What time are you off to fetch him from school? Have you got to ride your cycle?'

'Yes. My petrol coupons are nearly all gone, I can't waste them

285

on a sunny day. Look, Nanny, here comes Sylvie. With a bowl of eggs too.'

'I'm bartering,' Sylvia laughed, near enough to hear Anna's remark. 'A bowl of eggs for a bowl of apples.' As she spoke she picked one up that had missed Anna's pole with its 'picking bag' on the end. 'Bliss. I wanted to see you anyway,' she went on as she crunched. 'Have you heard Lance's news? They certainly don't waste time. Jenny's having another baby. Actually it was Jenny who wrote; I heard this morning.'

'That's wonderful,' Anna the actress replied. 'They're pleased?'

'Over the moon, so she says. I'm blessed if I would be when their youngest is eleven already. You'd think she'd settle for what she's got.' Another bite of apple before she threw in a laughing: 'Typical American – not that I've ever been there, I suppose it's just the impression we get from some of those dreadful, sentimental films. Nothing Jenny enjoys more than parading her emotions. Thank God Lance never caught the habit. A blessed gift for the future, or some such tripe she calls it. She can't be far off forty, but she says she's fine. One thing to her credit, she never makes a meal of having her babies; I remember that with the other two. Now then, shall I take the eggs indoors to Ethel and use this bowl for the apples or have you something you can put them in for me?'

'You can have today's harvest if you can carry it; we've been putting the keepers in this box.'

'Smashing. I'll lay them out for the winter. Dee seems more settled, doesn't she? She works like a navvy, so we'll soon get some of those pounds off her, poor kid.'

So they chattered, Dee and her progress taking pride of place over Lance and Jenny. That's the way Anna wanted it; that's the way it had to be.

I'm being dog in the manger, she told herself as she let the conversation wash over her. I told him we could have no future; I told him it was what I wanted more than anything but it was a pipe dream and that's all it ever could be. And what did I expect? That he'd pine his years away, that he wouldn't have the guts to look on what we had – had? have? – as a glorious interlude. Duty, responsibility, obligation, those are the things that have to be our guiding star. He knows they're mine, so why should I feel like this that he has made them *his* too? That's what happened – duty, responsibility, obligation – that's what he's clinging to. We didn't ask for it to happen, him and me. There was no other way. And now there's no other way but to take the hand that's dealt. His old life pulling him back . . . did he remember me while he was making love to Jenny, giving her a child to cement their future?

'I'm taking the trap into town,' Sylvia said. 'Wakey, wakey, Anna, did you hear?'

'Sorry, I was just thinking I'll soon have to start off to get Christo.'

'Proof that you weren't listening.' Sylvia said it teasingly, but remembering Lance and Jenny and the tripe she'd talked about their 'blessed gift for the future' she surprised herself by putting an arm briefly round Anna's narrow shoulders. Poor kid, with Theo gone what sort of future could she hope for with this great place taking her time and energy? 'I was just saying I'm going to collect some barbed wire from Clements so I'll bring Christo home if you like.'

'In the trap? He'll like that.'

After she'd gone they carried on with their task for a while, but the warmth of the sun, the hint in the hazy air of autumn fruitfulness, had lost its healing power.

'It's the time of day when the air changes, child,' Nanny said, noticing Anna's sudden shiver that had nothing to do with temperature. 'Won't be many more afternoons like we've had today. Come on now, child, head up, shoulders straight. That's what I used to say to them when they were bairns and fell out of step with living. If I could get my hands on Mr Hitler I'd make him wish he'd never been born, all the upset he's brought. Happy as kings we all were before it all started.'

'We might have been, Nanny, but everyone wasn't so lucky. I won't let him down – Theo, I mean.'

'Do you think up there in the Better Land he doesn't know?'

'Let's go in, Nanny. I've a few things to see to.' In truth she hadn't, but she went to the estate office all the same. An accepted part of the family, respected mistress of the estate she truly loved, yet her greatest solace came from the hours she spent pounding the keys of her typewriter. At a time of paper shortage and economy it was unlikely that her first book would receive a fanfare of publicity when it was published the following January, but she had been commissioned for two more. So, when there was no

287

way of ignoring the dull grey of her future, she lost herself in the realms of fantasy just as she always had. Life had no high 'ups' and no desperately low 'downs' – simply a grey hopelessness that showed no light on the horizon.

And so it continued until a morning in November. The breakfast room was empty when Anna came to the table. Dee had already gone over to the farm, Thelma hadn't appeared yet and Kath had a tray in her room. The morning post was left on the salver by the side of Anna's place. One for Thelma from the solicitor, one for Thelma from Sam, one for Kath in the spidery handwriting she recognised as coming from Augustus, Sidney's cousin. The bottom one in the little pile was addressed to her: Mrs Theodore Sullivan. The typewritten buff envelope was crumpled, used-looking, the franking smeared and illegible; it gave the impression that it had been dropped and trampled on, left to lie somewhere in the damp. But that was nonsense, she told herself before her imagination completely ran away with her. Usually she slit her envelopes open with a paper knife, a habit she'd consciously adopted as part of her determination to be efficient in all that she did for the estate. She had no idea who the letter was from or what it contained but was certain it had nothing to do with Manningtor as with fingers that behaved like thumbs she tore the envelope open. Even before she unfolded the single sheet she knew the moment was important.

Chapter Fourteen

Where the letter had been held up she would never know, perhaps somewhere in Germany or France, or even caught in the corner at the bottom of some postal sack nearer home. All this time, he must have been waiting for letters that didn't arrive. So why hadn't he written himself? This was months ago – and then nothing. Surely he must be alive, surely the authorities who sent out this notification – for that's all it was – would have told her. Only at this point, as she read the official missive for the third time as if she expected to see something she'd overlooked, did the enormity of its message fully register.

Leaving her untouched and unappetising scrambled dried egg, she leapt two at a time up the stairs. Who to tell first? Aunt Kath? Thelma? Instead she passed both their doors and literally ran along the long gallery to the nursery.

'We've got to see to our teeth before we can be ready for school,' Nanny greeted her. 'You're early this –. What is it, child?'

'It's Theo. Nanny, you read it. I'll help Christo.'

So like his father, there was nothing Theo's son liked better than a break from normal routine so he led the way happily to the nursery bathroom, glad to show off how he cleaned his milk teeth, up and down, down and up, first the front, then the back before he rinsed and bared them for inspection . . .

'Something 'citing?' he asked hopefully, as she nodded her approval. 'Something 'citing for Nanny?'

'Something exciting for all of us, Christo – you, me, Nanny, the family, everyone at Manningtor. Your daddy is going to come home to us.'

'Today? Will he be here when I get back from school?'

'No. He can't come until after the war, but we can write to him; we've been sent his address. You could draw him a picture.'

'OK,' he answered, pleased to air what he heard as a 'grown-up' expression picked up at school and obviously at a loss to see what the fuss was about. Anna held his uniform gabardine raincoat for him to put his arms into, wrapped his scarf round his neck and passed him his school cap, smiling to see how as an outcome of Nanny's strict training he didn't put it on his head until he left the house. Uninvited, the memory of her grandfather sprang to her mind; he who'd been a stickler for good manners would have approved of his great-grandson.

'Bicycle this morning, Christo. You'll need gloves too.'

'I like bicycle days. I'll get my satchel and kiss Nanny goodbye.' That was something he never missed. But that morning his confidence took a jolt – he'd never expected that Nanny could cry.

'My poor darling boy,' she sniffed, mopping her eyes shamefully. 'What do they mean when they say "serious head injuries"? This is months ago – see the date, just this official note then nothing. How serious? Why has he never written to us? Doesn't that wicked Mr Hitler let them send letters even? Why don't our lot get on and finish the job off? The poor Air Force boys, the likes of him and Lance, they do their best. But what about the Army? There can be no end until those Nazis get chased back into their own country where they belong, but there's no sign of it happening. Head injuries, what do they mean, child?'

'It must be that letters aren't getting through from POW camps and hospitals. That must be why we haven't heard.'

'You say that – and God forgive me for doubting – but what do they mean when they say serious injuries? Then nothing . . .'

'I know what you're thinking. But Nanny, there would have been another official letter in all this time. It's months.'

'The lad'll be late for his class.' One final wipe and Nanny put her man-sized handkerchief in the pocket of her morning skirt.

That same day each one of them wrote to Theo. For none was it easy when the most plausible reason for his silence was one they wouldn't so much as contemplate. All his life Theo's presence had brought pleasure, his love of life had infected the atmosphere of the whole house. For months they had schooled

290

themselves to accept that he'd gone from them while never letting their memories of him become clouded by the gloom and austerity of the present. Now came this glimmer of light, hope to be clutched; and yet they were afraid to let themselves believe. That same question was at the back of all their minds: if Theo lived, why didn't he write? Even if letters brought out of prison camps were censored, even if they were infrequent, surely there could have been something.

Whatever it's like in some dreadful camp imprisoned by high barbed-wire fences and with guards watching every movement, Kath told herself, it would take more than any of that to break our darling rascal's spirit. If we could just have a peep at him we'd see how he is keeping everyone's spirits up. So we mustn't fail him, we must tell him all about home, let him know it's all waiting for him. Then, despite her determination, 'But why hasn't he written?'

Thelma's letter was a credit to her resolve to accept life cheerfully. It dwelt on their thankfulness that he was being taken care of, her trust that one day soon all this would be no more than a dark memory; he and Sam would both be home. She wrote of Anna's love for Manningtor and gave him assurance that when he came back to take up the reins he would find nothing had been neglected. Of the troubles with Dee, all she told him was that she'd never be an academic so it had been wiser to let her leave school and help Francis on the farm.

Sitting alone in the estate office, pen in hand and blank paper in front of her, Anna stared unseeing out of the window. Until this moment it had never occurred to her that this would be the first letter she'd have written to Theo. *'My darling husband, Your brother and I are lovers . . .'* Are? No, were. But that was the one thing she could never tell him. Try and remember those early days, try and feel the wonder of hearing his Riley draw up at the gate at Grandpa's; shut your eyes and take yourself back to that water meadow – to you that's what it was, only to him was it a scratchy cowfield. Think of the wonder of walking to church on that first Christmas Eve. So long ago all of it, it's like looking back at a fading dream; was I even the same person that I am now? How could I have been? That was before I knew Lance, before I knew there was a difference between 'being in love' and 'loving'. But Theo is alive (surely he is?) and a thousand times

I've thanked You. I'll never break faith with him again, honestly I won't – as long as he wants me. How much did he ever want me, really *want me* because I'm me, not because I was a duty? Is that why he hasn't written? This is where we're at, is that what he's telling himself? And where is he at? Where is his heart and mind? When he comes home I shall know – but until then I must try and hold on to the first wonder of falling in love with him. More than that though, remember the miracle of making love together. Then Lance – no don't think of Lance. Anyway it was all different with him – when he made love to me I knew it was because it was *me* he wanted.

'My dearest Theo,' she started to write. Words always came easily to her and as her pen flew across the paper she built a picture of his beloved Manningtor clearer than any artist could paint. The staff, the horses, Francis and the farm, the cottages on the estate, she wrote of all the things he knew and loved; and of Christo, reminding him of the football games on the lawn and the unchanging atmosphere of the nursery. So she might have written to a beloved brother.

So the year came full circle, another Christmas, another January showing no promise that peace was in sight. There were rumours that something was afoot further round the coast in the South Hams: people had been moved out so that a whole area could be used for training American troops. There was no doubt of the truth of the rumour, for Mrs Gibbons had a sister who had had to leave her home, yet even the local newspaper made no mention of it. In days when everyone had become used to being more than circumspect in spreading information, there was a feeling of being able to 'do one's bit' by saying nothing and pretending not to know. Why the Americans had to use an area where people lived when not many miles away was the whole of Dartmoor might have seemed to make no sense, but these were days when anything was believable. Life went on from one day to the next, shortages got tighter, treats and red letter days no more than a memory and a hope for the future.

It was halfway though the short, dull days of January that the next letter arrived, sent through the Red Cross, the unfamiliar writing on the envelope striking fear in their hearts. Since George Grant, their regular postman, had been called up his wife Beth had brought the post out each day from Moorleigh, delivering it by breakfast time.

'Here's the postwoman again,' Kath said as, soon after noon, she watched Beth pedalling up the drive as if the devil were on her heels, 'Are we supposed to call this the afternoon delivery? You can't depend on anything today. We used to be able to set the clock by the time the postman came.' Gloomy January was making its mark on her, she needed to find fault. The truth was that when the letters had come to Moorleigh to be sorted for the afternoon delivery, it was because not only Beth but everyone in Moorleigh cared about the handsome young squire and his brave little wife that she wanted to feel involved in bringing news. His sudden romance had created a good deal of gossip and speculation but local affection for him was genuine and, in local eyes, Anna had proved herself worthy.

Anna saw her coming too, recognised the urgency of her manner and saw that she carried no postbag, simply a single envelope. That's why she had the front door open ready as Beth charged up the flight of stone steps.

'Brought it straight up to the house, Mrs Sullivan. It looked to me like what you might have been watching out for.' Had it been a telegram she could have waited while it was read in case there was a reply, but a letter, even one with a Red Cross frank, gave her no excuse.

Sitting alone on the stairs Anna haggled the envelope open. Her first feeling was disappointment, for the handwriting wasn't Theo's; her second was dread. Then she started to read. Written by a German nurse whose grasp of English was excellent, it told her that Theo's head wound had left him with no memory. More than that, it had destroyed his sight.

Some days ago your letter was delivered, yours and more too, from your home. I read them all to him. It was wonderful. He had been lying there knowing nothing. Because I know some English I talk to him but it was as if he was lost. Then the letters came. The first time I read them I was not sure if I imagined that briefly he seemed to understand. So I read them many times, every moment I had spare I read them to him. He said words, elf it sounded like, crist perhaps too? I thought he must have meant Christo,

293

as you had written. I could not be sure, but we kept trying.
I talked to him about the things you wrote – and it was like a
flower unfolding (Does that sound silly? But it is the truth),
his soul is on the way back. He has started to talk, a small
amount, he cannot concentrate for much time. But he is
getting better, his memory is returning. You will understand
how it is he cannot write. If you continue to write about the
things to recall, then as soon as he can tell me the words
I will write his letters for him. Please try not to become
very anxious, he is greatly better than he was when he was
brought in. It is your letters that are giving him benefit.

Anna knew Kath and Thelma were waiting to hear what Beth
Grant had brought, but she needed the solitude of her bedroom,
hers and Theo's. Once inside it, with the door closed she sat
on the dressing table stool, reading it again, thankful for the
kindness beyond the bounds of the nurse's duty, thankful and
desperately sad. Theo, fun-loving, never cowed by any difficult
twist in life. This is where we're at . . . blind, Theo not to see
the blue sky, not to take his boat on the sea, not to race across
the country in his beloved Riley, not to hunt – didn't it add up
to 'not to have a life'?

Slipping onto her knees and turning to rest her head against
her folded arms on the stool, with every ounce of her strength,
with her whole heart, she begged that he'd get better. He was
starting to remember. But wasn't that almost worse than knowing
nothing, being some sort of a cabbage?

Theo, a cabbage. Please God, You can perform miracles, You
can help him get better. I beg you, with all my heart and soul,
don't do this to him. Remember what a swagger he had when he
first got his wings? Yes, of course You do. Then he got shot out
of the sky. You let it happen to him, You could have saved him.
No, I didn't mean it like that, I'm not blaming You, I'm trying
desperately hard not to blame anyone, but just to beg, to plead.
Help him, bring him home, make him whole. Please.

So the months went by, letters from Manningtor telling him
every smallest detail, letters from him penned by the faithful
nurse proving that the fog around his mind was clearing.

When in June Allied Forces invaded France hope had a great

boost; surely the end must be in sight. But it was hard to hold hope high when each week it became more apparent that, though no one doubted what the end would be, there was still a hard-fought battle ahead. There was talk of Hitler having a secret weapon, and evidence of it when the first of the flying bombs landed in London and the South-East, soon to be christened 'doodlebugs', and followed very soon by something even more deadly, the flying rocket. Both were pilotless and merciless. So less than a year after the pupils from Chiltern House had left Manningtor, once more the furniture lorries trundled up the drive. They had returned and with them a new intake of junior students. As the short days of winter cast a cloud of depression, it seemed hope had been premature. As they moved into the year 1945, it took every ounce of moral courage to believe that somewhere only just over the horizon surely must be peace.

But had there ever been such a spring? In those last few weeks of hostilities each day brought some new revelation, new promise – as the Allies entered concentration camps new awareness of the unimaginable horrors, new determination that on the ashes of the past a better future must be built.

In the Easter holidays Chiltern House once more left Devon, everyone knowing that this time the move would be permanent. The end came in May, the 8th of May, Thelma's forty-fifth birthday. Everyone, even Christo, went to Moorleigh church that evening. Bells hadn't been pealed for years but that evening their clamour filled the air, a sound of thankfulness. In Deremouth, in the region of the much-bombed dock, drinkers from The Jolly Sailor, and at the top of Quay Hill The Seaman's Rest, danced in the street.

Sitting in the pew next to her mother, Dee wore her Women's Land Army uniform. She had never consciously wondered when her ambition to join the ATS had faded; probably when she knew herself to be useful and necessary on the farm. So instead she'd enlisted in the Land Army and continued working on Home Farm, sharing a bedroom in the farmhouse with three other land girls.

But it's all over now, Dee let her thoughts stray while the Vicar's sermon made the most of the unusual sight of such a large congregation. The others will all go home. What about me? Francis will want us until he can get men again, but then what? And Mum, what's she going to do when Dad comes home with Pretty Pam? If Sam extends his commission like he says he probably will, then there will only be Mum and me. A year or two ago, such a thought would have appalled her. It was the war, she concluded, it changed everything, everyone. That and the fact I'm grown up now, I guess I feel sort of responsible for poor old Mum. In her eyes Thelma had never been young.

Next to her Thelma was letting the sermon wash over her too. Her thoughts were much on the same lines as Dee's. She must find somewhere to go. To say anyone regretted the war ending would be wicked – and not true. But it had given her a purpose. Now what? What and where?

And Anna, where were her thoughts? Poor Reverend Brightman had lost her as surely as the other two. The prisoners were sure to be the first to be brought home. Help me make life good for him, she pleaded. He won't be the same as when I first met him, he won't be Aunt Kath's fun-loving rascal, how can he? But am I the same? Of course I'm not, I was just a kid ready to fall in love with the first handsome man I met. But he was more than that. I swear I'll be a good wife to him, I'll try and make up to him what he's lost. And what about what I've lost? That letter from Lance the other day, *'war drawing to a close'*, *'times that will stay with me always'*, and even reminding her of their dreams in a veiled way that would pass unnoticed should anyone else read his letter, *'wartime was time for planning, looking to a golden future. Now surely we can say our duty is done, the things that seemed so distant can easily be within our reach.'* Then a brief sentence that the baby was growing daily, Jenny over the moon with the new addition.

There was no doubt what he was telling her; it might mean nothing to Aunt Kath or Thelma but to her it was obvious. Word for word she remembered what he'd written and, just as clearly, what she'd replied in the letter she'd addressed to him at the air base. What they had found had been perfect, it had been as right as the fit of Cinderella's glass slipper. But that was yesterday, as far removed as everything else over the last unnatural years. And that's how it must remain, a time capsule of perfection. Visualising the single page she had folded so neatly and put in its envelope, she closed her eyes as if that might black out all feeling. Instead it brought memories alive, a kaleidoscope flashing through her mind: dinner and dancing on the night they'd let themselves see ahead to a cloudless future; the strength of his presence when her grandfather had died; the joy of his being part of the household at Manningtor; the fear each time a squadron of fighters roared overhead or each time she'd seen a dogfight in the skies above Deremouth; the rightness of sharing so much of herself when she sent him away with her completed manuscript and even more of having him with her when she went to meet Edward Crighton. There she pulled her thoughts up sharply, frightened to remember the agony of guilt she'd known, believing Theo had been killed. Opening her eyes, she fixed her gaze on the vicar, who without her noticing had finished his sermon and was announcing the next hymn. 'I Vow to Thee My Country' came the lusty sound of voices. Again her eyes were closed as she stood silent. For his country he'd lost all that he loved in life. I have a vow, she pledged silently, and I'll make it here in church: I vow to make it up to him. He didn't deserve this, he's good, kind, he believes in duty and obligation; but it's not just that that makes him what he is, it's his optimism, his trust that nothing's ever so bleak that there isn't a bright side to it. That's how he was . . . but now? How can he bear it? Well, I'll show him (no, not show, I can never show him anything) I'll see that he is sure that 'wherever we're at' I'm there for him. I swear it. I'll not let myself yearn for the future we'd planned, Lance and me; whatever I'm giving up can't compare with Theo's sacrifice. She hardly noticed when the hymn came to an end and the rest of the congregation, with varying degrees of agility, were getting onto their knees.

Were they the only ones who followed their own thoughts as they sent up their joyous songs of praise? Perhaps not. But for everyone, they as surely as any, they knew that that summer evening had brought them to a milestone in their lives, the beginning of a new road.

The prisoners were the first to be repatriated, those who were fit passing more quickly through the transit camps for demobilisation than the disabled. It was early in June, an evening when with what was called Double British Summer Time the sun was sinking behind the distant ridge of Downing Wood a few miles to the south-west. Christo was in bed, his heavy curtains tightly closed in the hope of persuading him the day was over. Not so different from her days at Wickley Cross, Anna was sitting on the grass, knees drawn up to make a 'table' for her notebook. Tomorrow she would type what she wrote today, but it was too lovely an evening to shut herself away in the office. When her first book had received favourable reviews she ought to have been wildly excited; at one time it would have been enough to fill her life. She loved writing just as much as she always had, perhaps more, for now her characters were complete in themselves, no longer an outlet for her own subconscious loneliness. These last years had brought her out of the dream world she used to occupy.

'Anna! Anna! Quickly. It's Theo on the phone!' Thelma's voice brought her back to reality. Thelma wasn't built for speed, neither was she used to excitement; the combination of the two left her breathless and flushed.

Dropping her notebook and pen, Anna ran up the slope, across the forecourt, up the steps and across the marble-floored hall to the study.

'Theo?' By now even she was panting.

'The elf's been running,' he laughed.

'Where are you, Theo? I've been saving my petrol; can I come and fetch you?'

If his laughing tone had been anything but assumed, how could he have dropped it so suddenly. 'It seems they haven't finished with me yet – not that I'm any use to them. But there are medicals, assessments, all that sort of tripe. I'll let you know as soon as I can. Anna, is everything the same at Manningtor? Can't believe I'm almost there . . .' His voice trailed into silence, one she rushed to fill.

'With Christo around, how can everything be the same?' she laughed. 'He's so like you, Theo. Everybody delights in spoiling him – just like I bet they did you.'

The pips came as a relief: neither of them were prepared for the emotion that was so near the surface.

'I'll ring you again in a few days – as soon as I know anyth–'

She was left with nothing but the hum of the dialling tone.

That was on the evening of Wednesday. No call came on Thursday, or Friday. The hours of Saturday dragged by while they imagined every possible reason for his silence: something must have gone wrong in his medical check, an eye specialist might be planning to help him, the excitement of repatriation

298

might have triggered off his memory loss again – hope chased horror, horror chased hope. The glorious few days of sun had been overtaken by lowering cloud; a weekend of silence stretched ahead as Manningtor held itself in readiness.

'Who's that walking up the drive? You know, my eyes aren't what they were.' Kath said it without much interest; the visitor was very likely one of the staff. But her words were enough to bring Anna and Thelma to the window. Perhaps Thelma's eyes weren't what they had been either, or perhaps at the top of her mind was always the hope that one day Matt would come back or Sam want to surprise them.

Anna didn't wait to answer. Before the truth had dawned on either of the other two she was outside, leaving the great front door wide open behind her, then down the steps, across the grass as a short cut to join the figure advancing alone along the drive. That it could be Theo didn't come into Thelma or Kath's scheme of things; poor Theo had lost his sight, he would never walk alone.

When he heard the sound of her running on the gravel Theo stood still and waited.

'Anna,' he said as she came within earshot.

Then she found herself crushed against him; wordlessly he clung to her as if he'd found a lifeline.

'You didn't tell me,' she whispered, her face held so tightly against him that she could hardly breathe. 'I was going to bring the car.' In those few seconds he'd time to regain his composure, his hold loosened so that she could raise her face to his. Again, almost his undoing as his mouth found hers. But Theo wasn't easily defeated.

'Thought it would be a lark to surprise you –' how familiar that laugh was '– just walk in on you all.'

He'd done it often enough in the past and always it had irritated her. Now, as she drew back just far enough to look at him, he had no idea of the unfamiliar sensation that overcame her. Did she see him as the handsome young man who had swept her off her feet? Was he so different? Thinner certainly, and because of that there were lines etched on either side of his mouth; the scar across his forehead that told her more than his words ever would. That he was still handsome didn't come into her thoughts, only that while she could examine

299

him he could visualise nothing beyond what he carried in his memory.

'Aunt Kath and Thelma are waiting by the door – and Thelma must have rung the farm, I can see the others coming: Francis, Sylvia and Dee all running like mad. You're home, darling Theo.'

'It's got to be all right, Anna. It will be, won't it?' Suddenly he was a frightened boy again.

'This is where we're at, Theo. We can handle it, you and me together.' She saw how firmly he clenched his jaw, knowing the battle he fought; she ached with pity – or was it simply with love? She didn't question, simply linked her arm through his as they moved on up the drive. Typical of him, the white stick that had been issued was tucked firmly under his other arm. He was home.

If he'd shown the emotion he kept firmly repressed no one would have been surprised, indeed it would have been lost in Kath's tears, Dee's overexcitement, Thelma's gentle, unchanging devotion. But, instead, he played the role of the person he'd once been: their darling rascal.

'How did you get here? Anna has been hoarding her petrol so that she could collect you,' Francis asked.

'They didn't just turn me loose,' he said laughing. 'I was put on a train – wonder they didn't put a label on me like the evacuee kids had. The guard shoved me off at Deremouth and from there it was child's play. I took the station taxi and got put down at the gate. I wanted to surprise you all, just walk in on you. Anna never misses a trick though, she saw me coming.'

He went to the kitchen to 'see' the staff, insisting that he knew every step of the way and didn't want help. At dinner he felt for the rim of his plate, found his soup spoon and then gave no sign that he wasn't the same Theo who had gone away. The main course could have been more of a problem but on that Saturday evening it was nothing more difficult than a humble shepherd's pie so, once again, he came through with flying colours just as he did with rice pudding. And never once did he let his mask of pleasure slip.

By the time the three from the farm went home the clouds had gathered into what promised to be a storm. Air that had been oppressive was whipped into life with a sudden breeze.

300

Upstairs in their bedroom habit made Anna switch on the light and close the curtains.

'I won't do that.' As fast as she closed them, so she opened them again then switched off the light. She knew there was no logic in what she did, but it helped her to understand. Even now she had the advantage over him, for she could just make out the movement as he took off his jacket and tie, unbuttoned his shirt and pulled it over his head. For her, undressing was brief, a dress and scanty underwear. No use groping for a hanger for her dress, instead she threw it across the back of a chair then opened the window wide and leant out into the night air.

'Come and sniff the air, Theo.' Then, turning as he flopped onto the edge of the bed, 'Theo?'

'Christ!' Did she imagine anguish in the one whispered word. In a second she was in front of him, kneeling with her arms around his waist.

'You're home, things will get better. I wish it were me, it's not fair doing this to you.' An easy thing to say, but in that moment it was sincere.

'I want the truth. I want it, I dread it. Why did Lance go with you to London? Were you in love with him?' This was the last thing she'd expected to hear.

Help me, she begged silently, help me to lie to him. I've been a cheat, now make me a liar too.

'To London? But why not? He was on embarkation leave, he had friends to see and say goodbye to. Anyway, the publisher is brother to a friend of his. After my appointment I came back home to Manningtor, but he stayed there for most of his leave. Whatever are you suggesting? All this time, what have you been imagining?'

The seconds ticked by. Theo was silent yet, leaning against him with her head against his naked chest, she could hear the thumping of his heart and feel the tenseness in his body. Then he raised her to her feet, pulling her close as if he wanted to bury himself into her.

'Forgive me, for that and for so much more, Elf. If I lost you I wouldn't want to live. With you I can face anything.'

'You won't lose me, this is where we belong. And Theo, even if that nonsense you imagined had been true I would never have broken faith with Manningtor. It eats into your soul, doesn't it.'

'Thank God – for you, for bringing me home, for Christopher, for giving me a chance to make something of the future we shall share.'

'We've done it before, darling. Remember.'

'I remember being a blind fool. Pardon the pun,' with a mirthless laugh. 'I remember thinking that we had to make the best of things because we had no choice. My eyes could see, my soul was blind. Now my soul sees clearly.'

'Come and sniff the summer.' She pulled him to his feet. 'Then you'll really know you're home.'

Together they stood by the open window. The thundery rain had started. He couldn't see the vivid flash of lightning and she felt the nervous tensing of his body at the violent clap of thunder.

'A storm,' she said, 'it's been gathering all evening.' He probably didn't even hear her, her nearness was filling his whole mind just as the warmth of his hands was filling hers. In seconds they were both naked – there was nothing beyond the world of darkness that held them, darkness and touch. With unerring instinct he moved to the bed, drawing her with him.

What a moment for memories of Lance to crowd into her mind. Don't think of him, look to the future; don't cloud these moments with guilt. Forget everything but this, *this*.

Afterwards they lay side by side while the storm still rumbled and the rain poured from the guttering. Out of habit she made a mental note that tomorrow she must send Grant up his ladder to see what was blocking it, and then she realised the difference the day had made.

'Listen to the rain, the guttering must be blocked,' she said as she snuggled close to him, half expecting that he would already be asleep.

'I'll tell Grant in the morning. What am I saying? As if you need me to tell Grant.'

'Oh but I do, Theo. I've done my best, and I'll be your eyes, but Manningtor needs you.'

Her answer seemed to have satisfied him, but still he wasn't ready to sleep.

'I can't describe what it was like,' he said, taking her hand in his.

'The night you were shot down?'

'Oh God, no, not that. Even now I'm too much of a coward to

302

try to remember. Sometimes in my sleep there's no escape from it. I mean after that. How long I lay in a hospital bed, being looked after, not even remembering how to look after myself. Nothing. It was as if there was no past and no future. Nothing really registered. There would have been humiliation in being cared for like a baby, except that I hadn't enough understanding for that. There was someone – later I came to realise she was the nurse in charge of me, the German girl who used to write my letters. Her English was remarkably good; I later learnt that she'd lived here as a child, her father had taught German at a boys' school. It was like looking through a thick fog. For a moment it would clear and I'd see something – a large house, a person, perhaps you, perhaps Nanny, any of you, just flashes sort of pricking at my mind and leaving me in a worse hell than being just a *thing*. That was before I started to get letters. She would read them over and over to me, probing, trying to help me. Some of it was wonderful. Then I remembered a call from Alex, it nagged at my mind just when I believed I was finding my way through to some sort of sanity. Tell me again, Anna, what she said wasn't true, tell me.'

'I know what she said, she told me herself. Don't be angry with Alex, she believed she was protecting you. I wish she'd find someone to love, but I don't think she'll ever put anyone in your place.'

'Tell me, I want to hear you say it.'

'The first moment I saw you when I was straightening my handlebars, remember? That's when I fell in love with you. And Theo, I've never stopped loving you, nor ever could.'

To make love twice in the space of an hour showed that he had come home strong in mind and body. For both of them, the first time had been fuelled by the hunger of sexual deprivation, the second something deeper. For both of them it was a celebration of thankfulness: for him that this was the woman he truly loved and for her because she believed it was a sign that God was on *her* side, her lies and half truths acceptable and the way forward plain.

There were good days and there were difficult days, times when Theo walked with confidence in the place he knew so well and days when he was frustrated, hated having to accept help, fought a silent battle with self-pity.

When Lance returned to England to be demobilised he stayed in

303

London, simply phoning Manningtor to say that he was returning immediately to America but promising that once everyone got used to the ways of peace he would try and arrange to bring his family on holiday.

It was Christo's ninth birthday, one of those near-perfect late summer days when the sunshine was hazy and the air heavy with the scent and sounds of harvest from the neighbouring fields of Home Farm.

'I'm home, Dad,' he shouted, racing to meet Theo, who was crossing the lawn towards him. 'And I got in the team! We all got tested and then eleven of us were picked for the Soccer Colts. Not a reserve, but in the proper eleven.'

'That sounds like a good birthday present,' Theo held a hand towards him, judging by the sound exactly where he would be.

'Mum stopped on the way home and bought me a new pair of boots. Have they come yet, these visitors?'

'No, but I should think they must be almost here. Dee phoned just before they left Southampton.'

'I'd better get changed, I promised Dee I'd go over and help Aunt Thelma with the dogs. Mum's just putting the car away.'

'Good lad. Off you go.' He listened as Christo leapt up the steps and across the terrace to the front door, then he turned and started towards the coach house. After all this time there was no logic in this fear that occasionally, and for no reason throughout the years, would suddenly hit him, a physical thing that tied his stomach in knots and turned his arms and legs to heavy weights. The truth was, it had been that fear which had been the driving force that had made him write to Lance – or more accurately get Anna to type the letter so that he could sign it. If he heard them together then surely he would know the truth. Suppose there had been truth in what that child had told Alex (making love in the wood, that's what Alex had said; time and again and often in the happiest moments, the echo of those words would come to him) – perhaps Anna had stayed with him out of pity. If she'd confessed, if she'd told him that she'd had a brief and mistaken fling, then it could have been forgotten.

But pity! Dear God, don't let her give me pity, make her take me for what I am and love me as I am. Sometimes I know I'm bloody difficult, it's no use pretending. I do try – most of the time

304

I try – but it doesn't get any less frustrating, I can't get used to knowing what's round me and seeing nothing. People do, better people than me. And what sort of a life is it for her, always in surroundings where I can look heroic and walk around like any other man. But I'm not. It's knowing it'll never get better, that's what I can't stand. She drives me to Deremouth; we walk up the track to the cliff; I feel the wind; sometimes when it's rough I can hear the waves. But I'll never see it . . . never . . . never. Shows what a selfish toad I am that that matters more to me than that I can't see the children. She describes them, I build a picture, to me it's real.

'We're back,' Anna's voice cut through his silent meandering. 'Did you see the birthday boy?'

'Yes,' he didn't question her use of words. Some see with their eyes, some with their imagination. 'So we've produced a footballer.'

'And a ballerina too, if Deb's performance is anything to go by. She's giving Meggie a performance,' she laughed, 'Meggie and a couple of dolls. What a show-off.'

Deborah was three, born ten months after Theo came home; Meggie, the latest Sullivan, was not quite a year, young enough to make a useful captive audience for her sister.

'Hark, I hear a car,' Theo held his head up to catch the sound long before Anna would have noticed. Another minute and Dee turned in at the gate, blowing her horn to announce the arrival of their visitors. 'Well, here goes.'

'There's a welcoming host for you,' Anna laughed. But could a laugh disguise the way her heart was racing, the way her tongue wanted to cleave to the roof of her dry mouth. Taking Theo's arm she turned him towards the forecourt where the car was stopping to put down its passengers.

The next moments were a clamour of excitement. Anna had seen a picture of Jenny but she hadn't been expecting anyone quite so glamorous. She'd known she'd been nearly forty when four-year-old Jayne had been born, but like the American women she'd seen in the movies, she defied age. Her figure might have belonged to a model, her make-up was immaculate despite her drive from Southampton with a fidgeting four-year-old. Jayne would no doubt grow up much the same but at present she was a delight in a provocatively short dress that showed her matching knickers, altogether a very self-assured young lady. Competition for Debs, Anna laughed silently. The boys hadn't come. At an age when education came first, in High School where female attractions were a new delight, they'd been more than happy to stay at home with only a gullible grandmother to watch over them.

Only now, Jenny and Jayne greeted and scrutinised, could Anna avoid it no longer. She'd known that one day he would come back to Manningtor, yet even while she prepared herself to meet him, deep in her mind was that unfinished dream.

'Sister Anna,' she heard him say, his voice no more American, not a shade different. Turning she held out both her hands, her smile bright and welcoming.

'Brother Lance,' she laughed. 'Quite time you brought Jenny to Manningtor.' Was it a charade, was it Anna the actress talking? Looking at him she felt a shock of disappointment. Through the years she'd kept the dream alive at the back of her mind, yet looking at him she felt nothing. Surely this wasn't the man she'd dreamed of sharing her future with? That his dark hair was receding and he was wearing those rimless so-American glasses were superficial changes, for the clock had ticked on for all of them. Behind him she seemed to see a ghost of that fighter pilot in his leather flying jacket, scarf knotted at his neck, battered RAF cap. That was the memory she had treasured; this smiling man with his glamorous wife and pretty daughter was a stranger.

'Go see the babies,' Jenny bid Jayne. Then she turned her attention on Theo, the natural flirt in her taking no account of the fact her beauty was lost on him.

'So how are things, sister Anna?' Lance asked quietly. 'Letters tell one so little. I told you I'd come back.' Such loaded words. Like a bird whose cage door has been inadvertently left open, metaphorically she beat her wings, preparing to fly. She was free. A great wave of thankfulness washed over her.

'Things are good, things are *very* good. Think back to when I last saw you, and see just how good. Theo is home.' Then laughing, she went on, at the same time reaching out and clasping Theo's hand in hers, 'I dare say he's grown up a bit. Haven't we all? Grown up or got older. Either way, things are good.'

Having unloaded the luggage and turned the car, Dee slowed up by the side of where they were standing amongst the luggage.

'I won't hang about; I don't want to leave Mum to struggle for too long. Did Christo go to help?'

'He'll barely have got there, but he said he'd promised,' Theo told her.

'OK. I'll send him packing in time to do his homework. Cheerio all.' And amidst a chorus of farewells and thanks she was gone. A very different Dee these days. Having shed at least two stone of puppy fat she was still a well-built woman – to be willowy would be out of keeping with her hands and feet. The main change in her came from her ready smile and her feeling of confidence. It had been her own idea that when Brambles, a smallholding – a very small holding – fell vacant on Manningtor estate she and Thelma should rent it and she should breed chow-chows. Already from her first litter she had won a rosette in a local show. Her puppies brought in a profit, so far not large but it was a step on the ladder. The hardest part was the copious tears both she and Thelma shed when each furry delight was carried away.

With Theo and Anna keeping the nursery occupied, Nanny was in seventh heaven. But she always found time to welcome Kath, whose visits became more frequent. For of them all it was Kath whose life had lost its lustre. Matt and his Pretty Pam had settled in Northumberland; Thelma had moved less than a mile away but she'd thrown herself into this dog breeding scheme as wholeheartedly as had Dee and never seemed to have time just to sit for an hour and chatter. And Theo, what had become of that naughty rascal he used to be? Always late for meals, always with a winning smile. Oh, the smile was still there, but she was no fool, she knew that often it was no more than a shield to hide the poor darling's frustrations. But Anna was always there for him, she seemed to see ahead and make things easy for him. And so life went on. One of these days Kath's time would come and she would join her darling Sidney. She'd smile at the thought, then imagine him greeting her with 'What kept you? Couldn't you get Saint Peter to stamp your pass?'

Lance and his family stayed six days, then went on to London. As Jenny said, if she was to see England she couldn't spend her time in a Devon backwater. Lance laughed at her expression.

'Backwater it may be, but there's nowhere on this earth like Manningtor. Wait till we get back home, a mention of England and this is what you'll call to mind. It gets deep into your soul.'

On the morning they left Anna and Theo caught up on what they would have done in the office during the week: two accounts to be paid – Anna's task; a letter ordering the drive to be made up with fresh hoggin – Theo's words but Anna's typing. She knew exactly the state of the family finances, she knew exactly the constant drain on resources to keep the building to the standard they wanted, and she had a feeling of satisfaction in knowing that because of that 'other life' she lived, Anna Bartlett would be able to help. In five years she had become a household name: those characters who used to be hers alone – even those in the first book she had shared with Lance – now had a following on both sides of the Atlantic.

'There, that's done,' she stamped the letter.

'I'll take it to the post box if you want to work,' offered Theo the independent.

'Let's go together. It's nice out; we shan't need coats. We'll collect the children on the way.'

'Good. I'll tell Nanny.' He seemed determined to be responsible for something. This was one of his good days. They both knew life wasn't always so easy and, today, only he knew the reason for this lightness of spirit. Lance had gone. He hadn't needed eyes to know that for Anna there had been no pain or regret in the parting; he had seen it with his soul.

Watching from the window Nanny saw them going down the drive. There was very little Nanny Harknell missed and she too sent up a silent 'thank you'.